A PROPER
Charlie

Christopher Stock

A PROPER Charlie

Christopher Stock

MEREO

Cirencester

Mereo Books

1A The Wool Market Dyer Street Cirencester Gloucestershire GL7 2PR
An imprint of Memoirs Publishing www.mereobooks.com

A Proper Charlie: 978-1-86151-747-0

First published in Great Britain in 2016
by Mereo Books, an imprint of Memoirs Publishing

The address for Memoirs Publishing Group Limited can be found at
www.memoirspublishing.com

The Memoirs Publishing Group Ltd Reg. No. 7834348

The Memoirs Publishing Group supports both The Forest Stewardship Council®
(FSC®) and the PEFC® leading international forest-certification organisations. Our
books carrying both the FSC label and the PEFC® and are printed on FSC®-certified
paper. FSC® is the only forest-certification scheme supported by the leading
environmental organisations including Greenpeace. Our paper procurement policy
can be found at www.memoirspublishing.com/environment

Typeset in 10/15pt Century Schoolbook
by Wiltshire Associates Publisher Services Ltd. Printed and bound in Great Britain
by Printondemand-Worldwide, Peterborough PE2 6XD

Welcome to the working week
I know it don't thrill you
I hope it don't kill you
Welcome to the working week
You've gotta do it till you're through it
So you'd better get to it

Elvis Costello

Contents

CHAPTER ONE

Happy returns

I lay in bed and gazed sightlessly at the pages of the book I was holding. I hadn't taken in a single word. I'd already renewed the damn thing three times at the library and still hadn't managed to get half way through it.

To my left Melissa was engrossed in some chick-flick novel she'd borrowed from a friend at work. Her contact lenses had been removed, binned and replaced by glasses. Her granny glasses, as I called them. They were black and thick rimmed, which gave her a severe look which I only really cared for when we were indulging in a spot of role-playing fun of a Friday evening. Melissa Bennett; by day, mother of one and part-time journalist at the Gravesend free weekly advertiser and by night, strict geography teacher Miss Two-Globes. What a transformation. I kept promising I'd get her a better pair from work, but I still haven't managed to get around to it.

The wind was howling outside, making the fence creak with annoying regularity. It's been doing that since we moved here two years ago and I still haven't summoned the energy or motivation to replace it. I suppose I will wait until it completely falls down and then pay someone an overblown fee to replace it.

'Oh well, that's another one gone,' I said.

'Yep.'

'Another three hundred and sixty-odd days have passed almost without notice, taken for granted and waved on by,' I added.

'Uh-huh.' Mel licked a finger and turned a page.

'Forty-two. How the hell did I reach forty-two?'

'You did what all forty-two year olds do, my love. You were forty-one, you had a birthday, and now you're forty-two. It's not a mystery.'

She scornfully patted me on the hand and continued reading.

'What I mean is, how did I suddenly become old? One minute I was a fresh-faced teenager with the world at my feet, full of dreams, heady ambitions and a twenty-eight-inch waist, and the next I'm contemplating getting a pipe and a cardigan and I'm over the hill. Well maybe not over it exactly, but I can definitely view the other side from where I'm standing.'

She put her book down. 'Here we go, it's the same every year. Where has my youth gone? Why don't my trousers fit any more? Why is there more hair on my shoulders than on my head? Christ, you're not going to go through another crisis like when you turned forty are you? I don't think I can go through that again, all that not eating, detoxing and taking out gym memberships. How long did you keep going for?'

'A couple of weeks.'

'And how much did that gym cost?'

'Three hundred and fifty something.'

'So those six or so visits set you back fifty quid each eh? Well worth it!'

'The money is not the issue, my dearly beloved. It's the feel-good factor when you leave, all pumped up and exhausted after a full-on work-out.'

'Huh, as I remember you weren't exactly feeling good after your exercise sessions. No, in fact as I recall you were a red sweaty mass of pulled muscles, strains and BO. You even needed help with removing your own socks. Now be quiet, I've read the same line four times now. There is no need to fret, you are as young and beautiful now as the day you swept me off my feet. Oh, by the way, that gardening catalogue you ordered came today.' She turned back to her book.

I sighed. Didn't that say it all? Once I was into the latest gadgets, high-tech mobile phones, clothes and cars. Now it's seed catalogues, pension plans and a nice sit down. The other week some of the lads from work hired the five-a-side pitch at the local sports centre and asked if I wanted to play. I made an excuse that I was busy. A few years ago I would have jumped at the chance and been looking forward to it all week, even going as far as getting in a spot of jogging to boost my fitness levels. Now I'd rather get home from work, eat my tea and put my feet up for the evening. I suppose I shouldn't complain. Everyone ages and it's better than the alternative. OK, I may never have fulfilled my childhood dreams of fame and fortune, but who has? I guess I have accomplished most of the targets and goals someone of my age is expected to have reached. Wife: check. Ex-wife: check. Family: check. Steady monotonous job: check. Garden shed: check. It just seems like, well, that's it. It's all done. That there is nothing more I am going to achieve and now it's all about running down the clock. What is there new to experience? OK, probably almost everything, but the rut I'm in has now become such a bloody great trench that I'm finding it hard to pull myself out.

'Did you count my birthday cards?' I asked.

'No, why would I?'

'It wouldn't have taken you long, there were only five.'

'It's not the quantity, it's the quality that counts,' she said, turning the page.

'Quality? You must be joking. One from you, one from Colin [my almost step-dad] and his new bit of fluff, the apparently lovely Grace, another from the one cousin who actually bothers…'

'Yes, which is pretty good seeing as you can't be arsed to send him one on his birthday, or anyone else if we are going to be picky about it.'

'Never mind that, that's not the issue right now. What number was I on?'

'God knows. I'm trying to read my book.'

I ticked them off on my fingers. You, Colin, Marie, one

from Adrian and Suzanne, one from Mark and Anna and a home-made effort from Ellie.'

'Which obviously should take pride of place. It's those which have taken the most time and love to produce. Anyone can pop into a card shop, pull one off the shelf and part with their two ninety-nine without even glancing at the picture on the front, let alone bothering to digest the moving heart felt poem inside.'

'I don't know, the picture on the front was crap. I couldn't even make it out. What was it meant to be? Me? Leonid Brezhnev? Was it an angry piece of modernist art? Someone's Friday night barf up?'

'Charlie, she is five, what were you expecting, a Turner landscape?'

'Mel, I expect to know what it is I'm meant to be looking at, plus a certain standard of capability in the colouring-in stakes.'

'My, you are in a grumpy mood aren't you? Look, if you're on the verge of yet another mid-life personality crisis I think Ellie and I will take a six-month sabbatical somewhere sunny while you wrestle yourself out of it. Portugal, Turkey or Cyprus appeals, I could do with a healthy glow.' She peered at me over the top of her specs.

'What do you mean, another mid-life crisis?' I replied indignantly. 'When have I ever had a crisis?'

'At twenty, thirty, forty, now... in fact I don't think there has been a single period in your life when you haven't been going through some kind of self-induced drama.'

'You didn't even know me then, well not at twenty or thirty anyway.'

'Thank heavens for small mercies.'

'I am not now having, nor ever have had, a mid-life crisis,' I argued feebly. She raised her eyebrows once more. 'No come on, when have I ever started acting like I am trying to recapture my not so misspent youth? I don't try to dress younger than my years. I haven't got a medallion, a fake tan or a combover. I'm not carrying on with my young secretary, pretending to fit in with her trendy mates and going to night clubs and dancing till dawn.'

'Oh yeah, so what's that thing parked on the drive then?'

'Here we go again,' I sighed, picking up my book and pretending to read.

'Now help me out here Charlie. How many of us are in this family?'

'At the last count, three,' I replied.

'And how many seats does your car possess?'

'Two,' I said wearily.

'I rest my case, milord.'

'How many times do I have to say this? I've always wanted a nippy convertible. I took it for a test drive and just had to have it. You have the family car, I have mine. I don't understand what the big deal is. Just because I'm the wrong side of forty it doesn't mean I should give up on all my dreams, does it?'

'Of course not baby, but you have to remember you do have certain responsibilities, and giving some unknown boy-racer a burn up at the traffic lights is not one of them.'

'Whatever,' I said, knowing I was in an argument I couldn't win. 'Anyway, there is a huge difference in being in the throes of a mid-life crisis and simply being aware of your own mortality and the rapid passing of the years.'

She replaced the bookmark Ellie had made at nursery

and plonked it on her bedside table. 'I'm beat, are you ready for lights out?'

'Yeah, go on then.' She switched off and snuggled against my side. 'You know what I mean though don't you?' I said. 'I don't feel ready to be old. I still want to be feisty, naughty and slightly unruly.'

'No you don't. You think you ought to, but against your best rock and roll intentions you and I both know that secretly you would rather be at home with your PJs on, feet up, and a nice milky coffee on the go.'

'You think so?'

'Yep, with Poirot on the box and an early night on the cards, as opposed to raising hell where it's unpleasantly loud with loads of kids shaking their money makers until the early hours.'

'It shouldn't be that way though, should it?'

'Maybe not darling, but it's the same for everyone, remember? Today's beautiful teens who have not a care, a crow's foot or a stretch mark in sight will, with the passing of time, eventually be shuffling down to Tesco's in search of incontinence pants, pile cream and sleep-inducing hot chocolate.' She patted my hand.

'I guess that's true, but you try telling them that.'

'I know, when you're young you don't think of the future. Everything is here and now. Even the following week seems a lifetime away.'

'Then you get to our age and all you do is dwell on the past,' I grumbled.

'Don't be so maudlin. You still probably have more time to go than has gone,' she reassured me.

'Let's hope so,' I said. 'Do you ever think about death?'

'Only during conversations like this,' she said with a sigh. 'Go on, pass me the rope.'

'No seriously, are you afraid of death?'

'I have never given it much thought. Now we have our little girl all I think of is the future, hers and ours. What she will become, how we can help her fulfil her dreams, that sort of thing.'

'I know it may sound selfish, but when did life suddenly become all about others achieving their dreams and goals? What happened to ours?' I carried on.

'I don't know. When kids arrive they become your life and really take it over. I suppose we have to put our aspirations on the back burner while they're doing their thing, growing up and getting their own lives sorted.'

'But won't we both be too old, too comfy and crusty and past it to pursue whatever goals and dreams are still lingering by then?'

'Probably but in no time the grandchildren will come along and we will be silver-haired unpaid child minders while our own kids are forced to scrimp and save and work fifty-hour weeks to keep their heads above water.'

'Great!' I said. 'What a glorious future you have mapped out for us, I can hardly wait.' My spirits were sinking further. We fell silent for a while, her head on my chest, her hand combing through the soft hairs of my belly.

'Do you know what's number one?' I asked.

'As opposed to number twos?'

'You know what I mean. What's the top of the charts, the hit parade?'

'The hit parade? Blimey, you are old aren't you! I haven't heard anyone call it that since Pete Murray and Tony Blackburn.'

'All right, what's number one in the charts?'

'That girl group, I think,' said Melissa.

'I have no idea.' I confessed. 'I always used to know. I'd listen to the top forty count-down religiously without fail every Sunday evening when I was a kid, my finger hovering over the pause button of my tape deck to record any new entry I hadn't yet acquired, hoping the DJ wouldn't talk over the intro. Now I haven't a clue who's top of the pops.'

'Sorry to age you further pop-picker, but 'Top of the Pops' hasn't been on TV for about a decade or more. They killed it off when they realised just nine people and a goldfish called Peter were the only viewers.'

'You're kidding me?' I said, astonished.

'Sorry,' she said. 'Oh, by the way, while we are at it there is also no Father Christmas and Jimmy Krankie was really a middle-aged woman with gender issues.'

'More dreams shattered. Next you will be telling me there's no tooth fairy and you fake your orgasms.'

'What's an orgasm?'

'Ha ha, very funny I don't think.'

'I think maybe we should change the subject. Did you enjoy your birthday meal?'

'It was lovely. I've only visited the bathroom twice since we have been back,' I answered, not feeling exactly on top of my game.

'Well, it's your own fault. I did advise against that killer chilli-fuelled burrito. You know what a state your digestive system is in these days. Anyone who leaves a stink like you do in the toilet cannot be a healthy man.'

'One must suffer for one's art, my darling. There is no way I'm living on a diet of healthy salads and fruit and veg.

This boy lives on the wild side, between the coronary intensive care unit and the bog.'

'Well don't blame me when you're sitting on the toilet tomorrow with fourth degree burns and a repetitive strain injury.'

'Do I ever?'

'Yes, constantly. Whenever you get drunk on a Sunday evening while you are trying to stave off the dreaded attack of the Sunday night blues. When we are at a barbecue and you feel the need to break the quarter-pounder cheese burger eating record...'

'All right, all right, message received and understood. I am the master of my own downfall. Any psychological and physical problems are one hundred percent down to my own sweet self and you, my darling, are completely blameless.'

'I'm glad you're taking responsibility at last. I see this as a major step forward in your development. At this rate of progress I can see you becoming a fully-rounded adult male by the time you get your pension book and free bus pass.'

She snuggled closer, the warmth of her body feeling delicious against mine. Despite having a huge Mexican meal plus starter and sweet inside me I wasn't totally against the idea of getting jiggy-with-it with my ho.

'Mel, do you still find me attractive?' I asked, still feeling sore at turning another year older.

'Not particularly,' she replied.

'Eh?'

'Just joking, I find you more arousing than a Brad Pitt sandwich with a side order of George Clooney fries.'

'Well that's all right then,' I said.

'Ooh, I've just remembered there is one last present I've yet to give you.'

'Cool,' I said, reaching over to turn on my bedside light.

'No, don't do that,' she whispered. 'This is the kind of gift I prefer to give in the dark.' She slipped silently under the covers.

'Oh…ah…I see. Lovely, ouch! Careful darling, mind the teeth!'

CHAPTER TWO

Colin and Grace

Colin is my 'almost' step-dad. I guess you could say he is as near as damn it to being the real thing as possible without having actually been present at the time of conception. My real father, my dad, died of cancer when I was still wearing short trousers to school and was still of an age where anything seemed possible. There was no doubt in my mind that on growing up I would either be Manchester United's greatest-ever striker, a spaceman or at worst a member of International Rescue, primed to take over the running of Thunderbird 1 when Scott decided to move upstairs and help to run the family business.

A few years after my father's untimely and painfully

long-drawn-out demise, this boring, balding and short-sighted mole-like creature moved in. One evening I was sat down and told over a glass of milk and a jam butty that this 'friend' would be staying just for a few nights and that I should be on my best behaviour. In no time his slippers were parked by the front door in the space that used to be reserved for my real dad's, and although they never managed to summon up enough energy or morality to shuffle down to St Marks and make it legal, he remained at my mother's side until she passed away herself four years ago. Sad as it may sound Colin (legally or not) is my closest family relative. We are a small family; I have no siblings and precious few cousins. My aunties and uncles are not much more than names towards the bottom of a Christmas card list. Those that are still around I rarely get to see. In fact, since Mum's funeral I think we have only gathered the once, and that was at the predictable setting of the burial of some obscure second cousin whom I had hardly met. It's horrible really, seeing the generation before me disappearing one by one. At each gathering my uncles and aunties, who used to be so loud and proud and the life and soul, now seem increasingly worn, stooped and filled with less life and jollity at each occasion. And then it will be our turn...

Not that Colin is in any mood to give up and slow down. No way. In fact if anything he's more active and forward-thinking than ever. He's vice president of the bowls club, a major player at the local battle re-enactment society, helps out on several charity organizations, has an allotment and a gym membership and is the devoted grandfather always turning up with sweets, gifts and assorted Barbie accessories he obtains off his new fad, the internet. He's like a born-again teenager. It is because of Colin that I find myself dragged away from the comfort of my home and the brand new 55-inch wall-mounted Hi-Def television on which I was looking forward to viewing the big Sunday lunchtime kick-off on Sky instead of cheering on United in the Manchester derby. I am being summoned to one of those bloody awful 'family' pubs. You know the sort of thing, a greeting with a smile and a cheap packet of crayons, a clientele of families who always somehow seem more prosperous and happier to be there than you, and to top it all, god-awful service. The food is hardly Michelin standard either; two razor-thin slices of semi-warm beef submerged in a dreary puddle of tasteless congealed gravy accompanied by a couple of sorry-looking spuds with an apologetic helping of wet broccoli and nearly raw slices of carrot. This is what the Great British Sunday is all about. Then once we've drunk enough and have managed to digest the poorly-microwaved dessert, we'll tip the harassed waitress and tell her it was all yummy, before paying the inflated bill and grouching about it all the way home. Never mind, it's work tomorrow. In another seven days if the urge takes you, you can do it all over again!

We parked up and I looked in the rear-view mirror. 'Ah, she's asleep' I said. 'It would be a shame to move her. Let's go home and text Colin our apologies. I'm sure he won't mind.'

'Come on, you've hardly bothered to see him lately,' said Melissa. 'It's about time you gave a moment from your not-so-busy schedule to see how he is. It's always him who takes the trouble to come over or to phone. It's high time you showed an interest.'

'Mel, it is Sunday, the one full day off a week I get. The last place I would choose to spend these precious hours is here with Colin, being introduced to his ancient bit of fluff.'

'What's wrong with here? It's really family friendly. It's got one of those jungle gym soft play areas that Ellie can run around in when she gets bored and fractious. That way when you and Colin are semi-pissed and arguing the toss about yesterday's football she won't be whining and getting on your nerves.'

'OK, all right, anything for a quiet life,' I said, climbing out of Mel's sensible family car. I opened Ellie's door and gently stroked her forehead. 'Ellie, we're here darling. Do you want to wake up and see Grandfather and his new bint?'

'Charlie!'

'Sorry! Ellie, come on darling, it's time for lunch sweetheart.'

She came round, yawned and suddenly remembered where we were. 'Is Grandpop here yet?'

'Not yet darling, but he'll be here soon.' I released the buckle on her car seat and she slid down. She looked beautiful in a smart pink party dress, and as always my heart felt like bursting with pride. Melissa and I have made a beautiful girl. She is lean, thin and fairly tall for her age (so Mel tells me). She has a very fair complexion with huge brown eyes beneath the longest lashes I have ever seen. Blonde locks hang down in ringlets, framing her angelic face. I have no idea where her golden curls come from, as what is left of my own hair is mousy and straight, as is her mother's. Well I think it is; Mel dyes her hair so frequently and in so many different hues from platinum blonde to gothic black that I'm not entirely sure what her real hair colour is. It's possibly mule grey, but I'll keep that suspicion to myself for health reasons. My mum's hair was wavy, so maybe Ellie's curls are a throwback to hers.

How I wish dear old Mum could have lived to see her only grandchild. She was always asking me and my first wife Marie when we'd make her a grandmother, but for some reason it never happened and then within a few weeks of being involved with Melissa something clicked into place and we were blessed. I know it maybe was a little late in the day to start a family at thirty-eight but I can tell you one thing for sure; it's definitely better late than never and now here I am expecting number two. Well, not me exactly, but you know what I mean.

We entered and stood at a lectern which had a ketchup-stained sign attached, telling all us lucky punters to wait here and be seated. After a moment a flustered-looking assistant called Megan (I knew this from her name badge) asked if I had booked. 'Yes, it's a table for five in the name of Bennett,' I said. She checked her list from top to bottom, didn't find us and scanned it again. She found us, ticked us off with the pen attached by some hairy string to the board, picked up a handful of menus (and of course our complimentary crayons and activity sheet) and led us to our table.

'Can I get you any drinks?' she asked smiling, her pencil poised on her little note pad.

'Yes please, I'll have a Stella, my good lady would like a… what would you like babe?'

'Mmm, I suppose I'm driving home?' she asked.

I nodded, smiling. 'You're a trooper babe, a true Brit and

no mistake. No, but be honest, can you really see me getting through this with only a diet coke or an orange juice?'

She shook her head. 'I guess not,' she said and turned to the already slightly impatient Megan. 'An orange juice and lemonade please, no ice and a blackcurrant Fruit Shoot.'

The drinks were almost instantaneous, pity the grub probably wouldn't be. I necked mine down in a couple of minutes. It was heaven. The place was heaving already, with little identikit families filling every table dressed in their Sunday finery. All scrubbed up, trousers pressed, shirts ironed and children freshly bathed ready to greet friends, family and the world at large. How nice! How British!

I went to the bar for a refill, leaving Melissa to peruse the choice of grub on offer with Ellie. As expected there was just a spotty youth receiving training on his first day on the job and one other pissed-off looking barman trying to ignore the crowd of stressed punters staring at him with ten-pound notes scrunched up in their fists with knuckles turning whiter by the minute. Eventually I managed to catch his eye and order another pint.

As the golden liquid was reaching the top of the glass I spotted a podgy old git in an ill-fitting suit coming through the door – Colin. I turned to the bar guy. 'Can I have a pint of whatever draught bitter is the most drinkable as well please mate?' I bellowed. I called Colin over and handed him his drink. He looked around disdainfully.

'Blimey, I didn't expect it to be this busy. It's not even half twelve yet,' he said.

'There you go,' I replied. 'Welcome to the world of the family man. It's a bit different from the dark ages when I was in your care. They don't have men-only boozers these days where it's deemed OK to leave your kid on his own in the car park, locked inside a clapped-out Vauxhall Victor for hours on end with only a small bottle of R. Whites lemonade and a packet of crisps with the little blue salt sachet for company while you prop up the bar knocking back the Watney's Red Barrel.'

'Shut up Charlie, you always used to ask to come. At the time it was a little treat. Have you got us our table?'

'Yes, it's between a party of Asian men discussing an honour killing and a party of chavs celebrating their nineteen-year-old's third baby.'

'Knock off will you Charlie. It would be nice to have a happy family gathering without your depressing cynicism for once.'

'Sorry Col, from now on I will be chirpiness personified.'

'Yes, well don't go mad, there's no need to overdo it.'

'So where is the lovely Grace then? Don't tell me she's blown you out at the last minute? I did warn you of the perils of dating on eBay,' I said, almost finishing my second with several large glugs.

'She's outside finishing her cigarette, she'll be here in a minute.'

'Oh, a smoker eh? That must go right against your anti-smoking and fitness crusade.'

'She's promised to try and give up. It's not easy you know.'

'I'll take your word for it. Well, knowing these places it will take an age for anyone to come round and take our order so we may as well get another in while we wait. It's your round I believe. I'll have another lager with a scotch chaser on the side if you don't mind. It is a special occasion after all.'

Colin beckoned the spotty youth over. 'One bitter, a large glass of dry white, one Stella and a Bell's with ice please.' He turned to me. 'Don't get too pissed Charlie, I don't want you to embarrass me. This is important. I've become very fond of Grace in the short time I've got to know her and I would like things to go smoothly and without drama for once. No stand-up rows, walkouts or histrionics please.'

'No worries there Colin, I will make you proud. With my sharp patter, the Bennett charm and my ability to juggle pickled eggs I'll make an impression she will never forget. The occasion you are no doubt alluding to when I got naked and arrested was a one-off and solely due to high spirits and incorrectly prescribed painkillers.'

'Just be polite, courteous and civil, that's all I ask,' he said, pulling a handkerchief from his trouser pocket.

As he was handing over his money for the drinks, the door opened and in walked a vision of slapperness. Her age could have been anywhere from forty-five to sixty. Without carbon dating, guesswork was all that was available. She was bleached blonde, heavily wrinkled, especially around the mouth (no doubt from a lifetime's addiction to Marlboro), and over made up with blood-red lipstick and incredibly long false eyelashes. She tottered through the crowded eatery in a pair of outrageously high-heeled white stilettos, a black patent leather skirt, fishnets and a sheer white blouse which freely revealed the black lacy bra she wore underneath, which was manfully trying and failing to support a humungous bosom. This look was topped off with huge chandelier-sized dangly earrings. Bloody hell, I thought, it's the bride of Dracula.

I nudged Colin in the ribs and gestured towards the 'lady', who was looking up and down the bar apparently lost. 'Look at the state of that!' I said, shaking my head.

He looked at where I was gesturing, looked back at me, gave me a filthy look and hollered to the woman in question. 'Grace, Grace, over here love,' he said, beckoning her over.

Oh my fucking god!

The woman squealed, waved, came over and planted a huge kiss on Colin's cheek and another on my own. 'You must be Charlie,' she said.

'That's me,' I said, trying to break free. I could feel her foundation transferring to my skin and taste her perfume and ashtray breath at the back of my throat. Colin handed her her drink as I led us towards my family. As we approached the table Melissa's eyes met mine. I made a face. Her eyes widened and a broad smile spread across her face, which she desperately tried to stifle.

Ellie put down her drink and rushed towards her grandfather. He gathered her up in his arms and kissed her. 'Grace, this is my little angel Ellie. Say hello Ellie.'

Ellie looked at the formidable sight in front of her and promptly buried her head in Colin's midriff. 'She's just a little shy, that's all,' he said, handing her back to Mel. 'Grace, this is my son, well my stepson, Charlie, and his wife Melissa.'

She bent down to Ellie's eye level and gave her a kiss on the forehead, stroked her hair and exclaimed that she was delightful, her mighty white orbs threatening to escape at any moment.

'I'll just check Ellie into the play area. Come on Ellie,' said Melissa, smirking as she went.

We sat down with Grace on my left and awkwardly discussed our journeys, the restaurant, and the weather. There was a brief moment of awkward silence before Colin felt compelled to say something.

'Well, this is nice.'

'Mmm, wonderful,' I replied. 'So where are you from, Grace?'

'Originally I'm from Dagenham. I'm an Essex girl at heart but more recently I've lived all over the south east, Southampton, Gillingham, Northfleet, Hastings...'

'So you get around a bit?' I said without thinking. She nudged me heavily in the ribs. 'Charlie, what are you suggesting!' she sniggered.

'Nothing, nothing at all,' I said hastily, as Melissa returned. She picked up a serviette and wiped away a scarlet lip print from my cheek.

'Is she having fun?' I asked.

'She was until some horrible boy who is much too old and shouldn't even be in there fell on her. She's OK now though.'

We ordered a combo starter and our main meals. After nearly an hour of stilted conversation and refills, there was still no sign of our Mexican platter to share. I was already feeling pissed and had received several kicks from under the table from Mel when the alcohol was threatening to loosen my tongue a little too much.

'So tell me Grace, how and where did you two lovebirds meet?' I asked.

She downed her glass and rearranged her cleavage. 'Oh, I've kind of known Colin for a while now, from the Rotary

Club and then later we'd occasionally bump into each other at various competitions at bowls. He often used to partner my husband in the four woods. They won it three years on the spin a while back.'

'Oh yeah, what was his name?'

'Bishop, Frank Bishop,' she said, waving her empty glass in the air and obviously hoping for a refill.

'Frank Bishop? Wasn't that the funeral you went to a few weeks back?' I asked Colin.

'Well it was a while back now but yes that was him. A smashing player was Frank. A long wood, a short wood, it didn't matter to Frankie boy, he'd draw either, right on the button nine times out of ten. A great bloke as well, always ready with his hand in his pocket at the bar afterwards, not like some of them down there. Right tight sods some of them I can tell you.'

Blimey, I thought. Poor old Frank has hardly had time to settle into his new small wooden surroundings and his grieving widow has already identified, targeted and snared his unwitting replacement.

I stood up ready to get in another round and hollered the passing waitress once again. 'Hey love, any chance of some grub over here? I'm starting to feel a bit faint. I've been here for hours and the only edible thing I've seen is the handful of peas that whoever sat here before me spilt on the floor.'

She apologised and went off to the kitchen. 'Do you fancy a quickie Grace, before they finally arrive with our lunch-cum-tea-cum-supper?' I asked.

'Go on then, you've twisted my arm,' she laughed, reaching across to Colin, 'I hope you aren't going to take advantage of me on the way home Colly.'

'Colly, she only calls him Colly!' I slurred not so silently to Mel, before dredging my beer to make room for the next. Colin gave me daggers as I got to my feet. My goodness, what would Mum say? Probably that he was way out of his depth and that she was no better than she ought to be.

I was cut short by the delayed appearance of our waitress. Her name tab informed us that her name was Alicia and that she was worthy of four of the five stars available from management. What she had accomplished in her career in taking orders and clearing away plates to achieve them was unknown to me, and further still whatever misdemeanours she had racked up to stop her proudly sporting all five shiny gold stars I would rather not be aware of. If you are minus a star for not washing your hands after a quick visit to the loo or flobbing on the returned food of some awkward bugger, I think I would rather endure my meal in ignorant bliss.

'Sorry about the wait,' she said with not a hint of regret. 'Here's your combo starter for four. Do you require any extra sauces?' We shook our heads in unison. 'Enjoy your starter, I'll be back in a minute to see if you'll require some more beverages,' she added as if from reading from a prepared script.

As Grace sat opposite getting stuck into a deep-fried chicken wing, I studied her closely and chewed on a potato wedge I had dipped into the small pot of garlic mayo. There was definitely something unusual about her features, but I couldn't quite put my greasy finger on it. It wasn't the mountain of bleached white curls that were piled high on her head, nor the masses of powder, mascara and eye pencil that made her look like a gaudy third-rate drag act. OK she was a bit jowly and saggy, but what do you expect at her age? Whatever that was.

And then I got it. She had no eyebrows! Actually, that is a lie of sorts. For although she had either pulled them out, had them singed off or lost them in a freak accident, she had made up for it by drawing on a pair of replacements in black pencil. Unfortunately she was obviously not that good at art or working from a reflection, as the left one was sitting a good quarter of an inch lower than its fellow on the right. This was what was giving her a permanent quizzical look of disbelief and sarcasm. Think of Mr Spock going to a cross-dressing party and you aren't far from the mark.

Colin started spouting his usual mantra on modern-day footballers after I carelessly let slip that I'd viewed the repeat of Match of the Day over this morning's breakfast. 'Cloughie would never have stood for it that's for sure,' he stated while chewing on a small chunk of corn on the cob. The gaps in his teeth were filled with corn kernels and looked revolting. In a moment, I thought, he'll get a toothpick out of his pocket and have a good root around.

'Here we go,' I said, 'All our glorious yesterdays...'

'I mean it, half of them couldn't trap a bag of wet cement! It's a disgrace. I wouldn't give them a penny, let alone the hundred and forty grand a week some of those frauds are on. Half of them should be sowing mail bags instead of being worshipped like gods and it's gullible fools like you who feed it all with your replica shirts and Sky Sports money.'

'I'm afraid you will have to get used to this,' said Melissa to Grace. 'It's like a scratched record. Sometimes I think they disagree with each other just for the sake of it.'

'Do you like sport, Grace?' I asked.

'I used to play a bit of hockey in my school days but that's about it. I never miss an episode of *Strictly Come Dancing*. Does that count as sport?'

'Not really,' I answered. Out of the corner of my eye I saw Colin shake his head.

'I love that show,' said Mel. 'I wanted Hope to win and I couldn't believe it when they voted her off and kept that lumbering bloke in.'

'I like that Jeremy from breakfast TV. He's got a lovely bum,' said Grace, obviously feeling more at ease as she finished the remainder of her wine.

'Here's a deal,' I said. 'We won't discuss football, if you don't talk about Strictly Come bloody Dancing.'

Colin got to his feet and announced he was going to visit the toilet before getting some more drinks in. I was in pressing need to go myself and joined him at the next urinal.

'So, Charlie, what do you think?'

'Well, the tiling is substandard, the floor is sticky but on the plus side the lemony smell that's wafting from heaven knows where is putting up a manful job in defeating the stench of urine.'

'Don't be funny. Grace, what do you think of Grace?'

'She's quite... what is the word I'm looking for?'

'Vibrant?' suggested Colin.

'Yes, she certainly is that. How old is she?'

'Fifty-two,' he said, washing his hands 'Why do you ask?'

'What, all of her?' I said, smirking. Fortunately the sound of the hand dryer drowned out this flippant aside. 'That's a big age gap, isn't it? What's that, around fourteen years?'

'Love knows no boundaries Charlie. Age is irrelevant where affairs of the heart are concerned. Look at Bruce

Forsyth. His wife is thirty years younger than him and they've been happily married for decades.'

'If I was going to inherit a fortune accumulated from decades of lame Saturday evening game shows and chummy catch phrases, I think I could put up living with a rug wearing wrinkly telling me it will be OK tonight if I play my cards right.'

'That might have something to do with it,' he conceded.

We returned to our table. Our starters had been cleared away; Ellie was sucking her thumb and getting seriously sleepy on Melissa's lap. Grace's seat was empty.

'Has she done a runner?' I said. 'Oh I get it, she's had her starter, didn't like the company and now she's high-tailing it down the road with her thumb in the air looking for a new sugar daddy to purchase her main course and dessert? Never mind Col, It's better to have loved and lost than to have never loved at all. I think Aristotle said that. Well, either him or Girls Aloud.'

'Sit down before you fall down, you berk. She's outside having a cigarette,' said Mel tugging at my sleeve.

'I'll get us a couple of bottles of wine to have with our lunch,' said Colin and shuffled across to the bar.

'Will you behave yourself?' said Melissa as she laid Ellie down between two chairs she'd pushed together. 'I think you should slow down a bit before you cause a scene or say something you'll later regret.'

'I'm fine. Don't worry, I am in full control of all my faculties.'

'Yes, so how come you're sitting on Ellie's doll?'

'So that's what that is? I thought I had suddenly developed a serious case of piles,' I answered, pulling a small soft plaything from under me.

All at once Grace, Colin and our main meals arrived. Ellie was still asleep, so we carried on regardless. To be fair the food was not as bad as I had previously envisaged. My roast was tender, Colin's mixed grill was the size of a small town in Wales, Grace was getting stuck into her rack of lamb and even Melissa's veggie lasagne appeared to look almost edible.

Just then Grace spilled a spot of gravy onto her bountiful cleavage. I thought about doing the gentlemanly thing and dabbing it gently with a napkin. It couldn't have been too hot, as Colin noticed it before she did. 'You've spilled a little bit of gravy, love.'

He gestured. 'Oh balls,' she said, wiping it away.

'Lucky they were there, otherwise that would have landed in your lap,' I said.

'Charlie!' growled Colin.

'They do come in handy sometimes. They were a present from Geoffrey, my third husband. He was definitely a boob man,' said Grace, carrying on.

'What, he bought you some boobs?' I asked. She giggled like a schoolgirl, while Colin had a face like thunder.

'Not exactly, they're all my own but as the years and gravity have taken their toll they were in need of a little perk up, so he kindly paid for a slight uplift.'

'I've always wanted to touch a pair of fake boobs. You know, just to see what they're like,' I said.

Mel and Colin stared at me open-mouthed. 'Sorry, did I say that out loud? This meat is really tender,' I said, trying to change the conversation. 'So you've been married before Grace? Just the once or…?'

'I've been wed four times, Terry, Alf, Geoffrey, and

Frank,' she answered without a hint of shame, embarrassment or regret.

'Everyone does these days. There's nothing wrong with giving Mother Nature a little helping hand' added Melissa, trying to steer the conversation on to a different path.

'Well, why not? Colin is kindly giving me a partial face-lift and tummy tuck for my birthday,' said Grace.

'Blimey,' I exclaimed, almost choking on a roast potato, 'How much is that going to set you back?' I asked him.

'Three grand,' he said nonchalantly, chewing on a whole sausage on a fork. 'We're having it done in the Czech Republic. It's much cheaper out there. We're going to combine it with a short sightseeing holiday through Austria and Hungary.'

'Three grand?' I exclaimed, 'Jesus, when did I ever get a present like that?'

'I wouldn't mind getting a nose job but on seeing one being performed on television I don't think I could ever go through with it,' said Mel. 'They stick a huge great file up there and start sanding big chunks off.'

'Do you mind, we are trying to eat here,' I said.

'Sorry.'

'So Mel, when is your baby due?' enquired the heavily-painted one.

'He or she should arrive in around four months and I can tell you it won't be a moment too soon. Ellie was a stroll in the park compared to this little bugger.'

'It's probably a boy,' said Grace, 'I had awful trouble with my Wayne and Ant-knee [I presume she meant Anthony]. Morning sickness, piles, chronic back pain, blood clots, you name it, I suffered with it!'

I put down my cutlery. A walk down her gynaecology memory lane had suddenly stifled my appetite.

Ellie stirred and looked around. 'Well hello sleepy head, do you fancy something to eat?' I said. 'There's sausage, mash and peas for a special little girl.' She yawned and nodded her head, her hands reaching out for her mother.

'Oh isn't she adorable Colly?' exclaimed Grace.

'She is the most precious thing in the world,' he said smiling, while having another go on the toothpick. He pecked her on the cheek, got to his feet, staggering very slightly, and cleared his throat. *Uh-oh, I don't like the look of this.* 'I don't like to be too formal or stand on ceremony as you know, but I have an announcement to make' said Colin, his cheeks red and his nose even redder.

'Great, you're getting another round in. I think I'll have a short.'

'Shut up, stupid one. Now what was I saying? Oh yes, I'm not one for being too formal…'

'We know, that's why you walk to the paper shop in your slippers.'

'Shush Charlie!' hissed Melissa.

'But being here in the bosom of my family…'

'And there are plenty on show today,' I put in. I felt a pinch from my beloved.

'I can't keep our good news to ourselves any longer. I am delighted to tell you that last night I proposed to Grace and to my joy and overwhelming happiness she has accepted.'

I gulped down my umpteenth glass of wine. 'You proposed what exactly? A game of brag, a kitchen extension?'

'Marriage, you half-wit. Show them your ring, sweetheart,' said Colin proudly.

Grace extended a bony, waxen hand across the table. On her wedding finger was a rock of a size I had only previously seen on the fingers of Hollywood divas and premiership footballers' wives.

'That is gorgeous!' exclaimed Melissa. Even Ellie seemed impressed. I poured another drink from the bottle.

'That's not all Charlie. To make our special day complete I want you to be my best man.' It keeps on getting better.

'What will my duties be?' I asked.

'You will be helping me with the preparations, getting me to the church on time and organising my stag night.'

'A stag night? You are joking surely? Aren't you a bit on the mature side for a four-day break in Amsterdam and a tour of the red light district during which you contract something nasty you hope your bride won't notice before getting out of your head on pot?'

'Actually I was thinking of a couple of bitters at the Shoulder of Mutton before a sit down and moderately-priced buffet at the bowls club.'

'Congratulations,' said Mel and reached over for a hug and kiss with Grace. 'Are you having a hen night?'

'You bet. We'll get out of our heads in town on a pub crawl before going to the Ricochet club where we'll watch several strapping men take their kit off and half drown in baby oil! Say you will come?'

Mel nodded enthusiastically. I looked at Colin and shook my head in disbelief. I'll give it six months. He'll either be penniless or six feet under.

'Right, who wants pudding?' said Colin.

CHAPTER THREE

In the car

We were nearly home when I awoke. I still felt a bit pissed, but the urge to have any more had dissipated. My rapid lunchtime session had stretched well into the afternoon, leaving me with a tongue I was in no hurry to return to my mouth, plus the beginnings of a killer headache and the dreaded Sunday night blues, with only the prospect of another working week ahead of me.

Melissa looked across. 'Hello sleeping beauty, have you had a nice little snooze?'

I grunted and reached into her handbag for a mint or a packet of chewing gum.

'I don't know about you but I've had a really nice

afternoon,' she said. 'The service was a bit slow but we were in no hurry, were we? The meal was nice, even Ellie cleared her plate before polishing off all of her ice-cream.'

'Marvellous,' I grumbled.

'What's wrong?'

'Isn't it patently clear?'

'If it is I'm peering straight through it.'

'When my dear mother died I didn't get a single penny. No matter that I was legally her closest living relative, everything, the money in her savings account, the house and all her knick-knacks and bits and bobs went to Colin.'

'They did live together for twenty-odd years.'

'I know and I didn't really mind at the time, plus Colin did kindly direct five grand in the direction of my back pocket. The reason I wasn't too miffed was because I knew everything would eventually be coming my way anyway. That little nest egg was earmarked to keep us away from the poverty trap it's all too easy to fall into in one's senior years. I had planned to either sell the place and get a nice lump sum to live on or alternatively rent it out and live off the steady income that the old homestead would bring in.'

'You've got it all worked out haven't you?' said Mel.

'One has to think ahead darling. You all depend on me and my financial expertise and fiscal management of our funds.'

She laughed. 'Charlie, you are the worst person with money I know! I wouldn't trust you with the small change I find down the back of the sofa, let alone a whopping great inheritance.'

'Oh, so it's you who pockets all that is it? No wonder all I ever find down there are toast crumbs and Polly Pocket accessories.'

'So what's your beef?'

'My beef, my darling, is the fact that my precious little legacy is disappearing rapidly from view and sliding nicely into the handbag of a fifty-two-year-old, big-titted, false-eyebrowed, chain-smoking, chardonnay-swilling, grasping, husband-murdering bitch.'

'I know she's a little on the trashy side, but she seemed genuine enough to me. I think there's a real love story going on there.'

'Don't be so naive Mel. She's a gold-digging slapper who's hooked prospective hubby number five or whatever it is with the lone goal of fucking me over and feathering her own nest.'

'Don't swear in front of Ellie. You know how she picks up on everything she hears. I think you're being selfish Charlie. Is this because you are angry at Colin moving on from your mum?'

'Don't be ridiculous. Am I the only one who can see what's going on here? She doesn't give a flying...' I looked over my shoulder. Ellie was awake and smiled at me. 'She doesn't give a flying fig about poor old Colin. It's not love that shines in her eyes, it's pound signs.'

We turned into our drive. I looked up and noticed I'd left the light on in the bathroom. More money down the drain, I thought.

'You don't know that,' argued Mel. 'OK I admit she has a bit of a previous but haven't we all. Maybe it's going to be fifth time lucky for her. You don't know what's happened to her in her past. I know lots of women who always go for the wrong men and it never works out and yet they still go for the same type again and again.'

'Rubbish, I bet she did them all in and has already put an order in for her next dose of arsenic for poor unsuspecting Colin, or 'Colly' as he's now known.'

'You've been watching far too much television. They are merely two simple people in the autumn of their years seeking companionship and security. What is so wrong with that?'

'What's wrong my dear, sweet, gullible, naive and romantic fool, is that some over-made-up grasping strumpet is making a complete fool of Colin with the solitary goal of getting her claws into my inheritance and leaving me to look forward to a miserable fucking penny-pinching old age!'

'Language! There are small impressionable ears about,' hissed a displeased Melissa.

We parked on the drive, where I picked up my now wide awake little daughter and prepared for an evening of headaches, dull TV and sulking.

CHAPTER FOUR

The working man's blues

I make glasses for a living. Not the fun pint-sized type you drink beer from at the pub on a Friday night, but the kind you put on to see where you're going and to read the daily papers. The kind that the attractive female lead will wear as the role of a scientist or some other specialist and brainy position in a Hollywood movie. These are thought to lend her character depth, and let you know that she's not just some bimbo put in for a bit of eye candy. No, she's clever AND attractive, and an integral part of the plot. This tactic is also prevalent in the porn industry when the role of a secretary or teacher is needed.

It's a dull way to make a living, just like most other jobs I guess. Once you've mastered everything and performed the same series of actions time after time, whether it's putting a lens in a frame or attaching a nerve during microsurgery, it all becomes routine in the end. Yes, I caught you stifling a yawn and observed your eyes glazing over. I don't blame you; it is one of the dullest professions imaginable, but it is a means to an end and it pays the mortgage and keeps me in beer, etc, etc. What I do find fairly irritating is that when I tell people what I do they for some reason feel compelled to take off their own specs and hand them to me for inspection, usually informing me of the price they paid and where they purchased the damn things. Why, for heaven's sake? If I'm at a party and am introduced to someone who happens to be a mechanic or works on the cheese counter at Tesco, do I feel it necessary to quiz them on the fuel efficiency of a Ford Focus or whip out a portion of brie from my back pocket and ask them what they think? Of course not, so why do people pounce on me? Usually I give their glasses the once over, hand them back and say 'Yes it's a pair of spectacles all right, don't worry you haven't been duped.'

Still, the money is not too bad and as it's all I've ever done and I'm too frightened/un-ambitious/old/lazy to change now I suppose I should be content with my lot. Yes I am full of regrets that I was never a pop star with a long string of top ten hits and an even longer string of admiring groupies. Or that I never became England's leading goal scorer with a comfy future ahead of me appearing on a Saturday evening spouting off my irrelevant opinions on *Match of the Day*. Back in the real world there have been plenty of times over the years when I had the opportunity to climb out of my rut and do something I might actually have enjoyed and found a bit more of a challenge. Twice in the past I have been made redundant, only to fall back into the one trade I know and loathe. In conclusion, I am a lazy, lazy man.

I do recall, after seeing a small advert in the local paper, that I did, with much encouragement from my ex, summon up enough energy to apply for a job at a small independent brewery. I put on a clean shirt, combed my hair and nervously made the interview on time. Unfortunately, the salary was only a little over half of what I was then earning and I found it hard to concentrate on the interview questions, as the owner's wife, who was interviewing me, was wearing an almost see-though blouse and no bra. I wasn't offered the position. Maybe if I'd have talked to her face instead of her tits I might have got a call back, but as it was I never heard from them and my dreams of being an apprentice brewer were dashed before they had even started.

So there it is. For my sins I am destined to be a glazer of specs for the rest of my working days with no promise of parole or time off for good behaviour, and what with the bloody government deciding that there are far too many wrinkly types currently drawing their pensions they will have no choice but to raise the retirement age to a hundred and thirty-five and keep us working until we drop.

I have been working at this place for about a decade. It has gone under three different name changes and as many owners in that time, each bringing in their own directors, management structures and ideas to make the place profitable and ready to meet the optical world's needs for the twenty-first century. Our latest owners are a consortium based in Munich, where with typically German ruthless efficiency they are bringing in their own unique brand of cold, ruthless working methods. How times have changed since I first joined the profession twenty-something years ago. Back then you were paid weekly, receiving a small brown envelope stuffed with money which had just one corner of the notes exposed to count and be checked before it was ready to be ripped open and joyfully spent. Being just a small underdeveloped spotty youth, I had no mortgage, direct debits or bills to worry about. In my case my cash usually found itself heading towards the tills of Burtons, Our Price record store and the one pub they deemed I looked old enough to get served in. Fifteen quid each week was nabbed by my mother to pay for my keep before I had time to blow it all on jeans, Madness albums and Heineken.

Back then you could drink endless cups of coffee, smoke (though I never did) and eat whatever you had brought in or ordered from the canteen at your work station. The section in which I was placed (and I was the only male) was full of very frank-speaking and saucy ladies and it certainly opened my eyes to the opposite sex and the world beyond the playground and my bedroom. I never knew women swore, spoke about sex and men's willies and fell out with each other. I constantly felt embarrassed, which would result in a bright red face, known as a 'beamer', and the more my discomfort showed the more they'd try to increase my distress by talking about periods, vibrators, bras and the inevitable 'problems down below'. Back then in the early eighties, at the height of Thatcher's recession, there were three and a half million unemployed, and a kid leaving school with no more than a handful of moderate CSEs was expected to be grateful for any work he or she could get, no matter how mundane and dead end. And as jobs go they didn't come much more soul destroying than mine. From eight until four thirty I had to stand in front of a Dalek-sized object that smoothed the surface of the lenses and repeat the following sequence over and over again: 1.Take two lenses from the 'in' tray and place them in their corresponding lens holders. 2. Press the foot pedal and place the lenses and their holders in the machine. 3. Press the green start button and wait fifteen seconds for the smoothing process to finish. 4. Press the foot pedal to release the lenses. 5. Remove the lenses from the holders and place them in the 'out' tray. 6. Repeat two thousand times before knocking off time.

During the long, hot, never-ending summer afternoons I would often question the need for eleven years of schooling to train me for such a simple and mundane task. How were my algebra classes with grumpy maths teachers and double periods of geography meant to aid me in this? Surely a better way to prepare me for this mind-numbing task would to have had me staring at a brick wall for hours at a time or sitting outside in a steady drizzle watching the grass grow. Among the closely-knit crew of our department (they had all been there forever - Shelley was still known as the 'new girl' after almost a decade) there was Joan (her adopted English name – her real name was Karwinder but for some inexplicable reason this was deemed too difficult for the English tongue), and an old lady with a potty mouth called Phyllis who walked with a limp and always offered me a sweet when I entered her little lens inspection booth. These days that kind of activity would be called 'grooming' and some sort of custodial sentence would be offered as a deterrent. There was Ann, a spotty but attractive girl who I fancied and would probably have stood a chance with had she been five years younger and Lynne, a grumpy old hag who permanently seemed to have a wet fag hanging from her lips which she would occasionally remove with her pink marigold covered hands to take a sip of the coffee that one of her colleagues had fetched for her. She was the fastest worker in the department and had reached almost legendary status.

The lady who captured most of my attention however was Heather, a loud and brassy forty-something whose job it was to dish out my duties for the day. As you can imagine my sixteen-year-old hormones were in overdrive and many a fantasy was fuelled by a glimpse of her cleavage or the tops of her stockings when she bent over to pick up a stack of trays full of semi-finished lenses.

The person to whom I grew closest however was Pat, a forty-something mother of three. Over the next few years she became a maternal figure to me, and things I would never consider sharing with my real mum I would happily talk over and receive guidance on from her. She was softly spoken, with grey candyfloss hair and a toothy smile. She also ran a shop-from-home catalogue from which I bought my first electric guitar and amp (which always was full of reverb and distortion, which drove Colin mad) on which I gladly handed over five pounds and ninety pence a week to meet the payments. I suppose there is every possibility that getting on for thirty years later Pat is no longer alive and is now just a memory to the people who knew, loved and needed her.

Back to the present day. Our chief bringer of misery, the Darth Vader to my Luke Skywalker if you will, was our 'systems co-coordinator'. What is a systems co-coordinator, I hear you ask? Well, your guess is as good as mine. Judging by the miserable humourless bitch that filled the role there, her job description must have read 'bringer of despondency, provider of red tape and the introducer of pointless rules and initiatives that demotivate staff and waste time and money'. She strutted around with her nose in the air with her inbuilt radar on full alert for any transgressor daring to disregard company policy. The trouble was that she held all the aces, as I had previously found out. On one occasion I had sneakily placed a headphone in one ear to keep track on England's progress in the fourth test of a very close Ashes series. Spotting me with her hawk-like vision from across the factory floor, she marched over and informed me that I was not permitted any audio equipment, mobile phone or iPod on company premises. I looked up from the lens I was drilling and said disinterestedly, 'Yes I've heard that too but I think it's just a rumour,' and carried on with my work. With steam coming from her ears, she turned on her heels and stomped off. Within a couple of minutes the inevitable happened and I was invited by the Glazing Manager for a 'chat' in his office, where despite sympathizing with me and inquiring if Flintoff had reached his century yet, regretfully insisted that I play by the rules, remove my earpiece and run along like a good little boy.

I mention this as I can see her thin, bony form heading my way now. There was a cup of coffee sitting on my desk;

another banned luxury. Here we go: 'Charlie, what is that doing there?' she asked, pointing to the offending article. I stared at it for a full five seconds before replying that I didn't think it was doing anything.

'Don't try to be smart. You know the rules, no drinks or food are permitted to be consumed at your work station.'

'Look, I had to nip to the shops during my tea break and didn't get time to have a brew. I am tired, grumpy and in severe need of a caffeine injection. I promise to be extremely careful and not spill it.'

Her usually colourless cheeks flushed slightly, her blood-red lips puckering as she listened to my plea for leniency. 'If you are thirsty you could have visited the water dispenser. You will have to take an early lunch and drink it in to the canteen or pour it down the sink,' she demanded.

I looked steadily into her cold blue-grey eyes before picking up my nearly full and still steaming mug and lobbed it in a nearby bin.

'That was rather irresponsible wasn't it? What happens when the cleaners come to empty that?'

She looked around for any further signs of rule breaking and dissention. She wasn't disappointed. 'Are you aware that you are only permitted to have one personal item on your desk?' she said, quoting from the rulebook. I looked at the Manchester United football pendant and the family photo of Mel, Ellie and myself that was taped to the black inspection board in front of me.

'Oh my god!' I exclaimed with a generous helping of sarcasm, 'and all the time here was me with two! Bloody hell, I'm surprised the business is still running and that the place hasn't fallen down around our ears. What a decision though. What do I lose; the precious reminder of why I am sitting here making glasses for nine miserable hours a day, or the tribute to possibly the best football team in England? It's a toughie and no mistake. So what is it going to be? Am I going to be publicly flogged or am I going to get away with a private beating behind closed doors?'

'Just lose one OK, and while you are at it you can give this place a bit of a clean-up,' she said, wiping a skeletal finger through the dust and grime on the small inspection lamp above my tool rack. 'Also this belongs here,' she added, moving my coffee-flavoured bin six inches to the left so it was parked squarely inside the small area marked off by bright yellow tape. Yes, that is true, I kid you not. The world has gone health and safety mad.

'Did I see you on the stepladder earlier?' she asked.

'Possibly one of the jobs was trapped on the conveyor belt and caused a back-up of trays.'

'In future if that happens, just press the emergency stop and call for a manager. You are not allowed to climb up there until you have received basic ladder training.'

'Basic ladder training! What in arse's name is that?' I said.

'We have undertaken a full risk assessment and only qualified members of staff are permitted to use climbing equipment. I will email your manager about it,' she said, making a note on the clipboard that was permanently clutched to her bosom-less chest before flouncing off, in all probability almost orgasmic with rule enforcement pleasure.

Mark, my best buddy and long-suffering co-worker, shook his head. 'What that woman needs is a good hard cock up her desert-dry fanny to loosen her up a bit.'

'Well, it's not going to be mine, but if you're volunteering? Mind you, she would probably make you carry out a full risk assessment first.'

'No thanks. I think if I was faced with Ms Smyth in sexy undies, stockings and suspenders and her varicose veins glowing a delicate shade of blue in the subtle bedroom lighting, I don't think I would be able to reach full arousal.'

'Who would?' I replied, trying not to picture the scene too vividly. 'I imagine her tits would look like two fried eggs hanging on a nail.' I delved into the bin and peeling off some spent chewing gum, placed my mug inside the desk drawer which was marked as personal. Everything had to be labelled for some reason I was yet to fully grasp.

'I don't know, I can remember when you were allowed to have a bit of fun and a laugh at work. I think the powers that be must get together every so often these days and think up new ways to piss everyone off and lower morale. Anything that may slightly add enjoyment or happiness to our dreary day is banned or restricted.'

I sighed. 'Yes, it's crap isn't it. I am seriously thinking it's time for a change.'

'Hey, you can't bugger off and leave me here to die all alone.'

'What do you mean, on your own? This place employs over a hundred people. You'll have plenty of company to see out your final days with,' said Mark.

'Yes, half of whom are Indian and I can barely understand one word in three, and the rest are made up of grumpy post-menopausal woman who cackle like distressed hyenas and chavvy school leavers with whom I have nothing in common.'

'So you expect me to stay here with the solitary reason being to keep you sane?'

'That's what friends are for. It's a dirty job but somebody has to do it' I said.

'Dave and Jez had the right idea. They saw the way things were going and got out while the going was good.'

'I don't remember the going ever being good. We've moaned and bitched since day one. There was never a golden age,' I argued.

'Maybe not, but it was definitely better than this.'

'It's funny, but when you are a child you think adults are so different and grown up, another species entirely from you and your chums in the classroom, but when you think about it this place is not so far removed. There's still name-calling, playground feuds and petty jealousies' I said.

'I don't know, I haven't observed many games of hopscotch, British bulldog or 'What's the time Mr Wolf' lately.'

'What I mean is, just like at school there are small exclusive circles of friends and gangs. There are those who don't like certain people and others that pretend that they do then run them down to others behind their backs.'

'There are those whose entire working lives seem to be made up of moaning that someone else might be getting away with something they are not,' said Mark.

'I know, in fact sometimes I believe we were more mature and generous in spirit as children than what we have become. We are all big kids and tiny adults really.'

'Well, not us obviously, we are great, it's just the rest of them,' said Mark.

'Yeah, we're great and they are all bastards' I said in self-satisfied tones.

CHAPTER FIVE

I'm not being funny but...

It was a beautiful sunny morning. The day was hot without a hint of breeze, and even with the air conditioning full on it was still a shirt-moisteningly-hot drive down to the large ex-council house in which I was born and raised, firstly by my mum and dad and then, when Father sadly past away, Colin. I always enjoy going back, although in the last couple of years it's been far too infrequent. Nothing seems to change, although the house and garden seem smaller than when I was a child. There are far more cars now as well.

They are everywhere, parked bumper to bumper with one side up on the kerb, nose to tail and on both sides of the road. These houses were built in the late forties when having one car, let alone two, was still just a dream to the average working-class family. The only houses with off-road parking are those who have paid to have drives put in themselves in more recent times after Maggie told us that we should all have the right to own our own places. The fact that now there are no council houses left for the low-paid or young couples starting out was obviously an eventuality that was overlooked.

Many here still have large front gardens, which at this time of the year are abundant with green shrubs and flowers in full bloom. I read somewhere that the number of gardens that have been paved over is partly the cause of the frequent and widespread flooding we get nowadays. It's something to do with the loss of natural drainage. It's the wealthier owners on our road who have had theirs replaced by Tarmac, concrete and block-paving, but looking out of your front window what would you prefer to view, an azalea in all its glory bordering a perfectly-tended lawn or the boot end of a Citroën Picasso? Mind you, if it's your car that gets its wing mirror persistently knocked off by what's-his-name on his way home from the pub each Friday night, you'd probably say sod the flowers and get the council to drop the kerb and pay for a drive to be put in as well.

As the long road sweeps around, you approach the corner shop. OK, it's not actually on a corner, but you know what I mean. It sells everything from cans of chopped tomatoes to ex-rental Playstation games. You can get your phone unlocked, buy second hand gardening equipment, get the number of someone with an unwanted kitten and purchase a lottery ticket all in the one visit. It was here that I had a paper round at the age of thirteen until I left school. Back then the owner was a strange balding man who was a bit too partial to the fruits of the hop to get up every morning before dawn to organize half a dozen cheeky paper boys who had to get their rounds completed in time to catch the school bus. Often we'd be standing outside the unlit shop freezing our recently-dropped bollocks off for half an hour before agreeing en masse to go back home when with a collective groan we'd see his headlights on the horizon and realise we would have to do our rounds after all. Mine used to take an hour and a half and even longer on Fridays when many customers required the heavy local paper as well as their usual dailies. My sack was so heavy that it took all my strength and balancing ability to keep my bike upright. Blimey, that sounds rude! Actually, as I recall my nut sack was pretty trim back then. It's only with the passage of time that things have seemed to expand and droop. I was standing next to an old boy in the showers at the local pool the other day and his under-satchel would have passed for a 1970s space hopper. Same colour too.

Many a time on a Sunday morning, laden down by colour supplements, I would veer off under their weight and crash into someone's carefully-sculpted hedge. All that for four miserable pounds a week. That works out at less than fifty pence an hour. What a tight bastard! These days in the current climate of over-protective parents and sick paedophiles, the paperboy is an endangered species. About bloody time if you ask me! Our local paperboy these days is a fifty-something woman who flies out of her Ford Fiesta like Starsky and Hutch after a tip-off from Huggy Bear.

As I half expected, there was no answer when I rang the bell. I walked around the house along the narrow shaded path to the back garden. I could hear the drone of Colin's petrol mower before I spied him. His portly figure was dressed in a T-shirt that didn't quite make it to his waist, blue shorts and sandals. His spindly white hairless legs somehow supported the red, sweating tubby mass that was pushing the well-worn machine across the large expanse of lawn.

He caught sight of me, waved and killed the engine. 'Hello son, how are you?' he said, obviously delighted to see me.

'A bit hot and bothered, it certainly is a scorcher, though not as hot and bothered as you by the look of it, have you been at it long?'

'All morning. I'm nearly done, just got to do the top and run the strimmer round and I'll be done. You can give me a hand if you like?'

'No ta, I've got new trainers on and I don't want them all green and grassy.' I pointed to my gleaming white Nikes.

'What a surprise, Charlie Bennett turning down the offer to do some graft. There's some little lagers in the fridge, pour one out, I shouldn't be more than twenty minutes.'

I did as instructed and sat under the large green parasol at the freshly scrubbed white plastic patio table while Colin huffed and puffed in the noonday sun. What did Noel Coward say about mad dogs and Englishmen? The garden and house have undergone many changes since we first moved here in the mid-seventies. Then it had been empty for several months with many prospective tenants declining to take up residency, put off no doubt by the lack of any real heating, the dated and worn-out look of the place and the enormous overgrown jungle like garden that had obviously been a dumping ground for all and sundry for years. This didn't deter Mum and Dad however and they set to the task with relish. While Mum was in charge of decorating their new palace, starting with papering over the gaudy old painted walls of orange and dark brown with more subtle tones, Dad wrestled with the massive undertaking of the back garden. These days, when developers try to pack as many cheaply-built houses as they can into the smallest plot, it's hard to imagine the council giving anyone a garden that huge, but times were different then, people's quality of life mattered more and everything wasn't tied down to targets, budgets and the pressing need for 'affordable housing'. It must have measured around twenty-five yards across by about a hundred long. So overgrown was it that the initial clearing threw up some remarkable finds; a three-seater velour sofa in mauve was found behind a formidable clump of pampas grass, two broken mowers were upturned and lifeless under the remains of a demolished greenhouse and a rowing machine that would row no more was found when a substantial nettle bush was hacked down. The *pièce de resistance*, however, was the decomposing remains of a couple of slaughtered goats behind the top shed. Were the previous owners members of some kind of satanic sect? We never found out, although judging by the four baked potatoes left in the oven they had left in something of a hurry. Steps, paths and even a large fishpond were later discovered when the junk and brambles had been consigned to history. Mum put in some beautiful shrubs, while Dad created a large vegetable plot towards the top where he later added a greenhouse. This still left a large area for yours truly where in spring, autumn and winter it was a football pitch for me and my new friends, while in summer the goal was replaced by stumps and cricket was played (only with a soft ball though, anything deemed a danger to Dad's greenhouse was strictly forbidden).

Presently Colin was done, and while he was putting the strimmer back on its hook in the shed I returned to the fridge and got us both a drink. He sat down, red-faced and sweaty. He retrieved a crumpled hanky from his shorts pocket and mopped his glistening brow.

'The garden's looking lovely,' I said admiring his hard work.

'It doesn't get any easier. I'm getting too old for all of this. Grace is talking about moving to the Algarve. I'm beginning to think it's not such a bad idea.'

'And what would you do out there? You'd be bored stiff in no time. You know you would miss all the clubs and societies you belong to over here. You wouldn't be happy lazing around a swimming pool everyday topping up your tan. It's just not you.'

He said nothing and took a large draught of his beer.

'And you would miss out on seeing Ellie grow up and the new baby on its way,' I added.

'Maybe you're right,' he replied, shutting his eyes and raising his chin, feeling the power of the sun on his face. 'Maybe we'll just go for something slightly smaller, a nice little bungalow or something on the coast. Brighton or somewhere like that.'

'Colin, I don't mean to be funny or to poke my nose in

where it's not wanted but are you sure about all of this? Do you really want to marry this woman?'

'Obviously, otherwise I wouldn't be doing it. Why do you ask?'

'I'm just a tad worried, that's all. Look, I think she's nice in an obvious kind of way, but are you sure of her motives?'

'How do you mean?' he asked, avoiding my gaze and instead preferring to look at the results of his hard morning's graft. The lawn was a lush green that the head groundsman at Wembley would have been proud of and the flowers were picture postcard perfect.

'Right, I won't beat around the bush or pull any punches. You are, let's face it, a vulnerable seventy-year-old sitting on an expensive property with money in the bank, while she is almost twenty years younger, in and out of work with God only knows how many marriages behind her and living in a pokey council flat on a skanky estate filled with crack whores, pimps and abandoned shopping trolleys.'

I drew breath, waiting for a reaction. Colin doesn't blow his top often but when he does he goes bonkers. His face goes crimson; the veins pulse in his temple and spit tends to shoot out as he forcibly puts his side of things. But it didn't happen.

'Then I guess that's even more of a reason to put a bit of happiness back into her life,' he said.

'Mum wouldn't like her,' I countered, knowing that it counted for nothing.

He wiped the sweat from his brow with the back of his hand, 'Yes I know she's a bit on the showy side, common even by your mother's standards, but believe me Charlie she has a heart of gold and only my best interests at heart.' I said nothing and finished my beer. 'You do want me to be happy don't you, Charlie? I'm not good on my own. You can't expect me to pine over your mum forever. I loved her, still do, but I need to move on. I need company and I still want to love and be loved.'

'Of course I want you to be happy Colin. Christ I love you, you old bastard and that is why I don't want to see you being shafted by some money-grabbing black widow.'

'If you are going to insult my intended like that then you had better go,' he said, finally turning to look me in the eye. 'Did I interfere when you ballsed up your marriage? Did I ever put in my four-pennorth when you hooked up with Mel or started seeing that bird behind her back from the record shop? No, no I didn't. Fuck me, what makes you such a bloody expert all of a sudden? Your love life has been nothing more than a series of car crashes and near misses, and when you do finally somehow manage to land on your feet you contrive to do your best to throw it all a-bloody-way!'

Taken aback and trying not to admit that he was totally correct, I tried a different tack. 'Sorry Colin, that was uncalled for. You know her a lot better than me. Maybe she isn't just after what she can lay her hands on and is genuinely besotted with you. Maybe she is a soft and gentle soul behind all that make up and peroxide. Possibly you will spend your twilight years together going for long walks, picking wild flowers and helping one and another on and off the toilet. I want you to be happy, I really do.'

He sighed and said nothing. There was an embarrassing pause. 'Have you made a will by the way?' I ventured.

Colin smiled and nodded his head. 'Ah, I might have

known.' He laughed. 'So this is what this is all about. I should have known you wouldn't have driven all the way down here unless there was some kind of monetary interest in it for you. You don't give a toss about my feelings or welfare. You couldn't give a damn if I was marrying Grace or the woman from the paper shop with the hairy wart and the bald patch. All you are interested in is how much cash you may miss out on when I finally pop off.'

'Don't be so silly,' I replied. 'You are all the family I have and your happiness and welfare are everything to me. But…'

'Yes?'

'But however cold and uncaring it may sound, it is an issue. I didn't get a bean when Mum went and now when you tie the knot with the fearsome Grace everything will be left to her. Melissa, Ellie and me will get shafted, and I can't imagine her being a generous benefactor once she's pushed you off your Algarve balcony.'

'Typical Charlie, you haven't let me down.' He sighed. 'As usual everything has to be about you, you and you.'

'But Colin,' I pleaded, 'I can't believe you can't see what she's up to. It's so obvious. She's a cold-hearted old slapper who's spotted a vulnerable old sap and can see a free meal ticket to keep her in gin, boob jobs, tummy tucks and shopping trips from here to fucking eternity!'

Colin finished his beer and without looking in my direction, got to his feet. 'I'm just going to do a spot of weeding in the top bed. Make sure you shut the gate properly on your way out, won't you?'

I sat there, my forearms burning in the sun, already regretting my words and wondering if an apology would put things right. I watched Colin stomp off towards the top of the garden. He picked up a hoe and began jabbing at the ground angrily, his back towards me. I finished my beer. It was warm, flat and deeply unsatisfying. I picked up my car keys from the table, peeled my sweaty self from the chair and left him to his slightly stunted delphiniums and prepared myself for the long drive back home.

CHAPTER SIX

Well, what am I gonna do now?

Everything was as it should be. It was just another day like the thousands of others that had preceded it. I woke up as usual half an hour before my alarm was due to go off and groaned inwardly at the prospect of another working day. My head felt like it was stuffed with cotton wool due to the alcohol I'd enjoyed the night before and I was trying my best to hold in a fart that would have made the bedclothes rise up like the skirt of a hovercraft.

As always, I pulled on my crumpled clothes half asleep

before stumbling into the bathroom and dragging my seven-year-old electric razor across my chin while wincing with discomfort as it didn't so much shave my chin as pull the whiskers from it. I switched on the kettle then turned it off again, realising it was empty, and filled it with the minimum amount of water required. I then scraped Marmite across a couple of sorry-looking pieces of toast. One side was as pale as a Scotsman in winter and the other side resembled, in colour, taste and texture, charcoal. I turned on the TV, nimbly avoided breakfast television and turning instead to Sky Sports News to see if any major stories were breaking. I have no idea why I bother to do this, as this is also the last thing I do before turning in at night. What players United hope to sign between the hours of eleven at night and six in the morning during a closed transfer window I am unable to imagine.

As always my car managed to get me to work on autopilot with little or no help from myself and I stumbled across the firm's car park with the same amount of enthusiasm as a condemned man heading towards the gallows. As I prepared myself for another day of sameness and boredom, alleviated only by the desperate humour of my fellow inmates, I looked at my watch. Only ten minutes late, I'll have to be careful, at this rate I will soon be up for a promotion.

One thing that's noticeable about Huntingtons is that if you can survive the first couple of years, the soporific and coma-inducing monotony of the job has a tendency to suck your ambition and drive to do something with your life right out of you. With this being the case you will no doubt give up looking elsewhere for employment and become a resident of these dark and dingy walls until retirement or infirmity. There are many employees (mainly female and post-menopausal) who have spent over twenty years here and have loathed every minute and pray daily for a firebomb to turn the place to a smouldering wreck, yet here they remain, ready to gripe and bitch through another day.

I mumbled a 'morning' to Mark, placed my lunchbox into my bottom drawer, retrieved my tool rack, drill and sundries for the day ahead and placed them neatly in their usual places on my desk ready for action. As someone informed me when I was an impressionable sixteen-year-old school leaver, wet behind the ears and still filled with hope, good intentions and bubbling hormones, 'a tidy bench is a happy bench'. Yes, sad isn't it, being brainwashed by a dirty old man with questionable motives and stained overalls? Still, that's the folly of youth I suppose, misguided, innocent and vulnerable, like a lamb to the slaughter.

With my muzzy head slowly clearing from the preceding evening's dancing with the good lady Stella (as I get older I find I need a mid-week pick-me-up more than ever) I managed to negotiate the morning's tasks without breaking too many lenses, which is a common occurrence after a night of ale and a couple of double shots of whatever spirit we have lying about. Last night I was scraping the barrel even for me. Still, sloe gin and flat Diet Sprite isn't as bad as it sounds. I even managed to refrain from barking at anyone who dared to have the temerity to ask me a question about what they should do with the green plastic tray in their hand. You can probably guess what my standard response is (it's usually along the lines of 'bend over and I'll show you).

Just before eleven, as my morning tea break approached, I at last began to feel less grouchy and more human. Mark and I played our usual game of 'Who would you do?' This time our subjects were the tubby blonde on final checking or the stern-looking woman wages clerk from upstairs. We compared the amount of alcohol units consumed the previous evening and weighed up who had the nicest sandwiches for lunch, a game he constantly wins as Anna, his wife, really pushes the boat out, introducing exciting and exotic combinations like Brie and apple or hand-reared goose and truffles. Mine are crap and generally half-arsed, usually involving a cheese triangle and cold greenish mash potato leftovers from the furthest corner of the fridge. This is because Melissa makes me do them myself while she prefers to watch someone's life falling apart in East Enders. In today's battle of the box Mark won hands down. How can my Marmite and cucumber on stale and thin 'Happy Shopper' budget bread compare to his roast beef, horseradish, avocado and rocket salad on a freshly home-baked ciabatta? It's not fair I tell you. No wonder he's over six foot, handsome, well-nourished and healthy looking while I am stunted, blotchy, puffy and handicapped by a constant craving for crisps and grossly overpriced chocolate bars from the canteen's vending machine.

As I got to my feet I noticed many of the rest of my department heading like worried sheep, one after another, past the double bench that Mark and I shared and towards the corridor which led to the stairs and the upper floor. We exchanged quizzical looks as our departmental manager strode purposefully towards us. There was something in his poker face and focused demeanour I didn't like. Usually he's so laid back as to be almost falling over with a cheery joke and an 'I'll leave it to you lads to get on with things, you know what you're doing' kind of attitude, but this was totally out of character.

'Up to the boardroom boys, the Managing Director wants a word with us all, straight away now.'

'What's up Gerry, is it serious?' I enquired. Usually if an announcement is to be made we gather in a circle in the middle of the department, as we struggle to hear what's being said over the din of lenses being cut and the clattering of conveyer belts. It's either a minor moan from the production director about quality or figures, or both, or a dull speech lamenting the sad departure of some lucky beggar who's been granted parole and is leaving us for sunnier prospects and a better job. I have been here over a decade and can count on the fingers of one hand, well to be more truthful, count on the fingers on the hand of a careless farm worker who wasn't thinking and decided to trim his nails in the blades of his combine harvester, the amount of times I have been invited upstairs to the executive part of the company where men in large suits and larger salaries ascend to while we lower-class factory types get on with the mucky job of making the firm money. It's very 'Upstairs Downstairs' here with a definite 'them and us' attitude. 'Them' are the rich bastards who never get their hands dirty while 'us' are the idiots downstairs who beaver away, out of sight of the fortunate and executive, in case we offend them with our coarse words and offensive smell. Well that's our take on things anyway. They may work really hard on our behalf and think we are doing a great job, but unless we ever have any contact with each other how will we ever know?

'Get yourselves upstairs lads and you'll find out' said Gerry in a businesslike tone. As we joined the throng on our way to the inner sanctum (or the inner scrotum as we sometimes refer to it) I said to Mark, 'I don't like the look of this. I bet they're finally going to shut us down.'

'Na, I bet we've been taken over again. What will that be, three different owners in the last five years?'

'The last time we were bought out we didn't get asked to climb the hallowed stairs, it was just stuck on the notice board on a memo. Maybe the mystery dirty protester in the woman's toilets is at it again and they are asking for the guilty person to own up,' I replied.

'Oh I know, I bet we aren't getting a Christmas meal this year. Either that or they are cutting our Christmas bonus so they have the necessary cash to wine and dine our customers at the Savoy on free champagne and East European prostitutes.'

'I hear that this year while our directors and customers are enjoying their caviar and venison there will be a live satellite feed on a jumbo screen of us working away for pennies while they look on laughing as they swig champagne and nibble on truffles served on the behinds of lap dancers.'

'That wouldn't surprise me,' Mark answered as we squeezed into the boardroom with our colleagues. There we stood, we scruffy types at one side, a handful of office types mingled in between and the managers and directors all suited and booted on the other. There were many nervous jokes being passed around but I didn't feel like joining in, I'd been here before. I noticed there was a top of the range coffee maker and complementary treats on a table at the far end. How the other half live, eh? I bet they don't get nagged about company policy and health and safety directives. They probably wallow around naked and greased up swigging coffee and poking their John Thomases in the power sockets without fear of rebuke or retribution.

A nervous hush fell over the large wood-panelled room as we were at last blessed by the entrance of the latest Managing Director. He was a hefty, cheery man with a figure that had obviously experienced many a business lunch that had stretched way into the afternoon. His rosy cheeks glowed like a highly-polished apple and his brow appeared moist. He avoided all eye contact as he reached his position at the head of the table. Unlike his predecessor, he appeared fairly well-grounded and ordinary, with a word or two for us serfs when he occasionally took a prospective new customer on a tour around the manufacturing department to show off the latest piece of technology the board of directors in the homeland had reluctantly agreed to finance. He was known to all as the 'fat controller', after the rotund top-hat-wearing character from Thomas the Tank Engine, but today as with Gerry there was no time for jovial banter and witty asides.

He paused for breath before beginning his address. 'As you are all in no doubt aware, things have become increasingly difficult for the company over these last eighteen months, since the beginning of this latest recession and the economic downturn. Orders are down forty percent on two years ago, and fifteen percent below this year's budget. With competition at an all-time high in a very competitive market, it has been difficult for RX houses like us to compete with the cheap deals on the high street.

Independent opticians, who are our bread and butter business, are closing at an alarming rate or being bought out by the larger high street chains, which are our direct competitors. As you are all aware, we lost twenty people from various departments last year in an attempt to cut costs and be more competitive, and I feel we have achieved fantastic results due to your tremendous commitment and hard work.'

He paused, reached forward and took a sip from a glass of water in front of him. Was his hand shaking ever so slightly?

'Unfortunately the holding group which own the company have, after much discussion with our head office in Munich regretfully decided to shut down production here in the UK due to financial constraints and the weakness of the pound. They are instead going to offer our customers a service where all orders are to be sent directly to Germany and Croatia where costs are considerably lower than in the UK and then be delivered by express courier to their places of business.'

A collective shaking of heads and groaning filled the crowded room. 'So what are you saying?' piped up one of the less cerebrally-blessed members of the now no longer wanted workforce.

The fat controller's lip visibly quivered. 'It is with enormous regret that I must announce that Huntington's has now ceased production in this country. Representatives of our parent company are on their way over as we speak to catalogue, stock-take and redeploy the orders we have in progress.'

There were shrugging shoulders, resigned groans and

the odd swear. The now ex fat controller tried to lift spirits. 'I have been assured that all employees will receive four weeks' notice in pay and a generous redundancy package.'

'Yeah, like that's going to last five minutes,' said an angry bloke who stood directly across from where I was, towards the back, next to an Indian lady with a hairy mole.

'I'm afraid that there is really nothing else I can tell you. I am as devastated as you at this turn of events. I know orders have been down but this has taken everyone, us included on the board of directors, by complete surprise. All I can add is that it's been a pleasure working with you in the few months I've been here. I was hoping for a long and fruitful association with you all, but it wasn't meant to be. If you would all like to clear your desks, say your goodbyes and remove all personal belongings as swiftly as possible that would be much appreciated.

'Finally, I would like to add my best wishes to you all for the future, it's been a pleasure knowing and working with you all, it really has.'

With that he shuffled his notes like the reader on the *News at Ten* and made his exit, closely followed by his sheepish-looking fellow directors. We shuffled out in silent single file through the narrow corridor, a distressed collective, numb, heads spinning and each trying to take it all in. Five minutes before we had been solvent employees whose only worries were what to have for tea when we ended the day and would there be anything good on the TV tonight. Now, a few brief sentences later, our lives were upside down and back to front. Mark and I followed the rest, heads down in a despondent trudge back to our benches.

I stood looking for a few seconds at the expensive

Swarovski frame I had been carefully working on before I had been so rudely interrupted. I picked it up and gave it the once over. It was perfectly on axis with the yellow painted progressive markings horizontal, and the shining gold bridge was sitting flawlessly straight. Its many crystals sparkled in the harsh glare of the banks of artificial overhead lighting. This little beauty had cost its new owner well over five hundred at least. Usually my next step would have been to offer the left side to the frame and see if it would sit straight. If it did I'd add a washer and a nut and if not I'd re-drill the hole slightly until it was at the satisfactory angle. Not today though. No, instead I gave it a last longing look, kissed it, and then with all my might, I threw it across the factory. It sailed gracefully in an arc through the air before landing almost silently behind a bank of machinery.

'Do you feel any better for that?' asked Mark, as he loaded the contents of the outer reaches of his bottom drawer into a scrunched-up plastic bag.

I shrugged. 'Not really.' I sighed. 'Maybe this will help?' I picked up a pile of seven trays. Each housed two lenses, a customer's order and a frame waiting to be glazed. I held them at arm's length and let them fall onto the floor. They made a satisfying sound that turned many a head.

'Well?' he enquired.

'Na, still hasn't done it,' I replied, 'I'll try this.' Approximately forty more trays were sitting behind our desks awaiting our attention. With a grandiose gesture I swept the whole lot aside. Trays smashed, lenses flew, frames disappeared and chaos reigned. 'Yeah,' I said standing in a pose like Superman, 'That hit the spot.'

We cleared our desks and went to leave. Mark took time to say goodbye to everyone and anyone. I wasn't in the mood and just wanted to get out of there as soon as possible. Despite this, I stopped to take one last lingering look at the place I'd haunted for so many years. I took a picture on my phone, turned the corner and walked for the very last time down the narrow corridor towards the clocking-out machine.

Can you believe it? Many of my misguided ex-workers were still, even though they were now redundant, taking the trouble to place their cards into the ancient machine and clock off for one last time. Whether it was out of habit or duty I wasn't sure.

Mark grabbed my arm. 'Do you fancy a beer at the Leather Bottle? Come on, there's nothing to hurry home for is there?'

'Go on then, one last time. I suppose I might as well have a drink while I can still afford it.'

Two hours later found me leaning lazily against the bar of the nearest hostelry to our ex-place of employ, surrounded by glasses, bottles and empty crisp packets. Mark and I were joined by old Les, a brilliant glazer who'd been in the trade working for various companies throughout Sussex and Kent all his working life. In his day he was a real ladies' man and often illuminated me on his former conquests, glories, near misses and narrow escapes. Completing our not-so-happy party was James, a raw and acne-ridden seventeen-year-old who was employed to mind the machines at the far end of the factory. I believe this, our final day, was the very first time we'd engaged in conversation. On an empty stomach the alcohol was racing through me. Dark thoughts of impending poverty had overtaken the feelings of initial shock and fake bravado.

'Well, that's me fucked then. They might as well cart me off to the workhouse right now,' I sighed. The glass I was viewing the world through was not so much half empty as completely empty, and cracked into the bargain.

'Come on, it can't be that bad,' said the young spotty one.

'James, do you live at home?' I asked. He nodded. 'And how much do you pay your dear old, sweet, silver-haired mother for your keep?'

'A hundred and fifty pounds a month, but she doesn't always ask for it.'

'And I guess that Mummy and Daddy wouldn't kick you out into the cold, frosty and shit-filled gutter if you lost your job through no fault of your own?'

'No, I can't do much wrong in her eyes. She's pretty forgiving is my Mum.'

'Where in contrast I have a wife who is partial to very expensive shoes. I also have a mortgage the size of Jordan's boobs, a child plus another one on the way, plus many credit card debts and two unmanageable car loans. So faced with this new catalogue of facts I have placed at your fingertips, it may be more understandable to you why I am sitting here drowning my sorrows and shitting my pants with a face liked a slapped arse!'

'I apologise for my friend,' interjected Mark. 'He suffers from an illness called miserable bastard syndrome. I'm afraid its terminal and at present there is no known cure.'

'Is it only me who can see the gravity of the situation?' I said exasperated. 'We've been right royally fucked over big time by a load of Lederhosen-wearing fat German sausage suckers who've left us to starve to death in cold and poverty while they warm themselves between the thighs of fat Bavarian maidens called Helga.'

'Yeah, I must admit I'm feeling pretty close to rock bottom,' said Les, putting down his pint. 'There's no chance of me getting another job in optics. Not at my age. It's the scrapheap for me. The next time you visit Homebase on a rainy Thursday morning it will probably be me you'll see wandering the endless corridors, looking lonely and lost and trying to avoid difficult customers' questions like, 'Will this paint suit my bathroom and does my one point six bottom nut need to be flanged?'

'Exactly Les,' I agreed, reaching for my back pocket and my wallet. 'Great usage of the word flange by the way. We more mature souls among us can grasp the levity of the situation.'

I hollered for four more beers at the young girl serving, who was idly flicking through the texts on her mobile.

'This is typical of you Charlie. Every day you slope in with an angry grey cloud thundering above your head and the world resting heavy on your shoulders, cursing everything and everyone for the circumstances that have conspired to your fate, and now that change and a way out have finally been forced on you, it's all of a sudden the end of the world.'

'Come on Mark, can you really tell me you're not worried? You are in the same boat as me. You have a family to support, a mortgage and suddenly no means to pay it.'

'Of course I'm concerned, but let's have a little reality check here shall we? You and I have been talking for years about leaving and finding something more rewarding. Well now we have the chance, no, sorry, the *need* to do it, and with a healthy bit of cash to keep us going while we do.'

I pulled a face, took a long draught and tried to convince myself he was right. What's the point of worrying? What good will that do anyone? I will try to take a positive approach, I told myself before instantly dismissing this as crazy talk.

'So what are you planning to do?' I asked him. 'I'll probably stay in this profession; get a job at Vision Express or Specsavers or something.'

'Why don't you do that Charlie? With your experience and skills I bet you'd walk into a job,' said James.

I took a large swig and sighed, 'Do you know what? I've had enough. I don't think I can play this game any more. Yep, I can tell you one thing for definite. I am never going to glaze another frame again. I've had it up to here with all of this. I'm sick to death of lenses and stupid little screws. I have had it up to here with grey-walled windowless factories. I hate being a pawn in a game played by faceless businessmen from other countries. I can't stand sitting down knowing I'm going to be doing the same thing as I did the day before and the day before that and the day before that, and then tomorrow and the day after. Do you know how long I've been doing this?'

'Twenty-eight years? Ah!' said Mark, playing an imaginary violin. 'Twenty-eight fucking years!' I announced. 'Do you know how many days I have woken up and been looking forward with anticipation about the working day ahead?'

'None?' said Mark in the voice of someone who had heard this diatribe many, many times previously.

'That's right,' I spat. 'So I ask you to raise your glasses

in a toast.' I cleared my throat. 'Ladies and gentlemen, well, there are no ladies present, no change there. I say gentlemen, raise your glasses to Huntingtons, formally known as Dostinuk, formally known as… sorry I can't remember, anyway, what I really want to say is goodbye to the old and hello to the new, whatever it may be.'

I slurped, and through the stem of my glass I watched my brothers-in-arms do the same. Yes I know it sounds ostentatious, overblown and over the top, but sometimes the occasion gets the better of me and grand gestures seem wholly appropriate. I downed my glass, wiped my chin and made a further announcement. 'Right, I need a piss!'

On my return they were discussing the booty they had managed to sneak out of the door before we were asked kindly to leave for the third time. 'Well,' said Lecherous Les, 'I managed to walk out of there with a full complement of tools, just in case someone wants to hire an old glazer with a wandering eye and a gammy leg. I also managed to palm a Gucci frame that somehow found its way inside my locker a while back, and two or three phone numbers of some of the more flirtatious and lonely woman of the factory.'

'Shit, I never thought about taking advantage of the situation. I should have grabbed loads of goodies to flog on ebay,' lamented James.

'The folly of youth,' I said, placing a reassuring hand on his narrow, sloping shoulders. 'I meanwhile managed to make off with my bits and bobs, three frames – one of which is a very desirable Oakley sun spec that I was about to work on before we were so rudely summoned upstairs, some booty from our stock cupboard and two packs of A4 printer paper,' I boasted proudly.

'Not bad my dear Charlie, though compared to my rich haul you appear to be a mere beginner, still wet behind the ears with downy bum-fluff clinging to his chin.'

'Oh yeah, come on then big boy. James has folded and I've laid a pair of Kings. What have you got to trump them?' I said, raising myself to my full swaying height of five feet ten.

'Have you ever, as I have, my dear ex-colleague and slightly pissed friend, admired the recently installed top of the range Hewlett-Packard laser printer that the mincing guy from IT installed a couple of weeks ago in the rear office? You are kidding me? You haven't? It is currently sitting in the boot of my car beneath a red and black check picnic blanket simply itching to be connected to my home PC.'

'Serves the bastards right' said Les, kindly passing the barmaid a crisp twenty-pound note. As happens on occasions such as this, our beery chat and memories wandered back through the years to people, events and incidents from the distant and not-so-distant past. There is nothing like a black event or an ending to spark off a journey into nostalgia and a joyful look back into all our yesterdays. We spoke of boozy nights out and momentous fuck-ups, the many co-workers who had come and gone and where we thought it had all gone wrong.

'I tell you who was a right weirdo,' said Les.

'That doesn't give us much of a clue, this place has been not as much a glazing house, as a rest home for the inadequate, the social misfit, and the physically deformed.'

'Alan Bathurst,' said Les.

'Blimey, you're not wrong there. He was a deeply troubled man, make no mistake, and no doubt a probable danger to the general public.'

'Who was he?' enquired James, leaning on the bar, heavily lidded and three sheets to the wind.

'He was a very strange man indeed,' said Les.

'Not half,' I said. 'He had this strange interest, some kind of hang up, whether it was sexually motivated or not I'm not one hundred percent sure.'

'A hang up about what exactly?' asked James.

'The old, the dying and the dead. That's right; he had tried and failed to get a job at every undertakers' in town and believed it was his destiny to become a mortician.'

'Do you remember that time he was off work and we found all those weird magazines and books in his desk?' asked Les.

'Yes, they were full of pictures of murder scenes, decomposing bodies and hacked-off body parts.'

'He was always telling me about the time he was out with his dad and puppy in the local woods and dear old Fido started sniffing and nosing around some body parts that had been poorly hidden.'

'That's right, and since then he's been obsessed with doing it again. He loves the smell of police tape in the morning.'

'Still, the clincher in his dead body fetish was his girlfriend.' I said.

'He wasn't doing a Norman Bates, was he?' asked James.

'No, but he wasn't far short.'

'I don't follow?'

'At the time I believe he was around a couple of years older than me, around the mid-thirty mark,' I replied. 'Whilst his girlfriend, and this was no minor fling by the way, they lived together, had joint accounts, the lot, was way into her seventies.'

'You're kidding?'

'No, and what's more she wasn't a youthful, glamorous, young at heart type of old girl, she was seventy going on eighty and looked like she'd had a bloody hard life and was older than her years.'

'So as you imagine, we all thought, dirty little fucker, we know your game. You are hanging on until she turns up her toes, grows cold and waxy and then-bingo! She'll be carried down to the basement for a homemade autopsy and a fulfilment of all his twisted needs and desires,' said Mark.

'I suppose it takes all sorts to make a world,' said James.

'Oh yes, and the proof was alive and in Technicolor within these walls. Do you remember that bloke, he only lasted a few weeks, he regularly came to work with his pyjamas clearly visible beneath his clothes?'

'How could I forget,' said Les. 'Even more disturbing was the fact that his place of choice to eat his lunch was the sit-down cubicle in the toilets.'

'You are kidding me?' said an amazed James. 'Even when you are on the plop you wouldn't want to spend a second more than necessary in that awful, awful place.'

'No, as amazing as it sounds, come one o'clock you'd find him sitting in the left cubicle with the door open as happy as a pig in shit (literally), digging into a packed lunch of processed ham and pickle sarnies with a packet of beef Monster Munch resting on the toilet roll holder and a Penguin bar to follow placed on the cistern that his mother had lovingly prepared for him the night before.'

'I wonder what became of him,' said Les.

'Who knows? Soon after that he got the bullet. Amanda, the one with no tits but the biggest arse in the northern hemisphere, felt him rubbing himself against her from behind during someone's birthday presentation. He was swiftly sacked and marched away from the building by three sniggering security staff.'

'He's probably an MP or something big in the city by now,' I sighed.

'Mind you,' said Les, 'For every oddity that's picked up a screwdriver or operated machinery over the years there have been some marvellous characters, men and women who've brightened up the long day and made it just about bearable.'

'I got on well with Tiggs' I said. 'He would always lighten the day with his amazing stories and tales of the miraculous things that happened to him on an almost daily basis.'

'What, old Billy Bullshit? He used to wind me up something chronic. How he couldn't see that we knew it was all a pack of lies is a mystery.'

'I could never understand why he felt the need. Did he really believe I would admire and respect him more if on his way back from his holiday in Costa Rica he was upgraded to VIP class and spent the entire flight playing pontoon with Mike Tyson and Jonathan Ross?'

'I suppose it is within the realms of possibility,' said James.

'The trouble is,' interjected Les, 'I am closely acquainted with his Aunt Belinda who used to work in sales and she reliably informed me he'd spent the week with his parents in a chalet at the slightly less glamorous settings of the Camber Sands branch of Pontins.'

'Yeah, he couldn't half come out with them. He told someone I knew that he was a director here and spent most of his time abroad setting up multi-million pound deals. Once he told me he was the lead singer in a group and was on the verge of signing a major contract with EMI. He gave me a copy of his demo tape and asked my opinion.'

'Was it crap?' asked Les.

'No, it was awesome. The songs were good, catchy in fact. They were playing in tune and some of the guitar solos were as good as you will ever hear. Unfortunately, the tape in question was 'Band on the Run', by Paul McCartney and Wings. I don't know what I found most insulting, the fact that I, as a bit of a self-confessed music nut, would not be able to recognise one of the most prominent singers of the last century, or that I would be gullible enough to take in the fact that three weeks after buying his first keyboard he'd be on the verge of rock n' roll superstardom.' I shook my head.

'Over the years he told me he was in the same class and sat next to Lewis Hamilton at school, was an ex-Olympic class gymnast, had the original C3P0 from Star Wars costume in his bedroom and had written three episodes and a Christmas special of *Only Fools and Horses*,' said Mark. 'He was a very, very sad man indeed.'

'When did he leave?' asked James.

'A couple of years back. He said he'd landed a substantial part playing Eddie Murphy's sidekick in a new blockbuster movie being shot in Hollywood.'

'And was that the last you saw of him?'

'Yes, although someone from surfacing spotted him stacking shelves in the Bromley branch of Superdrug.'

'That's the fickle world of Hollywood for you. One minute you're on set surrounded by stars, flunkies and make-up girls all wanting to sleep with you and the next you are pricing up bottles of conditioner and being asked the whereabouts of panty-liners.'

'I wouldn't scoff, that will probably be me in a few months when I've blown my redundancy on supermarket scotch and scratch cards. Either that or handing out leaflets on double-glazing in the entrance of some supermarket,' said Les.

"I'll probably be in the car park rounding up the stray trolleys, so I'll pop in occasionally and keep you company. Why don't you join us Marky boy? I can just see you on the checkout.'

'Not sure about that mate. One thing I will be stipulating though is the need for a better class of totty to work with and brighten up the day. It's all bow-wows and old biddies here.'

'That's a bit harsh. There have been some cracking bits of stuff that have worked here over the years, Alice on plonking, Tracy on order-entry, and who can forget Sara from accounts?' said Les.

Mark and I looked at other and shared a smile. It was all water under the bridge now. 'Mind you,' he continued, 'There have been some right old monsters as well, lest we forget.'

'You're not wrong there old mate, do you recall that mother and daughter combo from a few years back? They thought they were Britney and Christina, when in reality they were about as attractive as Eric and Ernie.'

James' eyes lit up - at last something from the not-too-distant past, 'Oh yes, Martha and Delilah, what a couple they were! Delilah dressed exactly the same as her mother, like a fifty-something frump with a weight issue and size ten feet, jammed into unflattering and impractical fake leather black stilettos.'

I turned to Les, 'Do you remember scabby Carol?'

'How could I forget such a monstrosity, or anyone else who worked with her for that matter?'

'What was her story?' asked James.

'She was about four and a half feet tall with the face of an old man and the body of a slightly stunted nine-year-old,' I replied.

'That was until her boob job, when she returned from two weeks off sick with a massive pair of bangers,' added Les. 'Anyway, she was the most annoying, smelly and utterly repulsive individual I have ever been unfortunate enough to be introduced to.'

'The trouble was, the poor mare suffered terribly from an incredibly aggressive form of ringworm and skin irritation.'

'That's right, especially on her legs, which were forever wrapped in dirty bandages.'

'What's more,' I butted in, 'she'd itch, scratch, and pick the scabs throughout the day before popping them into her mouth when she thought no one was watching.'

'Do you mind, I'm trying to eat a packet of pork scratchings here,' said Mark.

'I tell you who was a right old brazen monster,' I said.

'Who?' they answered in unison.

'Sheila.'

'What, old BTLT?' replied Mark, swaying ever so slightly.

'What do you mean, BTLT?' asked James, pausing with a cheese and onion crisp resting on his tongue.

'Well, I'm afraid the lady in question had an unusual physical abnormality.'

'Sounds heavenly, what was it?'

'Her left breast was the size of a satsuma...'

'Or maybe a clementine.'

'Whereas its compatriot on the right was more like an over-ripe melon,' I went on.

'I still don't get the BTLT thing?' said James.

'Big tit, little tit,' Mark, Les and I explained in unison. 'Mind you, that was the least of her worries, what with her slack jaw and googly eyes. You never knew if she was looking at you or peering over your shoulder at someone else the other side of the factory.'

'I used to hate being next to her when we sat in the canteen at lunch. Her mouth never seemed quite capable of closing completely and it made a noise akin to a washing machine with a full load,' I complained.

'I suppose she'll be one of those lonely and unfortunate people who sadly die a virgin.' Les almost choked on his beer. 'You must be joking! She was the biggest bike in town! Blimey, at her interview when she was asked if she possessed any special skills she proudly boasted that she could put her boyfriend's condom on his knob with her gob.'

Mark cleared his throat and in a hushed reverential tone that befitted the situation, made an announcement. 'Friends and colleagues, well, ex-colleagues as of today, I have something which I need to get off my chest, something that for some time has weighed heavily upon me and I guess if ever there was a time to unburden oneself of one's misdemeanours and errors of judgment this has to be it.'

'Go on,' I said, 'We are all ears.'

He took a deep breath. 'You all know me as a man of taste and discretion, sensitivity and a shrewd eye when it comes to affairs of the flesh.'

I belched loudly, and Les nodded as did James. 'You're not wrong there mate, only the fittest ladies need apply or maybe the odd plain Jane at a push when the constraints of time are against you. Only when the landlord down the pub is clearing his throat before hollering last orders will you consider allowing a lady of less than perfect features sample the contents of your boxers.'

'That is true, so it will amaze you when I confess that in a moment of weakness and arousal due to too many cocktails and not enough sex, I succumbed to Sheila's less than obvious charms.'

'You have got to be fucking kidding,' I said on the verge of pissing myself with laughter. 'You, the only man to make George Clooney envious have swapped fluids with BTLT. This is just too precious for words. And to think all this time I have looked up to you and gone to you for advice during my many problems I've encountered with the fairer sex, when all the time you were tubbing the creature from the black lagoon!'

'I was never tubbing her, as you so delicately put it. It was strictly a one off, a brief aberration in a lifelong career of impeccable shagging.'

'Yeah right! Go on then, let's have the grisly details. You're just lucky I haven't eaten yet.' I hollered to the barmaid, 'Hey darling, cancel that bag of scampi fries will you?'

'Regrettably, to be honest I can't really blame the evils of alcohol or poor nightclub lighting. One Saturday morning during a stock take in a near empty factory I was unfortunately partnered with BTLT.'

'Sorry mate, that is no excuse and you know it,' I said.

'I know, anyway there we were, counting discontinued frames and checking them off on the list when she suddenly threw down the box she was holding and said, 'Fuck this, life is too short. I fancy you, you probably fancy me, and we are both feeling as horny as hell. There is nobody around, why don't we just get on and do it?' Whereupon she hitched up her skirt, ripped a hole in her tights, she wasn't wearing any underwear incidentally, put one of her sturdy legs on a frame carousel and said, 'Go on then, shove it up us!'

I hesitated for a moment then thought, what the heck, no one will know and I did the business. There, I'm glad it's out in the open.'

'Wow!' I said. 'This is a bit like confession. My son, you are absolved of your sin. Say three hail Marys and have a couple of vicious wanks and your sins of the flesh will be fully absolved. Right, my shout I believe gentleman.'

'Hang on Charlie, while we are getting things off our chests I'd like to unburden my heavy load if I may?' said Les in an ominous tone.

'Go on then, but it's going to have to be a corker to top that little lot,' I said.

'It can't top it I'm afraid, but it is definitely on a par,' he said. 'If I remember, Sheila joined our happy little band a few weeks before Christmas several years back now. Anyway, she was new, shy and a bit of an ugly duckling so I decided to take it upon myself to take her under my wing, so to speak.'

'You dirty old man,' said James.

'No, it was nothing like that. Anyway at the Christmas party BTLT got totally off her head on Smirnoff Ice and Pernod and black, and me, being the department head and a gentleman and being rather pissed myself, foolishly offered to escort her safely to the bus stop.'

'You dirty old man,' reiterated James, glassy-eyed and in danger of slipping off his stool.

'We were nearly there. She was stumbling, mumbling and trying to grab my nuts when she suddenly exclaimed that she had to 'go'.'

'What? Go, go?' I asked.

'Yes.'

'This is brilliant, carry on.'

'Well, she looked up and down the road and seeing no traffic she dropped her knickers, squatted on the floor and emptied her bladder.'

'You are joking!' we said in unison.

'I wish I was. I turned away in embarrassment, walked a few yards down the road and waited for her to finish. The next thing I knew a river of piss was making its way past my feet and down a handily-situated storm drain.'

'I love a bit of romance, me,' I laughed.

'So what did you do Les, get her on the bus and beat a hasty retreat back to the party?' asked Mark.

'I should have done Mark, I should have done, but before I knew what was happening we were in a secluded shop doorway, my trousers were ahoy and her slack jaw was wrapped around my wotsit, slurping and sucking like a milking machine gone cranky and awaking feelings that I hadn't experienced for many a year.'

'Fucking hell!' we exclaimed as one.

'The next thing I know it's six the next morning, I'm naked in her bed, with her limbs all over me, a screaming hangover and frantically thinking of a plausible explanation to excuse my not coming home to my missus.' The pub was empty now except for us recently unemployed. The lunchtime crowd had taken their leave while the workers were still busy at their desks, computers and machinery.

'How are you getting home Charlie?' asked Mark.

'Fuck knows, anyway pretty soon I doubt I'll have a home. I'll be a wandering gypsy, selling heather and siphoning off petrol during the sleeping hours and selling it on the roadside in my rags with Melissa at my side offering executive hand relief in the back of a 1997 Mondeo.'

'That's what I like about you Charlie, you always keep a sense of perspective and a cheery outlook.'

'Never mind that,' I said. 'Gents, as this is apparently an afternoon for confession and tales of the disgusting, I believe it's my turn to toss my hat in the ring and claim the match ball as it were and admit my own part in the remarkable Sheila's sexual march across the factory floor. Do you remember Dave, the old maintenance guy who'd been there since the year dot?'

Mark and Les nodded, while James shrugged. 'You know James, he had wild bushy eyebrows that were making friends with his combover and a keenness for traction engines?'

'He was a good old boy was Dave,' said Les, lifting his pint of bitter in a half-hearted gesture at a toast to our forgotten and fallen ex-comrades.

'Anyway, we were at the Spread Eagle for a nice retirement celebration' I went on. 'All his chums from work were there as well as his family when in walks BTLT in a micro mini-skirt, her jugs practically out and saying hello to anyone who'd pass within gawping distance. Before her arrival the chitter-chatter was hushed, polite and anchored in the past and centred on the happy years that Dave had seen in his years of hard graft and service. Then Sheila gets her drink from the bar, sits in the middle of the hushed throng, crosses her legs revealing cold looking thighs and pink knickers and begins to dominate the conversation. In no time we are all privy to the details of her sex life, including the previous Saturday night when she took two blokes home from her local working man's club. She also recommended the benefits of nipping down to the chemist's sharpish when the itching between the legs becomes more than just an inconvenience. As you can imagine the crowd soon thinned out and before long there were only a handful of us frequenting the snug and still listening to Sheila's sexploits.

'As you know my bladder is not the strongest and I could put off nature's call no longer. When I returned I found my so-called mates had made a timely escape and I was left alone with BTLT, who was pissed and needing a lift to the station.'

'I remember,' said Les, 'I was just making a swift departure when I heard you calling me a bastard as my tyres squealed like Bodie and Doyle as I made a speedy exit from the car park, laughing all the way home.'

'Git! So there I was in a catch twenty-two situation. We drove to the station where we found there was a forty-minute wait for her train. I turned on the radio to help kill the time. She had a better idea however and before I knew what was occurring she'd removed the previously mentioned pink drawers, placed them in her handbag, had reclined the chair to its fullest extent and assumed the 'Take me I'm yours' position, and then I too regretfully succumbed to her dubious charms.'

I was expecting to hear gasps of surprise and shock at this almighty disclosure, but there were none.

'Sorry to burst your bubble Charlie, but that's old news I'm afraid. Everyone in the whole place knows the gory details of your evening of passion in the back of your motor. I think she told anyone who'd listen the very next day,' said Les.

'Jesus, how embarrassing! I don't think I can stand going back there tomorrow,' I said.

'Well, that's lucky then,' said Mark.

CHAPTER SEVEN

The agony of choice

'So, when was the last time a downturn of circumstance forced you to consider your career options?' asked Melissa, as she peered over my shoulder to witness the progress or lack of it in my attempts to concoct an exciting and believable curriculum vitae.

'Would you believe that this is the first? I joined optics immediately after finishing school. The only other profession in which I have had any experience in is the localized distribution of news and media.'

'You mean you had a paper round,' said Mel.

'I believe my CV makes it sound a much more challenging and pressurized role. I had targets to meet and an important service to provide. If the moany old biddy at number 5 didn't receive her *Daily Mail* and the *People's Friend* on a Monday heads would roll, don't you worry about that!'

'Mmm, it all sounds incredibly stressful. I bet you had to unwind when the job was done with a full can of Tizer and a Snickers.'

'They were called Marathons back then, and in my eyes they still are by the way, I don't handle change very well,' I replied.

'I would never have guessed.'

'When I was made redundant previously, a like for like job at Huntingtons was offered to me before I'd even decided what to blow my redundancy dosh on.'

'If this is all you know, why don't you get a job at Vision Express or Specsavers?'

'Mel, I have been making glasses for close on a quarter of a century. I hated it almost from the day I started and I hate it now. I'm sick of it. If I ever see another pair of specs it will be too soon. The time has come for me to finally climb out of my comfort zone and embrace new beginnings and horizons which hopefully will lead to fulfilment, contentment and huge bundles of wonga.'

'If you were single and living at home darling and had no ties or drains on your resources it wouldn't matter what you did. You could take a year out and travel up the Amazon looking for a new species of tree frog. You could write the novel everyone is supposed to have inside them, you could even move to Albania to learn how to play a nose flute and it wouldn't matter. Unfortunately, you are a father of one, soon to become a father of two, you have a mortgage bigger than the national debt of a mid-sized South American country and a wife who has her heart set on the kind of lifestyles she reads about in the glossy magazines that litter every checkout till in the land.'

'Cheers babe, there's no pressure then,' I sighed.

'Well, why can't I be a WAG?'

'Do I look like Steven Gerrard or Peter Crouch? I'm sorry Mel, but the chances of me ever earning a Premiership footballer's wage of a hundred and fifty grand a week with my limited ball skills and age handicap are slim to say the least. With my qualifications I'll be lucky to earn the type of salary to make you a' – I thought it out - 'a WWGHCFB.'

'What the hell is a WWGHCFB?' she asked.

'I would have thought that was blindingly obvious? Melissa my love, you will be a WOMAN WHO GETS HER CLOTHES FROM BOOTFAIRS,' I said.

'Every little girl's dream!' she said. 'I bless the day you walked into my life, staggering under the weight of a dustbin-liner full of dirty washing and a hundred different hang-ups which would slowly reveal themselves to me over the following weeks like a child playing a poorly-planned game of hide and seek.'

'So my dearest darling, take a good long look at the man in front of you. What, and be honest, do you see me as?' I asked.

She pulled a face 'Mmm, Exactly how honest do you want me to be?'

'Honest enough to direct me towards the career my not inconsiderable talents deserve but not so brutal as to shatter my already fragile confidence,' I said.

'Hmm… This is a tricky one, what qualifications do you hold?'

'Well, I can drink most people under the table and have an inside leg measurement or thirty-two inches,' I said proudly.

'Sorry darling, but I fear that will cut very little ice indeed with any prospective employer. What did you leave school with?' she asked.

'I departed that awful, awful place with very little I'm afraid, just a dirty PE kit, a hatred of Geography and its teacher and a lifelong fascination with sixteen-year-old girls in navy blue short skirts.'

'Sorry Hun, but I think you'll need slightly more than that to forge a promising future in the city or as the head of ICI. Where are your O level certificates? Still at your ex's place or did Colin use the back of them to jot down the numbers of a tasty Chinese menu sometime in the distant past?'

'What certificates? Thanks to my cousin putting in a good word for me down the glasses factory I had already secured a position and didn't feel the need to cycle up to the school and collect them,' I admitted.

'Charlie, you are, as I am discovering on an almost daily basis, a complete arse of the first order. Are you seriously telling me that you attended school for a dozen years or more and then when it came to the pay off and the chance to finally leave with some reward after all the years of study and toil you put in you couldn't be arsed to pedal the mile and a half up there?' she said incredulously. 'That is so like you it could have been written and traced as a blueprint for the whole of the rest of your life.'

'There's no need to take that tone. It's hardly held me back, has it, and if I'm totally in the dark about my qualifications or the lack of them then surely any prospective new employer will be in the same boat,' I suggested cheerfully.

'You are a one-off Charlie, and no mistake,' said Mel. 'So come on then, what have you put down so far?' She leaned over my shoulder, her chin resting gently on it. I love being that close. She smelt gorgeous and I again blessed my fortune that she loved a loser such as me.

I cleared my throat, 'Charlie Bennett, age 39.'

'Whoa, whoa, whoa my boy! That's incorrect for a start. I believe you to be forty-two. In fact I'm sure a look at your birth certificate will verify that beyond all reasonable doubt.'

'Mel, I admit to not being an expert at this sort of thing, but even I know that you have to twist and garnish these things with half-truths and enormous dollops of bullshit. I will surely be a more attractive applicant if I'm in my thirties as opposed to a slightly soiled and weatherworn forty-two.'

'You don't think the Inland Revenue will cotton on that your details are incorrect and contact your employer then?' she sighed.

I shrugged off her concern. 'Possibly so, but by then, my dear sexy wife, I will be nicely ensconced in my new position and proving to be an invaluable and totally indispensable member of staff. It will be passed off as a clerical error or an oversight on the dear old human resources department.'

'OK, I accept you may just get away with it. What else have you got?' she asked.

I cleared my throat. 'Qualifications: O levels in Maths,

English, Geography, Commercial Studies, Technical Drawing, History, Home Economics and Woodwork.'

'And in the real world, which of those did you really pass?'

'It is a long time ago babe, and my memory on the subject is rather hazy to say the least, but at a guess I would estimate that I passed all of them with top grades with probably many more I have forgotten about and have failed to list here.'

'Right, so a top of the class student who obtained seven O levels decided not to further his horizons and progress on to further education, whether it be A level, college or university, but instead settled for a bottom-of-the-rung dead-end job at the glasses factory? Call me over-suspicious and cynical, but somehow that doesn't quite ring true to me.'

'OK, I admit my recollections of that far-off time are cloudy at best and academically I may have not fulfilled the promise my talents had undoubtedly hinted at, but I'm pretty sure these are the results I deserved,' I said. She raised her eyebrows and gave me a 'You don't fool me' smirk. 'OK, OK, I just about scraped woodwork and history. Are you happy now? But if I took all these courses and exams now I'd pass them with ease, and let's face facts, any new employer will have the good fortune of getting me as I am now, the confident and learned man about town with bags of experience who has seen and done it all. Not the spotty clueless youth I was back then suffering with raging hormones and constant lesson distracting erections.'

'Well I agree there is something in what you are alluding to, but...'

'Look, I know what I'm doing OK, I'm not bloody typing

this sodding thing out again!' I said. I was rapidly losing interest in the damn thing.

'All right, calm down, OK, so qualifications aren't your ace in the hole. Never mind, we will simply concentrate on positives and focus on the things you are strong on and the experience and knowhow you can give your new employers.'

'Right-oh, now you're talking!'

I nodded and stood aside to let her take control of the keyboard. She stood with fingers poised waiting for me to start. I smiled. 'Well, go on then, tell me what you are good at,' she said impatiently. I slid a hand gently from her shoulder slowly towards her breast. She grabbed it and put it back.

'This is serious, Charlie. Get the work done first and then it's playtime later.'

I liked the thought of that. I deliberated for a moment, struggling for a glimmer of inspiration. 'Not withholding modesty, I think I can announce without question or debate that no one can hold a candle to me when it comes to lounging on the sofa and watching sport on television while drinking beer and occasionally blowing off,' I said.

My ever-patient wife sighed and patted me on the hand. 'I'm sorry to disappoint you my love, but opportunities for employment that would harness those skills you have just outlined are few and far between, and seeing that we are about to traverse shit creek without a decent flush I suggest you take this a bit more seriously and stop mucking about.'

'That's a pity, because mucking about is another of my specialist subjects.'

'Charlie!'

'You're so right, sorry. Well, let me see. I would say that

I am a highly professional, self-motivated ambitious go-getter. I have great personal skills and leadership qualities and the ability to think on my feet during any crisis or emergency the job, probably any job, may throw at me,' I said in best middle management speak.

'Mmm, that's odd. It just goes to show how little I really know you, even after a full five years together. I would have put you down as a half-arsed bodger who needs a rocket under his arse simply to climb out from beneath the sheets in the morning. Someone who doesn't give a toss about anything work-related as long as his wages are in his bank account on the first of every month. Someone who if a problem arises would pretend not to notice, look the other way and then blame someone else.'

'Flipping heck, you really have my number don't you?'

'Oh yes,' she said. 'I tell you what, why don't you leave the CV bit to me and concentrate on finding the position that appeals to you and is tailor made for your, er... let's say, unique and rarely appreciated skills. There's the local paper in the kitchen, it's usually packed with ads, why don't you have a browse through that and see what takes your fancy?'

I retrieved the paper from beneath a dirty plate, wiped off the spillage of my egg sandwich and opened it at random whilst getting comfy on the sofa. 'Mmm, let me see now... oh! This looks interesting, "Attractive older blonde seeks well-endowed man for afternoon fun. Disabled gentlemen also welcome." Well that's not a bad starting off point. I don't mind working for a woman boss, I'm free most afternoons and I can easily put on a fake limp if required.'

'Nice try Casanova, but if I were you I would leave the

personal column to those desperate enough to require the services of an afternoon slapper of no discernible taste and head onto the jobs section.'

'No hang on; there's no need to dismiss this without giving it at least a little consideration. Maybe we should be thinking a little outside the box here. Let's face it, there must be hundreds of rich lonely women in this locality who are dying for some attention and companionship from a handsome guy such as I. Hey, maybe I could even persuade some rich old widow to leave me her house and fortune on the basis of a part-time relationship, the odd shag and maybe a foot rub every other week?'

'Good effort Charlie, but I don't think I want to be married to someone whose job description is to keep aged woman in massages and pity-sex. Also when the teacher asks the kids what their Daddy does for a living, I don't want Ellie to have to say her father is a rent boy.'

'Mmm, yes, that might make parents' evening a bit awkward. She goes back in a couple of weeks, doesn't she? Blimey, where has the time gone? One minute she's a tiny helpless baby who could fit into the palm of my hand and the next she's in her uniform behaving like a little madam and playing kiss chase.'

'Yes, it has gone quick. Before we know it she'll be an out of control teen who won't listen to a word I say while bringing home a succession of undesirable, spotty and gangly boyfriends back to her bedroom.'

'No she bloody won't!' I said firmly. 'She will forever be Daddy's little angel, helping with the washing up and making me snack treats on demand.'

'So you don't think she'll turn into a crack-crazed slapper

who'll sell the furniture for drugs and put you in a home at the first opportunity?'

'Stop it,' I said, seeing a picture in my mind's eye that upset me greatly. 'She'll forever be my perfect little girl.'

'I'm just joshing. Now, is there anything else that you might be interested in?' she asked.

'Busking?'

'Be serious!'

'Gambler?'

She shook her head. 'I can whip your sorry arse at any game you care to mention – pontoon, dominoes, chess, draughts, gin rummy, Monopoly, the lot. I don't think I want to leave our future, savings and house in the hands of someone who thinks it's a viable risk to twist on nineteen on a game of twenty-ones.'

'Good point, well made.' I scanned the job section. 'Well at first glance there are at least half a dozen vacancies for experienced dental nurses. Mmm, I wonder why that is. Is the job really demanding or do they all get head hunted and end up going abroad?'

'Sorry to be sexist, but that is and always will be a girl's job. What else is there?'

'You're right, that is sexist. I can suck slobber out of somebody's gob as well as any girl. This is the twenty-first century love. Gender doesn't come onto it. Hang on, that's a thought – maybe I could become a househusband. Teach me how to use the washing machine and I'd have no problems. Run the Hoover round, a bit of ironing and heat up something from the freezer for tea, job's a good 'un!'

'Nice try, but no deal mister. I give up work in December to have bambino number two. We need at least one of us to be bringing some money into the house,' said Melissa.

'Point taken. Ah, this is interesting – 'train as a driving instructor. Work the hours to suit you and earn up to 30k a year'. Mmm, I think I'll put that on the maybes pile. I can just see myself teaching vulnerable teenage girls how to apply the handbrake and put the seats into the reclined position.'

'Do you know Charlie, I believe within five years you will be a fully paid-up, card-carrying member of the Dirty Old Man Club. You are not going to be a driving instructor. For one thing it costs a couple of grand to train and take the exams and secondly with your track record I wouldn't trust you as far as I can throw you.'

'Baby, I am a changed man. I have learnt from my mistakes and am an older, wiser and more trustworthy fellow.'

'I'm glad to finally hear it,' said Melissa.

'Still, training and starting from scratch may well be the track I am forced to take. Hey, what about taking an IT course? Computers are everywhere these days. Even in the optics business. It's so unlucky that I was just leaving school when the new technical age was dawning. My generation has been left behind. All I can do on our laptop is manage my i-tunes library, send emails and look at women doing naughty things without clothes.'

'Ah, so that's what you're up to when I'm at aerobics. I've often wondered why the browsing history has been wiped clean on the laptop and you look more flushed than I am when I stagger in.'

I changed the subject. 'No, proper computing like spreadsheets and stuff. Microsoft Word and Powerpoint are a mystery to me. A closed book. Well, actually a book I have yet to have the opportunity to open. Blimey, the calculator was the cutting edge of science when I was at school. We even had to still use logarithm books to work out how long and pointy our triangles were in maths.'

'Poor you. Still, I bet it was a real boom when they replaced the quill with the fountain pen,' laughed Melissa.

'Mel, I know I have been keeping a brave face and appearing to be not too concerned and fairly positive about losing my job, but in fact I'm worried. Really scared and worried. I have practically no qualifications to speak of, I am the wrong side of forty, and have an ever-increasing family to support while at the same time the country is on the brink of the biggest recession in recent history.'

Melissa sighed and gave me a comforting smile followed by a reassuring hug. I felt her rapidly increasing bump come slightly between us. 'I know babe. I'm worried too,' she sighed. 'I've rearranged my hours so I can take Ellie to school before doing longer hours at the office until you get settled in your new job. I know you may not want to, but I do think you are going to have to swallow a couple of large mouthfuls of pride and take something that's not really you until something bigger and better comes along.'

I squeezed tighter. 'And what if it doesn't?'

CHAPTER EIGHT

Sweating palms and unwanted advice

Freshly bathed, shaved and hair-washed, I stood for a good ten minutes in front of the wardrobe, pondering what would be the most appropriate attire for the gig in question – my first job interview, to be held at The Laminator's HQ, which is situated about twenty minutes from our modest little three-bedroomed house. Now what to wear? Firstly, I have to look smart, well turned out and confident. But also, as the job entails mainly manual labour and no doubt a lot of time crawling around on my hands and knees fitting flooring, my persona has got to scream out, 'This chap looks like a hard-working, salt of the earth, blue collared kind of a guy. The type of employee I can rely on to do a first-rate job in the shortest possible time. Not some half-arsed slacker who'll spend most of his day drinking lukewarm tea from a flask in the back of the van.'

I decided not to bother with a tie, as that seemed a bit officey to me. I thought I'd settle for my smart black trousers and a smart but casual white shirt, open at the neck. Yes, that should strike the correct balance between endeavour and respectability.

Half an hour later I was parked up outside my destination, a smallish unit tucked away at the back of a sprawling industrial estate. Yes, it does sound strangely exciting and romantic, doesn't it? The kind of place where empires are built and life is a raw-arsed jet-ride to stardom and fame, or conversely where a shattering fall from grace could descend into broken dreams and oblivion. My appointment was for two-thirty. I waited until two-twenty-five, nervously counting down the minutes. I was sweaty palmed and anxious. I need this job; I must not screw this interview up.

On entering reception, I could see that only a small part of the building was partitioned and office-like. Through a large glass window I was able to view its massive interior – it was really just a glorified warehouse. Enormously high racks housed pallets full of what I assumed were laminate flooring, rolls of linoleum, hardware and other supplies. Dotted around were a few workers and the odd forklift truck. No one appeared to be racing around or breaking his or her back trying desperately to get an urgent order out on time. This looks like my kind of place, I thought to myself.

When I announced my name, the receptionist, a friendly-faced woman in her fifties with a white streak in her brunette fringe, passed me an application form attached to a small wooden clipboard and offered me a seat. Next to me on the small, water-damaged orange sofa was a kid in his late teens who was filling out an identical sheet of paper. Ah, so this is the opposition is it? He was dressed in ripped jeans and a Motorhead T-shirt, all in black. He looked painfully thin and weedy and I found it hard to imagine him being able to lift a roll of lino out of a van without being crushed. He had a grey tattoo of a skull on fire beneath his left ear and had so many zits on his face that I was tempted to play dot-to-dot. Charlie boy, we have it made here, I thought. All I have to do is to keep my cool, be polite and keen and surely the job is in the bag.

I had only written my name and age when the lad turned and spoke to me in little more than a whisper. 'Here mate, how do you spell 'straight'?' He asked.

I glanced over at his form. There were many angry blue crossings-out and what looked from where I was sitting a doodle of Snoopy in the margin.

'Why, what do you want to put?' I asked.

'Wanna say I can start straight away,' he replied. He smelt of baked beans and sweaty feet.

'How have you spelt it?' I asked.

'S T R A T E.'

'Yeah, that's right,' I replied, and continued filling out my own questionnaire. Huh, if this is all I am up against I should walk it.

I chewed the end of my pen while figuring the best possible answer to each question. As I had done earlier with Mel and my CV (which I had forgotten to bring owing to my rush in getting out of the door after spending ten minutes deciding on what shoes would be the winning option) I had made up my academic achievements to sound appropriate to the vacancy on offer. I told them of my sterling service in the line of duty at my previous employers and my marital status. Right, that's that sorted. Now, what about hobbies? What can I put here? I don't engage in any kind of organised sport these days, I don't do jigsaws or make model planes (and if I did I think I would probably prefer to keep that to myself), I don't go hill walking, indulge in morris dancing or fishing, or do judo. I hate gardening and DIY, and the day I join one of Colin's battle re-enactment days will be the day I know I have become a target of my own humour.

Come on, I have to put down something, but what? Giving Melissa Dutch ovens when I'm one over the eight? Moaning about the limited offerings on television? Growing new and varied kinds of foot fungus? Blimey, this interview lark is not as straightforward as I had first hoped.

My thoughts were interrupted by Mrs Silver Streak calling out, 'Duane? Duane Russell, Mr Pratt is ready to see you now.' I wished him good luck and set about completing my form before spending another ten minutes nervously looking at my shoes, out of the window and at the receptionist doing her paperwork.

Presently my rival emerged from Mr Pratt's inner sanctum with a smile and a nod in my direction. Now it's my turn...

Mr Pratt was a spindly-looking man with horn-rimmed

glasses, a wispy grey moustache and an effeminate manner. His handshake was limp, moist and unappealing, much like the man himself. 'Good afternoon Mr, er… Bennett' he said, looking at the form I had passed to him. 'Please come through.'

He ushered me into his cramped office. It all looked very dated and a bit tired. Disposable coffee cups filled the bin and a wall planner which had many different colours of stars arranged on it was pinned to a large corkboard. I sat on the seat, which still radiated the heat from Duane's skinny posterior. After a forced friendly preamble concerning the weather, my journey and my ease in locating the place, we finally got down to brass tacks.

'Now Mr Bennett, tell me why you would like to work for me?'

What kind of poxy question is that? Because I need money! Because if I don't find work before too long my family and I will shortly be evicted from our comfy existence and be moved to DHSS land and live in a run-down government-funded bed and breakfast, surrounded by the hopeless, the helpless and East European asylum seekers eager to take a free bite from the British way of life.

'Mr Pratt, ever since I was a small child it has been my dream to lay laminate flooring and affordable budget linoleum,' I answered, knowing as the words spewed forth from my mouth that this was a quite preposterous thing to say. He chortled, shifted in his chair and glanced around his office, trying to find the right words.

'Come, come, Mr Bennett, we both know that isn't true. In my formative years my dreams were of trains, signing professional forms for Crystal Palace and running away to join the circus. Never once did I get excited by the prospect of tongue and groove.'

Speak for yourself, I thought. I can't stick Crystal Palace. I tried to blank out thoughts of Mr Pratt's wiry, leotard-covered body flying across a trapeze and came clean.

'I apologize. The thing is Mr Pratt, I am pretty nervous. This is my first proper interview for a dozen or more years and I am a bit out of practice. I have an ever-growing family to support and I need to find employment as soon as possible. Please let me assure you that I am a hard worker and a thoroughly committed employee. I won't be here today and gone tomorrow, my track record I believe shows that. I'm great with my hands and feel ideally suited to your company's needs.'

He sat back in his chair and studied my application form, occasionally raising an eyebrow and glancing across in my direction. 'I agree, you seem perfect for the position advertised. Some may say that possessing nine 'O' Levels and a degree in microbiology might be overegging it slightly, but I always think a good education grounds a man in whatever trade or situation he finds himself in.'

I congratulated myself on my creativeness and barefaced lying.

'I see you are also a thespian?' he said.

'What did you call me?' I said getting ready to lamp him one.

'A thespian, Mr Bennett! An actor, you tread the boards and wear greasepaint. I myself am a member of the Chatham Players. Why it was only last Christmas that I was, if I do say so with all modesty, a very convincing ugly sister.' That wouldn't have been much of a stretch, I thought.

'What production are you currently working on?' he asked, full of interest.

'I'm one of the pink ladies in an experimental production of *Grease*,' I replied sarcastically before thinking.

'I say, that sounds a challenging role indeed. If you ever need any make-up tips, don't hesitate to give me a call.' He handed me a business card. 'Now, back to the matter in hand. As you are aware I am after a trainee carpet layer and flooring fitter.' I nodded, glad to leave his love of the theatre behind. 'You are a married man with a family, Mr Bennett, and any vacancies with the prefix trainee are never going to be too well paid.'

'Yes, I understand, but...'

He cut me short. 'It says here that your expected salary is in the region of twenty-five thousand pounds a year.' I nodded. 'Mr Bennett, if I paid my fitters, even my most experienced and valued fitters, that kind of money I wouldn't be sitting here in my nice swivel chair talking to you. I'd be out of business.'

'I am prepared to take a small drop,' I said, feeling my prospects slipping away.

'Yes but I...'

'I really am fairly flexible on salary,' I added.

'I appreciate that, I really I do but...'

'When I say flexible I really am talking bending over backwards,' I pleaded.

'I am sure you would and it is most admirable. But the reality of the harsh world of business dictates that unfortunately the awful chaffing ropes of financial realism binds my hands and indeed yours. Duane, the young man who was occupying that very chair not ten minutes ago, will work for minimum wage. Can you honestly tell me that you could afford do the same?' I shook my head. 'I thought so, and as lamentable as it is I'm afraid it is his number I will be calling to offer employment.' He rose from his chair and offered me his hand. It was still limp, still wet and uncomfortable to grasp. 'Thanks for coming Mr Bennett, I am sure you will soon find suitable employment to harness your undoubted talents.'

I mumbled a thank you and made for the door of his cramped little office. 'Oh, and good luck with your role in Grease, I am sure you will make an admirable pink lady.'

I smiled weakly and shut the door behind me. Cursing everything and everyone from God, fortune, John Travolta and Olivia Newton-John to the sudden summer downpour outside, I entered the sports and social club I was a member of, determined to drown my sorrows and discover if there really wasn't an answer at the bottom of a bottle.

'Hello Charlie, this is an unexpected honour. You don't usually grace us with your presence till late afternoon at the earliest. Have they cancelled 'Diagnosis Murder' on the sad old gits with nothing else to do channel?'

'Fuck off, Ralph!'

'Is it a day's holiday then?' he continued, unfazed.

'Less talky, more poury, OK?' I growled.

'That will be two eighty please,' he said.

'If you must know, I have been made redundant and have spent the last half hour being interviewed and patronised by a wet lettuce of a man who promptly informed me that asking for a living wage that my family and I can scrape by on is near lunacy.'

'When were you given the boot?' He asked, loading the under-bar dishwasher.

'Two weeks ago tomorrow, and I am bored beyond tears already and yes, there is only so much daytime TV a man can take, I tell you. Yesterday I suddenly realised that I was watching a fifteen-year-old episode of Cagney and Lacy and couldn't even summon up the strength to cross the room and get the remote control. It's killing me, I can tell you. I know I used to moan about the crushing monotony of the daily grind of work, but believe me this is much worse.'

'That's because you're goin' aboot it the wrong way, pal,' said a large gentleman on my left in a Scots accent. 'Being a member of Her Majesty's long-term unemployed I can tell ye that if handled correctly and using the correct amount of savvy it can indeed be a fulfilling and challenging profession. Let me introduce mesel'. My name is Fulton Aloysius McQueen.'

Everything about this man was large and vociferous, from the purple corduroy trousers to the oversized battered floppy felt hat he was wearing at a jaunty angle. He gave off an air of Oscar Wilde mixed with Tom Baker's version of Doctor Who. He looked to be somewhere in his fifties, but it was hard to pin him down with much of his features being covered in wild untamed hair. He picked up his almost empty glass, downed it, and put it on the bar before placing an enormous hand in mine.

'And who am I addressing, sir?' he asked.

'Charlie Bennett,' I said, sighing inwardly. What is it about me that seems to attract nutters? No lie, but if I'm in a room with a large number of ordinary people mingling, the one weirdo with the knitted shoes and a collection of spittle in the corners of his mouth will latch on to me and inflict his keen interest in 1960s vacuum cleaners before whipping out his collection of photos and showing me his favourite.

This lunatic was a good six foot five, as wide as a garbage truck, and spoke with a Glasgow accent. His nose was as bright red as a tomato but as misshapen and wild as a head of broccoli, the result no doubt of a life's adoration of booze and brawling. There was a gleam in his eye and a hooped earring in his left lobe. His goatee beard was wild and silver and as thick as a hawthorn bush. If he shaved it off and offered it to you as a pan scrubber you would bite his hands off.

'Would you like tae take a drink with me, Charlie Bennett?' he boomed in a voice so broad and charismatic that it would have required balls of steel to refuse.

'Yeah, go on then,' I said weakly.

'Excellent!' He slapped me on the back, almost chipping my front teeth against my pint mug. He waved Ralph over. 'Hey pal, two lagers and two whiskey chasers. Right, I'm just off to the lavatory Charlie, get these in will ye.' It was a command, not a question. He strode off, leaving me open-mouthed.

Ralph laughed as he poured our drinks. 'Blimey, you've done it now. This guy has been coming in here for a while now and he's a complete nightmare. He's almost drunk the place dry. You won't be able to shake him off. If you leave here without being carried out I will be greatly surprised.'

I drained what was left of my pint and was contemplating a surreptitious exit when my new friend returned. 'Hey pal!' he called to Ralph, 'There's nae paper in stall number two. Sort it, will ye?'

Ralph took my ten-pound note. He is a bit of a kindred spirit is Ralph, the type of guy who has low expectations and generally fails to meet them. I guess he's the perfect barman, in a way. He'll listen, watch the world go by and not bother to try and make a difference.

'I love the glamour of the pub industry. It's pure Hollywood,' he said. 'Your good health sir.' He raised his whisky glass and drank it down in one before moving swiftly, and I must say gracefully, on to his pint.

'Yes, the secret of making a success of the predicament you currently find yourself in is structure and discipline. After many years of suffering the rigidity of the nine-to-five routine of the working man you have understandably become programmed to a schedule, my friend. When this is removed you feel bored and at a loss as to what to do with your day.'

I was warming to him. 'Yes, you probably have a point there.'

'I ken that of which I speak, man. I was a toolmaker for thirty-five years. I was never off sick and often failed to take all my holiday allowance. Then one day I was deemed surplus to requirements. I was pushed out o' the door without a thought from my employers for my many years' service or my future. The sterling work and devotion I had given had counted for nothing. I was the wrong side of fifty in a shrinking industry with no other apparent strings to ma bow.'

'Yeah, they're bastards the lot of them,' I agreed, feeling my scotch chaser warming my throat and making me shiver.

'Bastards to a man! You are totally and without argument correct. Anyway, I was like you at the beginning;

lying around all day, mooching from room to room, going to the odd interview and generally waiting until evening opening time so I could drown my sorrows. I was depressed, I was broke and I was a mess.'

Ralph interjected, 'That was ten years ago and nothing's changed,' he laughed.

'Fuck off you little prick, and sort out that convenience. My bowels are of a particularly loose habit today, possibly due to the out-of-date chilli dog I consumed last eve, so I dinna wish to be languishing in there with only a cardboard tube for salvation. You might also, while you are at it, take a wallpaper scraper to the dried-on shit that's clinging to the side of the bowl.'

Ralph pretended not to hear and carried on serving another customer. Fulton Aloysius McQueen slurped his pint and wiped his bearded chops on the back of his hand. 'Now, where was I?'

'You were broke, bored and down in the dumps.'

'That's right. So I thought to myself, "Fulton, it's time to take control of your life". Now I have a rigid structure to my day. I have a purpose and I have a function.'

'Are you still looking for work?' I enquired, trying manfully to keep up with my hard-drinking companion, who now had just a dribble left in his glass.

'Nae point son, my skills are lamentably no longer in demand and also my day is far too full to fit in distractions of that nature.'

'So how do you manage financially?' I enquired.

'On my wits, the State and the small legacy left to me by a distant aunt,' he boomed before summoning Ralph to refill our glasses. 'Each morning I rise at ten and read a copy of the *Telegraph* which the paper boy kindly doesn't quite push through the letterbox of the flat downstairs.'

'What, you nick it?'

'Och no dear boy, I read and return it, having saved myself the princely sum of sixty new pence. I then dress and make my way to the café on the corner, where a senior citizen's breakfast, complete with limitless fill-ups of tea, is an attractive one pound ninety-nine. There I spend the morning warm and refreshed until opening time, saving on my heating, electricity, wear and tear on my kettle filament and at least three tea bags.'

'But how, with the relatively low salary the government are currently prepared to pay to us unfortunate unemployed, can you afford premium lager and scotch chasers?'

'With cunning, guile and with the help of friends and acquaintances such as your good self,' he explained before he informed Ralph that he had better hurry up as he was dying of thirst. Noticing I was checking my wallet and seeing the perturbed look on my face, he pulled out a roll of notes thick enough, if not to batter a man to death, then surely to give him a bloody good hiding. He extracted a crisp twenty-pound note and dropped it onto the bar.

'Ye see, it's nae good gettin' up in the morning without a purpose. Have a schedule or timetable that you can stick to as if it were a job. You will find that the time will pass much quicker that way. If you really get the hang of it you will soon wonder how the hell you managed to fit a full-time job into your day.'

'Yes, but fill it with what? I have nothing to do with my days except watching TV, drinking cans of lager and masturbating myself silly,' I said with the openness and honesty one is given to when sharing a drink with a giant Scotsman in a floppy hat with a beard that is as wild and unruly as a stag night in Amsterdam.

'All fantastic pastimes, I agree, but there is more. After my drinks here I am spending a couple of hours down the library, where the whole world of literature is literally at my fingertips. Then I will do a quick circumnavigation around the pond in the park to get the blood flowing and the old ticker racing before heading to the off-licence in search of a chat with the proprietor and a rare claret I had him order in for me. My next port of call will be Gerald, my bookmaker, to lay several well-informed bets on this evening's dog racing at Crayford, which will fund the day's expenses and give me a smug feeling of superiority in the knowledge that I have survived and enjoyed another glorious day in your nasty little country.'

I listened intently, ready to pull apart his life plan piece by piece. 'Firstly, Mr McQueen...'

'We have shared a drink, my friend. I believe that gives you the right to address me by my Christian name,' he interjected.

'OK. Firstly, Fulton, I am in a slightly more perilous position than yourself as I not only have to support myself but also my wife and one and a half children and secondly if you think this country is horrid you should fuck off back to Jockland, where I am sure they will no doubt welcome you with open arms.'

I don't know where this false bravado came from, but my legs weakened almost immediately, anticipating a forearm smash that would send me to dreamland and loosen several teeth. He laughed loud enough to be heard back in his native land and placed a muscular arm around my shoulders, possibly snapping a collarbone. 'Point taken Charlie, point taken son.' He downed the rest of his pint and placed his glass before me. 'It's your round, pal.'

I couldn't believe it. I had hardly made a dent in mine, yet his glass was as empty as a hermit's spare bedroom.

'Another two pints over here Ralph, you lazy little gobshite!' he shouted.

A couple of hours and what must have been half a dozen pints later I staggered through my front door and just about made it to the downstairs toilet. From there I managed to totter to the couch, where I threw myself down. Melissa sat in silent astonishment with Ellie on her lap, enjoying the children's channel on the television. My flies were ahoy and chilli sauce had created a new and exciting pattern on my shirt. I stared at the ceiling, willing it to slow down and stop spinning.

Mel got up and stood over me. 'Well, judging by the state of you, you've been out celebrating. When do you start?'

'I don't,' I admitted, belching loudly and giving off fumes of such eye-watering strength that she had to take a couple of steps backwards. 'The bloke said he would have loved me to join his happy little band of floor layers but unfortunately owing to the weakness of the pound and an outbreak of woodworm he had to pass me over in favour of an illiterate acne-covered kid called Duane who was willing to work for a shilling a week and all the wood glue he could sniff.'

'So why in the hell have you come home three sheets to the wind then?' she asked with a mixture of curiosity and annoyance.

'My dear, my love, my beautiful other half, I was coming straight home from my interview with Mr Pratt to do some more scouring on the internet for employment when in a moment of weakness I stopped off at the club for a brief half of shandy when I was accosted by a giant Scotsman with a hedge-sized beard, ready to dispense all the secrets of the universe and more. Then before I knew it we were new best friends and completely pissed. Well, I was, though he still seemed strangely lucid.'

She shook her head and frowned. 'Charlie, what am I going to do with you?'

Looking at her blurry figure I reached out and kissed her hand, 'Darling, for me you can do so, so, so much. But in the immediate short term you can fetch me a bucket or the washing-up bowl, I think I'm going to be sick.'

And I was.

CHAPTER NINE

The hand of friendship

With much prompting from Melissa and my own conscience I had decided to take another trip to Colin's, this time to apologise for my accusations and to give him and Grace my blessing for their upcoming wedding. I have never been much cop at this sort of thing, so as you can imagine it was a journey and task I was not keen to undertake. Still, as Mel had rightly pointed out, it was Colin's business and nothing to do with me. She said I should be happy he had found a new soulmate and be there for support and advice only if called upon. She also pointed out that he didn't need a doom and gloom merchant telling him he was being made a fool of by a blood-sucking harpy. Even if it was true.

The thing I really couldn't get my head around was that this new lady was the polar opposite of my mum. My mother was a home-loving, old-fashioned kind of a lady, never happier than in the kitchen with flour on her hands, making a home-made stomach-expanding pie while listening to Woman's Hour. Now OK, I admit I had only met Grace just the once thus far and first impressions can often be misleading, plus I was half cut at the time, but there is no way I could envisage her being the dutiful housewife with a rolling-pin in one hand and an iron in the other, making delightful sweet shortcrust pastry and perfectly-pressed slacks while listening to the Archers omnibus on the wireless. Stomach churning as it may be, the only apron I could imagine Grace wearing was a cheap and tacky French maid's outfit purchased from Ann Summers.

Suddenly images of Colin naked and handcuffed to the bed with a ball gag in his mouth sprang up in my imagination, with Grace in her saucy outfit standing over him and tickling his shrivelled privates with a feather duster. Ugh! I had to seek some kind of professional help. My imagination was far too vivid. I'd be having recurring nightmares about that for a week.

As I walked up the front path I admired once again the fruits of Colin's green fingers and many hours of labour. The grass was as flat as a crown green bowling green, and so carefully manicured it appeared that it had been cut blade by blade by a pair of nail scissors and a ruler rather than a mower. Beautiful beds bordered the lawn, packed with carefully-chosen flowers, which were picture postcard perfect, all in full bloom with not a weed or a dead head in sight. I wondered if Grace had lent him a hand since she'd moved herself in. Would she risk the finish of her French manicured nails amongst the slugs and dirt? Would she take her turn mowing the vast lawn at the rear, or join in the backbreaking sweat and toil on hedge cutting day when the ninety-foot by seven-foot-high monster that separated us from the neighbours needed taming? I couldn't see it somehow. I could however picture her sitting under the patio parasol with a large gin and tonic in one hand and a racy airport novel in the other, pointing out any missed bits to Colin as he sweated like a hog on heat struggling with a wheelbarrow laden with slaughtered hedge up the steep winding path towards the area behind the top shed where all garden waste met its final resting place.

I gave the bell a ring and waited... and waited. I rang again. Come on Colin, I know you're in, your car is on the drive. I tried again. Oh, so that's the way things are lying is it? He doesn't want to talk to me just because I may have indicated that his intended was a money-grabbing slapper who wanted to separate me from my birthright? Well that was just petty! There was no reason to be childish and pretend not to know I was here.

I yelled, 'Grow up Colin, for Christ's sake!' through the letterbox and turned to leave. Just then the door opened and there was Grace, dressed in a pair of skimpy white shorts and a navy blue and white polka dot bikini top whose tiny straps were straining to support the mammoth weight of her awesome, surgically enhanced bosom. She lifted the pair of huge, oversized Gucci sunglasses she was wearing to get a better view.

'Oh, Hi Charlie, this is a pleasant surprise, how are you?'

Slightly taken aback, I managed to murmur, 'I'm, er, good thanks.'

'And your lovely wife, Melanie, wasn't it?'

Wait till I tell Mel she'd got her name wrong. That will get her on my side.

'Actually it was Melissa. Where is Colin? Is he up the garden talking to his raspberry bushes?'

She waved a magazine across her face. 'Jesus it's hot! I'm sweating like a bloody... well you know what I mean.'

'It is a hot one all right, this summer is going on forever isn't it?' I agreed, peeling the back of my shirt from my sweating body. I was feeling slightly uneasy, though I didn't quite know why.

'So where is he?' I asked again, trying to hide my impatience and slight embarrassment at being confronted on the doorstep by my future step-mom in a half-undressed state. Her nipples were almost brushing against me, she was standing so close. 'He's popped into town for a few, er, necessities,' she said.

'Are you sure?' I asked. 'His car is on the drive.'

'He's taken the bus. Well, I have a hair appointment a little later, and it seems a waste not to use his free bus pass.'

How long have you had yours, I thought. 'I guess,' I said.

'Yes, we are all alone,' she said, with a sudden hint of menace.

'Yes, er... so what's he nipped out for then? A bulk buy of Odor-Eaters and a family bag of Werther's Originals for him and a tube of strawberry lube for you?'

'You cheeky boy!' she cackled, playfully smacking me on the back of the head. I could feel her hot overly-tanned body pressed against me for a second and she smiled slyly. In a moment of weakness I couldn't help taking a closer look at her cleavage. As I looked up her eyes met mine. Shit, busted! She smelt of cigarettes and coconut and Chanel and alcohol.

'I was just sunbathing out the back, would you like to keep me company while we await his return?' she asked. I went to look at my watch and was met with an empty wrist. I'd forgotten to put it on after my shower this morning. Grace was watching my unease and it seemed to amuse her.

'Yeah, go on then.' I was weakening. 'If he's not going to be long.'

Yes, I have to concede that she is alluring in an over-obvious slutty kind of Mrs Robinson way, and yes I'll even go as far as divulging that the thought of placing my head between her overfed puppies and shouting 'brrrrrrr' while nuzzling them was a thought I was trying to suppress and... calm down Charlie, don't forget, she is the enemy and must be kept at arm's length at all times.

I sat on the deckchair next to the sun lounger. It was indeed a beautiful day for taking one's shirt off. I kept mine on. She soon returned from the kitchen carrying two long tumblers topped with ice and mint and handed me one. 'Have a sip of this Charlie. It's a Mojito.'

'Oh yeah, what's in it?' I asked suspiciously.

'It's Bacardi with a dash of lime, a squirt of soda, plenty of fresh mint and a special secret ingredient of my own that must remain a secret.'

'Rohypnol?' I said under my breath.

'Sorry?' she asked.

I took a tentative sip, 'Mmm, lovely' I said, 'Most refreshing.'

I followed her through the French windows and down to the bottom of the garden where my mother would often be found enjoying the sun and doing the tea break quickie crossword in the paper during a break from her chores. I wondered what she would be thinking if she was to look down now. I guessed it would probably be something along the lines of 'She's no better than she ought to be.' A saying I admit I have never quite understood.

Grace got comfy on the reclining red and white striped sun lounger and let out a sigh of contented bliss. I placed my drink on the small wicker table that separated us and enjoyed the warmth of the late summer sun on my face as I shut my eyes and tried to think of something to say. With nothing coming I took another sip and my mind couldn't help wandering back to summer days gone by; me as a small child playing catch with my real dad before he passed away. Playing cricket with a green plastic bat he'd got from saving up his Green Shield Stamps, then in later years being told off by Colin for booting the football into the flowers and knocking the heads of his geraniums, or whatever the bloody hell they were. I'm sure it was always sunny then…

'Be a love and pass me the suntan lotion will you Charlie? I think it's sitting on the floor next to that fag packet.' I turned, reached behind me and found the small yellow bottle. It felt nearly empty – it had been a wonderful summer. I turned back round to pass it to her and got the shock of my life. JESUS CHRIST! SHE'S ONLY GONE AND GOT HER BLOODY TITS OUT!

'Cheers Charlie,' she said, taking it from my hand without noticing the look of stunned disbelief on my face. She carried on as if nothing was more natural in the world than stripping to the waist in front of your future stepson and covering your silicon-enhanced bosoms in factor number five. I had to admit they were a pretty impressive testament to modern plastic surgery techniques. There was no hint of scarring, and they sat high and proud like a couple of eager puppies begging for a treat. They absorbed the liberal amount of sunscreen being applied like a sponge. Thank God I had my mirrored shades on.

'So how are you and Melissa? Is everything going smoothly pregnancy wise?' she asked, still applying the cream without a hint that this was anything other than mundane or normal. 'Er, yes, she had another scan last week and everything seems as it should be.'

'And the sex?'

Slightly taken aback, I took a large swig of my cocktail. 'It's OK, a little uncomfortable for her but I suppose that is to be expected at this stage in her pregnancy I guess.'

She squawked loudly. 'I wasn't quizzing you about the ins and outs of your love life darling, I was simply enquiring if you knew the gender of your baby!'

I tried to regain my composure and conceal how foolish I felt. 'Oh, got you. No, we didn't want to know. I think it's nice to have a surprise on the big day.'

'Has Colin told you we've fixed a date for the wedding?'

'No, we haven't spoken in a little while. So when is it? When are you tying the knot?'

'It's all booked for Christmas Eve at one o'clock. It is going to be at St. Mark's Church. My boys are going to be ushers and Colin still wants you to be his best man despite your, er... let's say reservations.'

'I'm sorry Grace, it just came as a bit of a shock that's all.

This is why I'm down here, to apologise and give you both my full blessing.'

She moved the recliner into the sitting position and pushed her sunglasses onto her forehead. 'Now listen Charles. I am going to marry Colin whether you give your blessing or not. I know you don't like me, and frankly it bothers me little. I suppose you see me as some kind of threat. You'd like to paint me as some troublesome interloper out to divide the family and make off with the silver. Well, let me tell you there will be a few changes around here when we are married. They'll be no more free lunches and cars bought for you because you are hard up. You've been taking advantage of Colin for years. It's not as if the two of you are even related!'

'Excuse me!' I said, getting rattled, 'He may not be my legal father but that man raised me with my mother since before I was in long trousers. He helped me through puberty, got me my first job, saw me through the difficult times of my mum passing away and the end of my first marriage. You can't blame me for wanting to try and protect him from some peroxide bleached, multiple divorced tart with an addiction for expensive plastic surgery and lonely old geezer's money!'

She sat in stunned silence and put a hand to her head. A stray tear appeared almost as if on demand and rolled gently down her cheek. 'Why does everyone always think the worst of me?' she sniffed. 'All I want is to be given the benefit of the doubt. I love him, he loves me and we want to be together and make each other happy. What's so wrong with that?'

I suddenly felt like the bad guy. 'Look, I'm sorry. I didn't mean any of that. Please, please forgive me. I'm sure Colin would agree that I have a terrible gift for talking rubbish and upsetting people, often myself,' I said.

Her shoulders were shaking, and she suddenly burst into tears. I felt like a complete bastard. I got up from my chair and put a friendly arm around her to console her. 'I'm so sorry Grace. Please don't take any notice of my big stupid mouth. Once you're familiar with our little family you will soon realise you have to take practically everything I say with a big pinch of salt, especially when I've had a few. Believe me, you have never heard anyone talk as much bollocks as me when I am in the vice-like grip of Jack Daniels or Madam Stella.'

'OK Charlie,' she whispered, holding me tightly. Between sobs she added, 'Please believe me, I only want to fit in and make Colin happy.' I felt her mighty breasts against my chest. Her perfume smelt expensive and the gold she wore on her wrists, ears and fingers looked valuable and exclusive. This lot was definitely not from Argos. Yet despite this scene of emotion and her claims of devotion, I couldn't help but wonder what she saw in my dumpy little step-dad.

'I so wanted you to like me, Charlie,' she said.

'I do, I do,' I said, feeling her nipples trying to puncture my ribcage.

'You do know Charlie that I am closer to you in age than your Dad. There's only around ten years between you and me. That's hardly anything when you think about it.'

Ten years my arse, I thought. I managed to wriggle free from her clutches. 'What are you saying?' I asked. Her tears had stopped and her mood suddenly altered as if by a switch, 'Come on, you must have felt it, this sexual chemistry between the two of us.'

'Eh?'

'Let's put our cards on the table. I fancy you, and I know by the way you can never tear your eyes away that you have the hots for me,' said Grace. I was struck dumb, especially when I felt a hand wander from the small of my back to my buttocks.

'I really don't think that this is a good idea...' I stammered.

She made a shushing sound and put her finger to my lips.

She gently, and I must admit, expertly, slid her hand from my bottom around to my inner thigh. The thing that was happily snoozing in my boxers awoke almost instantly and uncurled with great interest.

'I am a woman and you are a man Charlie. If it doesn't hurt anyone else and it is our little secret, does it really matter?' Her head tilted upwards as she sought to kiss my lips with her own bright painted set.

'This is wrong Grace, so wrong,' I protested, but then she moved in for the kill and nuzzled into my neck.

'If it's so wrong, why does it feel so right?' she whispered.

At that moment Colin burst through the patio doors with a bottle of sparkling plonk and a bag of nibbles. 'Sorry I was so long sweetheart, there was a hell of a queue at the cigarette counter and I knew you'd kill me if I didn't come home with your Benson and Hedges.' Then he took in the sight of his prospective bride in all her topless glory in the arms of his stepson. 'What in God's name is going on here?' he exclaimed, his face filled with amazement and disbelief.

'Oh, Colly!' she screamed, 'Thank God you're back. He's

been suggesting all kinds of disgusting things! I couldn't get rid of him! He's an animal!'

I disentangled myself from her enhanced and oily body and stuttered my defence. 'This is not what it looks like, Colin. I only came down to make peace with you and the next thing I know your blushing bride-to-be is coming on stronger than an extra strong mint dipped in chilli powder!'

Colin was red in the face. 'Oh, I see. Not content with trying to split us up, you thought you would move in and try to grab her for yourself. What is wrong with you son? You have everything, a lovely home, a fantastic wife and a magical family. Is that not enough for you? Are you so screwed up that you have to be the centre of everything? Doesn't my happiness count for anything at all?' he shouted.

'Do you really think I'd risk my wife, my family and your trust for a five-minute knee trembler with that old boiler?' I spat, pointing to a horrified Grace.

'Colin, are you going to stand there and let him insult me like that?' she shrieked.

He shook his head. 'Piss off, Charlie, you're welcome here no longer. I will find someone else to be my best man, and to be honest, right now I don't care if I ever see you again!'

I shook my head, unable to take in this sudden turn of events. 'Fine!' I said and turned to go. Out of the corner of my eye I saw a smug, satisfied grin spread across the face of my stepfather's intended.

CHAPTER TEN

Four small walls

Friday night is no great thrill for the unemployed. Don't get me wrong; it's not a total flop. It's infinitely preferable to a Tuesday morning trip to Morrison's for food shopping or repainting a garden fence. It's better than endlessly flicking through the TV channels during a dull, long Thursday afternoon, trying to find something to watch that isn't about house hunting, home improvements or finding priceless antiques at boot fairs.

A few weeks back when I was still a working man (and it seems ages ago already), Friday night was the Holy Grail, a treasured and much lusted-after thing that dominated nearly every waking thought from about Wednesday onwards. But now, as I'm pretty much idle 24/7, Friday is more or less just another day. When something is free it's never as appreciated as much as when it has been worked for.

Here we are sitting in a recently-opened Mexican restaurant, packed to the rafters with forty guys and girls blowing off steam after their long hard week of toil and tedium. And here I am feeling a bit of an interloper, and frankly a bit of a fraud. I haven't sweated blood or paid my dues to get here. In fact I have to admit that this week I have probably spent more time lazing around in bed than up on my feet in search of new employment. I wouldn't say I've thrown in the towel, but I have definitely twirled it around my neck in a 'just got out of the gym and feeling flushed' kind of move. Yes there is no denying it, there is definitely more of the horizontal than the vertical about me these days.

So why are we here? Why is Ellie at her grandmother's while we are ensconced, quite happily I must admit, three sheets to the wind (in my case anyway, Mel is, as always, the designated driver. No prizes for guessing who designated her though) and in the mood to agree to go along with almost anything; nipple piercing, clog dancing, even talking in a South Devonshire accent and having my hair styled like the guitarist from Slade. Anything feels possible right now.

My beautiful wife took a small sip of her wine. 'OK Charlie, I must admit, much as I love your company and a cheap Tex-Mex deal for two, I must come clean. There is a reason for this nice little end of the week treat.'

'Sock it to me baby.'

'Let's have a little recap of our current situation, shall

we? I am going to give birth to our second-born just after Christmas. I will then be off work for six months. In our present circumstances, what with you currently still searching for a suitable job to match your huge, varied and undoubted talents, we will not even have the funds coming in each month to cover our mortgage, let alone the bills and supermarket costs and the expense of running our cars.'

'It's a bit of a pickle,' I agreed.

'Everything's going up, Charlie. Each week when I fill up the car and do the weekly shop I'm spending more and more. They lower tax on something small and then raise it on everything else and expect us ignorant buggers not to bloody notice. Soon they'll be trying to charge us for breathing the Queen's oxygen and walking on the pavement to get more money out of us.'

'God bless her!' I said and raised my glass. 'She's a wonderful woman.'

I was seriously pissed, as unknown to her I had starting my boozing session a full two hours beforehand by visiting the local corner shop and liberating a cold and shiny four-pack of Strongbow for a budget busting special offer of £2.99. I had wolfed the lot while watching three hours of crap on the bonus disc I received with my copy of 'The Return of the Jedi' on DVD.

Seriously though, who actually watches all this extra shit they seem to be obliged to spew out? Well, apart from the long-term unemployed such as myself, and the occasional over-enthusiastic obsessive fan, obviously? No lie, but when I was wasting a few hours the other afternoon wandering around the large and mainly empty isles of the Bluewater shopping centre I was gobsmacked to find an eight-disc copy of Aliens. Eight discs? What the hell could they possibly fill up seven bonus discs with? The deleted scenes? The alternative ending? The cinema promo and the directors' cut? That would probably fill another couple of discs maybe, let's say three at the most. So what the hell do they find to warrant another four discs or so? A forty-minute featurette on alien make-up? The apprentice electrician's video diary? The postproduction team's Subway favourite?

'So what are you saying?' I asked.

'I am saying, my darling, that I'm afraid you are going to have to swallow a large mouthful of pride and take something that normally you might consider somewhat beneath you.'

Just then our starter to share arrived. I tucked in with enthusiasm, pleased with the welcome distraction. 'Blimey, these chillis are a bit on the violent side. Nice but naughty. Come tomorrow when it's time to park one's breakfast I will no doubt be regretting hogging most of these.'

'I think I'll avoid them then,' said Mel, opting instead for a less challenging onion ring.

'Best thing,' I said, cramming my mouth with tortillas and dip, 'I don't want the sudden injection of spicy heat to induce sudden labour. It may delay the main course if the waitresses have to mop up around us to clear away your broken waters and other feminine-type goo you may spill.'

'Do you mind? People are trying to eat here. I'll be careful, I wouldn't want my discomfort and agonising pain to spoil your fajita enjoyment. Anyway, getting back to what I was saying, your redundancy money has all but gone. We have very little in the way of savings and I'll be receiving only maternity pay before long.'

'That's it Mel, you certainly know how to make the evening go with a swing.'

'This is serious, Charlie. I think it's time to take your head out of the sand and wake up to the scary and precarious predicament we currently find ourselves in.'

'Do I have to? I much prefer having my eyes closed and my fingers in my ears. It's a much happier place.'

'Why did I have to get hitched to a child?' Mel said, shaking her head. 'You can't keep getting pissed every day and arsing around with your silly new Scottish friend and pretending things will be all right if you pour enough lager down your neck.'

I took a deep breath, sat back in my chair and looked her in the eye. 'Mel, I have been giving this a lot of thought and there is something I just have to say.'

'What is it?'

'Can I have the last spicy chicken wing?'

'This is exactly what I'm talking about.'

'OK, OK, I will forgo all pride and take the first dead-end job I stumble upon. No matter that I possess twenty-five years' experience in my trade, a keen brain and a healthy work ethic, for our family's sake I will flip burgers, clean toilets or hand out leaflets on double glazing at the entrances of out-of-town DIY superstores to keep the wolf from our door. Are you happy now you have stripped me from all dignity, or is there anything else you would like to point out? That I have no future? That my DIY skills are sadly inadequate? Or maybe that my penis has a weird habit of bending towards the left? These are facts I am already well aware of, thank you very much.'

'You have sauce on your chin,' she said coldly.

'Thanks for pointing that out. You are most observant these days. I have sauce on my chin, I have no money, my friends are silly, my penis...'

'Can we leave your penis to one side for the moment? All I ask is that you start getting up before midday and start bringing some money into the house before the bank takes it away from us.'

'It's not easy you know. I have been trying. There is very little about. In case you haven't noticed, there is a recession going on. Right, I need the toilet, something on that platter has gone right through me.'

I stumbled from the table and managed to locate the convenience. While seated on the throne I tried to envisage taking a job I had no interest in for the sake of the money. These were dark days indeed.

I was just finishing the paperwork when I heard voices – female voices. A sudden fear sobered me up. Come to think of it I don't remember passing any urinals on the way to the sit-down cubicles. Oh fuck, don't say this is the ladies? Oh bollocks, this place looks and smells far too nice to be the gents. Bugger! Bugger! Bugger!

The girls chatted while they presumably checked out their appearances in the mirror. I held my breath. Stay cool Charlie, wait until they go and then swiftly make your leave. Only it wasn't that simple. Over the next fifteen minutes it appeared that every female in the place was emptying her bladder of the house wine she'd been enjoying. Either that or reapplying her make-up and having a bit of a gossip. There even developed a bit of a queue, with at least a couple of ladies commenting on the length of time the person in cubicle two (me) was taking.

My phone rang, making me jump. It was Melissa. 'Charlie, where the hell are you? Your main course has arrived and it's getting cold. You've been in there nearly twenty minutes, which is extreme even for you.'

'I'm stuck in the ladies' toilet,' I whispered.

'What's that? Speak up Charlie, I can't hear you.'

Putting on a slightly effeminate accent, I explained as inaudibly as possible my predicament. Her laughter echoed around the tiny cubicle. When she finally recovered her composure she added, 'Only you Charlie, only you! Well hurry up and make your escape. I'm getting lonely. If you're not out in five minutes I'm leaving you there.'

Presently the toilet fell silent and I gingerly unlocked my door, opened it an inch and peered out. The coast was clear! I was just about to leg it when two gorgeous girls, one blonde the other a redhead, dressed to impress in their late teens or early twenties strolled in. I hid behind the door, my heart beating fast. The blond entered the cubicle next door to mine; the other stood at the sink and checked out her appearance in the large mirror.

'So, are you really going to dump Rob?' she asked, presumably reapplying her lipstick. Her mate next to me replied, 'Yes, there's this new bloke Nick who works in accounts who is so hot it's almost untrue. I know he fancies me and I want to be single so he'll ask me out.'

'When are you going to tell Rob?'

'I was going to tell him tonight but he dropped a hint that he's going to buy me something nice and pricy for my birthday next week so I'll probably wait until after then.'

She flushed and joined her pal and they washed and left. I bolted as soon as they were out of the door and regained my place at the table. Mel, who had almost finished, looked at me, smiled and shook her head. 'Chow down Charlie, it's getting late and I'm tired. Some of us have to go to work in the morning.'

'But it's Saturday?'

'Needs must my darling, I'm afraid.' On leaving we passed the two girls I had observed in the toilets. It was against my better judgment, but I just couldn't resist it. I paused at their table and addressed their partners. 'Which one of you is Rob?' I asked.

'My name is Rob,' replied a concerned, fresh-faced and smartly-dressed man in his early twenties. 'What's up?'

'Nothing with me pal, but if I were you, I wouldn't bother pushing the boat out on a birthday present for this one.' I nodded to Blondie. 'She's going to dump you for Nick from accounts straight after. Enjoy your evening, people.'

We exited, leaving the four of them open-mouthed. My work here is done.

CHAPTER ELEVEN

The seat of learning

With ever-tightening financial constraints and Mel's boss ignoring medical opinion and letting her increase her hours of employment rather than reduce them, I have been duly privileged to take my daughter to school while my beloved taps away at her keyboard, thus increasing our monthly incomings by a few pounds a week. Although this small amount will scarcely cover my weekly bar bills at the club, I appreciate the sacrifice and hard work involved. It can't be easy being a working mother with a huge bulge that is growing ever bigger by the day. That and the constant war against the negative elements of pregnancy such as backache, swollen ankles and the fear of stretch marks, plus the ever-increasing chance of piles, must be a drag.

I must confess this addition to my daily list of chores was not a welcome one. The thought of trudging to and from St Mark's infants and primary school every day left me distinctly unexcited. The last thing I need every bloody morning is to stand around feeling a complete spare part, surrounded by a load of gossiping mums with their pushchairs and whining kids, all the while getting freezing cold waiting for Ellie's po-faced teacher to tear herself away from a pre-lesson fag and blow the whistle to call the herd in. I have grown quite accustomed to lying in my pit until ten before being overcome by the need for something to eat and to empty my bladder. Within ten minutes I am back under the duvet with a cup of tea, the morning's paper and three rounds of heavily-buttered toast. Unfortunately the axe has fallen on my life of idleness and slobbery. I have been given a whole new agenda to stick rigidly to.

'So, are you clear on everything?' asked Melissa, bolting down her muesli. We were all sitting at the dining table, a feat we usually only accomplish during Sunday lunch.

'I think so,' I replied, munching on the breakfast I was struggling to digest due to my lager-induced dehydration from the previous evening's excesses. I repeated the instructions she had already bored me to distraction with the previous evening: 'Leave home at a quarter to nine, teeth brushed, hair combed and with the correct shoes on, armed with her packed lunch and juice out of the fridge to be at school for ten past.'

'Don't forget her book bag,' reminded Mel.

'Right, are you taking all of this in Ellie?' I asked my beautiful little girl. I can't believe she's at school already. Where has the time gone? It only seems five minutes ago that Mel was creating a load of fuss squeezing her out. Ellie was far too engrossed in the C-Beebies channel to notice my prattling.

'And are you sure she's not going to get upset and cry?' I asked Mel, fearing the prospect of having to peel my bawling little Princess off my leg and shove her through the classroom door.

'She should be fine. She's been going in on her own for the last week and a half and she's been OK. Make sure you give her a last wave before she gets out of view and there shouldn't be any upsets. We've had a little talk and she said she's looking forward to showing you her school.'

'Cool, and what time does she come out?'

'Three-fifteen. Whatever you do don't be late. If you are, you are a dead man, understand? Against my better judgment I am entrusting my daughter's safety and welfare to your less than capable hands.' I nodded, half listening. 'And don't forget to double check she has everything when you pick her up; lunch box, book bag and coat.'

'I won't. I don't know why you're so concerned. I am quite capable of taking my daughter to school, you know. Sometimes I get the impression that you think I am a half-baked drunken idiot who's unable to carry out the simplest of tasks without you standing behind me.'

'Mmm,' was her only response.

Twenty minutes later found me hand-in-hand with my little girl walking through the autumnal streets towards her school. It was the first really cold day of the winter, and I soon regretted opting for my hooded tracksuit top instead of a coat. Ellie was fine as she skipped and chatted away happily.

'Daddy, I think you should be a football man. You always watch it and you know everything.'

'I'm afraid I'm a bit old for all that running up and down, darling,' I replied.

'You could be a secret agent. You like James Bond.'

'Yes that might be good, but what if some baddies get me, wouldn't you be worried?'

'Yes I would, but if they do get you, you could just tickle them like you do me and escape while they are laughing,' she said.

'OK babe,' I said, picking her up and attempting to tickle her through her coat.

The nearer we got to my daughter's school the more we were accompanied by a growing throng of Mums, the odd dad and children of different ages and sizes. By the time we reached the school gates it had become a heaving mass of pushchairs, parents and uniformed children. I felt alien and out of place. I found a spot at the rear of the playground and wondered what my life had come to. A couple of months before I had been a successful and prosperous member of society with cash on the hip and without a care. I'd had a purpose. OK, I bitched about it endlessly and took it totally for granted, but I warn all you people out there who are unhappy with the daily grind that this is much, much worse. It's an abyss. A dark, dank bottomless pit filled with hopelessness, despair and a total loss of direction. Surprisingly, or maybe not given these troubled times of recession and ever-increasing unemployment figures, there were plenty of other men among the woman in the ever-growing crowd. Were they in the same boat as me?

Ellie spotted her best friend, a little dark-haired girl with a look of fun in her eyes and a Chelsea Football Club rucksack on her back. Ellie was away and I was instantly forgotten. I felt a little disappointed. Here I was in a strange place and I had been left all on my lonesome, feeling like a fish out of water. Just who was the infant here?

I was summoned from my reverie by a holler of, 'Charlie, Charlie, over here!' Registering that it was my name being called, I looked around to see Melissa's friend and co-gossiper Sue, a woman in her early forties of slim build and a bubbly personality whom I had met a few times previously. She was dressed smartly (perhaps off to the office) with a bob haircut, sparkling green eyes and lips I wouldn't be averse to kissing. Next to her was a short woman in specs wearing well-worn leggings and a duffle coat. I had the feeling we had met at various kids' parties, school events and such in the past with nothing more than a smile or a hello passing between us.

Completing this little group was a great hulk of a woman with a mane of straw-like yellow hair and three prominent moles jostling for position above her upper lip. She must have been a good couple of inches above six foot, with a bust size nearing three figures. I felt tiny and wimp-like as I approached. Unlike me, she wasn't regretting on not putting on that extra layer. No way! She was warm enough in a pair of tracksuit bottoms that she was constantly hitching up around her waist and a white sleeveless top that was straining to contain the contents. The only covering she needed on her muscular arms was her scary-looking collection of tattoos. An inaccurate and poorly-drawn portrait of a person I guessed was supposed to be David Beckham was positioned on her toned left forearm and a catalogue of what I assumed was her ever-lengthening list of offspring on the other. Her right biceps sported a six-inch picture of Freddie Mercury in full flow, while on her left was an indiscernible grey-green blob that I couldn't make out. A skull on fire above her right breast completed the not too darn handsome ensemble.

What these three ladies had in common could only be their children, as there seemed little else to connect them; a go-getter working girl, a tired-looking homemaker and a contender for the Gravesend and District Female Arm Wrestling Team.

'Morning Charlie, how are you love?' asked Sue.

'I'm good, if a bit on the chilly side,' I replied. 'Is it always this cold, miserable and depressing up here?'

'Pretty much. Welcome to the exciting world of the school run.' She introduced me to her compatriots. The small woman was Claire, while her friend was named Sophie, which as I was about to find out was almost always abbreviated to Soaf.

Soaf spoke. 'We always stand here at the back of the playground. You get a good view here.'

I turned to observe the tired-looking school building, the kids running around like headless chickens in an abattoir and the collection of oddly-shaped, and I must confess ugly-looking, parents.

'Views of what, exactly?' I asked.

'Oh, there's always something happening,' said Claire.

'Really? And you stand in the self-same spot every day?'

'Twice a day,' corrected Soaf.

'You have much to learn Charlie,' added Sue. The school playground is a whole little universe of its own. It has its own hierarchy, code of conduct and even its own royal family.'

'You're kidding me,' I replied.

'Absolutely not! There are rules that must be obeyed, rivals to be slagged down and minor battles and tiffs carried out daily. Standing in someone else's spot is the equivalent of declaring war.'

'Blimey, I had no idea,' I admitted, suddenly feeling not quite as bored. Claire pointed to a small woman who was making sure the toddler in her buggy wasn't about to turn blue.

'See her?'

I nodded.

'Just before half term her son Zak smacked Soaf's Jonathan on the chin, right in front of her and she didn't say a word to the little brat.'

'That's right, and then when I went to have a go at her about it she claimed she didn't see anything.'

'So what did you do?' I asked, genuinely interested.

'I said it didn't surprise me that she couldn't see what was right in front of her face, which was why she didn't have any idea of what her old man is getting up to behind her back.' She laughed.

'And what is he doing? Playing away?'

'Not as far as I know, but it certainly put the wind up her. I imagine he was asked some pretty searching questions when he got home from work before eating a crappy microwaved meal and spending an uncomfortable and lonely night alone in the spare room.' She cackled like an overfed witch with bronchitis and a recurring cough. Bits were shaking and threatening to come loose and fly off. I was preparing to duck.

Looking around at my fellow mums and dads, I have to admit my heart sank. This was real life. This was my life. Forget television and the life the media would have us believe is being lived by the beautiful and slim-hipped majority, this was reality. This was what we really are. We are poor, unattractive and without aspiration to anything more than surviving until payday or giro day and meeting the mortgage payment for another month. You will not find anyone here stumbling out of a hot London night spot at 3am while putting a pissed hand up to try to block the unwelcome snapping of the paparazzi or getting into the back of a stretched limo and giving the society page a glimpse of a dewy gusset. No sir, all we can hope for is for the working week to pass as quickly as possible so we can celebrate the arrival of the weekend with a box of cheap supermarket Stella, a fish-and-chip supper and if we are feeling slightly indulgent, a battered sausage on the side. Are we less deserving than some rich city boy who makes ten grand a week, of which a quarter goes up his nose in coke and the rest on his riverfront mansion, fine dining and East European prostitutes? No I don't think so either.

At that moment a woman with startling flame-red hair and multiple piercings joined our merry band. 'Christ I thought I was going to be fucking late. I was arguing with some frosty faced bitch about blocking her drive and I lost track of the fucking time. Are the little bastards going in yet?'

'Here we go,' said Soaf. Just then a short, stout woman appeared from the warmth of the building and blew hard on a red whistle. The children, including my own, froze and almost zombie like, robotically formed lines behind symbols painted on the grey playground beneath their feet.

'She loves to drink from the furry cup, that one,' said Claire, raising an impeccably-groomed eyebrow in the direction of the whistle blower. Blimey, the girls are talking dirty to me. I belong already!

The children went in row on row. As instructed by Melissa I was ready to wave to Ellie as she followed her school chums into the busy and brightly-painted classroom, but she never turned to bid farewell to her doting father. There was a sense of anti-climax on my part.

So, what now then, a second breakfast and a half-hearted wank to Lorraine Kelly? With one eye on the clock during the rest of the day I made it in plenty of time for the afternoon pick-up. Well, that and the fact that I was bored out of my skull with nothing constructive to do and precious little money to spend.

The sun had decided not to bother to show his face that afternoon, preferring instead to hide away behind angry and heavy-looking clouds. There was a cold easterly wind whistling across the grey tarmac of the school playground. The mums and dads were once more standing in their regulation places on the grey tarmac chattering away like cellulite-covered clockwork toys. What do they find to talk about? What have they been up to in the last six hours? What can possibly have happened to cause such enthusiastic outpourings that keep each circle in a state of such engrossment day after day, term after term and year after year? Is there a new brand of dishwasher tablet on the market? Was there a three for two offer on baby wipes down at the local supermarket? Was the milkman seen paying a thirty-minute house call at Cheryl's at number thirty-two?

Anyone would think they were meeting up again after a twenty-year absence, not six bloody hours. Christ, this is the first day of this and I'm already bored stiff and hating it. Either I am not getting it or I'm just a miserable bastard... Yeah well...

As I looked around the rapidly-filling schoolyard, one thing struck me; I have never seen so many unattractive, if not downright ugly people congregated in such a small area in my whole life. Jesus, where were this lot spawned? Most of this lot look like they only crawled out of the slime and learnt to walk upright this morning. God knows what the lovely people at OK magazine would say if they caught sight of this lot. No wonder this part of North Kent is looked down upon by the great and the good. It's a sea of sloping brows, stretch marks, Chatham facelifts (where the woman's hair is pulled back so hard the features are raised and stretched to form the look of a bulldog being dragged back by its leash) and knocked off and second-rate market gear.

I mentioned this to Sue, who I must admit didn't belong in this category at all. She was tall, long-limbed and willowy with a body that belied the fact that she'd had two or three kids. I leant over.

'Sue, have you ever noticed how grim this lot are?' I whispered in her ear.

'Mel told me you were a bit of a snob. Don't be so judgmental Charlie. I know a lot of this lot fairly well due to the PTA, the football team, dance classes and birthday parties and they're for the most part good people. It's about time you learnt that outward appearances can be very deceptive. OK, I admit some of this crowd tend to look a little frayed around the edges but the majority are warm, good-natured people with hearts of gold who will do anything to help and give you their last pound if you needed it.'

'Yeah, or rather head-butt you and rip it from your unconscious hand' I scoffed. 'What about him over there?' I asked, pointing to a red-faced, unshaven ape of a man whose jeans were exposing a good inch and a half of hairy bum crack. He stood stern faced and growling, all tattoos and testosterone ready to thump anyone who dared to look at him in a funny way.

She smiled smugly. 'Well, I think this little example proves I am right. You should never judge a book by its cover no matter how tatty or gaudy. That, Charlie, you might like to know, is Bob Elms, the nicest and gentlest guy you could ever wish to meet.'

'Yeah, he's only assaulted three policemen and a Salvation Army lady this week. After this he's off to his weaving and head breaking class.'

'Charlie, I have great pleasure in telling you that he is a lovely soft teddy bear of a bloke. He's on the PTA, voluntarily drives the mini-bus for the old dears at the rest home around the corner on their days out, and at last year's Christmas jamboree and fundraiser he gave up his free time to spend four hours on the cake stall selling chocolate brownies and fairy cakes.'

'Yeah, right,' I said doubtfully.

'Which he baked himself!' she added.

'OK, OK, you got lucky this time, there is always an exception that proves the rule.'

'Do you think so? Right, what do you make of her?' she said, indicating a group of young women standing beneath the netball hoop.

'Which one?' I asked.

'Her facing us with the purple woolly hat on.'

'Well my dear Watson, my first impression is that she appears warm and friendly. She has checked on her toddler in the pram twice in the last few minutes, so I would assume she is a caring, loving mother who would always put her children first. The buggy looks new and fairly expensive, so I would deduce that her husband has a good job, maybe in the city, or possibly he runs a small firm installing false ceilings or heated toilet seats. They are not short of a few bob. Yes, her coat and shoes look expensive and new, so I wouldn't think there are any money worries. I can also see her driving a people carrier that is religiously cleaned inside and out every Sunday by her husband, whose name is probably Kevin. They reside in a three-bedroomed house in the better part of town with an adjoining garage and a recently constructed conservatory, probably south facing judging by her tan, which has still to fade fully. They are looking to move up the housing ladder in the next couple of years, depending on how his business is doing. They spend a fortnight each summer in Greece but are considering going somewhere else as it's becoming too much of a tourist trap and they wish to avoid the poorer class of Brits who are dragging the place down with their boozy antics and shop doorway shagging.' I paused for breath and got a minor round of applause.

'Charlie, you leave me almost speechless! You can tell all that from a pushchair and a bobble hat?'

'Pretty much, my deductive powers are pretty sharp,' I said. 'I can sum people up in an instant. I guess some would call it a gift, but in reality it's a poisoned chalice. When you can look into a person's eyes and peer deep into their soul and see all their failings, secrets and weakness of character it makes it difficult to trust people and make lasting friendships. It's a curse Sue and a heavy burden, one which I carry manfully and without complaint, but it's a burden all the same.'

She laughed out loud, 'Melissa is so right, you are so full of shit it must be starting to overflow. For your information that girl is called Hannah and she has three daughters by different one-night stands. She lives with and sponges off her poor kind-hearted mum, who is used as a freebie meal ticket and baby sitter. She spends most evenings in the Crown getting gullible blokes who aren't aware of her dreadful reputation to buy her Pernod and blacks in the hope that they will be getting an easy shag. She is a habitual user of what I believe are called class A drugs and is regularly to be found at the doctor's, who has the repetitive job of handing out treatments to clear up her STDs.'

'All right, one point to you.' I scanned the playground. 'What about that shifty-looking creep over there? He looks like a complete perv if you ask me. What is he doing here? I don't see him as a family man or a reluctant uncle helping out a family by picking up little Ben because Mum and Dad are having to put an extra shift in at the factory or office. No, he's definitely an undesirable, no doubt on the police register, and he gets his kicks by filling his trouser pockets with pick'n'mix and hanging around the school gates waiting for an opportunity to fulfil his sick and sordid fantasies.' I took a closer look. 'That's it!' I exclaimed. 'I know where I've seen him before. He was on *Crimewatch* a couple of weeks ago. Yeah, that photo-fit they did nailed him completely. He lured some girl away from Brownies and fiddled with her or something equally sinister.' I pulled out my mobile phone. 'Shall I phone the authorities and get the SWAT team down here?'

Sue raised her eyebrows to the heavens, 'I wouldn't if I were you Charlie. That's Mr Drake, the headmaster.'

'Well, if you're sure,' I said feeling slightly foolish. 'So do you know everyone in the school then? Pupils, parents, the lot?'

'More or less, either directly or by rumour and reputation.'

'Go on then, give us some juicy gossip I can impress Melissa with.'

She looked around until she found the person she was looking for. 'You see that tall blonde in the fur coat, short skirt and boots?'

'What, her who looks like she's just flown back from warmer climes with an orange tan and too much make-up?'

'Warmer climes my arse. She spends at least two mornings a week beneath the sun bed at the tanning and pampering parlour in the village. And that's before having a full facial scrub, her legs and fanny waxed and her nails done.'

'Well, you have to admit it's money well spent. She's definitely a cut above the rest of the downtrodden track-suited inbreds... er, present company excepted of course.'

'Charlie, she is completely fake!' said Sue. 'Fake eyelashes, fake tan. Her hair colour is out of a bottle and even her tits aren't real. She's known behind her back as Mrs Plastic.'

'OK, OK, so she's had a bit of help from the chemist and the silicon industry. Blokes don't care what it's made of as long as it's easy on the eye, I'm afraid. So what about her?'

'Well, she has a lovely husband. He may not be the best-looking guy in the world, and granted he's a tad overweight, but he's a smashing fella. He owns a small building firm and works around the clock to fund her lifestyle of shopping, pampering, eating out and paying for a wardrobe with more designer labels in it than Posh.'

'He and I share a bit in common then,' I said. 'Well, apart from owning a building firm and having pots of money.'

'And is Mrs Plastic grateful?' she asked.

I shrugged. 'No, she treats him like shit whenever they are out and has had at least three affairs to my knowledge. I wonder if she fancies a fourth.' I was admiring her long slim legs and leather mini-skirted arse.

'I think she's a little out of your league funds-wise Charlie. If rumour is true, her last conquest, some big hitter in the banking sector, bought her a Range Rover.'

'Mmm, so a packet of cheese and onion and a swift half of Foster's followed by the promise of a quick fumble behind the gas works is unlikely to impress then?'

'I wouldn't have thought so.'

'So what is the latest gossip that will have my other half salivating over?' I inquired.

'I have it on good authority, from two different sources, that she is booked in at a top private Harley Street clinic next month to undergo a full vaginoplasty operation.'

'Sounds revolting,' I said. 'What is it?'

'A face-lift for your fanny,' said Soaf.

Fortunately, to save me from embarrassment and

further ridicule, Ellie's teacher and her assistant appeared right on queue and led the children from the sanctuary of the cosy and warm classroom to the bitter cold and us, the loving parents. I waved enthusiastically and she responded likewise. She looked scruffy and carefree as she waved her lunchbox and a freshly daubed painting. I felt a surge of pride envelope me. Gosh, this must be what it must be like to be an attentive and caring parent. I took a mental note to take more interest in Ellie and not bawl at her to get out of the way of the telly when I am trying to watch re-runs on UK Gold.

'Hello babe, have you had a good day and have you got everything you went in with? Mum will give me the sack if you've forgotten anything.'

She smiled, nodded vigorously and reassured me that everything was present and correct. I opened her backpack. Inside was her book-bag, along with a lunchbox, a letter from teacher and her mittens. Good, there should be some Brownie points here surely. If I can't get my leg over tonight I never will.

We were just about to turn and go when I was summoned by a teacher. 'Mr Bennett. May I have a quick word with you?'

My spirits shrank and disappeared. 'Ellie, what have you done? Have you been naughty?' I whispered. She gazed up with a face of pure innocence, 'No Daddy.'

We followed Miss Crankshaft back through the classroom door and into the inner sanctum of her classroom. There was a smell that took me back several decades to when I was a small child in short trousers with the whole world was ready to be explored and conquered. Paintings and models made by the boys and girls were stuck on the walls. I searched for one of Ellie's creations, but I couldn't spot one. The tiny tables and chairs made me feel like a giant.

Ellie's teacher was young, tall and attractive. She wore dark trousers and a pale top that sported a splash of red paint just above her left breast. It was hard not to stare. Her hazel eyes sparkled behind a pair of small black plastic framed glasses. I wouldn't object to a spot of detention with her, I thought.

'I'm afraid, Mr Bennett, that we had a bit of a situation this afternoon during our potato painting session. From what I gather Ellie accused another child of spoiling her painting. A commotion ensued and Ellie I'm afraid hit the poor boy in the face with a large potato.'

I looked down at the sweet little girl at my side. She looked at me defiantly.

'Was he hurt?' I asked Miss... whatever her name was.

'He was very distressed I'm afraid. The matter was noted in the accident book and his parents notified. Ellie and I have had a little chat about it and things are sorted, but I thought it best that I put you fully in the picture. This kind of behaviour can easily escalate if unchecked,' she said matter-of-factly.

'I do apologise, it is most unlike her. I will have a strong word with her when we get home and try to get to the bottom of it. It's not in her usual nature to be unruly so I am sure it was probably a case of six of one, half a dozen of another.'

On our way back to the car I asked Ellie if she really had hit him. 'Yes, Daddy, I was doing a picture of me, you, and mummy and for no reason he put his green potato on your face.' 'That doesn't mean you can go around throwing potatoes at people, sweet heart.'

'Sorry daddy.'

'Did he cry?' I asked.

She laughed, 'Like a big baby! Boo-hoo-hoo!'

CHAPTER TWELVE

Women's bits

Sitting in the passenger seat on our way to the local clinic I was in a rotten mood and sulking like a five-year-old who's had his favourite toy taken away. Mel and her ever-growing baby bulge were squeezed behind the steering wheel. She commented on a closing-down sale poster in a window while we were stuck at a red light. I didn't reply.

'Don't be like this, Charlie. How often do I ask you to put yourself out and do something for me for a change?'

'I just don't get it, that's all. When you were pregnant with Ellie and were surely in need of pre-natal classes you were never interested but now, one child on, when we know what it's all about, you suddenly decide it's imperative that we leave the warmth and comfort of the sofa on a frosty Wednesday night to listen to some nurse spout off about contractions, stretch marks, pain relief and nappies.'

'Two hours of your time Charlie, that's all I'm asking.'

'It's the final game of the group stages in the Champions' League tonight Mel. We need at least a draw and I'd purchased six cans of premium lager, two tubes of Pringles and a tub of reduced fat hummus to help me get through all the drama. But now thanks to your selfishness I am going to be sat in a draughty hall surrounded by a load of fat women.'

'Do shut up Charlie. You really are starting to sound like a scratched record.'

We were one of the last to arrive and Mel was definitely the oldest mum-to-be there. The midwife was a hard-faced sturdily-built lady in her early fifties who was obviously about as keen on being there as I was. There were only five bulging ladies present and one other male of the species, a spotty youth with a bum-fluff moustache who wore a sex pistols T-shirt and baggy jeans that hung so low his crotch was level with his knees and in imminent danger of sliding clean off his almost arseless body. Oh, to be young once more, with a twenty-eight inch waist and your whole life ahead of you.

The evening began with the midwife illustrating the birthing process using a plastic pelvis and a small flexible doll.

'Excuse me,' I asked with an arm in the air and a straight face, 'but will the baby come out like that one wearing clothes or will it be naked?' This comment ensured I received a dig in the ribs from my good lady wife.

'No, the only thing baby will be wearing is amniotic fluid and blood. The usual baby dummy I use has gone missing and this was all I could get hold of at short notice,' said the midwife wearily. 'There's always one, isn't there?'

'Yes, and it's always him I'm afraid,' said Mel.

'Don't worry dear, there is still a fifty-fifty chance that baby will take after you and not Dad.'

'Yes, I'm keeping my fingers crossed,' she said.

Next we sat on worn green gym mats on the dusty floor. The dads knelt behind the mums-to-be as they practised breathing, counting and pushing – all things I can confidently announce I am already proficient in. Out of view and very much behind her back I managed to sneak out my phone and catch up on the latest football scores on the web. 'That's it Mel, you're doing brilliantly! That really is some top class breathing you are doing there. Mmm, still nil-nil, sounds proper tense.' Who says blokes can't multi-task?

Next on the agenda was pain relief. We had a go on the gas and air and then I strapped a TENS machine to my arm and turned the dial up to maximum. I went into spasm; Mel shook her head sadly and took it off me, telling me 'Grow up for God's sake, why can't you take anything seriously?'

After being met with a negative response at my request of an epidural we were paired off and given a large piece of paper to discuss and write down the pros and cons of the different antenatal topics we were soon likely to face. Pain relief was one, baby's first days was another I overheard, but predictably ours was breast verses bottle. Mel and Sydney; funny name for a girl but there you go, they got on like a house on fire and were soon discussing teats, formula milk and cracked nipples as if they were part of an exciting future. Sydney's partner however remained silent, and evidently would, much like me, prefer to be somewhere else.

I offered a hand. 'All right mate? My name's Charlie.'

'Rob,' he replied after a short pause. At closer quarters I could see that he was very young, indeed, still in his teens and finding this all a bit overwhelming. After half an hour's bonding through the frankly arse-clenching embarrassing situation we found ourselves in we were both in need of some fresh air and a break.

'Do you fancy a fag?' he asked.

'No, but I think I'll join you outside for a few moments. All this talk of placentas and afterbirths is making me a bit queasy to say the least.'

My fellow parent-to-be was shit scared of the mess he was in. He barely knew his partner and definitely didn't want to be tied down with her, or anyone else for that matter.

'I can't believe it. I only did her because I couldn't land her mate. Now I'm stuck with her, her family's getting heavy and there's bloody no way out. I should be at uni now getting a degree, shagging anything with a pulse and drinking myself unconscious, but instead I'm stuck with this fucking shit!'

I tried to think of a consoling response. but could come up with nothing. My years of experience (or lack of it) gave me little in the ways of wisdom to help the spotty nurk. In fact, if I were in his shoes, knowing what I know now I would probably be even more pissed off than he was.

'Don't worry mate. OK, your immediate future has slid down the pan, ready for a double flush, but in a dozen years or so you may have enough free time and cash for a couple of jars and a set meal for two down the Indian. That's if you can get a babysitter of course. She seems like a nice girl, your other half?'

'I suppose so. I was more interested in her mate, to tell the truth.'

'Nah, she's a little cracker. You should count your blessings. You could have been saddled with a lot worse, believe me.'

'You've left it late to start a family, haven't you?' he replied, idly checking the texts on his mobile.

'We already have one, but yes, a bit like yourself it wasn't part of some great plan. Things just happen. There's no rhyme or reason to it. Who was it that said that plans are something we make while we live our life?'

He shrugged, 'I dunno, Snoop Dog?'

'I wouldn't have thought so, but you get the general idea. The thing is, you can have your life all mapped out in your head but it's both pointless and worthless. We have as much a control over our destiny as your newborn will have when she decides to go and dirty her nappy or not.'

'So this is it is it? I'm seventeen and instead of meeting the world head on with angst, enthusiasm and a libido the size of a lion I'm suddenly told, sorry, pause all of that. From now it's a non-stop diet of responsibility, a steady job and sensible haircuts while your chums are missing lectures, getting laid and having the time of their lives before it is too late. Fucking marvellous! My whole life fucked, due to one pissed-up party shag that I can barely even fucking remember!'

'It will all sort itself out. Things always do,' I said, immediately cringing at my own platitudes. Christ, I am sounding like Colin! Jesus, it's true, eventually you will become everything you mock and stand against.

His phone beeped and he pulled it out of his pocket. 'You're right fella, there is always a silver lining to the darkest cloud.'

'What do you mean,' I asked, feeling proud that my experience and knowledge of the world could indeed help my fellow man. 'Have you had a positive result on the DNA test?'

'Na, my mate has just texted me that Man U are two down already. Fucking magic! I can't stand those cheating northern monkeys.'

My sympathy and desire to console and encourage this poor wretch disappeared in an instant. I rejoined the group of bulging and swollen mothers with a cloud above my head and a face of thunder. 'Are we nearly done? I need a drink.' I growled at Melissa.

'What, another one?'

'Don't start!'

Half an hour later we were back in the car with the radio tuned to the footy channel. United had pulled one back, but by the commentary it looked unlikely that an equalizer was forth-coming. I was tense, dry and tetchy. Melissa was chatting non-stop about the baby class, which she had evidently enjoyed and found instructive and rewarding. She was just enlightening me on the benefits of breast pads when the commentator from Old Trafford screamed at the top of his voice that Rooney and United had scrambled a last-minute equalizer and that surely now they would be heading towards the knockout round of the Champions' League. I screamed with gay abandon and banged on the horn repeatedly. The evening hadn't been a complete waste of time after all.

'Yes, yes, yes, get in there you fucking beauty!' I roared. 'Come on babe, let's go for a couple of drinks and an Indian to celebrate.'

'No thanks, some of us have to go work in the morning.'

She turned her head away and stared out of the window into the pitch-black gloom of the country road. In an instant, the chasm of what we each valued and found important was laid out for each to digest. Neither of us spoke again until I wished Mel a good night before I turned off the bedroom light.

CHAPTER THIRTEEN

The night shift

So it has come to this. I, Charlie Bennett, who once upon a time was promised a glittering future by the school's career adviser, who said, and I quote, 'He has the talent and drive to succeed in whatever field he fancies' has been reduced to this: a nine-hour night shift at a grotty, mass-producing budget food company for the basic minimum wage. Soon, while my beautiful wife is snug under the covers all warm and wrapped in silk, I will be standing knee deep in offal, making sausages or picking the gristle out of supermarket own-brand steak and kidney pies.

This is what our increasing poverty has driven us to. Out of devotion to my family and the wish not to have 'NO

FIXED ABODE' as our address on my future child's birth certificate, I have swallowed several helpings of pride and agreed to take a job here while I look for something more challenging, well-paid and permanent.

Having misjudged the journey time from our humble dwelling to the place of my new employment, I sat in the car and waited for 10 pm to tick round whilst listening to the crazy views of the weirdos on a talk radio station. After enduring the opinions of Keith from Watford who wanted all unmarried mothers to be sterilized or shot, I decided I could take no more and that I would show some willing and go in early. I guess it's always a favourable idea to make a good first impression in any job, even one as (hopefully) temporary and as cruddy as this.

I bounded through the reception door, full of purpose and motivation, and gave my name to a bloke reading a newspaper on reception. He grunted and looked at a sheet of paper on a clipboard. 'There's no one of that name down on here. Are you certain you're meant to be starting tonight?'

I nodded. Why does this always happen to me?

'Who's your supervisor?' he asked.

'I can't remember the name of the bloke who interviewed me. It only lasted two minutes. I think he was northern. He was bald, tall and thin – a bit like a pool cue with the white ball balanced on top.'

'That will be Terry. He doesn't work nights, I'll get the night shift supervisor.' Off he disappeared. I sighed inwardly, wishing I were anywhere else but here.

Presently a guy in his late fifties approached me with an outstretched hand. He spoke incredibly slowly and clearly and at a volume one notch below shouting: 'My-name-is-Barry, I-am-the-line-leader-of-the department-you-will-be-working-in.'

I nodded and smiled. Is he retarded or does he think I am? 'Did-the-agency-send-you, have-you-brought-your-form?' 'No. My-wife-sent-me-and-I-have-no-form. Is-that-a-problem?' I shouted back.

'You're English!' he exclaimed.

'Yes-I was—born-and-raised-here. Is-this-going-to-be-a-problem?'

'No, no, not at all! It's a godsend, that's what it is. It's just that we haven't had any new English employees for ages. They usually send us people from Eastern Europe, plus the odd Pole and Indian. Not that we are in any way racist. Oh no, we as a company embrace the whole spectrum of creeds and colours from around the world. It's just a shock that's all, hearing an English accent. We haven't had a home national start here for months. The pay's shite, the hours are long and the conditions aren't much to write home about. Huh! Listen to me putting you off before you've even got your hairnet on! Follow me and I'll kit you out and show you your duties.'

Within minutes I was decked out in plastic bag things that covered my trainers, white cotton overalls and most humiliating of all, the promised hairnet. I was led to a room about thirty feet square, covered from floor to ceiling in plain white tiling. A conveyor belt entered through a hole in the wall on one side and disappeared out of another. In between stood four incredibly bored-looking people slopping food from large steaming metal containers into small foil trays that trundled past them at a fair rate of knots. No one spoke, smiled, or even acknowledged my presence. A warm welcome it most definitely wasn't.

I was placed in between a swarthy-looking unshaven guy in his mid-twenties who looked ready to commit a serious assault if I dared to look at him in a funny way, and an old chap whose enormous belly almost prevented him from ladling his peas into their allotted space on the trays passing by. 'Right, I am going to put you on mashed potato,' he said, as if this was a truly sought-after position that I was incredibly fortunate to walk into. He passed me a ladle. 'One scoop and one scoop only. Make sure you place it in the left-hand corner of the tray and try not to spill any over onto the other sections. We have Gerry on inspection tonight and he is most particular on any kind of merger of foods. The chap before you kept on spilling potato onto the peas. God, what a night that was. They almost came to blows!'

He demonstrated a few times before handing me the ladle, then nodded towards the next silver tray as it passed. I scooped the lumpy grey mush into the correct compartment without spillage, merger or outright miss. He looked genuinely delighted with my first effort.

'Well done, I can see you are a natural. If you need to visit the toilet, press the red button and someone will take over. If one of the others (he pointed to my co-workers) has beaten you to it you will have to tie a knot in it and wait. You are allowed one toilet break per half-shift of no more than five minutes. Any extra time taken will be queried and possibly deducted from your pay. Your break time is three. You get half an hour. Any questions?'

'Is there a canteen?' I asked, 'I might start to flag by then and need some sustenance to keep going.'

'Yes, if you can call it that. There is a brightly-lit, soulless room at the back of the factory. It has four tables, a microwave that is in badly need of a clean, a kettle that takes fifteen minutes to boil and three incredibly overpriced vending machines. Anything else?' I shook my head and prepared to scoop another load of mash. 'Good, I'll drop by a bit later to see how you are getting on.'

Within forty seconds I had mastered the 'task' assigned to me. The unappealing and frankly inedible-looking slop was hitting my allotted compartment in the TV dinner tray with remarkable accuracy. By golly, my first shift and already I was putting the guy whose job it was to provide a small portion of overcooked carrots to shame. There were half a dozen of us on the chain gang. I tried to make eye contact with my fellow inmates, but there was nothing doing. They were statuesque, silent and possibly in some kind of catatonic state. They may even have been brainwashed to prepare them for the task in hand, so zombie-like were they. Each wore headphones and was lost in his own private universe. My God, this was going to be a long night. That is if I manage to see the whole shift through to its bitter end. Come on Charlie, stay strong, remember why you are putting yourself through this purgatory. There is a wife, a daughter and a large female gut relying on you to put pride to one side and bring home some much-needed cash.

I sighed and shook my head. And there I was foolishly thinking making specs for a living was dull. Blimey, compared to this my previous career was a wild and exciting roller coaster ride. It is so true what the saying says – you never appreciate what you have until it is snatched away from you.

Just then, a short man sporting closely-cropped grey hair and a goatee beard to match flung open the door (or the escape route) and strolled confidently in to join our not-so-happy little crew. The guy to my left immediately handed him his ladle and moved along the line to the small wizened black guy whose job it was to provide what looked like some kind of non-identifiable brown slop, possibly stew, into our hearty meal for one. This was done without acknowledgement, smile or a word spoken. The stew man left, no doubt looking forward to a cup of coffee from the canteen machine and perhaps a little cry before slitting his wrists.

Grey hair and grey beard eyed me up casually and without warning shook a long, loud fart from his tightly-covered arse.

'Another cup of tea, vicar?' I said under my breath while questioning the hygienic implications of dropping one's guts in an area of food preparation and making a mental note to myself to breathe through my mouth rather than my nose for the next few minutes.

He turned to me with an expression of surprise mixed with joy and relief. 'Do I detect my own native tongue or has my double espresso and half a packet of Jaffa cakes befuddled my brain and laid waste to my senses?'

'I'm English, if that's what you mean,' I said.

'My dear boy, how delightful to make your acquaintance. I would shake you warmly by the hand, but I fear the time spent grasping your delightfully-formed paw may make you misjudge your aim and a poor unfortunate pensioner or care home resident would have to go without carbohydrates with their beef cobbler, and that would weigh heavily on my conscience, leaving me with a troubled night of restless sleep and umpteen trips to the bathroom. My name is Francis Longworth, how do you do?'

Slightly taken aback by his outrageous campness and what I'm sure was a touch of eye shadow, I smiled brightly. 'I'm Charlie, Charlie Bennett.'

'Is it OK if I call you Charles? I do like things to be proper. I hate sloppiness.'

'Be my guest. It's nice to see a friendly face and hear an English accent when you start a new job.'

'You are so right. And this is such a treat for me! Ben, he was the last English-speaking chap in this godforsaken hell hole of a department, quit nearly three months ago to return to Newcastle University to resume his degree in fine art. I fear what the mass-produced food industry has lost, the world of canvas, bristle and paint has gained. No doubt he is currently sketching the outline of a young unemployed northern youth in charcoal, surrounded by cherubs and wailing fallen women, the lucky boy. Still never mind, we must move on. So tell me Charles how has fortune dealt you such a poor hand that you find yourself among the dead and dying such as I?'

I told him my situation and he listened intently, nodding and cooing in equal measure.

'My poor darling boy, this must be a terrible strain for you. We will have to make you as welcome as possible so your burden is as light as one of my salmon and goat's cheese soufflés.'

Despite, or maybe because of, his outrageous gayness, I was warming to my new colleague immensely. 'So how have you managed to wind up here Francis?' I asked him. 'You are obviously a man of experience, culture and taste. Surely you belong a million miles away from this place, spending hour upon hour shovelling overcooked veg about?'

'My dear, dear boy, it is a tale of woe from start to finish. It deserves to be made into a Hollywood blockbuster, or at least a three-part mini-series staring dear Kev Spacey and Daniel Craig. I gave everything, Charles; my heart, my soul, my money and my trust. And how was I treated?'

'Er... poorly?'

'I was cast adrift, equipped with neither a compass nor a first aid kit. He left me broken hearted and more or less destitute. He took my savings, he took Lancelot, my devoted springer spaniel, my Portmeirion dinner service, the furniture and everything else I once held dear. I am a husk, Charles. An empty shell left to the mercy of life's cruel and vicious tide.'

'Men are such bastards.' I concurred.

'You are so right my dear, but where oh where would we be without them?'

I shrugged. Just then a sturdily-built, rosy-cheeked woman in her early fifties breezed in with a cheery smile. She was pushing a trolley that housed three large metal cooking pots. 'Hello love, let me take that for you,' she said, replacing my almost empty barrel of slop with a steaming full one. 'How are you this evening Francis?' she asked my new friend.

'I had one of my heads this morning and I was concerned mightily that it was going to develop into a full-grown migraine, but after a lie down in a darkened room with a cool flannel pressed to my throbbing brow it melted away into nothing more than an annoying niggle. How are you darling? Has your David shown his face since he liberated the money from your purse?'

'Yes, but he's denying it of course. He must think I'm bloody stupid. I ask him, so, where did you get that new iPod from then? Oh, I found it, he says. Jesus, it makes me so cross. I'll be glad when he gets put away again. Then at least I can have a bit of peace and know for sure that when I get home the TV will still be there.'

'You poor, poor cow,' he said. 'You're too soft, that's your problem. A few more clips around the ear would do that boy no harm at all. I'll have to come round for a cuppa and a Hobnob. I'll soon put him straight.'

I found it hard to imagine Francis sorting out a burly hoody with authority issues. He was pushing five feet six in his Cuban heels and weighed less than nine stone. He was thin and wiry, without an ounce of fat on him and about as intimidating as Orville the Duck.

'Gosh, how absolutely brutish of me! I haven't introduced you to my new friend.' He turned to me. 'Charles, please say hello to Pat, a dear friend and the maker of the lightest lemon sponge drizzle cake available this side of the Thames. Pat, this is Charles, a sympathetic listener, a father of one with one on the way, who is scooping his mash for his family with not a thought for his own pride and sanity.' I nodded a greeting.

'Hello love, when is it due?' she asked. 'Early January,' I replied.

'Not long then, what are you hoping for?'

'We already have a girl, so a boy would be nice.'

'You wouldn't say that if you knew my David, the bloody little shit. Still I expect you'll be a better influence as a father than my Mick ever was. Bloody shithouse he was. Still he's gone now.'

'Oh, I'm sorry,' I said, feeling awkward.

She laughed and patted my hand, 'No, he's not dead love! I kicked his sorry arse out of the door when I caught him shagging my bloody sister. It was the best thing I ever did.'

'He didn't deserve you, love,' chipped in Francis.

'I make you right Francis. I haven't looked back. He can rot in his tatty little mobile home from now until eternity for all I care. Now I would love to stop, chat and slag him off further, but if I don't get the mash to the shepherd's pie lot before they run out, my goose will be cooked and that bitch of a line leader will have another excuse to give me a bollocking. See you later boys.' She made a hurried exit.

'She's lovely is Pat. Give you her last fiver or cigarette she would, but she's a fool to herself. Those boys of hers run her ragged.'

Over the next few hours Francis and I discussed many topics. From the Prime Minister to I'm A Celebrity, he had an opinion and an insight on everything and everyone, each delivered with his unique flowery style.

'I don't get it. I know the country is in recession with unemployment rising and opportunities few and far between but I am sure you could get a much better job than this bollocks. How long have you been here now?' I asked him.

'Mmm, it must be getting on for three years now.'

'Are you seriously trying to tell me that in all that time you haven't been able to find anything that's better paid and more rewarding than scooping grub for ten hours a night?' I asked incredulously, worrying for my own future prospects. He winked; whether it was a come on or cheeky secret I wasn't sure.

'It has its compensations Charles. I can watch Jeremy Kyle and Cash in the Attic during the day and listen to Abba Gold while I work as well as keeping one or two other irons in the fire that compensate for the poor hourly rate and lack of sunlight and stimulating conversation. Present company excepted, of course.'

Eventually it was time to change out of our gear, remove our hairnets and take our leave. My back and feet ached and the last couple of hours had dragged dreadfully. Francis was off working elsewhere and despite my best efforts my other co-workers didn't want to (or couldn't) engage. As our shift trooped out we met our replacements coming in the other way. It wasn't hard to figure out who were the happiest. While we were chirpy and moving quickly out of the door, the lot who were hauling themselves in against their will were silent and morose with not a smile between them. I guessed in a matter of hours the roles would be reversed once again. They would be the happy lot while our shift would be dragging our heels and wondering why we never got the breaks and wishing we'd have taken school a little more seriously.

After a brief 'How was it?' from Melissa, to which I just grumbled a response and shook my head, I was on my own once more as she left to take Ellie to school and herself to work. The house was cold, untidy and empty. Ellie's half-eaten breakfast cereal was congealing in her bowl, while a lipstick ring on a mug and a burnt and discarded crust were all that proved Mel had been there this morning. I suddenly felt sad, lonely and without purpose.

I entered the kitchen and threw open the fridge door to see what we had in there that was quick to make and easy to scoff. There was a jar of marmalade, a half-open tin of anchovies, some tired-looking salad and Ellie's school packing up goodies that were exclusively intended for her. On the top shelf on their sides were four cans of Stella, which Mel had bought for consumption at the end of the week as a reward for all my efforts. The imaginary angel at my shoulder tried to tell me that if I resisted and waited for the end of the week I would not only win approval from Mel for being such a hard-working sober goody-goody, but the golden nectar held within would taste that much sweeter after a week of sobriety.

Feeling righteous and strong, I shut the fridge, flopped on the sofa and scanned through the TV channels to try to find something worth watching. Less than ten minutes later I returned to the kitchen and pulled out a can of lager. As my finger slid under the ring pull I glanced at the clock. It wasn't even nine in the morning and there I was ready to get on it and wipe the day away. Shaking my head, I returned the can to the fridge, whacked up the heating and had another go with the TV remote. One hundred channels later I decide that staring at the wall would be far more entertaining and educational than watching the lamentable offerings of lame seventies re-runs, shopping channels and make-over shows. I finally admitted defeat and while making a mental note to cancel our satellite subscription I wearily made my way upstairs to bed.

Drawing the thin cream-coloured curtains made little difference to the brightness of the room. If anything it appeared even brighter. Is that possible? Surely that must go against all the laws of physics? By an hour later I had counted sheep, recited the alphabet backwards, listed every one of Elvis Costello's albums in chronological order and drawn imaginary ever-decreasing circles in the blackness of my scrunched-up eyes, but sleep was as imminent or as likely as a blow job from Mother Teresa. I'd known it wasn't going to be the easiest thing in the world to suddenly shift my life from day to night, but I hadn't thought it would be this difficult. I wondered how Francis managed to drift off. He was probably sound asleep now, clad in snuggly pyjamas and a pink furry eye mask. I would have to ask him his secret. How do you switch off when the world about you is at its busiest?

After another hour I finally gave up and played some computer games and made myself a bacon butty for breakfast/lunch. I watched a black and white film I remembered from years before starring a fresh-faced young star who had since grown old and died. I was yawning uncontrollably and I think I might even have drifted off for a couple of seconds. As my next shift was approaching with the speed of an express train whose driver needs a wee, I returned to bed and finally slept.

I awoke with a start. Mel was giving me wet kisses and urging me to wake up. She was in her pyjamas and holding a cup of tea. 'Come on sleepy head. Ellie's in bed and you have a little over half an hour before you have to be in work.'

My red and tired eyes forced themselves open. 'You have got to be kidding me. I've only just got off. I'm knackered!'

'It's half eight. Get your arse out of bed and get in the shower!'

Feeling in probably my worst mood ever, I stood once

again in my designated spot with a giant spoon in my hand and mashed potato at my side. My compatriot however looked as fresh as a daisy and full of vim and vigour.

'Call me a cynical old queen but I never thought you would be back. You are a trooper Charles, a real trouper! How are you this dark and storm threatened night?'

'Fuck off,' I growled.

'Oh dear, I will have to try and lift your spirits somehow. Ooh, I have brought in my mix-tape of Celine Dion and Wham's greatest hits in my locker. Would you like to listen to it? It always gives me a lift.' He started to shrill the theme tune to *Titanic*.

'Francis, if you don't stop in the next five seconds, not only will your 'heart not go on', but it will be stopping permanently and very suddenly when I beat you so savagely with my ladle that it will take your dental records and blood type just to identify you!' I said menacingly.

'I say, someone's a grumpy grot! Do I detect a lack of sleep and a less than enthusiastic bent to tonight's work?' he asked. I scowled and carried on slopping. 'Did you read *The Sun* today? I couldn't believe what poor old Ant's partner turned up in at the latest Harry Potter flick. I know she wanted to make a splash and get into the next morning's papers, but Christ there are limits! I could have told her that that dress was far too tight, clingy and see through for someone of her age and build. The poor dear looked like an overcooked sausage that had forgotten to be pricked on its way to the frying pan and was in danger of splitting open under duress! The poor dear! I bet she has spent the entire day in floods with the phone pressed to her ear trying to find consoling words from her friends and hangers on. We may scoff Charles, but believe me, a celebrity's life is nothing more than a fragile shell that's ready to crack open and become nothing more than yesterday's garbage at any moment. Yes, to us mere mortals, from the outside it might appear to be a non-stop carnival of celebrity parties, fashion shows and West End film premieres. Yes it must be marvellous rubbing shoulders with Richard Branson, Naomi Campbell and Kate Moss, and I'm sure having cocktails with the Beckhams and having dear little Tom Cruise on speed dial must be dreamy, but is it worth the price that has to be paid?' He carried on without drawing breath. 'Could you cope without any kind of private life whatsoever? Would you want the dreaded scum of the paparazzi following you about 24/7, with their devilish telephoto lenses homed in on you, ready to snap you off guard exposing a cellulite rippled thigh, a picking of the nose or heaven forbid an early morning departure from an establishment that isn't the family home? No Charles, those poor, poor dears suffer more than we will ever realise.'

'Francis?'

'Yes dear?'

'Fuck off.'

He pulled a face. 'Charming!'

Half an hour of tense silence later, my guilt at my outburst got the better of me and I made an effort at friendship and reconciliation. 'Sorry about my little outburst earlier mate. I'm finding the changes my life is going through at the moment a bit challenging. What with the new job, and the worry of the drop in salary and the new baby on its way and everything...'

'I understand,' he said. 'It's not the easiest thing to take in your stride without a stumble or an unsteady step here or there. But as I hinted at yesterday evening there are perks to be had that make the whole spirit crushing shift almost bearable.'

'Oh yeah, and what's going to happen? Am I going to discover an extra-large lump in my mash which turns out to be fifty grand in used readies? Or maybe that miserable old git of a supervisor is going to trip up, fall arse over tit and drown in laughing boy's vat of brown offal which is laughingly disguising as beef stew?'

'Nothing as exciting as that I'm afraid.' He tapped the side of his nose. 'Charlie, although we are only recently acquainted my instincts tell me, and I am rarely wrong, that you are a fine upstanding citizen of this once proud and brave nation. As honest as the longest of days, a believer in charity and doing right by his fellow man.'

'Absolutely,' I replied. 'I believe in always doing the right thing, playing fair by my fellow man and knowing that what goes around comes around.'

'Indeed, indeed, so let's just say hypothetically that a chance arose for you to leave here tonight with a whole leg of lamb, a huge bag of pies, some chops, a few quiches and a large side of beef to handsomely enhance your paltry wages. Do you think your conscience could bear the guilt that this great institution has one or two items less than it thinks it has, or would it lie heavily on you like a big fat girl you've picked up at closing time at a down-market pub in a small parochial village?'

'If I had been asked this delicate question a few months ago I would have said "Shut up, you small, poofy, yet likeable queen, you can shove your side of beef and budget family pies where the sun rarely shines".' He was ever so slightly taken aback. 'However Francis, times are hard, the government is about to drop and so is my missus, so if a leg of lamb was somehow to find its way into the boot of my car I would say three hail Marys or three hell Marys, I'm not completely clear on the correct terminology and despite being neither Catholic nor religious I would fool myself into thinking that it was either an act of God, fate or chance, and purchase a large jar of mint sauce from the service station on the journey home.'

'Excellent! So keep your wits about you and when I give the signal, move swiftly, keep your head down, remain silent and stick close. It's imperative we remain professional and leave nothing to chance.'

'Blimey! What are we doing? Robbing the Bank of England or whipping a couple of bits of meat? We're hardly the Krays are we? On second thoughts, wasn't one of them meant to be a bit... you know?'

'Charlie, do me a little favour will you? Give your silly mouth a nice little holiday, preferably somewhere quiet, the Isle of Mute is very nice this time of year I am told. Just concentrate on the job in hand and everything will be fine.'

'Right-oh, oh, what's the signal, you didn't tell me?'

'Signal?'

'Yes, the signal that I should put down my ladle and put on my ski-mask.'

'Oh, let me have a think. I know, when I start whistling 'The time of my life' from *Dirty Dancing* hand your ladle to Pat. She will fill in while we slip out. Just stick close and follow me. OK?'

'Understood,' I said.

We carried on in silence for a few minutes until I asked, 'Er, how does that go, the *Dirty Dancing* song? I'm not particularly familiar with that movie or its soundtrack.'

'My poor love, you don't know what you're missing. It's a fantastic movie! The number of times Kevin and I have spent cosy evenings curled up on the sofa with a fruity red, a box of chocs and a supply of man-size tissues at the ready must run into the dozens! Remind me before we go tonight to bring it in for you tomorrow. I have the new remastered edition with two bonus discs containing hours of extras. It's simply to die for!'

He started singing *I've Had The Time Of My Life* with huge amounts of volume and emotion. Even our friends, the silent and emotionless foreign workers, looked slightly embarrassed and ill and ease as they turned up the volume on their personal stereos. As the shift wore on I was beginning to think that the criminal master plan had been either forgotten or delayed for another night when, as it was nearing four o'clock and I was in a state of semi-consciousness, the woman introduced to me as Pat the previous night and another woman I had yet to make the acquaintance of entered as silently as ninjas (except that they were in overalls and hairnets – OK, maybe not as cool and threatening as the dreaded Japanese assassins, but you get the idea). They wordlessly took our spoons from our hands. Francis whistled his theme tune under his breath, tipped me the wink and with stealth and no little excitement I followed him out of the door and through a maze of brightly-lit corridors.

A heavily-set man wearing what I assumed to be

butchering gear approached from the other direction. Shit, are we busted? He winked at Francis without paying heed to myself and taking out a ring of keys from his pocket he unlocked the brushed steel door at the end of the passageway and promptly turned around and disappeared the same way he had come. Christ, how many people were in on this thing?

After a final look up and down the corridor, we entered. Inside, the chill and brightness hit me like a heavyweight knockout blow. This was evidently some kind of holding area where the frozen goods were kept before delivery. There were large racks and trays of every conceivable frozen product imaginable. It was like the entire frozen section of Sainsbury's but magnified a few dozen times. Instead of thirty packs of frozen sausages, there were three hundred.

'We have three minutes and no more,' said Francis as he retrieved four large folded up plastic carrier bags from the pocket of his overalls. He passed me one while pointing in several directions, his breath visible in the frozen air. 'Over there are the butchered carcasses and joints. On this side are pies, sausages, pre-packed bags of chicken breasts and the like. If you fancy the ready meals like the budget slop we dish out night after night, they are in that big steel cupboard in the corner, although if you still fancy feeding that muck to your family then you should have your brains tested.'

In no time our bags were bulging. Mine contained packs of chicken, premium sausages, a few quiches and several super-sized Sunday joints I would normally never be able to afford.

Then came the second thoughts. What if I get caught? What will Mel say? Or maybe more seriously, what will the judge say? What will be my defence? 'I'm sorry your honour, please show mercy. I am an honest man who was cruelly led astray by a smooth talking and extremely persuasive old poof. Please let me keep my liberty and be at my wife's side as she gives birth to our child, even if there is a ball and chain tethered to my foot. Go on Judge, there's a few lamb cutlets in it for you if you let us off.'

'Are you set?' Francis asked.

'I think so.'

'Right, let's go.'

I stood behind my partner in crime as he opened the heavy door a couple of inches and peered out into the corridor. He turned to me and with a point of the finger bade me to follow him. As we re-entered the corridor the butcher man and yet another accomplice approached, took our bags without a word being spoken and disappeared. We returned to our workstations and resumed our ladling. The whole operation had taken less than five minutes. I wasn't quite sure what had just happened and I didn't ask.

Our shift ended, we changed and headed to our respective cars. 'Do you know the Black Horse pub? It's about two miles from here off the main road,' asked Francis.

'Yeah, I've been there a few times. It won't be open now though sadly,' I said.

'I'm not thirsty. Meet me in the car park in ten minutes and I'll give you your share of the meat.'

'Ooh-er! I bet I'm not the first bloke you've said that to!' I quipped.

'Do you know what Charlie?' He grinned, 'You might just be right!'

Fun as that episode was, a week was all I could tolerate. By Friday I was so deprived of sleep that I was nodding off at my feet. Stolen meat or not, I could take the monotony no more. Our section leader was not disappointed; in fact he congratulated me for sticking it out the whole week. By all accounts my length of service was well above the average term of stay, in fact another week and a half and I would have qualified for a line leader's role, which came with a name badge and a special blue hat. Given these attractive promises I almost had a change of heart... but I didn't.

Mel was surprisingly understanding, given the fact that we were back on the breadline. I wasn't given a tongue lashing for giving in so quickly and not sticking it out. She could see the defeated look in my eyes at the start of every shift, the tiredness in my gait and the hollowed look behind the eyes.

'Charlie,' she asked me at the start of my well-deserved weekend, 'I was in our garage yesterday evening having a tidy up when I noticed that our old chest freezer that hasn't been used since last Christmas was on and humming away,'

'Oh,' I said, as she handed me a coffee. I fluffed my pillow and got comfy. 'Can you pass me the remote, babe? Soccer Saturday is on in a mo.'

She changed channel for me. 'Yes, and to my surprise it was full to the brim. It is literally jam packed with lamb, beef, chicken, about a dozen packs of pies and at least two hundred mini sausage rolls. What have you got to say for yourself?'

I took a large draught from my drink and considered my response. 'You can never have enough mini sausage rolls, babe. Parties, weddings, or a surprise visit from friends, mini sausage rolls are always a dependable buffet standby.'

'And these came from where, exactly?'

'Ask no questions and I will tell you know lies, sweetheart.'

'You are a bad influence and example to your children, Charlie Bennett!' she said, hitting me with a pillow.

'Watch it! You nearly had my coffee over then,' I exclaimed. 'Actually, all this talk of food has given me a bit of an appetite. If you look behind the chicken and mushroom pies and under the quarter-pounder beef burgers you will find a couple of rather handsome looking large black puddings. Be a love and bring one in will you while I dust off the frying pan. It's been an awfully long week and if there is anybody that deserves a hearty fry-up breakfast it's this fella. What do you fancy sweetness, poached eggs or fried?'

CHAPTER FOURTEEN

The man with the plan

Mel hardly had time to get her feet through the door before I leapt like a man with a purpose off the sofa and rushed to greet her in a flurry of hugs, kisses and promises of a brew and a nice bit of tea to follow. She was slightly taken aback by my enthusiasm and also by the tidiness of the kitchen, which was at odds with the usual state of affairs. Normally she would come home after a hard day's slog to find this morning's breakfast things still lying in situ, with further coffee cups and teaspoons in the washing-up bowl. An open margarine pot with a knife stuck in it was also a familiar sight. Today however it positively gleamed, with surfaces polished and all things tidy and not even a solitary item of cutlery at the bottom of the washing-up bowl to spoil the overall effect.

'Someone's been busy,' She remarked, with eyebrows raised.

'Nothing's too much trouble for you, sweetness,' I gushed, as I poured out the coffee.

'You're in a good mood too. And sober! What's happened, have you got some good news to share with me?'

'Uh-huh. I've got a feeling that everything is going to be OK.'

'Congratulations!' She shrieked. 'I knew you'd find a job if you actually put your mind to it. What is it? When do you start? God I'm so relieved. I've had so many sleepless nights worrying about how we're going to cover the mortgage and pay the bills.'

'Er, it's not a new job exactly,' I said, trying to bring her down as gently as possible.

'It's not? Well what is it then?' She replied, looking crestfallen. She took her drink into the sitting room, gave Ellie a big hug and asked her how her day at school was. Ellie gave her usual response, which was that she couldn't remember and could she watch The Simpsons later if she tidied her room.

'We'll see,' said Mel before putting on her slippers and picking up the TV mag to ascertain if there was anything worth watching later. 'Come on then Charlie, let's hear it. What is the latest get rich quick scheme you've come up with? I hope it's better than that last one where you were going to hand paint murals on kids' bedrooms. How much did you get for painting that Chelsea badge on Kate's son's room?' (Kate is the woman who lives three doors down.)

'Twenty-five quid, and all the coffee I could drink. I'd forgotten about that. She was incredibly pleased with my work.'

'Yes, pity he changed his allegiance to Spurs a week later.'

'I offered to paint over it and redo it as a Tottenham one, but she wasn't keen.'

'And how long did it take you?'

'From about start to finish, including planning, measuring and preliminary sketches, about a week.'

'I'm sorry sausage, but in the real world of grown-ups, bills and bank loans, twenty-five pounds a week isn't quite going to cut it,' she said condescendingly.

'I know, I know.' I felt slightly disappointed at her lack of positivity.

'Well go on then, pitch it to me,' she said, sounding like those executive types on the telly who shoot down young entrepreneurs who try to convince them that their invention of a self-heating tin of soup will make them all rich. Well, the contestant rich, them even richer. Actually that's not a bad idea – self-heating soup. I must jot that down in case I need a plan B.

I began, 'Well, I'd just finished watching Jeremy Kyle and then, finding nothing on until Quincy at two fifteen, I decided to go to the garage and mend the puncture on Ellie's bike.'

'Good God it's non-stop pressure with you unemployed types isn't it. No wonder you have to have a good drink now and again to unwind.'

I carried on regardless. 'Whilst I was looking for the puncture outfit I found that old portable wireless and put it on.'

'I can't see where this is going, but carry on,' she said.

'That was when serendipity, or fate, came in to play. The knob was missing and I couldn't change the station.'

'And you fixed it and now you want to be a traveling radio repairman, traversing the length and breadth of the country making sure poor bored lonely housewives don't miss out on listening to *Woman's Hour*?'

'Are you going to listen or what?' I said, slightly annoyed.

'Sorry, carry on.'

'It was stuck on Radio 4 and there was a programme about probability and mathematics.'

'You're going to train to be a maths teacher?'

'What, with my patience? I don't think so. No, they were talking about the Martingale system.'

'And what is that when it's at home?' she said, picking up the TV guide and rapidly losing interest.

'Let me show you,' I said, pulling a handful of coins I'd collected earlier for this very demonstration from my pocket. I picked a shiny two pence piece out and placed it onto my thumb. 'Heads or tails?'

Melissa folded her arms, crossed her legs and tilted her head to one side.

'Come on, indulge me,' I pleaded.

'Tails,' she huffed.

I spun. 'Tails it is,' I said and put it on the arm of her chair. 'Right, as I lost I am going to double the bet. Heads or tails?'

'Tails.'

'Are you sure? You called tails last time. Odds are all pointing to a heads.'

'Tails.'

I spun again. 'Tails again! Well guessed, you win once more. Now as I lost again I will double up once more. Are you going for tails again or you going to change?'

'Heads.'

I flicked the coin and slapped it on the back of my hand. 'This is your lucky day, heads it is.'

'Charlie I don't mean to be unkind but I know of no one who has supported their families by playing heads or tails, specially someone as bad as you. You are already...'

She counted the small pile of coins on the arm of her chair, 'Fourteen pence down.'

'No matter,' I said confidently, 'I simply double up again. So come on then for sixteen pence, heads or tails?'

She sighed again. 'Hadn't you better get dinner on the go or are you going to persist with these childish games all evening. What have you got planned for later, a game of British Bulldog followed by a couple of goes of hopscotch? I tell you what, Ellie darling, can you fetch your skipping rope? Daddy wants to relive his childhood.'

'You wound me not. Go on then, heads or tails?'

'Tails.'

'Ha, its heads, I win!'

'At last, now go and peel some spuds.'

'I think you're missing the point I'm trying to illustrate here. By doubling my stake each time I lost, I ended winning back all my losses plus winning my original stake. Therefore I am two pence up on the deal. I have made money!' I exclaimed proudly.

'Two pence, Charlie. This solves our money worries how, exactly?'

'After listening to that radio show I rushed inside and

fired up the Internet.'

'I've told you, you will go blind and get hairs on the palms of your hands.'

'Did you know that there are literally dozens and dozens of on-line casino sites?'

Her shoulders drooped; she smelt trouble. 'Casino sites?'

'More specifically, roulette games.'

'No, no, no, no, no! And if I ever find out that you've been gambling away what little money we do have I will take a large pair of bolt cutters to your privates before taking Ellie and leaving you forever!'

'But darling, I've...'

'I mean it Charlie. This time I'm really putting my foot down.'

I pulled out a sheet of paper. 'I studied a random roulette site this afternoon and had I placed a fiver on red on each spin of the wheel using my system in three hours we would have made just under two hundred quid. Two hundred quid babe!' I passed her my page of research. The first column was filled with R, B or 0; R for red, B for black and 0 if the ball landed in the house zero. In the next was my stake and the final row was my profit.

She glanced at it before handing it swiftly back.

'You are so naïve Charlie. Don't you think if it's that easy to make money then everyone would be doing it and all the casinos would have gone bust?'

'Ah, but not everybody listens to Radio 4 my love.'

She put on her most serious voice combined with a threatening manner. 'I mean it Charlie. This is not the way to solve our problems. Promise me that you will forget all about this.'

'But haven't I just shown you that we can't lose? Babe, this is a mathematical certainty. Truly we can't lose. This is the break we've been waiting for,' I pleaded.

'No, this is the end of this conversation. If you do this you lose me and you lose Ellie. I've put up with a hell of a lot lately, but do this and it will be the final straw. Understood?'

I nodded.

'No Charlie, I want to hear you say it and I want to hear you mean it. Promise me you will not go anywhere near the computer and go on those gambling sites.'

'But babe...'

'Promise.'

'Ok, but I think you are really missing a trick here.'

'Promise, on mine and Ellie's life.'

I huffed, 'I promise on both of your lives that I will not go on any Internet gambling sites.'

'Good boy, you know I'm right. Now, get your cute little tush in that kitchen and cook me some pie and let's not have any more of this nonsense,' she said, slapping my backside before hollering up the stairs, 'Ellie darling, Dad's mended the puncture in your back wheel. Do you want me to put your bike in the back of the car so that you can ride back to Grandma's when you finish school tomorrow?'

'Yes please Mummy,' she shouted, running down the stairs. 'Thank you Daddy, Laura brings her bike in now. We can ride together.'

'Er, sorry love, I didn't actually manage to fix the bike. When I found the puncture kit I found that there weren't any patches and the glue had gone all hard.'

They looked at each other and both gave small shrugs. Ellie's shrug said 'Oh never mind,' while Melissa's said

'Crap Dad strikes again,' but that's no news, that's just the way it was. I felt small and pathetic. I am a loser. My little five-year-old daughter, who should hold me in the highest esteem and think that I, being her Daddy, can make anything possible, has already at this young and tender age sussed out that I am somewhat of a disappointment. This is so, so wrong. I should be her knight in shining armour, the man who makes the impossible possible, the kind of daddy who always comes through to make her proud and the envy of her friends. Well, when my fortunes change and I can afford the latest expensive toys, the most 'in' trainers and exotic holidays whenever I feel like getting the sun on my back, I will be number one. I'll buy her a car for her eighteenth birthday and hold her wedding on the moon if that's where she wants it. Nothing is too good for my little princess!

I spent a restless night eager to start on my plan of world domination. Mel was getting ready for work while I made Ellie a breakfast of Rice Krispies followed by chocolate spread on toast. While waiting for the kettle to boil I ate a knifeful of the sweet brown goo. It was horrible. I threw the knife into the washing-up bowl as Mel came down the stairs. 'Watch out, tank coming through!' I hollered.

'Ha, ha. If you think I'm big now wait until I drop. Do you remember how big I got with Ellie?'

'Yep, all you needed was a harpoon sticking out of your side and you could have passed for Moby Dick.'

'Right, I'm away. Don't forget to give Mrs Pearson the note, it's in Ellie's bag. Make sure she cleans her teeth properly after eating that rubbish and it would be great if you could summon up the will to push the vacuum around and sort out the recycling before the kitchen resembles a beer can museum.'

'No probs babe.'

She pulled me close by the neck of my old dressing gown and whispered in my ear, 'I meant what I said last night Charlie. If I find out you've been gambling away the little money we do possess you do know what I will do to you don't you?' Her grip left my throat and headed to my scrotum, which she squeezed menacingly.

'Message received and understood, my sweetness. Have a good day.'

She relaxed her grip and looked me in the eye. 'Don't let me down.' She kissed Ellie on the lips and no doubt got a taste of chocolate. 'Have a good day sweetheart. Work hard and do your best.'

'I always do Mum.'

'I know.' She grabbed her car keys and left. Why does life have to be played out in such a hurry? Why are we always late and in such a rush? Wouldn't it be lovely if we could all just slow down, take our time and get there when we do rather than when we have to?

I glanced at the clock. Blimey, we are behind. I picked up a brush and attempted to tame Ellie's wild curls. 'Come on slowcoach, are you going to eat that or make friends with it? We have to leave in ten minutes and you've still got your jimjams on.'

I returned from dropping Ellie off at just after half nine, kicked my shoes off and immediately fired up the computer. I logged onto 'Mega Casino'. A beautiful girl with long dark hair and shiny red lips welcomed me to the site. She was clad only in a sheer black camisole. She repeatedly blew me kisses with one hand and jingled a handful of chips in the other. These were casino chips by the way, not French fries covered in ketchup. That would be plain silly. She winked suggestively in an expression that seemed to be saying. By playing at this casino you are exciting, sexy, stylish, a bit of a dangerous playboy and could probably have me. Boy, was I easy to reel in!

I clicked on the 'create account' button and it asked me for a user name. Mmm, I want something sophisticated, modern and with a hint of menace and danger.

JAMES BOND, I keyed.

THAT USER NAME IS TAKEN.

I tried again, SAM SPADE.

THAT USER NAME IS TAKEN.

THE FONZ.

THAT USER NAME IS TAKEN.

CHARLIE HUGEMEMBER.

THAT USER NAME IS TAKEN.

You have got to be kidding me! I know, MONTE CARLO SECRET AGENT 007.

THIS USER NAME HAS TOO MANY CHARACTERS.

'Flipping hell! All I want to do is join. What's next, an initiation ceremony followed by bloodletting and branding?

CHARLIEASTONMARTINDB5.

USER NAME SUCCESSFUL.

Hoo-bloody-ray! Next came the nitty-gritty, how much to deposit into my account. I was well aware that to carry my plan through I would need a fairly substantial bank roll. I deposited £200, which would probably plunge us well into the red. Sorry Mel, but sometimes you just have to trust me.

I joined the table. The last three numbers had been black. I took a big breath and put a fiver on red. The ball was spun one way and the table the other. After what seemed like an eternity the ball finally came to rest.

BLACK 35

OK, no problem Charlie, remember the system and double your bet. Right, this time a tenner on red.

BLACK 11.

No panic. Stay cool Mr Bond £20, red it is.

BLACK 2

I felt hot and lightheaded. OK, Charlie, you may panic a little bit but stay strong. I used the mouse to drag my next forty quid on to the red and crossed my fingers. Time stood still and my legs felt wobbly. Despite this I stood up and paced up and down in front of the computer screen shouting COME ON! And GET IN THE RED YOU FUCKING SHIT!

The result appeared on the screen and I felt sick.

GREEN 0

'Green? Fucking Green! I don't fucking believe this! This is fucking fixed, it has to be. Jesus! Yesterday when I was practising it was as easy as pulling fivers from beneath the pillow of a sleeping baby. Now it's for real it's more like pulling fucking teeth. What the fuck is going on? The two hundred quid I had five minutes ago was now down to a hundred and twenty five. Christ if this goes tits up I am a dead man.

That's seven spins since the last red. What are the chances of that? I tried to calculate what they actually were in my head, but my mental arithmetic skills were woefully inadequate. Reluctantly I doubled my last bet to eighty quid, thus leaving a pathetic £45 in my account. The wheel span and I left the room. I couldn't bear to watch as my marriage, my bank account, and my fate was left to the jiggling and bouncing of a small white ball. I went to the fridge, pulled out a lager, opened it and downed four or five large glugs. It was ten in the morning.

I caught my reflection in the toaster as I chugged on my beer. I didn't have any sympathy for the sad, broken wretch that stared back at me. Christ, what was I thinking? Bloody hell Charlie, you know this kind of thing never goes your way. If anyone was ever going to have an unfathomable run of bad luck it was going to be you. What made you think this was going to be any different? Why couldn't I listen to Mel? Why couldn't I just stop and think before rushing in? If only I had a head on my shoulders. If only the knob hadn't broken on that shitty radio. If only I hadn't been made redundant. If only...

I finished my can and threw it in the general direction of the recycling pile and slowly made my way to the computer. I was resigned to my fate and was already planning to eat humble pie and beg Colin to give me a loan to cover my losses. If he transferred the cash through the online banking thingy the mortgage would clear, there would be no threatening letter from the bank and Melissa would be blissfully unaware of my latest folly. OK, this was not how I wanted this little scheme to end, but at this stage it is all about damage limitation.

I took a deep breath and braved a look at the computer screen. The next spin was already under way, with the ball still circling the polished wood of the virtual table.

I looked at my balance.

£205

I've won! I can't believe it! I've only gone and bloody won! I raced around the room punching the air and leaping around like a lunatic using language that ladies in the twenties would have fainted at. I hadn't felt elation like this since Ole Gunner Solskjaer put the ball in the Germans' net back in '99. I am out of jail and a fiver richer. And I have learnt my lesson.

This was a moment of epiphany. This is far too much stress for such little rewards. I logged off and turned the computer off. A lesson learnt and a narrow scrape. A massive weight had been removed from my shoulders. I put on the TV and made myself some coffee. Jeremy Kyle's rotund trailer park guests however failed to hold my attention. I grabbed a packet of Monster Munch and scoffed them whilst giving the houseplants a watering. I opened some junk mail that had been lying on the kitchen worktop for a week or so. I skimmed through it before tearing it up and throwing it in the bin. After watching the arse end of an old black and white flick I turned the channel to Bargain Hunt.

God, this is so boring.

I thought about the adrenalin rush of earlier. The moment when my brain registered that I had won, and that I was a winner. That feeling of relief and euphoria was almost intoxicating.

I looked over at the computer. I looked at David Dickinson. His face glowed as invitingly as a Mediterranean sunset.

I looked back over at the computer with its red glowing standby light.

The people on *Bargain Hunt* were looking at a small

silver figurine of a troll blowing a bugle.

On the Internet a gorgeous seductress was waiting to blow me kisses and make me rich.

I fired up the computer again. Then I turned it off. Had I not learnt anything?

An advert came on for miss-sold personal loan insurance. Nuts to this bollocks! I'd rather be shamed and penniless than live this life of dreariness and death by slow lobotomisation.

Come on Lady Luck, where the fuck are you? Game on!

A few days later Ellie and I sat parked up in my car outside a large detached house a mile or so from home. It was on a quiet leafy road well away from the town centre with neither a cider drinking bum nor a petrified dog turd in sight. It was one of those mock Tudor mansions that people who work in the city and drink wine rather than lager live in. The type of gaff that would always be beyond our price range, whether I was still working at Huntington's or not. I guessed it was at least seven bedrooms with maybe room for a study or games room. Oh that's a thought. My own room with a pool table, XBox on a jumbo TV, a bar and even one of those cool retro jukeboxes…

'Are we going to be here long Daddy? I don't want to be late for swimming club,' said Ellie.

'Not long babe, Mum will be here in a couple of minutes. We'll have a quick natter then take you swimming. Do you fancy having dinner in the club afterwards?'

'Yes please Daddy,' she exclaimed excitedly. Kids are so easily pleased. 'I'm going to have macaroni cheese. It's even nicer than Mummy's!'

'Don't tell Mum that, she'll kill you,' I replied in fake alarm. I pointed towards the large house. 'Ellie, would you like to live in a place like this?'

She looked at the house and screwed her nose up. 'Not really Daddy, I would miss Jane and Sarah and I would probably lose all my toys because this house is too big.'

Just then Melissa's nine-year-old Astra pulled up behind us. 'Do you want to stay in the car or get out?' I asked Ellie.

'Stay in,' she said as she resumed the game she was currently into on her DS console. I stepped out and bent down to kiss Mel. 'Good day babe?' I asked.

'Not one of the best,' she said. 'So what is the mystery? What on earth have you dragged us out here for?'

I turned towards the house. 'Let's have a quick look' I said and strode past the 'For Sale' sign down the perfectly-paved front path to look through one of the big bay windows. Inside was a front room the size of our entire ground floor. How the other half live, eh?

'Yes it's lovely Charlie, I'll have one for every day of the week and two for Sundays. Are you going to tell me what this is all about? I've had a shitty day, my feet ache, my back aches and the baby keeps pressing on my bladder so I keep needing a pee. All I want to do is get home, have my tea, run a bath, climb into my PJs and put my feet up.'

I continued smiling. 'Good I'm glad you like it, because I'm going to buy this house.'

'Of course you are sweetie. Then next you're going to win the Spanish Grand Prix in a go-cart and reform the Tweets and take *The Birdie Song* back to No. 1.'

'Most amusing! Right, I'm going to tell you something now and I don't want you to get mad and fly off the handle.'

'Oh God, what have you done now?' she said with that familiar sound of dread in her voice. 'Christ, don't tell me that you and that big Scottish lunatic have gone and robbed a post office or something?'

'I know you thought it wasn't a good idea, but I decided to test my system at the roulette table after all.'

'I knew it! I bloody knew it! What the hell is wrong with you? Well that just shows what a promise from you means! Bugger all!'

'It's OK darling, if you just let me finish.' I tried to calm her down with a cuddle but she was having none of it. 'You promised Charlie, you fucking promised me. So that's it, is it? We are in the red and you've blown all my wages. My wages that I earn while you lie at home all day on your stupid fat arse, feeling sorry for yourself!'

'Will you just shut up for a minute and listen for once in your life?' I shouted back.

She folded her arms tightly and cocked her head to one side, 'Go on then, but this is going to cost you a bottle of wine from the offie on the way home.'

'No problem at all,' I replied.

'And a family-sized bar of chocolate.'

'Anything you want, my darling.' Her mood was softening.

'I'll probably need a foot rub as well.'

'I can do that. The rubber gloves and gasmask will be on standby, just give me the nod.'

She smiled and reached for a kiss. It was lovely.

'Come on then, my sadly misguided gullible husband, tell me the worst.'

'For the last four days whilst you have been at work and

for a bit after you've gone to bed I've been using my system on the casino site. I deposited two hundred quid...'

'Two hundred? Two fucking hundred? You fucking stupid fucking bastard!' She slapped my face. It hurt. She turned her back on me and walked towards her car.

'Will you bloody listen? My balance when I left home half an hour ago was one thousand seven hundred and forty-five pounds!' I shouted.

She stopped and turned round.

'Darling,' I said reaching out to hold her. 'That is a profit of over fifteen hundred quid. Fifteen hundred quid! Multiply that over a six-day week and it's three grand. Over a month and you're talking twelve K. For a year of sitting around all day and placing bets I will be on close to a hundred and fifty thousand quid a year. Jesus, that's more than enough to make all our dreams come true!'

I held her in my arms. She was silent. 'Go on then, say something.'

'We'd better get going or Ellie will be late for her swimming lesson.' She disentangled herself from my embrace and made for her old banger.

'Babe, this time in six months you will be driving a Merc!'

'We'll see.' She got in and after a couple of coughs her car sprang into life. She drove off, but not before checking out the house one more time.

It was early Saturday morning and all was well with the world. Ellie was downstairs watching kids' TV. Melissa was enjoying a well-deserved lie-in after the week's exertions, whilst I was in the half-decorated nursery amongst the paint pots, rollers and dustsheets. I was sitting on a stool in front of my laptop gamely employed at the roulette table while listening to country music on my iPod. I can't explain why it always seems to play country whilst I'm gambling, it just seems to fit somehow. I didn't hear her approach but enjoyed the feel of Mel's arms around me. Her squeeze was warm, welcome and reassuring. I was topless, still wearing only the boxers I'd been to bed in, and I could feel the firmness of her breasts pressed into my back. She nuzzled the nape of my neck and licked my ear.

'Hmm, beautiful,' I said, turning around to kiss her.

'Glad you liked it,' she said, still slightly sleepily. 'You're up early for a Saturday, darling.'

I smiled and tapped the screen of my laptop. 'There's not much point lying around when I could be up earning. Do you like this?' I asked pointing to my current balance.

'Bloody hell!' she exclaimed. 'You have been busy! Two thousand five hundred! Is that pounds or dollars?'

'It's pounds my love. Each one of my poundingtons has a nice little picture of the Queen herself on it, God bless her. Now get that sexy little ass of yours into the kitchen and cook me up some breakfast, and none of that healthy crap neither!' I slapped her hard on the rump. 'We high fliers need plenty of fuel to keep us rolling. I need eggs and I need sausage. I will also be requiring three rashers of your streakiest bacon and a generous helping of the blackest of back pudding.'

'OK master, it's your arteries you're blocking.'

At that moment the little ball on the screen landed on black and added a further five pounds to my account. 'I'm not doubting you, oh holy one, but don't you think it would be a good idea to bank some of that money just in case something does go wrong?' she asked.

'OK honey, I tell you what, when I reach the big three grand I'll bank it and start again.'

She kissed me again and set about cooking a breakfast fit for a tycoon. Twenty minutes later she returned bearing a tray fit for a king. 'Right my lover, we have egg, we have bacon and we have sausage plus black pud, beans and a slice of bread and butter. We also have a nice cup of tea and a small glass of orange juice. Does that suit, my lord?'

I didn't reply but simply stared sightlessly into my computer screen.

'What's wrong babe?'

I grunted and pointed towards the part of the page that showed my current balance.

'Zero?' she asked, disbelieving.

'Zero,' I replied in a voice lower than a mouse's whisper that had a sore throat and was worried he was being overheard by a secret agent mouse with listening gear.

'What happened?'

I sighed so heavily I almost imploded. 'Fourteen reds in a row, that's what happened,' I said in a voice devoid of any life or emotion.

'And you were on black?'

I didn't even dignify that question with an answer.

'So, you're telling me that in the time it took to knock up this breakfast you have gone and lost two and a half thousand pounds?'

I nodded the smallest nod imaginable to man.

'I suppose that I won't be handing in my notice this week then?' she asked.

I shook my head, 'I wouldn't, no.'

She gently placed the breakfast tray on the floor and left oh so quietly, shutting the door behind her.

Mel was no more than half a dozen steps down the stairs when she heard the sound of a fully loaded breakfast plate smash against a bedroom wall with the almost inhuman force of a man whose dreams of mansions, a glorious future and a way out of a life way too small had been shattered.

CHAPTER FIFTEEN

A day in the life

I gazed out of the kitchen window, past our meagre front garden, the frost-damaged knee-high garden wall and out into the street beyond. I had been standing there in my reverie for the best part of twenty minutes with only a young mum wrapped up in jeans, moon boots and a heavy dark coat passing up the road. She pushed a pushchair up the steep climb, finding it an ordeal against the freezing wind. A small child was with her, wearing a large woollen hat pulled down low on his head. With one mitten on and one mitten off he obediently followed his mother a couple of steps behind. I leant forward to keep them in view for as long as I could. The wind blew, the trees shook, and life went drearily on.

I had dropped off Ellie at school, returned, washed up last night's supper things and this morning's breakfast plates and mugs. The small hand of the neon Simpsons clock on the kitchen wall (which Melissa hated and dismissed as tacky) was pointing directly at ten. I wouldn't have to leave for the school until just before three. That left me with five whole hours to fill. A huge five-hour void of nothingness, crap on TV, snacks, cups of tea and mooching about. I really didn't know how much longer I could keep on doing this. Surely everyone needs a purpose, a reason to keep going and get out of bed in the morning? OK, I suppose I could do a spot of housework. There is dusting to be done and it surely wouldn't kill me to drag the Hoover around. But what's the point? It will only get dirty again and Melissa will do it at the weekend anyway, no matter what kind of a job I make of it. It's weird in a way. The more bored and restless I become the greater my lethargy and tiredness increases. If I carry on at this rate, by Christmas I will be bedridden and unable to support my own weight without a crack team of care assistants feeding me through a tube and lifting me on and off my own personal commode. I would give the grass a last mow of the year but it looks like it rained last night...

After flicking through the channels at least twice to find something to watch I finally plumped for a thirty-year-old episode of Starsky and Hutch, and would you credit it? It was the one and only episode I can ever recall watching all those years ago when I was a young bright-eyed boy with my whole life ahead of me. I turned the television off and read the flyer that had been poked through the letterbox, which informed me this was a great time to replace my existing windows with state-of-the-art new ones, and returned to the kitchen, where I once again stood at the sink and admired the view of the world outside. It was now almost ten thirty. With a sigh of defeat I opened the fridge and took a large bite from the huge block of mature cheddar that was in the door. Then I spied the large collection of bottled lager that Melissa had purchased during the weekly shop for the forthcoming weekend. Surely she wouldn't notice if I sneakily helped myself to one little beer, would she? 'No, of course not Charlie,' I said to myself.

As I poured one into my favourite glass, my spirits began to lift. Once the froth had subsided I realised that after a decent-sized glug I could probably fit in another bottle, thus giving me a full regulation pint. I opened the fridge and retrieved another bottle. Just one mind, and that will be definitely it…

My daughter poking me in the tummy brought me back to consciousness. My eyes parted slowly. My mouth was dry, my head throbbing and I still felt really pissed. I quickly sat up on the settee, my feet accidentally making contact with the three empty bottles that were standing on the floor. Well, I say empty. One was still half full and it sprayed its foaming contents across the floor and the expensive and highly-prized rug which Mel had hauled all the way from a pre-me trip to Morocco. I quickly wiped it with my sock. Oh fuck! I was in the shit now. My plan before oblivion hit was to end my one-man party early, go to the corner shop and replace the many beers I had consumed before eating something, sobering up and brushing my teeth.

Melissa knelt down and spoke to Ellie. 'Darling, I want you to go to your room and grab your three favourite tops,

trousers, knickers and socks. Get your Barbie, Nintendo and teddy, lay them on your bed and I will be up in a minute.'
'Why Mummy?'

'Just do it sweetie, quick as you can. We are going to stay for a sleepover at Grandma's.'

Ellie nodded and disappeared upstairs.

I stood up; the room swam slightly as I tried to defend myself. 'I am so sorry babe. I nodded off during the test match and the next thing I know you are here with Ellie and I'm knee deep in shit.'

She took a deep breath, opened the patio doors and threw the rug onto the patio outside. 'I love you Charlie, I really, really do but we can't go on like this.' Was that a tear escaping from those pretty eyes? 'I'm having a baby soon; I haven't got the strength or time to look after another one. You are a forty-two-year-old who is acting more like a two-year-old. It's lucky that my boss is so understanding and that I was able to leave at the drop of a hat and go and pick up our daughter when the school called.'

'I'm sorry babe. This was a one off. I was having a bad day and feeling really down. I was having a party for one and it kind of got out of hand. It won't happen again I promise you. There's no need to go to your mum's.'

'It's not fair that everything has to fall on my shoulders. I'm pregnant, hormonal, the only breadwinner and on top of that my husband has given up, thrown in the towel and become a trainee alcoholic. I just don't need or deserve this right now.' She called upstairs to Ellie to get her toothbrush and pyjamas.

'It's not my fault I lost my job!' I shouted. 'It's not easy out there you know. Just in case you haven't picked up a newspaper or switched on the news lately you might be interested to know that there is the little matter of the worst recession in living memory going on at the moment. Everyone from the brainiest brain surgeon down to the bloke who cleans the soggy fag butts from the public bogs in town has been given the elbow. If you check out the faked government statistics you would realise that it's only you and a welder in Aberdeen who are still engaged in full employment. Everyone is fucked off, screwed and considering taking up busking as a step up on the career ladder.'

'That is bullshit Charlie, and you know it. Since you were made redundant your job seeking has consisted of half-heartedly glancing at the local Friday free paper every other week. That and the CV that I nagged you to do and eventually ended up finishing for you, plus one visit to the job centre where you decided the jobs were crap and the people were all wankers!'

I ran my fingers through my hair and tried to get my wits about me. 'Babe, you are living in the past. Everything is online and digital these days. I have my fingers in dozens of web-based pies. My name and CV are out there, any day now my emails will be bulging, inviting me for interviews for attractive opportunities.'

Mel got up and immediately went into sarcasm mode. 'Oh, they will, will they? Gosh, that's jolly good then. And there was me being stupid and worrying that this little one' - she rubbed her swollen belly – 'would be born homeless and living on the charity of strangers. What an idiot I have been. All this time I have been resigning myself to losing our home and having to live with my parents in their poky little box room and all this time you are on the verge of being headhunted by some big boys and major players who will make us financially solvent and put us on the fast track to easy street.'

She approached my laptop, which was illegally downloading a rare Bob Dylan bootleg album and the latest Bond film. 'Right, let's have a little look shall we? What captains of industry and commerce have you been in contact with today?'

I felt nauseous and slightly panic stricken as she checked my web browser history. She pressed a few keys and then remarked, 'I say, this is odd Charlie. According to today's internet log the only sites you have visited are, and I quote, 'Bra Busting Babes', 'Big Titted Milfs' and 'Tanya Young's 50inch DD's'. Oh and some movie you seem to have downloaded called, 'Tiny Asian babe gets - WHAT? With a baseball bat?' Mmm, I can't see any obvious career opportunities there but, hey, what do I know about staff recruitment?'

I started mumbling an apology but was cut short by my daughter entering the room with her little case in hand. 'Mummy, can I take my colouring books and pens to Grandma's?'

'Of course you can babe. Wait in the kitchen for me and I'll get your packed lunch stuff for tomorrow.'

'Come on Mel.' I pleaded, 'I've said I'm sorry, you know it won't happen again.'

'You're bloody right it won't,' she said. 'Sort yourself out. I will phone you in a week.'

They both kissed me, Mel on the cheek followed by my daughter on the lips. The door slammed and the car sprang into life and roared off up the road. Soon there was silence.

I turned on the television and stared sightlessly at the screen. I felt incredibly sorry for myself, as the house seemed to grow huge and silent around me. I sent my love by text, cleared up the mess from my afternoon's folly, and then opened the fridge to start again.

CHAPTER SIXTEEN

Women

I stood, or rather slumped, against the bar and stared at the long row of different-coloured bottles, all hanging upside down with their optics fitted and waiting to be pressed. I have often imagined coming in with a wad of dosh and seeing how far along the line I could get through before passing out, becoming someone's new best friend or getting in a fight. Not today though. I was on the beer, my third to be precise. What better way to while away a wet Thursday afternoon in November before darkness descends at four and I can start on the evening session.

My pint was at my chapped lips when an almighty slap on the back brought glass to tooth with a painful jolt. I checked for blood and turned to give the perpetrator a piece of my mind. It was my old friend Fulton.

'Hey there Charlie boy, how are you? In fine fettle I hope?' he boomed.

'I was peachy before you spilt my beer and nearly chipped my front teeth,' I replied.

'Get that man a beer, I'll have a large malt with a large malt chaser and whatever my friend here enjoys,' he said to the bored, heavy-looking woman in her fifties behind the bar. Her make-up was as half-hearted as her bar work. She reluctantly dragged herself away from her word-search book.

'What scotch do you want?' she asked my huge Scottish friend. 'The one with the fat dumpy bird on,' he said, pointing towards the nearly empty bottle of Famous Grouse. 'So, how are you, Mavis my little pudding?'

'My legs are playing up again.'

'Bloody awful thing legs, what are they good for?'

'Standing up, moving around, filling out your trousers, giving your arse something to look at...'

'How many has Plato here had?' he asked the far-from-lovely Mavis.

'Three or four,' she replied, as if I wasn't there.

Fulton downed his first in one gulp, picked up number two, indicated a free table (of which there were many) and bade me follow. Mavis handed me my pint and I joined him. He immediately pulled out a pen, picked up a beer mat and jotted something down before handing it to me. 'Fine Art, 2.30, Plumpton, tomorrow,' I read.

'It's like printing money. Lump on and ye'll eat like a king for the rest of the month,' he said. He stared at me.

'Now Charlie, by using my powerfully-honed powers of deduction, I can tell by your demeanour, alcohol intake and body language that all is not flowers and roses at Bennett Towers just now.'

'Mel left yesterday, taking my daughter, two bottles of white and the smoothie maker.'

'Huh, smoothies, I ask ye. Do ye think this great nation explored, conquered and ruled three quarters of the globe by drinking smoothies? Everyone's gone soft in my opinion. Do you think Robbie Burns, Robert the Bruce, Winston Churchill and others of that ilk drank smoothies?' I shrugged. 'No way pal, it was ten pints of heavy, a few double chasers and then off into battle, swords sharpened, guns blazin' and fearing nothing more than possible decapitation or a screaming hangover the following morn.'

'Precious as it was, it's not the loss of the smoothie maker that has reduced me to this sorry state, Fulton.'

He stroked his mighty beard and said, 'Well thank Christ for that Charlie boy. Smoothies, I ask you! Huh, along with breadmakers, melon-ballers and ice cream machines, they can rot in hell as far as I'm concerned. Do you know what my sister got me for Christmas a couple of years back?'

I shrugged. 'A sporran cosy? A Sainsbury's Taste the Difference organic haggis?'

'A popcorn maker! What the flying fuck would I want with a popcorn maker?'

'Are you a habitual popcorn eater?' I enquired.

'No.'

'Are you or have you ever been a casual user of popcorn?'

'Never!' he growled.

'So I guess you have never been, for example, sitting in

the back row of a darkened cinema with a beautiful woman sharing an overpriced bucket of popcorn whilst sitting through an arse-achingly boring chick flick with the sole purpose of getting into her drawers later in the evening?'

'Not my style, Charlie boy. I don't need tricks or props. My looks and charm have always given me a massive advantage when it comes to the ladies.' He raised a cheek off his seat and farted loudly before wiping his beard with the back of his hand.

'So I gather it is currently gathering dust at the back of the kitchen cupboard, unused and unwanted, without ever popping a single kernel of corn?' I asked.

'Not a bit of it, ma friend. By mid-morning on Boxing Day it was on eBay attracting many bids indeed. With the fourteen pounds plus the fiver I charged in postage it helped make Hogmanay an almost unforgettable night. Well actually, that is a lie of sorts, as by the time I awoke on the late afternoon on New Year's Day everything had been forgotten. The events of the night before, the drinks I had consumed, the bars I had frequented, the ladies I had kissed and where I had left my mobile phone and wallet.'

'Oh well, at least you didn't waste it,' I replied. I gazed out of the window, though there was nothing to look at but our own reflections and those of the handful of others with nothing else to do on this depressingly miserable afternoon. My companion hollered for a pint of ale, which duly arrived.

'So tell me Charlie, why has the lovely Melissa departed the family home to leave you to cope on your lonesome?'

'There is no one particular issue, Fulton. It's a combination of many tiny details that on their own are mere bagatelles, small differences of opinion that aren't enough to disrupt the harmony and give and take of the home but when added together can cause friction, animosity and tension.'

He belched loudly, drew heavily from his glass and wiped the back of his huge weather-beaten hand across his mouth. 'You should never under estimate the little things in life, young Bennett. These are the building blocks that all existence is based on. A slight niggle here, a sharp word there and before you know it the seeds of a microclimate of deep hatred and long-term loathing are sown. My Aunt Martha at my Uncle Alex's funeral confided in me that she'd hated him for as long as she could remember and do you know why? What could make a placid and shrivelled-up old lady vent her spleen at the wake of her departed husband of forty years?'

I shook my head. 'No idea. Had he been unfaithful years ago and although they carried on as they tended to do in those days she could never get over the hurt and betrayal?'

'No Charlie, what made old Auntie despise her poor dead spouse was the fact that he constantly sucked on his back teeth while watching the television! Forty odd years of trying to concentrate on *The Sweeney, Minder, Bergerac* and *Poirot* with a guy who keeps slurping on his dentures can really grate on you over time. That and the fact that he used to keep putting his marmalade jar back into the fridge even though it was empty. He also kept holding his breath while he was sleeping before suddenly exhaling loudly.'

I was puzzled. 'So you are saying that more often than not it's not the big things like infidelities, lack of love or the hateful words that wound and damage a long-term relationship, but the small things that often pass by without scarcely being noticed?'

'Absolutely! Couples tend to pull together and rally round during trauma and cases of infidelity. Even discovering your partner is a secret cross-dresser with a weakness for mini-skirts and gold sequinned slingbacks can strengthen a marriage when the problem is addressed head on and talked through. Whereas living with someone who constantly leaves a single teaspoon in the bottom of the washing up bowl or leaves their toenail clippings lying on the arm of the sofa can drive even the most understanding nature over the edge.'

I took a thoughtful draught of my beer. Maybe he had something there. The fact that Mel always has the remote for the telly on the arm of her chair and not mine is a constant irritation to me.

'So what is it that gets your old lady's hackles rising, Charlie boy?'

I stood up and prepared to get another round in. I pulled out a crumpled fiver and a handful of shrapnel. 'Well, if I was to be brutally frank and honest, not with just you but with myself also, I would say that the minutiae of the friction between us that has led to this temporary split lies in the fact that I am a crap father, a lazy work-shy sod and a compulsive wanker who thinks of himself and himself solely.'

My burly, foul mouthed drinking pal sucked the dregs from his glass and handed it to me. 'Yep, that's probably it,' he said.

By six the bar was filling up with drinkers sneaking in a quick one on their way home, and our table was full of dead and empty glasses. I was totally pissed, having trouble focusing and visiting my friend the urinals at ten-minute intervals, yet my partner in crime carried on as if each drink was his first. Maybe he was as drunk as me; you never can tell when you are one over the eight. You tend to be clinging on to sobriety while trying to kid on that you are as sober as when you blew the froth of your first.

'Have you ever been married Fulton?' I asked.

'I have indeed. In fact, much to my regret I still am.'

'Blimey, I had no idea. So where is she?'

'My wife of over thirty years is currently ensconced in a high-rise flat on the edge of Glasgow with a limp-wristed accountant who my children call Dad and I call Desmond. Well, either that or limp-wristed prick.'

'Do I take it that this is still an open wound after all these years?' I enquired.

'You must be joking! I would rather live with the Loch Ness monster or Noel fucking Edmonds!'

'Come on now Fulton. It's pretty obvious that only someone deeply wounded and still holding a grudge and a broken heart would come out with an answer like that. What happened? Did you catch her in bed with your best drinking buddy, or even worse, a lifelong Rangers fan?'

'There was nothing in particular that ended our fifteen years of dull and unfulfilling wedlock. There was no painful betrayal. There was no coming home unexpectedly and catching her in the arms of the guy next door or shagging a supply teacher from West Bromwich. We didn't argue or quarrel over soft furnishings, watching *Sportsnight* or the extent of my drinking.'

'Was her family continually sticking their noses in?'

'Her relatives kept a safe distance and there were no money worries to speak of.'

'So what caused you to split from...?'

'Angela. There were no surprises left, Charlie. Our life had fallen into such a trough of monotony that life had become as about as interesting as a three-hour lecture by a local weatherman on the subject of cloud formation and rainfall statistics over southern Belgium. Day after day, month after month and year after dreadful year was mapped out in front of me. Monday, back to work, Sundays leftovers for tea and an evening in front of the box. Tuesday, egg and chips and if I was lucky some mushy peas. Wednesday I was usually able to sneak off to a match or the club to watch it on the big screen. Thursday was her bingo night, which in turn made it my favourite of the week. I'd grab a six-pack and a take-away curry on the way home and watch a mucky film. Friday would be our night out. God, how I hated them! We would sit in almost total silence in purgatory, drinking our drinks and looking at other smiling couples enjoying themselves while we sat tight-lipped and going through the motions. My weekends were usually spent at the footy or in my shed reading the *Sporting Life,* drinking cans of Special Brew and waiting for the clock to tick round so we could start the cycle over again once more.'

'Sounds amazing. So what made you two red-hot lovers finally decide to throw in the towel and go your separate ways?'

'St Mirren.'

'St Mirren?'

'St Mirren.'

'What about St Mirren?'

'St Mirren verses Hibs in the Scottish Cup third round replay.'

I was perplexed. 'Fulton, for the life of me I can't see why a minor football match between two shitty Jock soccer teams would bring about the end of a marriage well into its second decade?'

'Celtic were having a poor season, Rangers were in and out of form and the green and whites were looking like genuine contenders, so I had one eye on the TV and I was pressing a radio against my ear to monitor our progress. I looked over at my Mrs and I saw her ugly square podgy feet, a resting place for aggressive fungal infections, hard skin and bunions, squeezed into her stinking pink slippers. I saw her blotchy fat white legs and her sagging tits which were on their way to merging in with her belly. Above that I looked at her double chin, which was then housing a red, ripe and angry zit. She was sucking on the end of a biro and studying a word search. A word search, I bloody ask you! There is a whole universe filled with majesty, wonder and things to be discovered out there. There is philosophy, art and mechanics. There are books to be read, sights to be seen and emotions to be felt. There is science, architecture and nature. There's moving verse and majestic cathedrals built to the glory of God. There are leafy glades filled with bracken, plays by Shakespeare and jazz on the wireless. And what was that dozy cow doing with her free time and ghastly feet? Doing a bloody word search! Can there be anything more pointless and banal?'

'That's a strong statement coming from someone who was listening to St Mirren versus Hearts,' I argued.

'Hibs,' he corrected me. 'Anyway, after looking her up

and down I turned off the radio, got to my feet and exclaimed, 'Angela, you are without a doubt the most unappealingly dull and ugly woman I have ever clapped my eyes on. You are totally without grace, style or beauty. You are nothing more than a distasteful lump of nothingness. Your cooking is bland and forgettable, you never have anything to say of any interest and in the sack you are about as sexy and exciting as a vegetable Cuppa Soup that's been lying at the back of the cupboard for the whole of living memory.'

'Tell me, have you worked for the diplomatic corps long?' I asked.

He ignored me. 'Do you know what she said?'

'Hmm, now let me see. Did she say, 'You smooth-talking charmer! Wait till the adverts come on and I will rush upstairs and switch on the electric blanket'?

'Nope, she sucked on her biro and said, 'just because your team are losing there is no need to take it out on me. Talking about the kitchen cupboard though, the milk is on the turn and there is a packet of strawberry Angel Delight somewhere. If you fancy some, I can quickly whip it up in the ad break?'

'Mmm, I love a bowl of Angel delight. It's a bit of a guilty pleasure isn't it? A bit like Arctic roll or wanking to fat birds on the Internet.'

'Well Charlie, that was the final straw. If all she could come up with to save our marriage was a bowl of gone-off strawberry Angel Delight I knew that things had reached the point of no return. So without a word I packed a bag, slammed the door behind me and drove south of the border.'

'What, Mexico?'

'No, Carlisle.'

'Oh well, at least you avoided bandits and a dicky tummy.' I was wondering if a packet of pickled onion Monster Munch would spoil my appetite before the bacon butty tea I had planned. 'So since then you have been celibate, a bachelor boy and a taker of three cold showers a day?'

'I've had my moments with members of the opposite sex, don't you worry. The trick is not to get involved. If you think with your prick and not your heart you will find life a lot simpler.'

I got to my feet to order another round. Mavis saw and began pouring. 'But what about love, companionship, and the deep bond between a man and a woman?' I asked Fulton.

'That is in technical terms bollocks, Charlie. The fundamental problem with the human race is that from the time each new person squeezes itself from the confines of the womb, he or she is wrongly programmed into doing what is deemed the norm and what is expected. It is drummed into you that you have to be sensible and good and get a job and get married and have children and all the other stuff. By forty if you haven't got a couple of kids, a nice pension to look forward to, your own house, a garage and a weird compulsion to wash your car every Sunday morning you are thought of as slightly disappointing and not quite fitting in.' He got to his feet, 'Right, I need a piss,' he announced and left me to my beer.

While he was gone I pondered his words. My head was swimming from the alcohol, my misery and the words from my Celtic friend. He returned with a double for himself and a half for me. I was already lagging behind and feeling a bit sleepy.

'I've been married before you know,' I said.

'Oh yes, and what caused the end of that romance? Apathy, adultery or Angel Delight?'

'No, just stupidity on my part I'm afraid. Without realising what I had, I threw it all away. Still I guess everything happens for a reason, or so they say.'

Fulton laughed out loud. 'That's just crap that people without balls or choice pretend to believe in and to reassure themselves that things are going to turn out all right. Life isn't about happy endings, Charlie. Your days won't conclude in some nicely-scripted happy finale full of smiles. It isn't like some crappy film where shit happens but it all works out in the end. There will be good bits if you are lucky, along with a lot of boredom and a whole lot of crap to wade through before one day you drop dead and it will all be over. But don't worry, because while you are getting used to your urn or hole in the ground your family and friends will be dressed in their best suits and singing hymns, chewing the fat and making plans to meet up more regularly because life is shorter than you think. All the while eating crappy dried-up overpriced buffet food at the local boozer.'

'So what's the point then? If this road we were put on, all without asking I may add, is nothing more than a hard uphill slog filled with pain, heartache and what appears from my angle at least to be more lows than highs, why bother?'

Fulton leaned back and ran his thick sausage-like fingers through his greying bushy beard.

'Now you're asking old son. What is it all about? Why are

we here? What is it all for? The meaning of life; that particular conundrum has puzzled the wisest philosophers and sages since the dawn of time.'

'So I guess two pissheads like us wasting away a dull and gloomy afternoon are unlikely to stumble on the true meaning of life then?'

'Maybe, maybe not Charlie boy, but if you can just accept that there isn't a big plan, that there is no pre-ordained purpose or destiny set out for us, just a series of random events, then things begin to make sense. Yes, good things will happen to bad people and vice versa. Yes, it will rain on your holidays, yes Rangers will more often than not beat Hibernian, and yes you will get your heart broken from time to time. Don't get me wrong, there will be glories and wonderful moments scattered here and there along the way, the trouble is we tend to forget these or take them for granted. That is our nature I'm afraid.'

I listened to his words and attempted to take a little comfort in them. 'So in a way what you are saying is, there is no point cursing one's luck, fate and the world as we are all going to die anyway.'

'Now you're getting it Charlie boy. It takes a strong man to shrug off life's disappointments and laugh when you've just skidded through a pile of dog shit. You can either curse God, your bad luck, your eyesight in failing to see the steaming pile in the first place and let it put you in a bad mood, or you can shrug it off, spread what's stuck on your nice pair of white Nike trainers on the kerb and move on.'

'You mentioned God, are you a believer? I believe most of you Jocks are?'

'No, though it was a constant and long-lasting

disappointment to my folks that I was not and never would be. They tried their best. I was hauled off to church every Sunday in my best togs, hair slicked down and knees scrubbed, while they praised the Lord and listened to all the awful things that would happen to them if they didn't. I was sent to Mrs McCredie's Sunday school to learn about fire and brimstone, angels, devils and the evilness of temptation. My best friend Tommy Johnston spent his Sunday mornings having fun, playing football and knocking on doors and running away. How I wished I could swap places.'

I emptied my glass and checked the contents of my pocket for a mislaid fiver, but no dice. 'So despite their efforts they never converted you then?'

'No chance Charlie boy. In my opinion religion is for the weak, the dying, the delusional and those who have yet to subscribe to my way of thinking. Just think about all the Sunday mornings wasted in a Christian's life, praying, singing hymns and wearing out the knees of their trousers on the offchance of some fairy tale actually being true about a big guy with a flowing and fulsome white beard inviting your spirit, whatever that is, back to his pad for an eternal holiday. It's so outrageous it's laughable.'

Noticing the absence of Her Majesty's head from any of the bits of paper I pulled from various pockets, Fulton told me not to worry and he'd get us one more round plus chasers before taking a casual stroll to the Chinese on the corner, where we would procure a set meal for two plus prawn crackers to go to eat back at his place where he had a newly-opened ten-year-old malt and a mucky film recently downloaded on his hard drive.

When we got up to leave, I stumbled and the room swam.

'See you soon Mavis,' said my burly Scottish friend as I swayed behind him. The night was cold and misty as we made our way down the high street. All around us life was going on as normal. People were heading home from work, tired, sweaty and thinking what to do for tea. Others were going to bars for a rewarding drink after their toil. People were muttering under their breath that their boss was a tosser or that the new girl in human resources had the peachiest arse. Me? I was trying hard not to let on to my hard-drinking buddy that I was three sheets to the wind and having a ball despite feeling incredibly sorry for myself, and that I was able to laugh off the fact that I was currently home alone and jobless. I tried to kid on that I wasn't missing my little girl and in very real danger of depositing the contents of my stomach over Fulton's size thirteen tatty brown boots.

Fulton's flat was in a large Edwardian house that had been carved into flats years ago. The hall carpet was bare, stained and uninviting, and the forty-watt bulb that hung without a shade from the ceiling only emphasised the depressing dinginess and despair. Welcome to bedsit land. Is this where I am heading – cast adrift from Melissa and Ellie in an ocean of despair, living off microwaved dinners for one with socks drying over the back of a chair facing an electric heater that has only one bar on, as that's all I can afford?

Just inside the unlocked communal front door Fulton searched through the collection of mail that sat on a small semi-circular table and picked out his. There were stacks of junk flyers from local takeaways, double-glazing manufactures and other local companies that interested no one and were left unread and unwanted. I followed up the wide staircase, our meal wafting oriental splendour as we went. I couldn't wait to get stuck into those sweet and sour king prawn balls.

'Wipe your feet,' said Fulton as he rummaged around for his keys. After twice shuffling through the pockets of his heavy knee-length coat and a quick check of his trousers, he located them. Welcome to your future, I said to myself. A grotty flat with mould growing rampantly, shared ablutions, dirty linoleum and windows so filthy you don't even need curtains. A home so small you can make a fried egg sandwich, bang the TV to get a better picture, mend a puncture on your bike and fill in a claim form while hardly leaving your cold, stained bed.

Only it wasn't like that. No sir. I was as wrong as Clive Sinclair was when he thought people would jump at the chance to squeeze into a shoebox with wheels and drive to work. I had expected Fulton's flat to be as unkempt as his beard, but it was actually the kind of large, bright bachelor pad that you would expect some whiz kid stockbroker to call home. There wasn't a trace of a drying sock or rising damp. The room was light, bright and airy. The neutrally-finished walls were adorned with original paintings he'd picked up over the years. On one wall was a giant bookcase housing books on every subject imaginable. There was Oscar Wilde and Doctor Johnson. There was Chaucer and Hardy. There were encyclopaedias, guides to antiques and books about nineteenth century farming methods. There were the collective works of Shelley, Conan Doyle and Jamie Oliver. There were film guides, books about Scottish football and great heavy tomes on the subjects of poetry, art and various not-so-famous battles.

He adjusted the lighting, turned on the largest, flattest television I had ever seen outside Curry's and signalled to me to put our food on the dining table. He disappeared into what I presumed was the kitchen and reappeared with plates, cutlery, and wine glasses.

'Charlie, grab that bottle of red that has been breathing on top of the fireplace will you. I imagine that will go down a storm with the ginger spiced beef.'

I stood, or rather swayed, opened mouthed. 'How?'

'How what, Charlie son?'

'This place is a palace. I'd kill to live somewhere like this. Some of those books are probably worth more than I used to earn a month. You probably paid more for that stereo than we did for our car. Your television is the size of a pool table and that leather settee could accommodate most of Western Europe.' I took the slug of wine as he handed it to me. It was the nicest I had ever tasted. The on-offer plonk I got from the supermarket tasted like hooker spit in comparison.

'This is gorgeous!' I enthused.

'It should be. My contact in the wine trade said that this particular year was the nicest available for forty quid a bottle. I got a nice little reduction as I bought three cases, used cash, and passed on my inside knowledge of a dead cert bet on a first-time-out horse at Linfield Park.'

'So how can you afford all this? You haven't done a day's work in living memory, yet you live like a king. I get made redundant after twenty-odd years' hard toil and within a matter of months my world has fallen apart, the house is in danger of repossession and all I can afford to eat is toast and whatever I can scavenge from the roadside and the back of the freezer. Do you know what I had to for dinner last night? I had two chicken and mushroom crispy pancakes, a tin of peas and a vanilla choc ice.'

'Ah, I remember crispy pancakes. I often used to eat them in the seventies.'

'Judging by their flavour, the cardboard texture and the way they made me want to barf, the ones I had were baked in the seventies. I was just glad they stayed down.'

'Do you remember Arctic Roll?'

'I think so. Didn't they have a big hit with *Do the Hucklebuck*?' I said, digging into my meal.

'Idiot, that was Coast to Coast, but I believe the original was by the Birdies a decade earlier, lyrics by Roy Alfred and music by Andy Gibson,' he replied while spooning another portion of egg fried rice.

'How the fuck do you know that?'

'I read it in a book.'

'So what's your secret?' I persisted.

He paused, and thought for a moment. 'Take advice from the wise, ignore the ignorant, don't worry what others think and if it feels right do it. Other than that, do what makes you happy, measure twice and cut once and never back the nag with the sheepskin nose band.'

With a belly full of noodles, some undetermined meat and yet more alcohol inside me I joined my host in front of the cinema-sized television. As he flicked through the hundred odd channels, two thirds of which were gambling, shopping or showing an advert, I further took in my surroundings.

'Do you miss your missus at all?' I asked.

'No way pal! She was about as attractive and as feminine as Joe Bugner. She had hands the size of coal shovels and farted every ten minutes. Now, call me a chauvinist and an unenlightened male but I think a woman should be demure, pretty and fairly silent bum wise. I can turn a deaf ear to the odd accidental pop off when she thought she was alone and out of earshot whilst doing the washing up, but cracking off giant foul-smelling guffs while I am endeavouring to watch Top Gear is an entirely different matter.'

'I don't think I have ever been downwind or within earshot of one of Melissa's anal eruptions,' I mused.

'Huh, I bet she wishes she could make the same proud boast of you. Have you finished with that?' he said, pointing to my plate. I nodded and watched him slide my leftovers on top of his own before tucking in. 'So when are you expecting her back?' he asked.

I shrugged. 'When I've grown up, secured a job and can prove I am a good role model and competent father.'

'No time soon then,' he replied, chewing hard on a rubbery piece of beef. He extracted it with a forefinger and thumb and threw it in an empty silver foil tray. 'She'll be back sooner rather than later pal. It's not as if she's caught you playing away or defrauding her for her savings, is it? As long as she knows you are looking for work and cutting back on the booze everything will be back to normal before you know it. Shall I open another bottle of this or shall we move on to the malt?'

'Scotch I think,' I said feeling slightly brighter.

'That's the spirit, and until she comes back you should treat this time positively and take advantage of the situation. You can safely do all the things that irritate her and get her hackles up. You can drink beer in the bath, you can pick your ears, nose and feet whenever the need takes you and wipe it wherever you want. You can let fly with gargantuan rasping farts whilst eating your dinner. You can safely snore without getting a jab in the ribs. You can go days without shaving, and enjoy porn openly and without shame. I tell you Charlie, opportunities for this level of freedom come along very rarely to the married gent. Enjoy it while you can.'

CHAPTER SEVENTEEN

Friends reunited

For the third time that evening the phone rang. It was the same unknown number, and for the third time I ignored it. What idiot would try to get in touch with me when United are playing live on the telly? Do they really think I would get up out of my seat and risk missing a Rooney wonder-strike for the sake of telling some prat in a call centre, 'No, I am not interested in your five windows for the price of three offer. And no I haven't considered upgrading to a premium package that would give me twenty-four hour support and a shiny new set top box. In fact I am so 100% sure that I am not interested, you can take your set top box and stick it somewhere the signal doesn't get through!'

The strutting Italian ref blew the half-time whistle and the two teams trudged back to the dressing rooms, one for a pat on the back and a Jaffa Cake and the other for a flying tea tray and a few choice words. Unfortunately for me it was my lot who were facing the hairdryer treatment. I was in the kitchen preparing a half-time sandwich and a lager when the phone rang once more. If the only way I am going to get some peace is by answering the bloody thing, then I suppose I will have to endure some pre-scripted sales patter before telling the prick to fuck off. I picked up the receiver and got in the first word. A tactic that is always vital in discussions of this nature. 'Look pal, I realise you have a job to do and are probably stuck in some Godforsaken windowless dreary call centre cell and all for the minimum wage but take it from me, I am not looking to buy a time share in the Algarve. I don't want to switch credit cards and as for wasting five minutes of my life to help with a customer survey, you have about as much chance as a man with no hands having a successful career as a pickpocket. So why don't you do yourself and me a massive favour by deleting me from your list and never call this poxy number again. All right sunshine?'

'Bloody hell treacle, you're a bit tetchy aren't you? Blimey they are only one down with the second half still to play.'

'Mark?'

'How are you doing, you grumpy old git?' he asked.

'I'm not too bad. Sorry about the verbals. You know what I'm like when the reds are playing.'

'I should do after all these years. So how is it going? What has it been now, three, four months since we were slung out and discarded like yesterday's rubbish?'

'I suppose it must be,' I replied.

'So what are you doing work wise? Have you stayed in the optical trade or have you branched out into another sphere entirely? What are you doing for pennies now? I somehow always saw you as either a male escort or an underwater welder.'

'There's nothing permanent at the moment. I have many, many irons in the fire obviously; it's just a case of pulling out the right one. I don't want to be too hasty and plump for the wrong option and regret my future career choice. This is a crucial time; I don't want to fuck it up.'

'I applaud your caution and mature attitude Charlie. What type of thing are you leaning towards?'

'Er, I was seriously thinking about moving into financial management. You know the type of thing; advising clients on long and short-range investments, where to put their money and so forth, advising on share issues, pensions and property portfolios.'

'Blimey, that's a bit of a turn up. When I was speaking to Melissa yesterday she indicated that you were living in Shit Street, had no prospect of any work on the horizon and that you spent much of your time getting pissed with some weird Scottish character.'

'She said that? Ha, what a little josher she is.' I laughed. 'No, things are on the up Marky-boy, no question about it.'

'I see. Well, I should have a word with her if I were you old mate. For some reason the story she spun me was that you were out every day getting pissed.'

'Naaa.'

'Yes. And that you've done your redundancy money and that she's been forced to leave the family home in despair hoping that this might finally pull you out of your self-indulgent 'the whole world is against me' bullshit attitude and do something about it instead of wallowing in self-pity all of the time.'

'OK,' I conceded. 'There may be an element of truth in some of that. So, you've spoken to Mel? Where?'

'She was passing my shop and I spotted her and called her in for a chat.'

'You have a shop?' I spluttered, disbelievingly.

'Uh huh, and I tell you, she has the right raging knock with you pal. How long has she got to go before she drops, a month, two at the most? How much of your redundancy money have you got left to spend on baby's booties, bottles and bibs etc?'

'A couple of hundred at the most I'm afraid old mate.'

'What! You got over five grand. Where has it all gone? I've hardly touched mine,' he asked disbelievingly.

'Yeah. Unfortunately a few of my investments weren't as profitable as I'd hoped.'

'Enlighten me.'

'Well, unfortunately while Mel was at work I got hooked on on-line poker and roulette. I lost nearly all of it on a run of such chronic bad luck that it would make you weep.'

'Christ, no wonder she's fuming.'

'She doesn't know yet. For all she's aware I'm only a couple of hundred down.'

'Fuck me it gets worse! Well, I was ringing you up to offer you a job but I suppose working in my shop is never going to be as attractive as being a top financial advisor brokering multi-million deals, taking clients out for three-hour booze-fuelled business lunches and bringing Wall Street to its knees.'

'Let's not be hasty. Let it never be said that Charlie Bennett wouldn't do a favour for an old friend. So what is it that you are managing? Is it a sex shop? Are you in need of a promising new dildo salesman with an in-depth background knowledge of lubrication and dirty mags?'

'You wish! No, when we got made redundant I was fortunate enough to get a technician's job at Express Specs at Bluewater.'

'Yes, I think I know it,' I replied, keeping one eye on the TV. The players were back on the pitch and ready to go for another forty-five minutes.

'Well, last week the store manager was given the sack for nicking frames and selling them on ebay. Guess who they have appointed as their new, young and dynamic replacement?'

'You're kidding me? You are such a jammy bastard. Why don't things like that ever happen to me? You get handed an empire and all I get given is a ladle and a sodding pile of mash.'

'What are you talking about? Here I am ringing you up out of the blue and offering employment, self-respect and the security you and your family need at this crucial time.'

'I'm not a charity case you know,' I said as United ballooned another chance over the bar.

'Never said you were pal. But after working next to you for a dozen or so years I do know you're a stubborn prick who often lets his pride and over-inflated sense of self-importance get in the way of a glorious opportunity.'

'Go on.'

'Now that I'm the manager I'll be far too busy to spend time glazing. I'll be initializing promotions, having meetings with senior management, helping out with the dispensing and keeping a close eye on the day-to-day running of the place. Therefore I will need someone I can trust to turn out the highest quality standard of product possible so that my customers will be so delighted they will come back time and time again for more of the same and tell all their friends how wonderful we are. That man is you Charlie! What do you say?'

'Oh, FUCK OFF!'

'What?'

'Not you Mark. It's that fucking dick of a ref. What a prick, that was a stone wall penalty.'

'Forget the football for a moment Charlie will you?' he pleaded.

I thought for a moment. 'What's my salary?'

'Twenty grand a year.'

'Twenty? Is that all? That's a five grand drop.'

'Plus benefits.'

'Such as?'

'Long lunches and knocking off early when we are quiet and extra cash when we meet the targets set by head office.'

'I must admit I am slightly tempted Mark. Saying that though, I do have an interview next week at Tesco as a warehouse assistant.'

'Wow, the big time!' he said sarcastically. 'How on earth can I possibly compete with that? Come on Charlie, it really is a no-brainer and don't forget, you get your wife back into the bargain. Oh, and there are reduced food vouchers for the food court.'

'Hmm, on reflection I happily accept your generous offer. That, combined with the fact that we have just equalized, has put a smile on my face and hope where there was previously none. Do I have to come in for a proper formal interview?'

'Na, no need mate. Just turn up at the store Monday at nine prompt, it's between Mothercare and one selling overpriced gadgets for blokes with too much money and too much time on the top floor. Oh, and this is not the factory Charlie. I don't want you wearing that baggy pair of stained tracksuit bottoms you wore almost daily for the last five years and one of your United shirts. We are all called upon to be the public face of Express Specs. We need shiny shoes, smart trousers, a shirt and tie, OK? That is until you receive your uniform anyway. All clear mate?'

'Yep, no worries. You won't regret it pal, I won't let you down. I will be there Monday morning, bright, breezy and raring to go. Ta-da mate,' I said and hung up.

I sat back and enjoyed the second half. I can just see it now. This time next year I'll be the one with his own shop. In five years I'll have my own chain of outlets, a dynasty of my own making. I could almost picture my mansion in the country with its detached double garage, leafy drive and umpteen bathrooms on suite. When United wrapped up the game with two late goals it simply confirmed that my life was back on track. After all, what could possibly go wrong?

CHAPTER EIGHTEEN

Happy families

It's amazing what a single phone call can do for morale. No more was I the wretched loser whose perspective future was loneliness, misery and a life of regret. One conversation with my old friend Mark and suddenly everything was rosy in the Bennett garden once again. Melissa was once more by my side looking more blooming and even more radiant than ever and my little angel with the golden ringlets and the most beautiful smile was back home ready to bring light and laughter to my previous gloomy soul. So what better time to invite Colin and his intended round for a Saturday evening of fine wine, lovingly prepared food, nibbles and reconciliatory family bridge-building?

We had planned a simple meal straight out of our collection of cookbooks, often flicked through but rarely used. We were having a cheese and horseradish fondue for starters, salmon soufflé and sauté potatoes for mains and a buy-one-get-one-free frozen dessert from the Co-op to finish on. After that we'd enjoy an Irish coffee with the floaty cream and the After Eights I'd bought last Christmas but had never opened.

While I was trying to squeeze into my new trousers (purchased to wear on my first day at my new job on Monday), Melissa was standing in front of the mirror and applying her face and giving me the speech. 'Now you know why we are doing this, don't you?' she said, squeezing her eyelashes with a frightening-looking device that made me wince.

'Yes my love, we are extending the hand of friendship and family togetherness and burying petty squabbles and my small-minded jealousy,' I said tiredly. 'You have drummed it into me all day my love. No matter that some old slapper is turning my stepdad against me. No matter that the family fortune and my birthright will soon be in her evil bony grasp ready to be squandered on further facelifts, wigs and tummy tucks. It is practically irrelevant that my poor old Mum is probably spinning in her grave. None of that matters babe, as long as Colin and the Wicked Witch of the West are happy. We will suck up to them, invite them to eat our food, drink our beer and put fag burns in our sofa. We are in for a memorable evening.'

'Charlie!' she barked. 'This is exactly the attitude that led us here in the first place. Carry on like that and things are going to go from bad to worse. Just let it go will you?

They love each other, they want to be together and you are just going to have to accept it and get used to it. OK?'

'Sorry!' I kissed the nape of her neck. She smelt wonderful. I wanted her there and then. 'I shall be on my best behaviour, not a disparaging word or innuendo will pass my lips.'

My hand wandered from her shoulder to the top of her breast. She slapped it as Ellie called from downstairs. 'Be a good boy tonight and I'll let you have the keys to the sweetshop. Now run downstairs and see to your daughter.'

Almost to the agreed second there was a ringing at the front door and our guests had arrived. Colin had gone through some kind of Grace-induced makeover and was carrying a small bunch of flowers for Mel in one hand and a bottle of plonk in the other which he thrust into my hand before grabbing me, pulling me close and giving me a cuddle. To say I was surprised at this outpouring of affection would be an understatement. Colin was such a reserved character on the physical front that even a playful slap on the back seems an over-the-top show of warmth.

I disentangled myself from him, complimented him on his choice of aftershave and turned to Grace. As anticipated she was plastered in make-up, her enormous cleavage was more out than in and her little black leather mini skirt would have fitted inside a matchbox. 'Hi Grace, wow, look at you, you look... fantastic! Come on in and grab yourself a drink. Mel will be down in a mo, she's just applying some scent and a pair of clean drawers.'

'I don't bother,' said Grace. 'Let the air get to it, that's what I say!' She breezed past me in search of a drink.

'And that's a lovely tan, Grace. Have you been away?' I asked, admiring her almost orange glow.

'No chance Charlie. I tried to persuade Colly to take me away for a late summer break to the Algarve but he dug his heels in and said what with the wedding and honeymoon to pay for he couldn't afford it. This I got at the salon in town, love.'

'Very nice,' I lied, noticing the streaks, runs and overspray. It reminded me of the time I tried to fill and paint the wing of an old Morris Marina I briefly owned before it gave up the will to live and departed to the great scrap heap in the sky. Mind you, to be fair, that old rustbucket's bodywork had more original features than my prospective mother-in-law.

Ellie was showing her grandfather some of her schoolwork while I fixed the drinks and Grace chatted to Mel in the kitchen. This is your family life; some cheap supermarket booze, Jamie's salmon thingy and a frozen Pavlova for dessert, before the passing of the port and some heated topical debate on football, politics and the chances of the guy from breakfast TV in Strictly Come Dancing.

We were called to the table to enjoy our starters and a selection of dips. I was sitting next to Mel with Grace opposite and Colin by her side. Ellie, who had already eaten, was enjoying a packet of Hula Hoops in front of Hannah Montana on the box, a DVD she had only watched three hundred and seventy-five times before.

It was only when we were seated that I could really take in the 'new Colin'. Gone were the baggy jeans with turn-ups and several different coloured stains down the leg. No more was the faded and ancient Harley Davidson T-shirt my mum had bought him back in the nineties with the hole in the left sleeve. What's more, he was even cardiganless, a sight that was as rare as a happy Monday morning or a nice-tasting Pot Noodle. On opening Colin's wardrobe previously, you would be confronted with many examples of this much underrated and versatile garment. There were chunky ones and some lighter and thinner ones for summer. They came in black, beige, blue, claret and every other hue you could care to think of. There were those for blobbing around the house and a khaki one he favoured for the allotment. There were heavy ones in thick knit with leather buttons that kept the old sod warm when out doing some emergency repairs on the car in winter and a smart, thin, white one he wore when crown green bowling. But now here he was, hair slicked back (blimey don't tell me he's wearing gel), a new pair of smart leather brogues and a Ralph Lauren polo shirt in a fetching shade of lilac. The tattered pair of specs that I'd been encouraging him to let me change for years with Sellotape holding on the right side had been replaced by a designer pair that would have cost at least a couple of hundred quid. To cap it all, the most out-of-character item was a chunky gold identity bracelet that hung heavily off his wrist. I almost felt like asking him to undertake a speedy DNA test during the break between starter and main courses to verify that it was indeed actually him and not some doppelganger intent on getting a free feed.

'Not got your Christmas decs up yet? We put ours up on the first,' commented Grace. 'We've got a seven-foot Norwegian spruce in the sitting room, a backlit nativity display from Harrods in the dining room and on the front lawn a moving, waving, ho-ho-ho-ing Santa in an illuminated sleigh being pulled by a herd of reindeer. It's motion activated, so whenever someone passes the front gate the reindeer make galloping sounds, Father Christmas wishes you the compliments of the season and *Hark the Herald Angels Sing* plays for thirty seconds from the back of the sleigh. You should have seen the postman the other day. He almost shat himself when it started up!' She laughed.

I exchanged a furtive look with Mel. 'You can't get much more Christmassy than that,' I said.

'That's what I thought. Colin wasn't too keen but I managed to convince him. Well, we couldn't really leave it. Not when it was half price at only two hundred.'

Something lodged at the back of my throat. Mel slapped me on the back and I took a large draught of lager. Blimey, at this rate I'll be lucky to buy a round of drinks and a pickled egg with my inheritance.

'How are you doing my love?' Colin asked Mel. 'Blimey, look at you, you look ready to drop now.'

'I hope not, I've got another six weeks yet. Ellie arrived almost to the minute of the expected date, so this one hopefully will be just as obliging. At least I've finished work so I can take it easy now.'

'Are you still on for my hen night?' asked Grace.

'I think so. I won't be drinking but I'm sure I will still have a good night.'

'You bet you will, I've got loads planned. So how are you doing on the swollen ankle and stretch mark front? My two boys gave me a belly like a road map of Birmingham, the little bastards, bless their hearts.'

I put down my fork, deciding I'd had enough.

'I got some cream from Avon and it seems to be doing the trick. It's a bit pricey though,' replied Mel.

'Hey, if it stops your guts looking like someone's family tree it is worth every penny love. Have you got piles?'

Colin and I exchanged looks. We both felt uncomfortable. Women's troubles are not a source of good table banter. Even Melissa was taken slightly aback.

'No, I've avoided any trouble of that nature thus far,' she said, smiling awkwardly.

'Lucky you, my Anthony gave me a bunch of grapes that would have done a vineyard proud. I was pushing them back up for months afterwards!'

'Anyone fancy a top up?' I asked, making for the safety of the kitchen. I poured out another can, necked it half way down and opened another. Jesus, I thought, they'll be discussing sore breasts and fanny stitches next. I returned with a bowl of tossed green salad and tongs.

'Colin and Grace are spending their honeymoon in Antigua,' said Mel.

'Cool, did you manage to get tickets for the test match? I asked Colin.

'What?' said Grace, oblivious to the fact that her hubby-to-be would be spending five days of their newly-wedded bliss with the England cricket team and many drunken 'barmy army' fans. Colin shot an annoyed glance in my direction. 'We are there for three weeks my angel, a couple of lazy afternoons in the sun with a gin and tonic, a cucumber sandwich and a magazine while I watch the cricket won't kill you,' he said, knowing that she might very well kill him.

Ellie came in rubbing her eyes. She sat on my lap, snug

and cute in her Bratz pyjamas. After two big yawns I managed to persuade her that it was time for bed. 'Goodnight Grandad,' she said and reached up for a kiss. She looked at Grace. 'Goodnight.'

'Good night love,' answered Grace as she bent down and kissed her on the cheek. Mel wiped away the fire-engine-red mark she'd planted on her and led her up the stairs. There go my girls...

Grace rummaged around in her leopard skin printed handbag and pulled out a packet of cigarettes and a lighter. 'I'm just popping out for a fag Colly.'

'All right gorgeous,' he replied, scratching his crutch under the table. He topped up everyone's wine from the box and once more put an arm around me. 'Can I just say how glad I am that you invited us round. I know how family feuds can simmer and ferment when words are spoken out of turn and pride gets in the way. I know you have your doubts about Grace and she is a little different in character from your dear old mum, but believe me, she has a heart of gold and she has only my best interests at heart.'

'I just don't want to see you being taken for a ride, that's all. I know I take the pee out of you constantly, but you are all the close family I have and I know Mum would want me to look after you.'

'I know son. It's difficult, this thing called life,' he philosophised. 'When your dad passed away and I came on the scene it couldn't have been easy for you. No one likes change but it happens when you least like it or expect it. If I had my way I'd be here with your mother, but that is just the way life is.' He hugged me again and I swear there were tears behind his trendy new specs. 'Let's get that other bottle of red open, shall we? It's a very exclusive little number that is well worth savouring,' he boasted.

'Sure.' Just then the kitchen door opened and in hopped Grace, an electric blue stiletto held at arm's length. 'Charlie love, have you got any kitchen roll? I've bleeding well trod in some cat shit.'

The meal was a resounding success, and leaving the plates on the table we adjourned to the lounge. Colin flicked through the channels and Grace got stuck into the After Eights while Mel made coffee. I got the scotch from the cupboard and put a slug in each glass.

'Are you having a good time?' asked Mel.

'Yes, awesome.'

'There's no need to be sarcastic.'

'I wasn't being,' I replied. 'No, I'm OK. I'm glad they came. Your meal was lovely, any free booze is always welcome and I am glad we are all friends again.'

She kissed me, her belly almost keeping us apart.

'I don't suppose that if you're not too tired when our guests have departed you might entertain the idea of some very gentle fun and games of the mummy and daddy variety?' I enquired.

'With the amount of booze you are putting away? As soon as you get horizontal you'll be snoring your head off.'

'No chance babe, tonight is a night for love, simply because you are near me,' I sang.

'We'll see. If you promise to help me with the clearing up in the morning I might be swayed. I want it in writing though,' she said doubtfully.

'Great, if you do that special thing I like I'll even promise you an orange juice and a Sunday roast at the Cricketers.'

'Don't push it, lover boy. I feel as about as sexy and pliable as a fridge freezer.' She skilfully poured the cream onto the back of a heated teaspoon. It swirled into hypnotic patterns and floated perfectly.

'As long as you are slightly warmer than the aforementioned fridge it's a deal.' I said.

The more Grace drank, the more frequent became her sojourns out onto the front step for a smoke. I was anticipating a knee-high pile of dog ends to clear up in the morning. I poked my head out through the half-open door and asked if she wanted a coffee or a Baileys. She inhaled deeply and blew a long stream of smoke into the cold clear December night. It was freezing cold but she seemed hardened to the sub-zero temperature, as a true smoker should be. The only indication that she might have been a tad chilly were the bullet-like nipples that appeared to be trying to burst through her thin, tight white blouse and the scarcely-concealed black bra underneath.

'No, I'm all right Charlie,' she replied, flicking her cigarette ash onto my honeysuckle. 'I've still got half a glass of plonk here. Thanks for letting us stay over. Colin's not the greatest of drivers at the best of times and after a few beers and a glass of red it tends to be a bit of a white knuckle ride home. How he's never been pulled over and banned is a mystery.'

'Maybe he's got a guardian angel watching over him and the people in the opposite lane he tends to drift into. I remember one time when I was a kid, we'd been to see a relative, I can't remember which, but even as a child I could see that the once-full bottle of tea-coloured booze that he and some distant uncle were enjoying was now empty and that out of character Colin was shouting at the top of his voice, planning moving to Austria and telling everyone he loved them. Not just a little bit but really, really, really. I spent the journey home being thrown about in the back hiding under a coat with my eyes tightly shut praying to God that I would get home safely to see again my Six Million Dollar Man toy and my Scalextric set with the glowing lights and smoking tyres. When we did finally make it home he threw up on the garden path before becoming unconscious half way up the stairs, still wearing his nineteen-seventies corduroy coat with the sheepskin lapels that was much favoured by football managers at the time.'

'You're kidding! So the old git does have some devil in him,' said Grace, as she sparked up another fag.

'You better believe it. My mum left him there and went to bed in a huff. The following morning when I came down in my jim-jams he was still there. I shook him awake. His furry lapels were matted with dried vomit and he suffered with chronic back pain for days afterwards. He was in the doghouse for weeks.'

She laughed hysterically. 'Silly old sod!' She pulled hard on her cigarette and blew the smoke into the night. 'I do hope we can put that silly little misunderstanding behind us. It was stupid, rash and all in the heat of the moment. I have these crazy episodes from time to time love. The best thing to do is to just ignore me. That's why my life has been such a roller-coaster ride, Charlie. There has been too much booze, too many rows, too many husbands and far too little putting my brain in gear before doing what eventually almost always turns out to be the wrong thing at the wrong place and the wrong time. That's why I feel your father is so good for me. He's grounded, never flies off the handle and only has my best interests at heart. He's so different from all the other losers I've been involved with. OK, he's needed a little licking into shape but he is coming along fine.'

'You make him sound like some kind of project. Yes, I have noticed the odd subtle difference in his demeanour and appearance,' I said.

She smiled. 'Come on, even you must admit that he needed a bit of tidying up and dragging into the twenty-first century. If he had his way he'd be forever clad in baggy jogging bottoms, shapeless jeans, three for ten quid supermarket T-shirts and those bloody wellingtons.'

'I suppose he was a bit retro,' I conceded.

'Retro? He was fucking Antiques Roadshow!' She giggled.

'Well I must admit he is certainly cutting a bit of a dash this evening Grace. If it wasn't for the blackcurrant jelly he spilled down his shirt front he could pass for minor royalty or an ex-boy band member. I'm amazed at the level of influence you have over him. It took all my mother's powers of persuading, and promises of crates of ale to get him to change his socks daily, let alone to discard his favourite gardening cardy and start dressing like a twenty-something advertising executive.'

'All women have to do something to get you blokes to look like presentable members of the human race and not some kind of scruffy missing link who has only just learnt to walk upright without scuffing your knuckles in the dirt. I bet even Melissa had to make the odd adjustment to get you into line.'

'I can't deny that there is the occasional criticism and subtle change forced on me, such as refraining from cleaning my ear holes out with the tea towel and throwing away my trainers when the fumes emanating from the shoe cupboard become a bio-hazard. But hey ho, you wouldn't be women if you couldn't find fault with almost everything.' I shivered. I was nowhere as hardened as the formidable Grace. 'Shall we return to the warm?' I asked, starting to feel the need to pee. She put her fag out on the brickwork before flicking it towards the road. It landed somewhere on the front lawn. 'Yeah, go on then. I think I'll have a little drop of something to get me asleep before Colin starts snoring his head off. Oh, and can I just say that I am so pleased you are going to be our best man.'

'I couldn't let the old boy down. I know it means a lot to him.'

She ran her hands through her long, bleached locks and rearranged her mighty weapons of mass destruction in her skin-tight top. 'Absolutely, and it's not just that. Your replacement was going to be that pal of his, Ernie from the bowls club. The last thing people want to hear when they're enjoying a forty pound a head lobster buffet is some wheezy old fart's hearing aid buzzing and picking up the police radio. And you will look so much better in the photos.'

CHAPTER NINETEEN

Welcome to the working week

Monday

Surprisingly, for a man whose previous four months had been spent at leisure with heaps of noon lie-ins and nothing to do but mooch, watch TV and obtain record scores in numerous computer games, the sound of my seven o'clock alarm going off was as annoying and unwanted as it had ever been. Melissa turned slowly towards me, her belly the size of a bouncy castle. Without opening her eyes she requested that I haul my lazy arse out of my pit and make her a nice cup of tea.

'This isn't fair,' I said. 'You get to lie in and wake up in your own time while I'm having to race around making breakfasts, do the school run and then work my fingers to the bone to keep you in the style you'd like to get used to.'

'Charlie, you have had a four-month vacation where you did nothing more strenuous than picking your nose. I think it's about time the bump and I were pampered and allowed to take it easy.' She grabbed my hand and pressed it firmly against her stomach. I felt little kicks and smiled. I kissed her tenderly on her forehead. Today was going to be a good day and a new beginning. I could feel it in every breath and every heartbeat.

'As this is the first morning of your maternity leave, would you like to celebrate the occasion with a bacon sandwich?' I said.

'Are you sure it won't make you late? You don't want to be tardy on your first day.' She yawned.

'No probs, it only takes a couple of minutes, I haven't got to be there till nine' I said, stumbling to the bathroom.

I opened Ellie's door. She was still snoozing, her long golden curls falling over her face. She was clutching her favourite teddy with her thumb in her mouth. I gazed down with a big smile on my face and wondered what she was dreaming about. Was she a princess in a big flowing dress living in a castle in the sky? Was she at the shopping mall with her friends, choosing make-up and giggling? Was she on a picnic with the Bratz girls and Hannah Montana?

I shook her gently, wishing I could leave her to sleep. She opened her eyes slowly and smiled. My heart swelled, broke and instantly mended itself again.

'Is it a school day today Daddy?' she asked.

'I'm afraid so,' I said, bending down to kiss her softly on the cheek.

'That's OK, I like school.' She slid out of bed, rubbed the sleep from her eyes and went to find her mother. I watched from the doorway and saw Ellie climb in beside her mother for a good morning snuggle.

'Do you want tomato sauce on your butty?' I asked Mel, brushing my teeth.

'Yes please.' She turned to Ellie. 'Daddy is getting the frying pan out, do you fancy a bacon sandwich or do you want something else?'

'Bacon, please Daddy.' I skipped down the stairs. Yep, today is going to be a good day.

One naughty breakfast later found me washed, shaved, showered, and picking through my wardrobe for the correct attire for my first day at my new job. It was only now that I was aware that my recent lifestyle of no activity, cheap lager and low-nutrition salty snacks had taken its toll on my waistline. Four pairs of trousers had already been discarded and were lying on the bed while I searched the wardrobe's depths for something smart that wouldn't feel like it was cutting me in half or in danger of splitting at an inopportune moment. The last thing you want when discussing frame shapes with a customer is to have the crutch of your slacks split open as you bend down to pick a pair of Ray-Bans from the bottom of the rack.

'I've got a freshly ironed pair of maternity trousers on my side of the rail if you're desperate,' said Mel, laughing and licking a stray daub of sauce from the corner of her mouth.

'Ha ha, don't get used to breakfast in bed. This is a once-in-a-lifetime offer only. Why didn't you tell me I was filling out slightly? I've been living in tracksuits with baggy bottoms and elasticated waists. I had no idea I was expanding at the same rate as you. Its lucky I've landed this job. Before much longer I would have grown into a blob of gargantuan proportions.'

'I'd still love you,' she said.

'Ah, would you?'

'No.'

'Cheers for that my love. I suppose I will have to plump for the black jeans. They've always been a bit on the baggy side with plenty of room around the crutch. The knees are a bit faded but I doubt if anyone will notice.'

Once I was fully dressed, I stood in front of the large wardrobe mirror and checked myself out. I resembled a large and untidy unmade bed. My trousers were tired, my shirt collar undone, as it wasn't able to circumnavigate my neck, and my tie was badly knotted, with the fat bit far too short and the thin bit hanging around my waist. They would take one look at me and shut me away in the back room, stuffing envelopes far from the sight and sound of the great British public. Oh well, I guess during my lunch break I could take a look around Burtons.

With great difficulty and at the third time of asking I managed to coax Ellie from the CBBC channel, got her to brush the bacon from her teeth and put her school uniform on. We stood in front of Mel, who was still comfortably reclining under the covers and now on her third cuppa.

'We're off now.'

'Don't you guys look smart!' (An exaggeration there surely.) She turned to Ellie. 'Has Daddy packed your lunch and got your book bag?'

'Yes Mummy I checked. See you later.'

'How are you – nervous?' asked Mel.

'No, not really, I'll be OK.' I bent down and kissed her. She grabbed hold of my tie and pulled me back for another before whispering, 'Don't screw up, Bennett.'

After dropping Ellie off at the front gates of her school and waving to her all the way to her lining-up spot, I made my way to my new place of employment. Unfortunately I had slightly misjudged the heaviness of the traffic, and by the time I'd parked up and figured out what floor the shop was on I was twenty minutes late, sweating and footsore. All around, stores were opening and early morning punters were itching to spend their hard-earned pennies on new shiny products and clothing they could probably do without. The shutters of Express-Specs were only half up with a scruffily, hastily written sign in black marker proclaiming that the store would today be opening at ten due to staff training.

I ducked under the blue-painted shutter and nervously approached my new colleagues, who were sitting around a small table at the far side of the shop. Mark, who was facing me, caught sight of my anxious approach and beckoned me over.

'Oh here he is, same as ever, twenty minutes late. Some things never change. Pull up a stool, Charlie. Everybody, I would like to introduce you to our new tech. He's the best there is, has a vast optical knowledge and will no doubt be able to help you out when faced with any of the more testing technical questions from head office or our customers. He is also occasionally extremely grumpy, lazy and a constant pain in the arse. Is that a fair description, Charlie?' He grinned. I felt my cheeks redden. I dragged a stool under myself and sat down and smiled. 'Yes, that sounds more than generous.'

He introduced the others in turn. To my left was a woman in her mid-forties. Her hair was pulled back into a clip with blonde highlights running through the darker strands. She smiled warmly and welcomed me aboard. This was Lorraine; she'd been in the optical trade for as almost as long as I had and was the senior dispenser.

Next to her was Mandy, usually called Moose, an extremely attractive twenty-something, and I found it hard to keep my eyes off her. She wore a thin white cotton blouse and a short black skirt which with her legs crossed, barely reached halfway down her thigh. Steady on Charlie, it's rude to stare!

To my right was Casey, who I guessed was slightly younger than Moose. She was, if you were being PC about things, not a natural beauty; chins, boobs, tummy and arse, she had an overabundance of everything, and as I would soon find out, that went for confidence and personality as well. Back in the seventies she would have been dubbed short, fat and ugly. She was struggling to reach five feet tall and probably had a similar size waist. Her chin, which blended seamlessly into her neck, sported a fresh necklace of love bites and her piggy eyes were almost hidden by rosy, chubby cheeks. She did have one redeeming feature – or should I say two - for bursting out of her staff-issue blouse were two of the largest breasts in the Northern Hemisphere. They were simply enormous! The size of a couple of over-filled shopping bags, they started somewhere under her armpits and reached down to her belly button. No doubt to give her poor aching back a break, she was resting them on the table in front of her.

'This one's nice Mark, a big improvement I must say,' she said, raising her eyebrows and looking me up and down.

'Sorry Casey, he's married and about to be a father for the second time,' replied Mark.

She winked in my direction, 'Oh I love a father figure, me.'

The girls giggled. I blushed.

'Right, carrying on,' said Mark.

The team meeting continued. I was struck at Mark's transformation from the scruffy slacker I had known previously to the go-getter store supremo. He definitely looked the part in his expensive tailored suit, perfectly groomed hair and shiny shoes. His tall athletic build and handsome good looks would probably have most female shoppers willing to part with huge sums of money with very little persuasion at all.

'I know I keep banging on about targets but we really have to push selling tints, anti-reflection coatings, hard coats and second pairs,' he continued. 'We were fifth in the branch tables last month and I want to see us push through into the top three next time. Don't forget there are plenty of incentives. Third for the year wins us a mini Waitrose hamper for each member of staff, the second a paintballing day and the first prize is a luxury weekend break at a spa of the companies choosing.'

'And no doubt an extra large cash bonus for you,' said Lorraine with a hint of cynicism.

'I'll share it around, don't you worry. We are a team. Let's not forget why we have come as far as we have in the few short months since I have been here. We were in the bottom half in June, now we are on the up and up. All of us pulling in the same direction is what has got us this far. One last good month and I am sure we can nick it. I know it's an awful cliché, but there really is no 'I' in team.' Mark was in full management mode now. I hardly recognized him.

'There's a 'U' in cunt though,' whispered Casey under her breath. I sniggered. She laughed. Mark frowned. I couldn't help picturing Casey done up in combats, charging around woodland with a gun in her hand, trying to find adequate cover behind a small sapling. She'd make a pretty easy target.

'We'd stand a better chance if we had a decent optician,' said Moose.

I thought it was time I made a contribution and showed some level of interest. 'What's wrong with him?' I asked, staring into her delicious green eyes.

She smiled and stroked a stray strand of dark brown hair from her eyes. 'Well, where does one begin?' she answered, turning to the rest of the group and shaking her head.

Mark put me in the picture. 'All Expresso Specs opticians are self-employed and are allocated by head office. Since we lost our last regular optician we have been allocated a well-respected, if a wee bit eccentric and unorthodox, OO called Brian Cox. I've tried having a word with the powers that be about getting someone else in but to no avail I'm afraid. He's on a contract, he has friends in high places and no other branch wants to take him off our hands. So I'm afraid for now and the foreseeable future we are stuck with him.'

'So what's the problem, doesn't he know what he's doing then?' I asked.

'No it's not that exactly,' said Lorraine. 'He knows his stuff all right and he never has to re-test anyone. He's been qualified for forty years and has even had numerous books published on the subject.'

'The problem is,' continued Casey, 'he's a hundred and five, completely bonkers, has three layers of dandruff on the shoulders of his jacket...'

Moose interrupted, 'He is forever coming in with his breakfast boiled egg clinging to his tie and white flobs of spit in each corner of his mouth that occasionally fire out when he gets animated and hit you in the face.'

'As you can imagine, the average punter finds one or all of these characteristics rather unappealing,' said Mark, clicking his pen.

'Added to this he can't seem to get it inside his soft head that we have a strict and busy schedule to stick to,' said Lorraine. 'Particularly on Saturdays when we are fully booked and rushed off our feet. Every twenty minutes he has a new person to test. People turn up on time and expect us to usher them through to the testing room at the allotted hour. They won't hang around for an hour because he's been sketching diagrams of the inner eye in multi-coloured felt tips or telling them about the time he was stuck at a train station in Kuala Lumpur for thirty-six hours in the monsoon season, wearing only a short-sleeved shirt, Fred Perry tennis shorts and a pair of second-hand deck shoes. No, they bugger off to Vision Express or Specsavers and leave us down on takings and behind on our targets.'

Mark nodded in agreement. 'I am aware of his shortcomings and I'll have another word with him when he gets in. Beyond that my hands are tied I'm afraid.'

'Good luck. I bet by lunchtime he'll be running forty minutes late because he's got talking to a patient about the Triumph Spitfire he owned in the seventies,' said Moose.

Casey adopted a gruff voice and began to take off the little-loved Brian. 'It was a thing of beauty. It had only a couple of thousand on the clock when I got it, I didn't spend another penny on her until I had to replace a wiper blade shortly before the jubilee in seventy-seven. British racing green she was, with the deepest shine imaginable to her. You almost felt like running up a flag and saluting before you put in the key and fired her up!'

'Not that you had to lock things away back then,' said Moose, continuing the impression. 'We knew our neighbours, cared for them as they did for you. You could leave your front door open in them days, blah, blah blah!'

We all laughed, though I must admit I felt the old boy sounded quite interesting and looked forward to meeting him. People like that are fine as long as you aren't in a hurry or have a bus to catch.

'One more thing,' said Mark, looking at his notes. 'A fortnight ago we were paid another visit from the mystery shopper and once again the report was less than favourable and I received a bollocking over the phone yesterday afternoon from the area manager.' He read the report in front of him. 'We scored a paltry three out of ten for customer service, four out of ten for store tidiness, three out of ten for technical knowledge and a miserable two out of ten for all round customer experience satisfaction.'

'What the hell is a mystery shopper?' I asked, perplexed. 'Is it some grey-rinsed old dear with a mask and a carrier bag ready to hit poor shop assistants with her magic brolly?' The three girls laughed. My first-day nerves were easing already.

'Nothing as exciting as that,' said Mark. 'The company hires, at great expense I am led to believe, the services of a marketing team who send someone anonymously to experience the Expresso-Specs customer service. They then give their marks on various categories and write a short report on the level of service and customer care we offered. This shopper's note read, 'I wandered around the shop for a full twenty minutes before I was approached and asked if I needed any help. When I asked for an eye test the young girl told me that I could be seen right away and that should stop the old git nipping down the pub until three and come back stinking of stale beer and cigars.' However I fear she was too late, as during my admittedly extremely thorough eye test the stench of alcohol and tobacco made the experience most unpleasant. Handed my prescription, I wandered around the deserted store for a quarter of an hour before finally another assistant appeared from a back room. Whilst trying on a frame I asked her opinion and was told that one of the frames on the next rack was more suitable for my 'chubby face'. Slightly taken aback, I asked her to get it for me. She replied she couldn't as she'd just painted her nails and they were not quite dry.'

Mark put the sheet of paper down and gave the team a challenging look. For once in my life I was scot free and in the clear. I felt rather smug.

Mandy suddenly succumbed to a moment of clarity. 'Oh

God, I remember! She was that fat old bird who kept hanging around a couple of Fridays ago. She was trying on a small eye size that made her look like a short-sighted overfed walrus.'

Mark tried the nice but firm approach. 'Moose, I know it's hard to keep a straight face but we have to be professional at all times. And please try to keep your beauty regime to your off-duty hours.'

'At least it's better than last time,' said Casey.

'Really, what happened then?' I asked.

'This bloke came in and complained that the side tips on his sunglasses were rough and making his ears sore. Moose snatched them out of his hands and said, 'You think you've got problems. I've just bloody split from my boyfriend, I'm overdrawn at the bank by a grand and I've just got my sodding period!'

I raised my eyebrows. 'That must have been nil points all round.'

The rest of the day passed smoothly. I spent most of it tidying up the lab, organising things the way I wanted them and getting to know the girls better. Mark instructed me on general procedure, the ordering of stock and how to deal with enquires from customers over the phone. These mainly consisted of booking eye tests, cancelling eye tests and checking whether specs were ready for collection. With Christmas only a couple of weeks away, trade was predictably light. Shoppers were much more concerned with getting last-minute gifts and stocking fillers than purchasing glasses.

I arrived back home at half six pleased with how the day

had gone and confident that a long-term future with Expresso-Specs lay ahead of me. Mel was waiting with a celebratory four-pack of lager and a hearty steak and kidney pudding. As the ring pull hissed I raised my glass and cuddled my wife.

'Baby, we are back on track.'

Tuesday

The shop was dead, with only a handful of people booked in for eye tests. Mark had given Moose an hour off to catch up on her Christmas shopping. Lorraine had gone to the bank, while I was holding the fort with Casey, who was restocking the frame racks. My lab faced the front window of the shop and I stared at the shoppers passing by the front of what seemed like my goldfish bowl. Occasionally people would stop for a moment and watch me work. Not for long though, as watching me work doesn't make the most riveting viewing. Especially since, as this was Mark's day off and I had nothing better to do, I was free to study and ring my viewing selections in the Christmas edition of the *Radio Times*.

Presently Brian meandered into the lab, hands in his pockets and at a loose end. His next scheduled eye test was not until three-thirty. It had only just turned one. He looked out at the passing throng of busy shoppers. He tutted and shook his head.

'Dear oh dear' he said.

I put a ring around 'Eric and Ernie; The Christmas Classics' in my TV mag and tried to ignore him.

'Every year it's the same,' he added, shaking his head.

'*Chitty Chitty Bang Bang* is on again Christmas Eve. I wonder if Ellie is old enough to appreciate the Cockney magnificence of Dick Van Dyke? Mm, I'll ring it just in case' I said, circling my selection.

'When will they ever learn?' he added.

'Mind you, that child catcher is a bit creepy though isn't he? I don't want her to have nightmares the night Santa is due. That will properly louse up Christmas. The last thing we want is her bawling and having nightmares about some paedo with a massive snoz when I'm attempting to sneak in her room and fill her stocking with presents whilst half pissed.' I scribbled though my selection.

'What's wrong with people?' he blew his nose on a crumpled hankie.

I rose to the bait. 'All right Brian?'

'I'm doing very nicely thank you. Not like that lot out there.'

I thought it wiser to remain speechless, having been advised by the girls not to engage in conversation under any circumstances with Brian if at all possible.

'Look at them Charlie, there they all are, rushing and running, twisting and turning like a load of rats trying to escape a flooding sewer. I can remember when Christmas meant something.'

'Oh yeah, and what was that?' I asked without interest.

He coughed into his hand, which he then proceeded to wipe down the leg of his trousers. He blustered, 'I can't recall what it was but it was certainly better than this, "buy three gifts for the price of two" imported Chinese tinsel and Aunt Bessie's instant irradiated honey-coated parsnips

Christmas we are all supposed to aspire to these days.'

I circled a Robert Mitchum film that I planned to tape on the early hours of Boxing Night. 'Yeah, shocking isn't it,' I said without looking up, 'Jesus must be turning on his, er, cross.'

'Do you know, I can still vividly remember one Christmas Eve when I and the late Mrs Cox spent a most memorable evening watching the sunset over the soot-stained brick houses of Barnsley. The mills were silent with folk indoors making dripping sandwiches and darning socks, ready to be hung over the fireplace. They were spending their evening praising the mercy of the good Lord above and drinking milk stout. The only sounds to be heard were the beating of children and the cracking of walnuts,' he mused.

'Sounds magical,' I said.

'It was Charlie, it was. The night was filled with the wonder of half-remembered Christmas carols and outside toilets being flushed. I can remember turning to my beautiful wife, her face upturned in wonder amid the steady drizzle as we exchanged a long and lingering kiss. I half expected to look up and spot a new star on the horizon, shining over the Gant Street abattoir indicating the second coming.'

'Blimey, it sounds like a Hovis advert. When was this, the thirties?' I asked.

'No, just a few years back. We'd broken down on the way to spend the festive season at a distant relative of hers in Ayrshire. The bloody RAC couldn't fix the fuel pump and we ended up staying in a guesthouse run by a woman with an intermittent cough and a limp. To be fair we couldn't complain about the room, the sheets were soft, there was an abundance of hangers and the breakfast was adequate. I could have done with another sausage but one doesn't like to complain.'

'No, one doesn't,' I said, returning to the TV mag. Brian was almost resplendent in a dark blue pinstriped three-piece suit. He looked like an out-of-shape geriatric gangster who couldn't get used to the fact that we were in a different century, they had invented the Pot Noodle, television was in colour and footballers earned more than six pounds a week. From a distance it appeared he was trying to grow a small toothbrush moustache in the style made famous by Hitler. On closer inspection it was merely an overabundance of nose hair trying to break free and make it on its own. His slicked-back hair reminded me of the collection of framed cigarette cards of old cricketers that Colin had halfway up the stairs. In fact, thinking about it, Brian is the only person I have ever encountered who made Colin look like a young upstart.

'What are you doing for Christmas, Charlie?'

'On Christmas Eve I am best man at my stepfather's wedding, and after that I will be binge drinking and eating anything within reach until the second of January, when I will return here bloated, hung over and wishing I had, as the adverts on television recommend, "Enjoyed Responsibly". What about you? Are you planning an emotional return to the dark satanic mills of Barnsley? Maybe even staying at the same bed and breakfast as before? Now you are widowed you might stand a chance of copping off with the landlady with the lazy eye.'

'It was a limp, Charles.'

'Oops, my mistake,' I replied. He was caught unawares

by a loud, unannounced sneeze. He reached into his pocket and retrieved a large handkerchief and had a quick wipe round.

'No I don't think so. I wouldn't want to sully such a precious memory,' he reflected. 'No, this year my sister and myself will spend Christmas at home with the rest of the family gathered round. We are having goose this year; I've negotiated a deal with a friend of a neighbour who has a rather large smallholding.'

'Ooh er!' I retorted.

'Yes, he promised me his prize bird. He's been giving it lots of special attention and extra feed. I'm going round there later in the week to watch him chop its head off.'

'That should make for a memorable evening. Why not take the grandkids round and make a day of it?' I said.

'If you want Charlie, I'll jot down my recipe for chestnut, cranberry and sausage meat stuffing. It's a real crowd pleaser. If we have people over and they're not offered some stuffing I never hear the end of it.'

'Maybe you should phone your limping landlady Brian. I'm sure she would welcome a good stuffing. It is Christmas after all.'

'Charlie lad, my stuffing shouldn't be restricted to the Yuletide season alone.'

'So you are up for a good stuffing fifty-two weeks a year eh? I will bear that in mind. Anyway the cooking at Xmas is Mel's job. I wouldn't want to step on her toes, you know how touchy about the rituals of Christmas women can be. A few years back she forgot to put the silver sixpences in when she made the Christmas pud. She really beat herself up about it. Now each time she serves it up she says, 'Don't worry I've put them in this year.' Yeah, like I'm bothered. There could be a plastic replica of Pat Jennings playing in goal for Spurs for all I care. By the time the figgy pudding is set alight I'm usually half cut, filled to the brim and ready to get horizontal for a snooze until five o'clock when I like to be awoken with a slice of Christmas cake and a cup of tea before the evening session begins.'

'Ah, tradition! It's funny how we all like to do the same thing year after year. Why we feel the need I have no idea. Why do people drink a snowball just because there is a tree in the corner of the room? Mrs Cox and I would never dream of having a Snowball at the golf club after playing nine holes, but if I dared to forget the Advocaat during the Christmas shop it would so ruin her enjoyment of Carols from King's on BBC1 – she would be beside herself. I could offer her a very decent sherry but the withering look of contempt she'd throw me would turn my mince pie to ashes.'

'You should have tried giving her custard with a drop of brandy in it instead. I doubt if she would have noticed the difference,' I said.

Wednesday

It doesn't take long to get used to a new job and build up a routine, does it? I had already worked out the best route and where to park. I knew the number of jobs that would be waiting for me to glaze when I first got in and when the rush would turn into a trickle before more or less drying up completely. I knew Lorraine would ask me how I was and what I had watched on the box the previous evening. I was already getting accustomed to the breath-taking beauty of Moose and the gravity-defying bosom of Casey. I knew I'd be going to the food court just after one and struggle to choose between a not-so-healthy chicken sandwich, overloaded with mayonnaise, or a more cardiac-inducing three-piece dinner from the state of Kentucky. I was also prepared for the friendly old Colonel with the chirpy smile and whiskers to come out on top.

Things were meandering along smoothly; our next eye test wasn't scheduled until three and the store was deserted. I'd ordered what needed ordering and glazed everything I could. The girls had tidied the storeroom and restocked the frame racks and had now decided to skive and keep me company in the lab. Casey dragged a stool under her enormous arse and started picking through the leftovers of her colleagues' lunch. Moose meanwhile leant on my workbench and observed the comings and goings of the people as they passed by the large window that separated them from us.

'How are you doing Charlie, have you settled in yet?' asked Casey.

'Yeah I'm cool. Are you having a good day?' I asked, pleased with the company. It had been a really slow day thus far.

'I'm bored stiff. I think we've taken about three hundred and fifty quid today if we've been lucky. Mark is going to throw a fit when he comes in later.'

'It's bound to be quiet this week, and the next I expect. It's the norm for the optical trade at this time of the year. Mark knows that.'

'Yeah, trouble is, it's been quiet for months now. If things don't pick up in the first three months after Christmas there is a good chance the twats at head office are going to cut their losses and shut this place down. Do you fancy a coffee?'

'Yeah, go on then. You mean there's a chance the store will be closing? How do you know this?' I suddenly felt a sense of dread. Bloody hell, just my luck.

Moose butted in, 'Because at a staff training day recently she got drunk and shagged one of the directors who told her during the 'having a cigarette and letting your bits dry out stage' that the money we are taking is barely covering the rent, let alone our salaries or making a profit.'

'Great!' I groaned. 'And there was me hoping for a long and settled stay here.'

'That's why Mark is so on edge. If this place folds he will be looking for another job, but if he can turn things around he will be the golden boy. It will be a huge feather in his cap. He will probably be given one of their larger superstores and earmarked for even bigger and better things,' said Moose.

I'd finished changing the colours in the tint bath and removing my rubber gloves, so I asked Casey to throw me the Mars bar that lay within her vicinity before she ate it.

'Are you married, Charlie?' she asked through her mouthful. I nodded. 'How come you don't wear a ring then?'

'I don't wear it when I'm working, Casey. I once caught it on a buffing wheel and it almost ripped my finger off.'

'I see, it's not that you're on the cop and looking for a bit of spare then?' She began trying to remove the pieces of corn from a tuna and sweetcorn sarny from between her teeth. 'Careful Charlie, if you don't watch it she'll add you to her collection of blokes she has done the dirty deed with. Mind you you'll be in good company there's hundreds of the buggers,' sniggered Moose.

'Hey, do you mind? I'm not a slag. It's not my fault boys like me and I like boys,' said Casey in defiance, her boobs wobbling as she laughed.

I was taken aback. 'Well I would have never have thought it.'

'Why not? Because I'm fat, is that it?'

'No!' I said. 'Yes!' I thought.

'Let me tell you, Mister Brilliant Technician, I have to fight off guys when I'm out clubbing on a Friday night. You blokes are so full of shit. Just because you are programmed from birth that the only kind of girl you should fancy has to be dead slim most of you are scared to let your true wants and desires bubble to the surface. Well I tell you, after a night of rocking and rolling with me in my bed you'd soon be back begging for more.'

'Yeah, if you say so Casey.' I said, rather taken aback.

'Do you think I haven't noticed you gawping at my tits at every opportunity Charlie?' she stormed. She shuffled off her stool and stood toe to toe with me. Her upturned face was level with my nipples and her humungous rack was threatening to push me out of the door. I felt myself turn scarlet. Then Moose laughed and the phone rang. Thank God, a distraction.

I looked at the girls and they looked at me. 'Well go on then Charlie, answer it!' said Moose, smirking and obviously enjoying my embarrassment.

I picked up the phone whilst still facing my tormenters. An oldish-sounding guy on the other end wanted to know if his specs were ready for collection yet. I went into the shop and after a couple of minutes, with great difficulty, I managed to log on, find his file and ascertain that his glasses were indeed ready for collection. Returning to the lab, I picked up the phone to give him the good news.

'Hello Mr Kenworth, yes your spectacles...'

'What the bloody hell goes on there? What is it you are running, an optician's or a massage parlour?'

'Sorry?' I asked, wondering what he was talking about.

'I was in the Merchant Navy for twenty-five years but I tell you that even from the hairiest Irish boiler man, I have never heard filth like that!'

'Filth, what filth?'

'Tell me, is this the optician's or have I accidentally rung one of those telephone sex lines?'

He was getting extremely hot under the collar and raising his voice to such decibels that I had to leave a safe distance between the receiver and my ear. 'This is Express Specs sir, and I can categorically confirm that any sexiness on our part is purely accidental, I can assure you.' I continued to apologise unreservedly but he still demanded that I give him my name, Mark's and the number for head office.

I put the phone down gently and turned to the girls. 'What was his problem?' asked Moose.

'God knows. What in hell's name were you two harpies chatting about when I was in the shop hunting for that old git's file on the computer?'

The girls exchanged sheepish looks. 'Er, Charlie, you do know you are meant to press the hash button when you have to leave someone waiting don't you? Otherwise our customers will not get to hear the delightful music we pipe down the line for them whilst we are helping with their enquiries.' Moose sniggered.

'Well, I do now,' I replied.

Casey snorted and began to laugh her head off. 'Are you telling me that he was listening to everything I said?' I nodded. 'Even the bit about bending me over the pool table and licking tequila from my arse crack?'

'Evidently,' I answered, and we all fell about laughing. I thought Casey was going to choke on the last remaining mouthful of my Mars bar she'd swiped whilst I was in the shop. After we'd calmed down I asked if we'd get into trouble when Mark got to hear of it.

'Doubt it,' said Moose.

'Good,' I said.

'Don't give a toss if they do,' added Casey.

I stood at the big window, our portal to the outside world, and watched the punters drift past.

Moose broke the silence, 'So, ten inches, eh, did it hurt?'

Casey shook her head. 'Na.'

Thursday

Today I was to stay by the tall and leggy Lorraine's side while she greeted the handful of people booked in through the day for eye tests. She was the senior dispenser and the unofficial person in charge when Mark was out of the store. I watched and took note as she smiled warmly and engaged them in general conversation and banter whilst entering the patient's information on the computer before ushering then gently into the dreaded Brian's clutches. The real skill of the job, and where the money was made, was the hijacking of the poor souls as they left the testing room after their eye examinations and convincing them that this was the only place in town to purchase their new specs to stop them from turning traitor and going elsewhere with their new prescriptions. I wouldn't say it was hard sell, but either Lorraine, Casey, Moose or Mark would be circling like vultures ready to nab them on their exit before they had the chance to escape the store. They would then be led gently towards the racks that housed the most expensive frames we sold before they had a chance to flee and slip through the net. Once sat down and given a cup of coffee, (whether they wanted one or not), the mouthwatering deals of 'Two for the price of one!' and savings and discounts on coatings would be offered. These appeared to be such a bargain and so tantalizing that they couldn't be passed up. (They weren't, by the way.) By the time the deal was done and the till was rung Joe Bloggs was now the proud owner of a pair of everyday specs, a second pair of sunspecs for their holidays and a pair of recreational sports specs with toughened Trivex lenses in case they took up squash or dry slope-skiing. All that plus a voucher for five pounds off their next visit if they persuaded a friend to drop by for an eye-test within the next three months.

I doubted if I could ever be as convincing and gushing, nor motivated and pushy, but it was a real eye-opening introduction to the cutthroat world of retail.

Later in the afternoon, when we were refilling the frame racks and having a bit of a tidy up, Lorraine asked me to fetch a new pack of price tickets. I searched the drawers in the lab but could find no sign.

'They might be in the contact lens fitting room,' she hollered. 'It only gets used once a week and it tends to be a dumping ground for deliveries before we get time to put them away. Follow me and I'll show you where they'll likely be. We need some of those 'Kids for Free' flyers as well.'

I followed her to the rear of the shop between the staff toilets and Brian's examination room. Sue opened the door, felt for the light switch and flicked it on. Illuminated before us was Mark, trousers hanging around his ankles with his pale backside a blur. Suddenly aware of our presence, he stopped in frozen horror. Bent over in front of him was Moose, blouse undone and knickers down by her ankles, frantically gripping the testing chair, her only means of support. Well, there are worse ways to spend a Thursday afternoon tea break, I suppose.

Lorraine quickly closed the door. Her cheeks were as red as a schoolboy's buttocks after he has just been given six of the best from the headmaster. In the safety of the lab I asked, 'Lorraine, do all members of our team undertake that form of team bonding exercise?'

'I don't know Charlie, but it seemed to be working. You can't get much more bonded than that.'

Friday

Ah, POETS day. The week had passed quickly. I felt jubilant at the completion of my first week. It had gone better than I had dared hope. I was happy in myself, happy in my work and all was well in the world. It was Mark's turn to work this Saturday and I was looking forward to spending the weekend with Mel and Ellie. I felt as though I was worthy once more. When I poured that first pint when I got home I would be able to do so knowing that it had been fully earned. I know we shouldn't be so brain washed and conditioned into thinking that unless we are bringing home a wage we are lacking somehow as a human being, (especially for a bloke) but unfortunately that is the way it is.

We were busy first thing and I even made my first sale as a trainee dispenser. My customer/victim was a woman in her thirties with big hair and an even bigger mouth. I even managed to talk her into buying a multi anti-reflection coat to help her with her driving. I felt confident, in control and a little like an ace salesman closing a six-figure deal as I rang it through the till. Well, four figures actually, £86.97. It may not be a store saver but it's a start. Mark was impressed as well and decided to cut me a little slack. Whether this was down to my sales technique or guilt about yesterday's shenanigans in the testing room I wasn't sure.

'How are you doing with your Christmas shopping, Charlie?' he asked. 'Are you getting it all done in plenty of time type chap, or are you like me, come Christmas Eve afternoon you hit the shops with a hastily-prepared list and a sense of blind panic and desperation?'

'I've got a few bits and bobs. I'm not at the panicking stage yet, but yes, there are more pounds to spend than days left to spend it in before Santa ho-ho-hos his way down the chimney,' I admitted.

'We can cover you if you want to take an extra-long lunch and get some done if you like.'

'Are you sure?'

'Yeah, no problem, you're not back in the factory now you know. There is a bit of give and take here, not the iron fist of repression. Oh, while you're out, you couldn't grab me something from the food court could you? I'm expecting a visit from the area manager, I'm flipping starving and I don't want to be out when he turns up.'

'No worries, what do you fancy, a healthy sub or something spicy and greasy? I believe the little shop on the corner are doing an Xmas offer on their large kebabs. For an extra quid you get another couple of slices of the elephant's leg, double the chilli sauce and a sprig of holly garnish.'

'Very festive! No, healthy please. The last thing I want is to breathe chilli and kebab fumes over Mr Timms. I know from my predecessor that he is a bastard of the first order.'

It seemed every other store in the whole giant centre was busy except ours. The lines to the tills were long and winding, filled with impatience and stern faces. As usual the freezing weather outside bore no comparison to the temperature of the shops, which were stifling hot, thus making people even more short-tempered and irritable.

After queuing up in the toy store for twenty minutes to purchase an accessory set for Ellie's favourite doll and a cuddly panda for our baby to be, I was close to breaking point myself. I was about to return to the sanctuary and wide open spaces of my own store when I felt a heavy hand on my shoulder. I spun around half-expecting to find a jumped-up store detective demanding to see a receipt for my goods. I was wrong. It was Fulton.

'Charlie, you soft southern bastard, fancy seeing you here!' He towered over me in big black boots, dark trousers and a white shirt with black tips on the collar. His large black knee-length coat was unbuttoned. He also sported a pair of black Ray-Ban sunglasses. He looked cool and a complete dick all at the same time. He put me in mind of a comedy Wild West sheriff who was as likely to shoot his own foot when quick on the draw than nab the desperado.

'Doing your Christmas shopping are you? There's a crackin' book at Waterstones I've just spotted if you're still in the hunt for a gift for me. It's a retrospective and in-depth study of Scottish national team managers since the year dot.'

'I'll add it to the list, Fulton,' I replied.

'Seriously though, what are you doing so far from the club? By this time on a Friday you're usually slumped at the bar on the way to being seriously depressed.'

'It may be news to you my old mate, but I am now back in full-time employment and I'm once again a creditable member of society. You catch me on an extended lunch break as a thank you from my boss for being first rate and awesome.'

'Is that a fact, Charlie boy?'

'Absolutely, I'm working at the optician's on the second floor.'

He ran his enormous fingers through his long grey goatee beard. 'I thought I hadn't seen you about this week. I put it down to either a lack of funds or trying to curry favour with the missus. How is she by the way? I couldn't help but get the impression that on our one and only meeting she was less than warm and pally in her demeanour.'

'I must confess that I doubt if you'll make the list of her top ten people to get to know better in the forthcoming year. This is probably due to the fact that I was pissed out of my head, singing 'Scotland the Brave' and vomiting on the side of the road on your first meeting with my better half thus far,' I answered.

'Yes, as first impressions go they could have gone better. I didn't mean to urinate over her foot, you understand. I hope you made that clear, Charlie. Talking of drink, do you fancy a cold one?'

I checked my watch, 'I don't know, my boss did say I could take my time but I don't want to take the piss. Especially on my first week.'

'He'll be OK. I believe there is a sports bar at the back of the food court, come on Charlie, I'm as dry as a nun's crutch.'

He strode off like a big cat that had just got a sniff of an antelope with a gammy knee, and I followed in his wake. The Home Run bar was a large long room, one side of which was open to the floor below. If you wanted you could lean against the polished chrome rail and observe the queue for the cinema whilst quaffing your beverage. On every available wall hung large flat-screen TVs showing the latest sports news but with no sound. This was provided by whatever awful radio station was being pumped out of the speakers. At the far end near the toilets were two pool tables. No one was playing. Filling up the space were a couple of games machines and a few brown leather sofas, plus some uncomfortable-looking stools and glass tables. It was modern, trendy, tacky and without soul.

A tall, willowy Australian barman finished loading spent glasses into a washer at the rear of the bar and asked our pleasure. Once again Fulton pulled his usual trick of shouting his preference before announcing that he needed to empty his bladder, thus giving me the privilege of getting in the first round. Had I the necessary cash on me for two Stellas, I wondered, reaching into my back pocket. Before pouring, the barman placed two small white circular napkins in front of me. I turned to look at the TV. They were showing the goals from the last round of matches and I guessed were previewing the upcoming weekend's fixtures.

'That'll be seven pounds sixty please mate.'

'Sorry?' I said, thinking I'd misheard. He repeated and unfortunately I'd heard correctly.

My Jock friend returned and downed half his pint before you could say 'Celtic forever.' He drew the back of his hand across his chops.

'So, are you happy in your new job?'

'Yes, it's going really well. I think I've turned a corner at last,' I said, enjoying my drink. I'd been dry all week and it tasted like a dozen beautiful angels dancing gently down my throat.

'Hey pal,' shouted Fulton to our bar host, 'When you've finished ironing those poncey doilies we'll have another couple of those over here.'

The barman looked over unimpressed and did a slow walk back to the pumps.

'Have you done much shopping?' I asked Fulton. 'Judging by the lack of bags I guess not.' He drained the remainder of his pint.

'I haven't many to buy for to be honest,' he said. 'I send the ex back money for the kids but I doubt if I'll get as much as a thank you, let alone a 'Merry Christmas Dad, how are you?' I send my dear old mum a Harrods hamper, my godson some vouchers and a distant niece a book token. To be honest I only bore the traffic today because I wanted to upgrade my phone and get a new pair of cowboy boots.'

'A gunslinger to the last eh?' I said as our reluctant Aussie laid out two more doilies before covering them with our drinks. 'When I was in the toyshop earlier I couldn't help noticing near the tills there was a neat little gun and spurs combo for £3.99. They even throw in a sheriff's badge. It's worth a look.' I sniggered.

'It's lucky I like you Charlie, otherwise you'd be needing the services of a good dentist in the next twenty seconds.'

'I'm only joking,' I said. 'Where's your yuletide spirit?'

'Christmas is for kids, hogmanay is the real deal.'

I finished my first and started my second. The cold lager sloshed around my empty stomach and made me feel festive and loose-tongued. 'You lot are so stereotypical. All you aim for is a double helping of haggis, a fight, a chance to get your sporran out and enough McEwan's to launch a liner on.'

'You may scoff laddie, but I bet it's more fun than you are in for. What is it? An evening in front of the television, a couple of sherries and a peck on the cheek from a great aunt once Big Ben has done its business, signalling that it's safe now for you to bid goodnight. That you have done your duty and seen in another year?'

'That's amazing! That was last year's New Year down to a T,' I said. 'The only thing you omitted was the overdone crispy duck and the sense of disappointment.'

'Talking of celebrations, that's another thing. I still haven't received my invite to the wedding.'

'I thought you were joking. Do you really want to come to see my stepdad spliced to the bride of Frankenstein?'

'Of course, Charlie boy! What was it you said? Two hundred behind the bar and all the free sausage rolls and quiche I can stuff into my pockets? I'm looking forward to it immensely.'

'OK, I'll get the green light and drop one round when I get five minutes.'

The bar was doing slightly better business. Couples were scattered here and there ready to take a break from the madness of the shops. They sat with their drinks in their hands with their bags safely resting close to the sides of their chairs, like masters keeping an eye on their tentative puppies. Some were showing off items they had bought which they couldn't really afford for friends and loved ones who didn't need or want the gifts in question. We all know this, but we still have to go through the agonising yearly ritual of it all. After all if we didn't it wouldn't be Christmas, would it? No one really expresses a love for turkey, but it will still be on our plates this December 25th.

Despite my half-hearted and frankly pathetic protests Fulton managed to talk me into a further two pints and a swift short before returning to my post. I was more than half cut and as jolly as an elf that knows he has the following month off, and was swaying like a reed in the wind. Mark was not back yet, the store was still empty and in my absence the only money that had been rung through the till was 49p for a bright yellow cord that some old dear had purchased so she could hang her specs around her neck and wouldn't mislay them whilst watching *Deal Or No Deal*. I began finishing the job I had started three and a bit hours previously, while members of the Great British public stood in front of the window to watch me ply my trade, something I was rapidly getting used to. I felt like an Amsterdam whore – all I needed was a red light. Come and get it ladies, you know you want me to glaze your glasses.

I continued working, pulling the odd funny face and smiling and waving. This they usually found disturbing, and it made them swiftly move on. Presently an attractive young mum paused and pointed me out to her little girl. She looked similar in age to Ellie. I smiled and waved back. Her mother smiled at me. Usually this would have made me self-conscious and bashful, but with my alcohol units in double figures I felt no shyness. I winked cheekily and waved back.

Then I remembered the panda toy I had bought earlier. I pretended to walk down an imaginary flight of stairs to an equally imaginary cellar. Once out of sight I fished the panda from my bag and began an impromptu puppet show. I had the black and white bear walking up and down my workbench, dancing a jig and waving back. After a couple of minutes of this pantomime I poked my head up to gauge their reaction.

Unfortunately, mother and daughter were nowhere to be seen. In their place however were Mark and some stiff in a dark pinstriped suit. Mark's face was frozen in horror, while the other guy had a face like thunder. He took a posh black fountain pen from his inside pocket, extravagantly removed the top and made what I imagined was a negative statement on the small clipboard he was holding. I staggered to my knees, threw the panda back into the carrier bag and carried about my business the best I could.

The suit and Mark spent the next half hour circumnavigating the store. He looked at the frame racks and the promotional posters and had a few words with the girls. He didn't enter my lab and bother talking to me. Was it because I was the new guy or are techs like me just not worth bothering with? Was I really, after being in this game nearly a quarter of a century, still at the bottom of the optical food chain?

They spent a further twenty minutes ensconced all nice and cosy inside the contact lens fitting room, presumably discussing the suit's findings. I hope Mark had cleared up any residue of the previous day's physical activities.

I made sure I looked busy when they emerged from the inner sanctum and watched them shake hands and bid adieu. The suit went towards the upper storey car park while Mark waved him off smiling with the exact amount of required reverence.

Once the suit was out of sight, Mark turned to me. He entered the lab before slamming the door hard behind him.

'How did it go?' asked.

He paced up and down the lab, seemingly incapable of forming the right words. 'An hour ago over my latte I was waxing lyrical about the fantastically professional, dedicated and experienced new technician I had managed to land. When I told him what I was paying you he wasn't happy, but I insisted that you were worth it. And what do I find when we get back from our hard-headed business meeting at Starbucks? My highly-paid man, in my words 'an outstanding candidate to be a future store manager' on his knees pretending to be Bluewater's answer to Harry bloody Corbett! What the hell were you thinking?'

'Oh come on,' I said, trying to defuse the situation. 'It's Christmas, I'd enjoyed half a lager, there was a cute little girl watching me and I got the notion to entertain her. How was I to know that you and that humourless android would be standing there?'

He shook his head and ran his hands through his waxed

hair. 'You just don't get it do you? This isn't a bloody game. We aren't back in the factory where safety in numbers could help hide the fact that you couldn't be bothered this particular day or you'd had one too many at lunchtime. This store is losing money hand over fist. We are hanging on by our fucking fingernails here. If things don't improve during January and February this place will be a clothes shop by March and we'll all be out on our arses!'

'OK, message understood and bollocking duly noted. It won't happen again. I will endeavour to be a model employee in the future.' What a knob he'd become, I thought. Christ, two years ago he squirted methylated spirits over Richard's shorts and then lit them as he bent over a grooving wheel. Blimey, it was only yesterday I caught him giving a member of staff a special Christmas bonus in the back room, and now he has the gall to take me to task over a puppet gag.

He looked out of the window and then down at his shoes. 'I'm sorry Charlie, I've got to let you go.'

'What?' I said, not believing my ears.

'Look, it's not me, it's Bainbridge. What he says goes. He didn't like the stunt you pulled. I tried to fight your case, but what could I say? He has a list of techs on a waiting list ready to take your place already.'

'Didn't you stick up for me?' I asked, feeling almost sick. How is it possible for things to turn around so quickly?

'Of course I did mate, but he wasn't having any of it. The stony-faced bastard tore several strips off me as well.'

'So that's it then is it?'

He nodded slowly.

'It's bloody Christmas Mark. You can't do this to me,' I pleaded. 'Our baby is due any day now!'

He once more found it easier to inspect his shoes than my face, 'There is nothing I can do.'

'Thanks mate,' I spat and barged past him, knocking his shoulder and spinning him round. 'Merry fucking Christmas pal!' I threw the lab door open and made my exit through the store. A grey-haired old lady took off the pair of cheap plastic frames she was trying on and glared at me. 'What are you fucking looking at?' I growled. She turned away and pretended she hadn't heard.

I passed the window. Mark watched expressionlessly as I strode to the underground car park in search of solitude and more alcohol.

I never saw or heard from him again. Shame.

CHAPTER TWENTY

Party party

I lay in the tepid bath; the bubbles had dissipated half an hour before. I was second in after Melissa, so the warmth had already gone and my attempts to top it up with some hot water had only ended in disappointment. Our immersion heater was shite. The harsh light of the sixty-watt bulb made the dingy bathroom seem even more tired and grotty than it was by daylight.

We'd been living there for the best part of three years and I still hadn't gotten around to painting over the insipid, dirty, aqua-coloured walls. The grouting between the plain white tiling was spotted with mould, making it look like Stilton had been used instead. There was no carpet, which further increased the second-hand feel of the place, just streaky beige linoleum that didn't quite stretch to the corners of the room and curled up at the edges like a tired sandwich.

When we had first made this three-bedroomed terraced house our new home I was filled with enthusiasm to renovate and decorate it into something modern, sharp and homely. In the first few weeks I was never seen without a drill, paint roller or spirit level in my hand. First we did the lounge, then Ellie's room, followed by ours. By the time I'd painted the hall and stairs the novelty had well and truly worn off. A new football season was on the horizon and the summer was still here, so I switched my attention to the small garden. All of a sudden I was a green-fingered junkie. Every Friday evening I was glued to *Gardener's World* on BBC2. Plant encyclopaedias replaced the football books on my bedside table and I became a regular face at the garden centre. I bought seeds, propagators and compost by the lorry load.

Unfortunately my horticultural interest lasted no longer than my doing it up craze. If you ventured into my garage now you would find my trowel lying somewhere forgotten and abandoned and covered in spiders' webs – Likewise my paint roller, which more than likely would have been poorly washed after its last outing and seized up through my idleness and neglect.

'It's nearly six Charlie, time you got out,' called Melissa from the bedroom.

'Can you get me a warm towel and maybe a roaring fire to stand in front of?' I yelled back.

'The best I can manage is a second-hand towel and two minutes in front of my hair dryer.'

'Beggars can't be choosers,' I said and dragged my body from the water. It ran down my lumps and bumps and made its way for the plughole. I quickly wrapped the damp towel that lay hung over the radiator and shivered. Hunched over like a man in his eighties, I joined Mel in the bedroom. She was smartly dressed in new black maternity trousers and a white collarless blouse. A blue towel was wrapped around her head like a friendly python. I felt the radiator; it was on, but only just.

'This heating's crap,' I said, endeavouring to rub some warmth into my body. 'The radiators need bleeding. My farts are hotter than that.'

She removed the towel from her head and made for the hairdryer on top of the chest of drawers. 'I don't doubt that for a minute,' she said, turning it up to full blast, her newly-dyed hair shining like spun gold in the hot blast. Her slight frame carried the weight of our baby manfully. She looked uncomfortable and unbalanced. What a strange thing nature is. Her body is being stretched to the limit and all kinds of chemical and hormonal changes are turning her world upside down. Me? I'm fine. It's her with the backache and tiredness. She's the one who was throwing up every morning during the early stages. She's the one whose ankles are filled with water. My tummy is stretchmark free and relatively flat in comparison. Yes, all in all we get off scot free. No wonder they nag us. It's payback time!

'Why are we doing this?' I asked.

'It's good to have a scrub every now and again Charlie. Otherwise we'd be humming like a spinning top. What's the matter? Has the shock of soap and water caused a sudden reaction?'

I lay on the bed, too cold to dress, wrapped up in my towelling shroud. Who cares that the sheets will become damp or we may be late? I admired Mel as she began to straighten her curls. She would never be tall enough, photogenic enough or have a good enough figure to be on the cover of glossy magazines or even stand out in a crowd, but there was that certain something about her, an inner beauty that shone through mere skin and bone that made my heart sing and my naughty bits twitch. I constantly wanted to wrap my arms around her and suggest all manner of grown-up activities. This was real beauty, not the airbrushed, cosmetically-enhanced one-dimensional beauty that looks so fantastic on the printed pages of magazines. This was real.

My angel spoke. 'Get your fat, wet, lazy arse off that bed and put some pants on. You have to be at Colin's in less than an hour.'

I sighed heavily and watched while she selected her make-up for the evening. 'I don't want to go, Mel. Admit it, you don't want to go either. Why don't we have a nice evening in? You can choose a DVD and I'll ring for a takeaway. A whole world of culinary delights is but a phone call away. What do you fancy? There's Indian, Chinese, Mexican or Italian. There's even some Polish place opened up where the baker's used to be. It seems quite popular, especially with Polish people I believe. I'm not fussy, anything will do me. There's nearly a full bottle of white left in the fridge as well. We could have a really good night. Just the two of us, what do you say?'

She lowered her head and kissed me softly on the lips. 'I would love to darling, that all sounds peachy, but unfortunately part of the deal of being an adult is responsibility. Along with staying up late, drinking alcohol and playing with boobies comes the downside, such as washing up, working for a living and doing things that you are obliged to do even though you would rather not. I'm sorry lovely boy, this is one of those.'

'This life is crap,' I countered. 'Next time around I'm coming back as a butterfly.'

'That's your answer to everything,' she sighed.

'Seriously though, I'm just not in the mood for any of this.'

She smiled, kissed me again and resumed straightening her hair. 'You and me both babe. I'm dog-tired, my ankles are the size of traffic cones, I'm as wide as a six-exit roundabout and my back is killing me. The last thing I feel up to doing is partying with Grace and a load of people I've never met.'

I discarded my towel and dragged myself vertical. 'You think you've got it bad. I've got to spend a precious Friday night out with Colin, the cast of *Last of the Summer Wine* and Graces' two idiot sons. Why they've been invited I haven't got a Scooby.'

'You'd better get used to it, honey. They will soon be family after all.'

'Don't remind me' I said, dragging a clean pair of trousers from their hanger. Now what shirt? They were lined up on the rail in strict order. The furthest left was plain, white and used for funerals, job interviews and weddings. The furthest right was a Hawaiian party shirt of many colours adorned with bikini-clad beauties and palm trees against a bright orange sunset. I plumped for a pale blue collarless number nearer left than right. I was in that kind of mood.

I was the last of our merry band to arrive at Colin's meeting place of choice, the Railway Arms, tucked behind Platform 2 next to a unisex hairdresser whose poster in the window boasted of a 'two for one pensioner offer every Monday'. On the other side was an ex-burger joint that had cooked its last takeaway and was now boarded up, covered in flyers and surrounded by dog shit, fag ends and several faded pages of a week-old copy of *The Sun*. The smoking ban had hit this type of back street drinking hole more than any other. This was a place where drink and tobacco were as closely linked as cheese and onion, salt and vinegar and crime and punishment. This wasn't the kind of joint that could reinvent itself as some kind of family-friendly gastro-pub where you and the kids could enjoy a relaxed Caesar salad, a surf and turf and something from the sweet menu. This place, along with hundreds like it, would soon be consigned to history, an anonymous, soon-to-be-forgotten dive where people would kill time while waiting for their train with a pint, a fag and a go on the fruit machine. It was dark, dingy, soiled and stained. It was also a bit of a squeeze, being no more than fifteen feet across at its widest point. It went further back than you thought though – a bit like a dentist's chair.

The bar was stretched against the wall across the left of the long and darkly-lit room. A couple of suited guys chatted quietly while waiting for their trains back home after their commute to work. I envied them on two counts; firstly because they were lucky enough to be employed and secondly because they would shortly be supping up and heading off. Other than Colin's cronies and the office guys the place was empty but for a nervous-looking couple of lads who judging by their youthful looks and acne-covered faces were enjoying a crafty under-age pint. The landlord I expected knew they weren't eighteen but was grateful for every penny he could ring through the till. As long as they kept their heads down and didn't cause any trouble they were probably OK.

I ordered a beer and approached the stag and his party, who were sitting around a couple of tables they'd pulled together at the rear of the bar. Colin saw me approaching.

'About bloody time Charlie! Blimey, this is a fine turn of events. The last one to show his face is my supposedly best man.'

'Better late than never.' I smiled and dragged a stool beneath me. Well what a group this was. Flanking Colin were, I guessed, a couple of his bowls cronies. I knew this as like Colin, they proudly wore club blazers and ties. The gent on the left had the shiniest head I had ever seen. Had he applied polish before he'd come out? It was so shiny that I could see a partial reflection of the side of Colin's own sparsely-thatched dome just above his ear lobe.

The other chap, I later discovered, was the bowls club captain. Had Colin invited him to gather some brownie points I wondered? He drank gin and tonic and was as frosty as the ice in his glass. His appearance was immaculate, spotless and from another era and even the squalor and dreariness of the Railway Arms failed to taint him. The hair on his upper lip was grey and as stiff as his clipped replies. I wouldn't want to get on the wrong side of this man. If I were casting a Second World War movie he'd be nailed on for the part of the commanding officer sitting behind a huge mahogany desk weighed down with pips, stripes and a Home Counties accent.

Sitting on a pew under a grimy unwashed window with a depressing view of empty barrels, rubbish, a backyard filled with junk and a car that would never again feel the road beneath its tyres were a trio of sixty-somethings whom I knew Colin spent weekends engaging in various activities with, from fishing and battle re-enactment through to rambling and charity work. Each held a faded dignity, which wasn't enhanced by the grubby surroundings. They looked uncomfortable and out of place, like a spent condom sticking to the sole of the Queen's shoe.

The brothers Grimm, Grace's two precious boys, sat with their backs towards me, suited and booted and ready to make to an impression. I could smell their aftershave from a penalty kick away. They turned their bull-like necks when Colin made the introductions. Even in their seated positions I could ascertain they were well clear of six feet tall, as wide as my pine-effect wardrobe and almost identical. To each other I mean, not my wardrobe. Grace had told me they were both employed as bouncers. It looked as if they were born for the job.

Wayne thrust an outsized mitt in my direction. My own hand looked like a doll's in comparison, but despite my fears he didn't decide to crush it. His handshake was soft and friendly, as was his brothers. Ant-knee was a couple of years junior to his sibling but despite this his hair was shrinking away from his temples more than his elder brother. This was only noticeable at close quarters however, as both scalps had made friends with unguarded clippers. They were big, bad, bald and threatening looking. What dipped their appearance into the realms of comedy was the wraparound shades they both wore. The fact that it was December and dark and we were in the gloomiest pub in Kent whilst hanging around with a group of geriatric bowlers didn't matter to these guys, the look was everything. They'd watched too many movies, spent too long in the gym and tried too hard. What they thought about being there I couldn't imagine, though I guessed Grace had summoned them and they would never, ever say no to their mother.

Colin did his best to raise the atmosphere above funereal. 'The train leaves in ten minutes lads, who's up for a quick double down their neck before it pulls in?'

Wayne, Ant-knee, shiny-head and I were the only takers.

Melissa found the large town centre pub surprisingly busy at this early hour as she slowly made her way through the throng. She ordered an orange juice and lemonade and looked around for Grace. She heard her before she saw her. A loud and unmistakable cackle rose from behind a gang of blokes and spread itself across the ceiling. At least a dozen women dressed to impress were banging shot glasses onto a table in front of them before cheering and downing them in one. It was a themed pub with posters and memorabilia attached to the walls and ceiling, and it was trendy, overpriced and overrated. That didn't matter to the punters enjoying their Friday night jolly up. They were here to get drunk, get laid or hopefully both.

Mel hollered a shrill hello in the direction of Grace, trying to compete with the loud pulsating bass of the sound system. After three further lung-busting attempts she caught her attention and was greeted with the wave of a spindly hand in her direction.

Grace leaned over the crowded glass-strewn table and planted her ruby-painted lips on Mel's cheek. 'So glad you've managed to make it love. I'll chat to you in a second but I'm dying for a pee.' She headed off for the ladies.

Mel felt self-conscious amongst her fellow hens. They were all either twenty-somethings and gorgeous or on the wrong side of fifty and desperate to blend in and assume the look of their younger, thinner and less worldly-worn counterparts.

After what seemed like ages, Grace and a workmate returned with a tray of drinks each. 'Dig in girls. I've got the slippery nipples and Rita has sex on the beach and the screaming orgasms. What's your pleasure, Melissa love?'

Mel waved her glass. 'I'd better stick with these. I don't want baby coming out tiddly.'

'Oh you don't want to listen to that load of bollocks about not drinking while pregnant. When I was expecting my boys I was legless most weekends and I smoked forty a day. In fact, If I'd have had my way I'd have been hooked up to a drip full of vodka throughout the entire bloody ordeal.'

'Yeah,' agreed Rita. 'And she's not just talking about the birth, she means the conception and the pregnancy as well!'

The two cackled wildly. 'You're not wrong there Rea. Do you know it took twenty-four hours for Anthony to finally drag his sorry arse out and nearly as long for Wayne. Still you never know, you may have a quickie.'

She suddenly caught sight of someone she knew and drink in hand, pushed her way through the crowd of people at the bar to place an arm around a good-looking bloke twenty years her junior and give him a kiss on the cheek. Mel looked at her watch and sighed; it was going to be a long night.

The golf club was a brisk ten-minute stroll from the railway station. We must have made an odd sight as we walked in line down the narrow tree-lined lane to the car park and entrance of the Manor Golf Club, the most exclusive and toffee-nosed of its kind in the county. At the head was Colin in his newly-purchased designer gear, which made him look like a chav second-hand car salesman, while following close behind was the bowls club captain with his nose in the air, full of military pomp and Gordon's gin. Next came the three old stooges struggling to keep up with the Captain's long and raking stride, and bringing up the rear were the two bullet-headed brothers with their sloping shoulders and knuckles dragging in the gravel.

The large clubhouse was set on two floors. On the lower were the changing rooms, lockers, various rooms marked 'PRIVATE' and a large shop selling everything to do with golf, from hugely expensive sets of clubs down to branded baseball caps, so that even the most feeble of Sunday morning hackers could pretend he could look and play like Tiger Woods.

We climbed a wide wooden staircase towards the restaurant and bar. On the walls hung large wooden plaques which told in gold lettering of the winners of the club's many competitions down the years; the Captain's Charity Cup, Men's and Ladies' Singles, the Montgomery Baxter Invitational Challenge Trophy and many more. At the top of the stairs was a large portrait of the current club captain. The expression on his face was smug and slightly creepy. He'd reached the top after no doubt many years of brown nosing and keeping in with the committee. I hoped it was worth it.

Next to a sign reminding members that no clubs or golf shoes were allowed in the bar area stood a steward who blocked our way.

'Good evening gentlemen,' he said, 'Can I help you?'

'Hello, I have a table booked in the restaurant,' said Colin, as he fiddled with the knot on his tie.

'Certainly sir, I take it you are all members?' he replied. He was smartly dressed in a dark green blazer and club tie. He was a tall man who obviously took pride in his appearance and his position at the club. His combover was almost convincing and the red threadneedle veins gave his cheeks a rosy festive glow.

'I am,' replied Colin, 'And these gentlemen are my guests.' He started towards the bar, but the steward had other ideas. 'I do apologise sir, but due to demand, Friday night is now exclusively for members only.'

Colin endeavoured to keep his cool. 'I'm sure you will find that this arrangement has been agreed and is down in the club diary. It was booked more than six weeks ago and I personally double-checked the arrangements earlier in the week. It was never mentioned then that there were any membership restrictions.'

The steward picked an invisible speck of fluff from his sleeve and glanced briefly at a large leatherbound book which lay open on a pedestal at his side.

'I do apologise sir, but my hands are tied. You are not down in the book and I'm afraid rules are rules and the committee are most insistent that the rules are adhered to.'

Colin was losing his cool, and he was also aware that he was beginning to lose face in front of his pals. 'This is ridiculous!' he said, raising his voice. 'The booking was made personally with the club secretary himself. I'm sure if you ask for his approval he'll give it.'

'I'm afraid the secretary isn't here this evening. If you excuse me I will have a word with the restaurant manager,' said the steward, and walked off.

Colin turned to us. 'Sorry about the wait chaps, you know what these kinds of places are like sometimes. It's all red tape, formalities and having to grease the correct palm.'

Through the half-open door I managed to catch sight of the steward exchanging hushed tones with his boss. They both looked us up and down, unsure whether protocol would be breached if we were to be allowed our seats in the restaurant. A third man was called over. He was wearing the same blazer as the others, though his was further adorned by two pips at the shoulders. I assumed this signified some greater power, but I was only guessing. He was a short, tubby, smarmy-looking man with reddened cheeks and coal-black slicked-over hair. I had seen his face somewhere before and it took me a moment to place him. It was the man from the portrait that hung on the stairs, the club captain himself. He looked us over in the same dismissive manner as the other two. He was obviously less than impressed with our increasingly hungry group. He whispered something, shook his head and dispatched the steward to relay the bad news.

'I do apologise sir, but as there is absolutely no record of your booking I am unable to seat you in the dining room. I am however able to offer you some crisps or sandwiches if you don't mind sitting in the patio area next to the driving range?'

'Are you kidding? It's twenty fucking below out there!' I said.

'I believe there is a heater.'

'Do you want me to chin him?' asked Wayne. His fists were opening and shutting in readiness.

'Better not,' I replied. 'Colin will lose his membership, the police will be called and we still won't be able to gain entrance,' I whispered in his cauliflower ear.

'Wait till the secretary hears about this!' said Colin, red-faced and furious. 'He will be livid, livid!'

We silently left, defeated and dejected. Colin pulled me to one side and whispered, 'Bloody hell Charlie, this has turned into a right shambles. What am I going to do? The Captain is fuming, the bowls lads are getting weary and Wayne and Anthony are spoiling for a fight.'

'Yes, I must admit things aren't going as smoothly as they might. As far as I can see we have two options. We can go back to the station and wait the best part of an hour until the next train comes and find somewhere in town to eat. Or there is the White Bear, which is about five minutes' walk from here. We can have a few drinks, something cheap and cheerful from the menu and try to laugh it off.'

Colin's face brightened. 'Good boy Charlie, I knew you'd come up trumps, plan B it is. He turned to his stags in semi triumph 'Come on men,' he ordered, cheering up no end. 'There's a cracking little boozer just around the corner. The ale is cheap and plentiful and the cheesy chips are the best in the parish. We are not going to let that stuck-up git ruin our evening, are we?'

'Not bloody likely!' said one of the bowlers, taking an oversized hankie from his pocket and blowing his glowing red conk.

'Of course not, come on men, the first round is on me, this way!'

By nine the fourteen girls were ordering their starters and giving the waiting staff hell. Innuendos flowed as readily as the wine. Grace had chosen one of the large chains of themed restaurants that are on the edge of every town these days. There will be a cinema, a bowling complex, a McDonalds, a Mexican, an Italian and possibly an American style 50s diner with checked tablecloths, movie publicity posters, small booths, gumball machines and overpriced ice-cream. This place was supposed to offer an authentic Mexican experience, though Mel was pretty sure that if she ever did get the opportunity to go south of the border she'd be unlikely to find anywhere like this.

Not that it was unpleasant. It had recently been refurbished at no small cost and was clean, tidy and offered a hint of El-something or other. The staff smiled throughout, despite the rudeness and impatience of many of Grace's friends and the occasional pinched bottom. Several helium-filled balloons proclaiming 'Getting Hitched' were tied to decorated weights and floated above the table. By now Grace was wearing a small white headdress and veil, which was swept back onto her peroxide blonde tresses. She also boasted a set of L-plates, one pinned to her back and the other just below her formidable cleavage, which looked even more puffed up and on show than ever.

On Mel's left was Grace's matron of honour Rita, and on her right a girl called Tracy. Rita was a redhead who wore her hair short. Although the restaurant was fairly dim she still refused to remove the oversized Prada sunglasses which were probably her trademark. She was tall, thin and as scrawny as her buddy. Her best points were obviously her long tanned legs, which were shown off to the max in a white micro skirt that only just covered her modesty. She was in her late forties and it was a place she didn't feel she belonged or wanted to be.

'I expect you've known Grace for years?' asked Mel, as the three of them tucked into a Mexican starter combo.

Rita endeavoured to remove a piece of sweetcorn from between her front teeth with a long and painted little finger nail. 'No, only a couple of years actually. She started working as a temp at our office and we just hit it off straight away. She's a right scream, especially when she's had a few. How that old fart she's going to get hitched to is going to handle her God only knows. How do you know her?' She picked up a chicken wing.

'She's marrying my father-in-law,' replied Mel, enjoying her discomfort.

'Sorry, I didn't mean to...'

'That's OK. Forget it. It seems odd though doesn't it that everyone here seems to be a fairly recent friend. There are no relations or pals from way back. It's almost as if she has no past or history that goes back more than a couple of years.'

'I suppose so,' said Rita, who was far more interested in procuring another bottle of wine than delving into her friend's history.

As the meal progressed Grace's almost manic cackling grew louder, and then just before desserts were due to be served a large hullabaloo erupted from the kitchen area. Out came a young member of the waiting staff carrying a miniature wedding cake topped off with sparklers and miniature naked models of a bride and groom. Behind him came three further waitresses banging trays loudly while singing the na-na-na-nas from the wedding march.

Rita leaned over. 'I set this up!' she said, exploding with laughter.

Grace stood up, swayed, grabbed the edge of the table for support and pointed a bony finger towards her matron of honour. 'You fucking bitch!' she screamed, laughing hysterically. Any other diners who had not so far been aware of the scene were now unable to ignore the fact that the fifty-something painted trollop with the blood-red lipstick and the foul mouth was about to walk down the aisle once again.

'Nearly there chaps,' said Colin, upbeat once more in his belief that the evening would not end in total farce. 'That jumped-up prat at the golf club will certainly be getting a piece of my mind when I next play a few holes that is for sure. I've got some pretty influential contacts on the committee and they will be incandescent with rage when I relay how we have been treated. I wouldn't be surprised if that bloody idiot loses his job over this.'

Yeah, that's likely, I thought. You've got about as much clout as a paper bag being tossed about in a force nine gale.

It was further to the pub than I had remembered, and some of the senior members were starting to feel the pace and the cold. Wally had already had to call for a rest so he could wipe his family-sized giant handkerchief across his wrinkled brow. The sky, which had grown heavy with snow over the last few days, was now beginning to relieve itself of its burden in big fluffy flakes. My toes were beginning to feel frostbitten. Jesus, I thought, if ever I needed a warming double scotch down my neck it was now. The uneven cobble stone path on which we strode was becoming increasingly slippery too, and it was clear that the slightest loss of balance from one of the more senior of our party could end up with a broken bone and a five-hour wait in the casualty department of the local hospital.

Just as mutinous mutterings in the ranks were beginning to surface, we turned the final corner and the pub came into view. At last, a drink, a sit down and a chance to get out of the blizzard.

'White Bear, get ready to welcome the stags!' exclaimed Colin like a commander in the D-Day landings. Only it wasn't the White Bear, not by a long shot. It was now called 'Freddie's Place'. Incredibly loud drum and bass music thundered out through the walls and I could feel the, thud, thud, thud, pulse across the slushy car park and through the soles of my soggy shoes. Colin's bowls chums stopped in their tracks and exchanged frightened looks. 'What the fuck?' said Colin. 'What the bloody hell has happened to the White Bear?'

Wayne and Ant-knee smiled, nodding their shaven skulls along to the bass line.

'God knows,' I replied, 'but what I do know is that we are all thirsty, dying of hypothermia and are unable to feel anything below our knees. It may not be ideal, but I really do think we should get inside and make the most of a bad hand.'

I pushed open the door and strode towards the bar.

Inside it was hot and humid. A dance floor ringed with golden coloured rope lighting occupied the left-hand side. It was full of writhing bodies bending and moving to the music, which was eardrum-shatteringly loud. I hoped the oldies would have the sense to turn down their hearing aids.

The bar was at the rear. It was long and made of what looked like chrome, and matching stools were set against it. They looked uncomfortable; maybe that was why most were unoccupied. The barman saw us approach and was ready to take our order. He was wearing a tight white vest and what looked like eyeliner.

'Nine pints of lager please,' I hollered.

'We don't sell draught beer, its bottles only,' he shouted back.

Trying not to stare at his pierced nipples, which stood proudly to attention beneath the thin cotton, I replied that bottles would be fine.

'Sol OK?'

'Yeah, whatever.' I turned to find that the rest of the guys had scurried to the quietest corner (if you could call having a five-hundred-watt amp spewing out hardcore rap within a foot of your earhole quiet) between a spiral staircase that led to an upstairs bar and another dance floor and presumably the toilets.

'That will be thirty-six pounds and fifty pence please.'

'What? You've got to be joking!'

'Sorry pet,' he said, smiling. I reluctantly handed over two twenty-pound notes, 'Thirty odd quid for nine tiny bottles of pissy Spanish lager? It's unbelievable. You certainly saw me coming.' I loaded them carefully onto a tray. He beckoned me forward so I was in earshot.

'Not yet sweetie, but hey, the night is still young.'

I returned and placed the tray before the stags, who were sitting like ice age exhibits that were slowly thawing out. Nobody spoke. Colin was taking in the surroundings and sadly shaking his head. He could probably have seen better if his specs hadn't been quite so fogged up. The oldies sat together on a long bench, hardly daring to look up in case of what they might see. The Captain looked as cool as ever. It would take more than a nightmarish evening such as this to make him lose his cool. The two brothers ignored their surroundings and simply picked up their drinks and chatted amongst themselves.

Old Wally sighed, discarded his long fawn mac, folded it and put it under the table. He picked up the nearest lager and observed it closely.

'What the dickens is this? There's something jammed into in my drink. Into all of them,' he said to no one in particular.

'It's lime,' I bellowed. 'You're meant to poke it inside to give it a bit of a continental flavour boost.'

'If I'd have wanted lime I would have asked for lime, wouldn't I? What if you don't like lime in your beer?' he shouted back.

'No one does, it's just a trendy gimmick. Get it out with your finger and lob it at that barman. That's what I intend to do with mine.'

Colin leaned towards me and whistled in my ear. 'Blimey Charlie, this gaff must be the trendiest place in town.'

I nodded. 'It's certainly popular. But I think there may be something you haven't clocked yet?'

'Well, whatever it is they certainly like the music up

loud. Look at that dance floor, it's packed. And the heat! Blimey, some of those guys are so hot and sweaty they've had to take their tops off.'

'That's the point I'm trying to illustrate Colin. Haven't you noticed that there must be about forty blokes in here strutting their stuff and yet I don't think I've seen more than a handful of women?'

Colin looked around and shrugged. 'There's nothing wrong with that. After all, look at us. Here we are, nine fellas out on the lash. When you're out with your mates talking football or expressing the virtues of a new socket set you've recently purchased down the market the last thing you want is a woman butting in and spouting off about the great pair of shoes she's just bought in the sales. Blimey, I get enough of that indoors.'

I pointed to two skinny guys who were dancing enthusiastically with each other and staring passionately into each other's eyes. They were tanned, toned, topless and sweaty. The taller, shorthaired one then grabbed the smaller guy, who was weedy looking and full of piercings, by his leather trousers, drew his hips towards him and ground his crutch hard against his own.

'Pardon me for possibly being guilty of judging a book by its cover and resorting to stereotype, but I get the impression that these two and most of the others in here are more than just chums talking over the weekend's forthcoming football fixtures.'

He looked around, and his jaw dropped so far it nearly had to be scooped up from the floor. Hello, I do believe the penny is finally dropping.

'Are you trying to tell me...?'

'I'm afraid so old chap. There is no denying the fact that you, Colin Bennett, the rough, tough man's man that you are, the lover of boxing and old-time football, the man brought up in an age when even an over-long handshake was seen as suspect is, at the age of sixty-whatever, spending his one and only stag night in a gay bar.'

I looked at Wally, the Captain and the rest as one by one the truth dawned on them. The Captain sat straight-backed and stiff-necked, his moustache positively bristling with distaste and disdain. Colin and his bowls buddies looked at each other with looks of pure terror. Some sat staring at their drinks wishing they were somewhere else, while others eyed the door, planning the quickest possible route of escape. The eyeliner-wearing bartender approached our tables and cleared away some empty glasses. He winked at me and asked if I was having a good time.

'Not as good as these guys.' I pointed. He placed a hand on my arm and bellowed in my ear, 'Yes, I bet those old queens don't get out much. What are you, their social worker?'

'Yes, something like that,' I said.

It was ladies' night at Leonardo's, the most notorious nightclub in the district. Without failure the local weekly paper would feature reports of violence, drunken behaviour or people going missing after a Friday or Saturday night. After being served cheap booze (even cheaper before eleven) for several hours, the partygoers were ready to fight, puke, break up, make up, get laid, burst into tears or search for a kebab shop that was still open. It left a heavy burden on the local police and its cheaper community policing volunteers to deal with. Mind you, the average kebab shop owner is a spirited and dogged breed. Who else would be willing to put up with all the shit that generally kicks off at chucking-out time for another fifty quid in the till? Is it really worth the risk of grievous bodily harm, verbal abuse and a good chance of having your front window kicked in for the sake of a few more servings of lamb fat, chilli sauce and overly powerful onions that you would probably sell the following day anyway? Maybe that's the Greek outlook. 'No matter how knobbily the young British male may behave on a Friday night, we are here to serve them till dawn! Our huge leg of compressed and congealed lamb will continue to spin for eternity! Our sabre-like knives will shine in the moonlight until the streets are empty of ignorant, racist, inebriated boys and girls with too much money and not enough responsibilities!'

Grace and her fellow hens each paid the special ladies' night price of fifteen pounds to the door staff to gain admittance. For that they would be able to help themselves to the free buffet, which was in reality no more than crisps, poorly-cooked chicken wings, a selection of whatever was on offer at the local discount freezer store and cheese sandwiches that tasted of nothing more than salad cream and margarine. They would also receive one complimentary drink and see the forty-five minute show, which comprised a third-rate local singer who would no doubt belt out something by Tom Jones to a dodgy home-made backing track, a female comedienne who would rip the piss out of all things male and best of all two oiled and pumped up gym junkies who would gyrate in their underwear before a final flash of nudity as the curtain made its descent amid screaming catcalls.

By now Melissa was tired and starting to flag. She'd had more than enough of Grace and her pals and was desperately thinking of excuses to get away without offending her future stepmum-in–law. She looked at her watch while they stood in the queue for the cloakroom. Half eleven, is that all it was? This evening was lasting forever. She wondered if Charlie was already home or on his way. She groaned inwardly as she imagined him putting the chain on the door before falling into an alcoholic coma from which he would never be aroused by shouting and the banging of the front door. Fumbling for her phone, she decided to send the stupid big lump a text, but then groaned as she observed the lack of signal.

It was a good job the punters didn't see Leonardo's during the day. By night it was a happening place with cheap drinks and coloured lights, filled with young and attractive bodies moving as one to the music and making the place come alive. Nine o'clock on a miserable Monday morning however was a different matter altogether. It was a sorry tale of faded glory, ripped seats and unidentifiable stains. The toilets were filthy despite the fact that judging by the lakes of piss on the floor it appeared they'd hardly been used. The carpet that had once been a vibrant blue was now greasy and grey and spotted with discarded gum and sticky patches that could have been anything. There are only so many times puke, spilt drinks, urine and blood can be cleaned away or brushed over before they become part and parcel of the building's very identity.

This didn't matter now however as it was party time, late at night and full of drunk and hyped-up clubbers ready to shake their thang to a throbbing dance track. The boys and their girls were in the main room while the majority of the single women were in the smaller enclosure ready to party and act naughty.

The huge roll of folded-up notes that had been donated by an ever-generous Colin for Grace and her friends to have a night to remember, the notes Grace had proudly held up for all to cheer at the beginning of the evening, had now been reduced to a couple of folded-up twenties. She stood at the bar, resting an arm on the sticky surface, slipped off and tried again. Swaying wildly, she asked the young woman behind the bar how many shots she could get with her remaining bankroll and was told that she was still serving another customer and would be with her in a tick.

Grace tried to get her mini-skirted bottom onto the high red bar stool. The first attempt ended in failure, with the stool skidding on the hard wooden floor, and she nudged an unsuspecting girl in the back. 'Sorry love,' she drooled. She decided to prop the bar up instead, a much wiser idea. The glass panel behind the bar reflected the optics, shiny and inviting. The people on the dance floor were also held up to view as if in Cinemascope. They were young and beautiful. Despite the inclement weather they had braved the snow and wind in very little attire. Skirts were short, and their youthful vitality, smooth skin and low mileage transported Grace into a reverie. In her day she had been the one all eyes had turned to. Her body had been to die for, athletic with a sensual quality that captivated all. She could have her pick of men and often did. She thought it would never end, but as the years passed the lines grew deeper, her once schoolgirl waist expanded, no matter what diet she adopted, and the gravity-defying breasts which had captivated any man with a pulse lost their oomph and decided it was time to take a bit of a wander south.

In a rare moment of clarity she took in her own reflection, and she didn't like what she saw. Her bleached, almost white locks looked straw-like and brittle. Her over-made-up eyes looked dark and weary and only drew attention to the bags under her eyes and the cheeks that were beginning to jowl, like a boxer dog that has lost its master. Her neck was scrawny and could have passed for that of a turkey waiting for the butcher's cleaver. Her ludicrous veil and bride-to-be L-plates only emphasized the overall look of a faded beauty still trying to cling on to former glories.

Where had it all gone astray? Christ, she used to date all the boys her friends could only wish for. She'd even for a short time been almost engaged (they had never got around to getting the ring) to a bloke who was now a star of East Enders. She thought of all the lost opportunities. If things had been a little different it could have been her living in a Tudor mansion with her face plastered all over the glossies, either showing off her lovely home and family or playing the wronged woman standing on the steps of the divorce court looking fantastic after securing a five-million-plus house settlement. Now she was the wrong side of fifty, with nothing to show from her life but her two boys and a meagre nest egg which thanks to the Chancellor was growing at a slower rate than her behind. And there she was now, celebrating yet another forthcoming marriage to a bloke she wouldn't have allowed to lick the shit off her shoes when she was in her prime.

The girl behind the bar finally took her order and filled

a tray with small multi-coloured drinks as requested. As Grace was waiting for her change she caught sight of three girls who were hardly old enough to be let out of school on their own, let alone to go to a nightclub. She saw them exchange furtive glances and whisper asides in her direction. Her anger rose, and she couldn't help herself.

'What's that?' she asked, necking a small blue drink in one glug. The tall thin girl pretended not to hear. The tubby blonde raised a bottle of lager to her fat, podgy lips. The strikingly beautiful girl who wore her dyed, Goth black hair up, smirked and said, 'Sorry, are you talking to us?'

Grace walked menacingly towards them, downing another shot. 'You looked at me and said something. What was it?' she growled.

The girl suddenly felt less confident. But she looked at her friends, and did not want to lose face. She replied, 'I was just remarking to my friends that I thought it was Christmas, but when I caught sight of you I realised I must be mistaken. I had no idea it was Halloween.' She laughed. The tall thin girl remained impassive and took a step back. The fat blonde sniggered and snorted. Grace nodded her head and smiled. In a split second her life flashed before her. She thought of the huge stately home she would never own with luxurious lawns and paid help. She thought of herself back in her glory years holding court. She remembered her beauty and how powerful beauty can be. She thought of Colin pulling his underpants over his swollen, extended belly.

With all the strength she could muster, she leaned back, then quickly threw her forehead forward and down to smash into the girl's nose. Despite her drunken state she could hear and feel the crack as the pretty young face disintegrated under the impact. As if in a dream, she felt hands pulling at her and angry cries ringing in her ears. She was unable to fix concentration on anything solid; there was blood, there were tears and there was regret.

The police arrived almost instantly, it seemed, and the ambulance was not far behind. It was just another Friday night at Leonardo's.

CHAPTER TWENTY-ONE

Here comes the...blimey!

My eyelids opened slowly as the knocking at the bedroom door tore me from my slumber. It had been two days since our adventures at the gay bar, and today was Christmas Eve. Today was the day to celebrate the anniversary of Christ's impending arrival at a stable in Bethlehem, and to witness the spectacle of Colin walking down the aisle ready to meet his doom.

We'd had a brilliant time the night before, Colin and I. The two of us sat up talking into the early hours about times and years gone by. We'd hardly mentioned Grace and the wedding. We had reminisced about my mum and my childhood and things I'd long forgotten had returned with crystal-clear clarity; day trips to the seaside and weeks spent at holiday camps. Collecting mussels and cockles at Seaford and having to be pulled from the grey oily sludge that threatened to drag you under at low tide. The numerous rows over homework and school and the times when he ran our local under-twelve's football team for a season and causing a huge row between the two sets of partisan supporters because while refereeing he had awarded a dubious penalty when yours truly went down in the box. He'd certainly mellowed in the years since my teens, when we had gone weeks without exchanging more than distrustful looks. We'd definitely forged more of a bond since Mum's passing, and when Ellie arrived it brought out a soft, attentive and cuddly side to his nature I never knew existed. He'd pop in every other day for a cuddle with his granddaughter, more often than not bringing with him yet another cuddly toy to lie at the foot of her crowded little cot.

Towards the end of the night we leafed through the family photograph albums stretching back to the seventies. I'd forgotten that he had once looked so young, handsome and athletic as he posed proudly with an arm around my mother's waist. He was a far cry from the podgy, bald, tubby little man he had since become. Still, what can you expect at seventy? Blimey, if and when I reach that age and I've still got enough embers smouldering on the old fires to entertain getting hitched to a sassy broad almost twenty years my junior I will think myself fortunate indeed.

Later as we sipped our brandies we listened to The Beatles 'Abbey Road' on Colin's old music centre, the one with the tape-to-tape deck with high-speed dubbing and

Dolby hiss reduction all hidden behind a smoked glass door, a piece of kit he'd had for what seemed forever. He grew quiet and solemn and I wondered what was playing on his mind; days gone by or days to come?

He saw me looking at him, smiled and sighed. 'One more and I think we'll call it a night Charlie.' He reached for my glass. I gulped down the remainder, 'Yeah, I suppose we should, you'll need your beauty sleep for the photos tomorrow.'

I awoke from a deep and peaceful slumber. Was that banging in my head or for real? There was a knock on the bedroom door and I groaned and ignored it. He knocked on the door again. 'Are you awake Charlie?'

I bloody am now, I thought. 'Yes, what time is it?'

'Just after nine, there's a dressing gown on the back of the door, pull it on and get yourself downstairs sharpish. Colin's famous full English breakfast is about to be served! How many slices of black pudding do you want?'

Call me squeamish, but the last thing I fancied after our alcoholic excesses of the night before was one of Colin's artery-clogging breakfasts, swimming in fat and accompanied by two rounds of coronary-inducing fried bread.

'Just the one for me,' I said diplomatically as I managed to haul myself upright. I pulled at the curtain and took in the day. Either there had been a blizzard during the night or we'd relocated to Lapland. Very festive I thought, as I tied my robe and headed downstairs.

Colin was dressed in baggy jogging shorts and an off-white T-shirt that was stretched tight across his chest. It bore in faded lettering the statement, 'I Ran the World.' Colin was not one for throwing things out. There would be little doubt that Grace, when she finally fully moved in, would swiftly consign it to history.

The kitchen was filled with smoke from the frying pan, which was spitting fat. The cheap transistor radio was turned up to the max, and the resultant noise made it sound like it was home to a small nest of angry wasps. I opened the kitchen window, turned up the extractor fan and lowered the volume of whatever 60s shite Colin was warbling along to.

'Ah, excellent timing Charlie,' he said as he slid half the contents of the pan onto a plate and handed it to me. The eggs were crispy and one of the yolks hadn't survived the bruising encounter with Colin's spatula. The black pudding had burnt on the bottom, making it the blackest black pudding I had ever seen. The tomatoes had caught a bit as well. But the sausages and bacon were fine and the orange juice was wonderfully cold and just what I needed in my dehydrated state. I gulped it back in one, immediately starting to feel better, and refilled my glass from the jug in the centre of the kitchen table. Colin shut the window I had opened, moaning that there was no point in having the central heating up on full whack if we were going to leave windows wide open.

I unfolded the newspaper and scanned the sports news, stopping every now and again to pick small pieces of eggshell from my tongue.

'Do you want a vest?' asked Colin.

'No thanks. Unpleasant as your cooking is I'd still rather

mop up my egg with a slice of fried bread than use one of your old yellowing vests.'

'Ha, ha, I mean for later. Its brass monkeys outside and you can just imagine how bloody freezing it is going to be in that church.'

'No, that waistcoat and jacket you're making us wear is thick and heavy. I think I should be OK.'

I turned to the television page in the middle of the paper and cursed my fortune. By two o'clock any other Christmas Eve I'd have been safely ensconced in my favourite chair with a large whiskey mac in one hand, the remote control in the other and a bowl filled to the brim of mixed nuts safely on my lap while enjoying *Raiders of the Lost Ark* or some other perennial family favourite. Instead I would be freezing my knackers off and singing hymns in St Mark's. Still, I supposed there was a bright side; the free bar and buffet at the reception, for one.

Colin glanced at the kitchen clock. 'I expect Grace is at the hairdresser's already. Then I believe it's onto the nail bar and then into Boots for a full makeover.'

'It will have to be a full makeover if she's going to hide that broken nose!' I said, scanning the fixtures. 'Will we have time to call in at the bookies on the way to the church? There's a six fold accumulator that I want to invest a tenner on.'

'Certainly bloody not! This is an important day for me Charlie. It is not going to be cheapened by stops off to Ladbrokes, the pub or anywhere else.'

'Actually I was going to suggest a slight detour so I could pop into Coral's, you get better odds there and occasionally if the manager is in a good mood, complimentary coffee and biscuits.'

'Bloody hell Charlie. This is my wedding day and you're treating it like a casual trip to Sainsbury's!'

'All right, whatever, I just hope for your sake that my selections don't come in, otherwise I will be looking for compensation that could well run into four figures.' Colin collected the plates and placed them on the draining board before filling the washing-up bowl. He looked out of the kitchen window to the front garden beyond. Only the odd tuft of grass here and there was visible piercing the blanket of snow, and the shrubs and the small apple tree were straining under the weight of what had been delivered throughout the previous couple of days. Large snowflakes still scurried busily down and the heavens looked heavy with more of the same.

'I wouldn't bother with your gambling', he said. 'They were saying on the wireless earlier that loads of games have been called off already. Come three o'clock everything will have been postponed.'

'Does that go for your wedding as well?' I said hopefully. If he heard he didn't answer.

Colin spent the rest of the morning rushing around like a headless chicken, and as the chosen hour approached he became more and more frantic. He'd rung twice to check on the cars and had nipped to the florist to pick up our buttonholes. He'd double-checked with the management of the Park Manor Hotel to ensure that there would be no repeat of the debacle at the golf club and that they were expected and everything was in place. I on the other hand lay on the sofa in my pyjama bottoms and flicked through the *Sporting Life* until nearly midday, helping myself sneakily to the ginger wine.

Eventually I could put up with Colin's whining that I'd 'better get a move on' no longer and ran a bath. Forty minutes later I was shaved, scrubbed and standing before the old-fashioned mahogany-framed full-length dress mirror in Colin's bedroom. Not bad I thought, not bad at all. My shoes were polished and the dark grey and flatteringly-cut suit we'd hired from the shop in the high street fitted perfectly. I adjusted the knot in my tie and stood side on to the glass and admired my reflection. I had never worn a waistcoat before, not even at my own two weddings. I looked good. A little like a gangster. I pretended I was Al Capone and pulled some Mafia poses. 'Are you talking to me?' I growled and cracked my knuckles. Wait until Mel sees me. She will be well impressed. I'll wager that when we get back to our room at the hotel she won't be able to get her knickers off quick enough. Then I remembered her huge belly bulge and the infant ready to spring from her some time in the next fortnight. Oh well.

I grabbed my jacket, top hat and gloves and made my way downstairs. My cousin Jackie, her husband Dave and their kids were in the kitchen chatting with Colin over a coffee. I'd always been close to Jackie when we were kids and although it was rare to meet up these days (especially since Mum died) we always clicked straight away, as if it had been mere days rather than years since our paths had last crossed. Jackie was small and petite, much like Mel with blonde hair and hazel eyes. She was dressed in an indigo jacket and skirt combination with a small black hat perched effortlessly on her head. What is it with weddings and hats?

As I stooped to kiss her on the cheek I noticed crow's feet

around the eyes and a slight slackening of the jowls that I hadn't spotted on our previous meeting. I wondered if she was thinking the same about me.

'Wow, look at you!' she exclaimed.

'Thanks,' I said giving her a twirl.

'I see Mel's taking good care of you,' she said, patting my stomach.

'She certainly is. So how are you guys?' I said, opening the fridge and handing a beer to Dave. Jackie glared at her spouse. 'It's a bit early for that isn't it? You've got plenty of time to get pissed and show me up later.'

'Chill out Jack,' I said, opening a can for myself. 'It's getting on for half twelve and anyway it is Christmas after all.'

'OK, but take it easy Dave. I don't want to spend my Christmas morning hoovering out the vomit from my back seat like I had to after your Christmas do.'

Dave nodded and winked in my direction. 'So how are you Charlie, still supporting those losers Man United?'

'I wouldn't call three trophies in two seasons losers Dave. Blimey, the last time Spurs won anything their fans couldn't celebrate properly because of the threat from the Luftwaffe and the rationing.'

Dave is a typical Spurs fan. Average build, average height, likes a beer and is too cocky by half.

Just then Colin came in with my Auntie Vi close behind. She was dressed in a floral number and left a red imprint of her lips on my cheek. I admired Colin in his suit. His large round tummy seemed determined to escape from the enclosed confines of his trousers, and every few seconds he tugged his waistcoat down to cover it. He only needed a long cigarette holder and an unfurled umbrella and he would be a dead ringer for Batman's arch-enemy, the Penguin.

We chatted self-consciously for a few minutes before we saw, treading gingerly up the front path, a tall, thin man dressed in light grey and wearing a peaked cap.

'Colin, why on earth are we going by hired car?' I said. 'Surely that privilege is reserved solely for the bride.'

'They had an offer on – book the Rolls Royce Silver Ghost and they let you have a vintage Bentley for half price. It seemed too good an offer to turn down. Anyway, it's nice to travel in style isn't it?'

The church of St Mark's, where I may or may not have been baptized (records on the event are sketchy to say the least), is situated across town on a steep and winding narrow road, flanked by large and very expensive three-storey houses. The road is aptly named Mount Zion and is so steep that oxygen is advisable when attempting to climb this muscle-tearing killer of a hill. During the slow drive, Colin grew increasingly quiet and gave monosyllabic answers to all questions or jovial observations. It was more like a journey to the crematorium than the celebration of two happy lovers tying the knot. Lost in his own thoughts, he preferred to turn his head and stare at the blizzard that was bouncing off the windows. All the roofs were white and icicles hung from the gutters. The illuminated houses looked inviting and warm and straight off a Christmas card, while tree lights twinkled and kids played in the snow. It felt almost Dickensian.

A small gang of urchins cheekily bombarded our car with snowballs. After one particularly large missile impacted with a dull thump against the windscreen, our driver stopped and with all the compliments of the season flowing through him he slammed on the brakes, leapt from his seat and yelled at the assailant, 'Throw another one of them and you'll feel my boot up your bloody arse, Christmas or no Christmas!'

'Fuck off!' The cheeky little scamp replied before no doubt heading off to a bus shelter to down a can of cheap supermarket cider. I love the festive season.

Half way up our ascent to the church it became apparent that more and more cars had failed to make it all the way up to the summit. I spotted our own car abandoned a good three feet away from the curb at an angle that suggested that it had slithered to an ungracious stop and was unwilling to go any further. A hundred feet further up I spotted my beloved and our daughter treading carefully through the slush. Poor Melissa must have been finding it particularly difficult to balance with her near fully-formed baby sticking out a foot in front of her. Ellie held her hand tightly and looked incredibly beautiful in her new dress with her school coat over the top in an attempt to keep her warm. I could see her face turned up to the sky to try and catch the falling flakes of white in her mouth.

I leaned forward and spoke to the chauffeur. 'Can you stop here mate? There are two over there who could do with a lift.'

He shook his head briskly, 'No chance mate. If we stop this thing this is where it will stay. Unless you fancy walking the last quarter of a mile we've got to keep ploughing on.'

'Fair enough,' I said as we slowly chugged alongside. Ellie waved enthusiastically and I replied. Mel looked on disbelievingly as I shrugged my shoulders apologetically. 'See you at the top,' I mouthed silently through the window.

St Mark's is by far the largest church in the parish and our meagre wedding party scarcely made a dent in the row upon row of empty pews. A few had decided to risk a severe case of piles and take to their seats early, whilst the rest were huddled in front of a lukewarm radiator at the far left-hand side, near the small nativity display the children from the Sunday school had fashioned from paper, paint, glue and a few stuffed toys brought from home. Joseph was played by a stretch Armstrong toy and Mary was a small Beanie Baby Panda.

After a few polite greetings and firm handshakes, Colin and I wandered to our places at the front. On the way down to our pew I saw from the back a huge shape I recognized. I had invited him, but was surprised to see him all the same. I slapped him playfully on the back. 'Nice to see you Fulton, glad you made it!'

'Aye son, I said I would,' he said.

'Marvellous, I'm glad I've got someone to neck a few with at the bash afterwards. Ooh, and I see you've come in fancy dress as well. You look lovely! Mind you, the bridesmaids might be a bit put out that you're wearing a nicer skirt than they are.'

'Ha ha' he replied sarcastically. 'This is the famous McQueen tartan, my lad. Generations of great warriors have proudly worn this as we've trounced the English from Bannockburn to Brighton and from Hamden Park to Wembley. If you look up on YouTube the time we smashed you in the mid-seventies I'm the third Scot from the left swinging on the broken cross bar.'

'I might just do that. Mind you, by the state of it you haven't had it cleaned since,' I said, pointing to a dark reddish stain to the left of his sporran. 'Is that the blood of an unfortunate England fan you lamped with a broken McEwan's bottle as you were going over the top?'

'No, sorry to disappoint you, but that's not blood Charlie boy. I was feeling a wee bit peckish on the way here so I stopped off briefly and got a bacon sandwich from a van in a layby. The bloody tomato ketchup was a bit over-enthusiastic in leaving the bottle and decided to fecking spray me.'

'Never mind Fulton, the flattened furry animal you have dangling from your belt helps to hide the worst of it. What is it? Roadkill?'

'Oh, so you're a comedian now are you?' he replied.

'Seriously though, there was no need to put on your favourite skirt and risk freezing your plums to the pew. Even that purple suit of yours would have done.'

'Don't worry about me lad. Let me tell you, my kilt will be a great conversation starter at the reception. I'm bound to create a good deal of interest with the ladies once they've downed their free sherries and in no time they'll be begging to know the answer to the age-old question.'

'What, why are the Scots so reluctant when it comes to getting a round in?'

'No, they'll be more interested in what if anything I am wearing underneath. By the way, what will the talent be like? Are there any attractive single ladies of the more mature variety invited?'

'I wouldn't bank on it' I said. 'Now where are my manners – Fulton, this is Colin, the condemned man. Colin,

this is Fulton, a big hairy Scotsman.' Fulton's huge mitt
wrapped around Colin's podgy one. 'Pleased to be here pal,
all the best.'

'Thank you for coming Fulton, we'll have to have a drink
together afterwards. I belong to a battle re-enactment club
and I am sure you can give me some pointers on a few
details regarding uniforms and such.'

'No problem pal,' said Fulton.

We made our way down the aisle and sat in our places in
the front row in hushed reverence before the pulpit, the eyes
of God and an almost unconscious old woman slumped in
front of the mighty church organ. She was wearing a heavy
cardigan over a floral dress. Occasionally she would rub her
hands together and bend her fingers backward and forward
to keep the circulation going. The last thing she wanted was
for her hands to freeze up over the keys.

Colin remained quiet as he sat hunched forward in his
seat, his hands between his legs and his eyes focused on the
scuffed brown tiled floor in front of him. I placed an arm
around his shoulders. 'Cheer up old mate. This is supposed
to be a happy occasion, not a flaming funeral.'

He straightened up and decided to look at the stained-
glass windows instead. Was that a stray tear rolling down
his cheek?

'Hey come on Colin. What's up? It's not too late if you're
having second thoughts. There's bound to be a back door we
can slip out of. OK, we'll probably have to move abroad and
change our identities to escape the wrath of Grace when she
sends Wayne and Ant-knee to exact retribution, but I reckon
I could get quite used to living out the rest of my days in Rio
surviving on whatever you have left in your pension.'

He smiled, pulled an enormous white handkerchief the size of a bed sheet from his pocket and blew his red nose. 'No, it's not that Charlie. I was just thinking that it should have been your mother that I am sitting here waiting for.'

I nodded, 'I know. Hey, why didn't you ever get round to doing the decent thing? Bloody hell, you had long enough.'

'We always meant to but never quite got around to it. Once we even got as far as booking the church, but then something happened and we had to cancel. Money was really tight in our early days. I can remember one time only about three weeks before the intended date. We'd booked the room above the Crown for the reception, the car, the flowers and the whole caboodle and then the boiler blew, the car needed a set of tyres and that was that. It was a pity really.'

That's ironic, I thought. For the sake of one old boiler you are now getting wed to another.

'If there is a heaven, and your dear old Mum is up there perched on her cloud looking down on us all, I wonder what she is thinking,' he said softly.

'She's probably thinking, what on earth are you doing you silly old fool? She's only after your money and somewhere to live. She's no better than she ought to be, that one.'

Surprisingly he didn't take offence and chuckled, 'Yeah you're probably right.'

Just then Dave tapped me on the shoulder. There's a slight hitch Charlie,' he said nodding towards the church entrance. I followed him back down, once more acknowledging the suits and hats with polite smiles. He opened the heavy door and an Arctic blast took my breath away.

'They've shut the road off. No one can get up or down. There's cars abandoned all over the shop,' said Dave.

I raised my eyebrows, 'Well, well, maybe there really is a god up there and he's granted the old man a last-minute reprieve.'

'I think you've spoken slightly too soon mate.' He pointed a frozen finger down the hill. I squinted through the heavy flakes that filled the air, and then suddenly, like one of those scenes in the movies where Sylvester Stallone or Arnold Schwarzenegger emerges triumphantly from a smoke-filled hellhole having saved the day, Ant-knee appeared. The climb was steep, the weather atrocious, and the path knee-deep with snow, but this slowed him not one bit. He strode up the precipice like a giant in an ill-fitting bouncer's suit. In his arms lay the ghostlike form of his dear mother. If it hadn't been for the fag she had on the go she could have been an angel fallen from the skies.

Forty or so yards back came the bridesmaids, who, without a burly bruiser to carry them, were not finding things quite so straightforward. The four attendants, from the oldest, who looked more ancient and weatherbeaten than George Burns, to the youngest, a little girl of about nine, they were struggling manfully to stay upright. On their feet were borrowed wellington boots. Their long puffball dresses were held waist high in frost-bitten fingers to avoid the drifting snow. If it hadn't been for the wellies it could have been a major turn on, especially with two of them wearing what appeared to be stockings.

I whipped out my phone and videoed their approach. If this didn't bag me two hundred and fifty quid from *You've Been Framed*, nothing would.

I returned to a nervous Colin's side and reassured him that everything was fine. Presently the little lady in the heavy knitted cardigan, who was now wearing a pair of fingerless gloves, received the signal to activate her organ. She attacked it with gusto, and the opening chords of the Bridal March filled the depressingly empty church. Joints that were stiff and reluctant to move were forced into life as the congregation stood as one to greet the bride. Colin and I moved to our marks. As she walked slowly down the aisle, I and I'm sure eighty percent of the rest of them, silently sang 'Here comes the bride, all fat and wide' along to the music. Come on, it can't just be me surely?

Once next to her groom, Ant-knee, who had the honour of giving her away (again - I guess it was his turn) lifted her veil. The vicar took a step back in surprise. I had to stifle a snigger, and even the groom himself was a little taken aback.

Grace smiled at Colin. Her right eye was many different hues of the colour purple and swollen to a worrying degree. Her nose, which may or may not have been broken, was distorted, puffy and misshapen. There was also some kind of medical tape stretched across the bridge that was holding the thing together. Fair play to her though, this had not removed her usual look of brazen glory. As always, her lips, like her nails, were vampire red. Her hair was freshly bleached, backcombed and the size of a small privet hedge perched daintily on her head. I wondered who was responsible, a hair stylist or a gardener. Her prize bosoms as usual were more out than in. In fact due to the extreme cold, the whiteness of the dress and the deathly pallor of her skin, from the back of the church it almost looked as though she was naked.

The Reverend Tring welcomed us to his church and to this 'happy occasion.' We rattled off the first three verses of *Jerusalem* (I bet Colin picked that one) and a couple of prayers before getting down to the nitty-gritty of the service.

'In the presence of God, the Father, the Son and the Holy Spirit we come together this day to witness the marriage of Colin Rogers [Baron Greenback lookalike and serial cardigan wearer] and Grace Harper [Shameless slapper and peroxide addict] to pray for God's blessing on them to share their joy and love. The gift of marriage brings husband and wife together in the delight and tenderness of sexual union [Thanks Vic, that's one image I could sure do without] and joyful commitment for the rest of their lives [Shouldn't be long then]. It is given as the foundation of family life in which children are born and nurtured [I think that ship has already sailed Vic, but do go on].

'Marriage is a way of life made holy by God and blessed by the presence of our Lord Jesus Christ, with those celebrating a wedding at Cana in Galilee [I wonder if the old dears wore hats at that do?] Marriage is a sign of unity and loyalty [are you listening Grace? What number is this? Four, five six, or have we stopped counting?) It enriches society and strengthens community. No one should enter into it lightly or selfishly but reverently and responsibly in the sight of Almighty God [and a depressingly small and frozen congregation who are praying for a speedy service so they can leave this freezing monument to the glory of God and move onto the reception to warm their bones and get pissed].

'Grace [broken nose and eyebrows by Crayola] and Colin [waistcoat so tight that several major organs are on the verge of failing] are now ready to enter into this way of life. They will each give their consent to the other and make solemn vows and in token of this they will each give and receive a ring.

'We pray with them that the Holy Spirit will guide and strengthen them [or failing that, other spirits such as Jack Daniels or Gordon's Gin may take up the slack], that they may fulfil God's purposes for the whole of their earthly lives. [What God's purpose is in bringing these two together only he knows. From here the only plan seems to be to shaft me over my inheritance.]

'First I am required to ask those present that if anyone knows a reason that these persons may not legally marry to declare it now.'

I shut my eyes and crossed my fingers. Please someone say something.

BINGO!!!!!!

To my amazement there was a shuffling at the back of the church and a small man dressed in tweed and clutching a cloth cap in his hands stood up and put his hand in the air. The congregation sat rubbernecking in stunned silence before turning back to the Reverend Tring, who didn't appear to have a clue what to do next. Well, I suppose this doesn't come up very often. I bet they don't prepare you for this at vicar school. Sorting out an argument at a jumble sale or gently rebuffing a lonely widow is probably as tricky as it gets.

Slowly, the man made his way down the aisle. As he got nearer he appeared to become even smaller, shrinking almost apologetically. He was a touch over five feet tall and no more than nine stone and wringing wet. His jet-black hair was styled into a razor-sharp parting and plastered to his head with half a jar of hair preparation that gave it a look of 'bloody hell, it isn't half raining out there'. His shoes were shiny and as neat as his perfectly-groomed moustache.

Grace and Ant-knee exchanged a worried, knowing look. The bride turned back to the vicar with a face like thunder, muttering cuss words that should never be uttered in such a place of worship. I spotted Ant-knee flexing his muscles, forming his hands into fists and puffing out his huge chest in a posture that said if there was going be trouble he would not be found wanting.

'Hello Grace,' said the man, in a strong Yorkshire accent.

'What the bloody hell are you doing here?' Grace said in a voice which was not much more than a whisper.

'It's all by chance really. My niece Karen – you remember Karen, the one with the lisp and large record collection of Cliff Richard? Well, by chance she moved down here last June and attends this church. She spotted you when you and your intended were here having your banns read. She took a picture on her camera phone and sent it to me.'

'And you are?' questioned Colin.

'Oh, do excuse me.' He held out a thin freckled bony hand for Colin to shake. My name is Geoffrey, Geoffrey Wilde. You see this lady,' he turned to Grace, 'is my wife.'

Colin, who had been growing redder and redder, loosened his tie and gulped. 'Don't be daft mate. Is this some kind of joke?' He turned to face me. 'Is this your doing Charlie?'

I shrugged and shook my head.

'We were married a little over eighteen months ago at St

Luke's near Doncaster,' Mr Wilde went on. Two weeks after the honeymoon my bride disappeared and I haven't seen hide nor hair of her since... well, until now that is. I came home from visiting my sister Shirley to find she was gone. As were the wedding presents and the money in our joint savings account.' He seemed almost apologetic.

'Tell me he's making it up, Grace?' Colin pleaded. His bride-to-be looked at the floor.

'We're still legally married I'm afraid,' said Mr Wilde. 'I did start proceedings to end our brief marriage on line but I'm hopeless at using a mouse and filling in all those forms.'

'Well, Grace?' Colin said, more urgently.

Grace looked at the mysterious interloper before turning back to Colin and nodded.

'You fucking bitch!' he yelled and knocked the bouquet from her hand.

'Watch it,' said Ant-knee, pushing Colin persuasively in the chest. He staggered back against the side of the front pew, his specs askew.

That did it for me. 'Just fuck off, will you!' I shouted at Ant-knee, squaring up to him. 'Take your Neanderthal brother and your saggy witch of a mother and fuck off!' In a flash I felt his fist connect with the side of my jaw. It hurt. Like fucking hell. Dave ran forward to confront him, and ran onto another hammer-like punch. His legs folded beneath him and he bade goodnight, probably with some of those cartoon birds tweet-tweeting in a circle above his head.

Then it all kicked off big style. Grace cuffed Geoffrey around the head, Colin leapt at Ant-knee and Wayne grabbed me in a headlock. The Reverend Tring held his hands out and tried to appeal to everyone's better nature.

'Please everyone, can we try and control ourselves and remember where we are,' he pleaded.

Just then I managed to wriggle free from Wayne's vice-like grip and caught him with a well-aimed knee to the groin. He yelped like a puppy at the vet's and launched a vicious right hand in my general direction. I managed to narrowly avoid the blow and watched as if in slow motion as he followed through and caught the vicar squarely on the nose, which promptly exploded in a very fetching splash of crimson. Wayne stalled in disbelief before being leapt upon by Colin, who jumped on his back and thrust two fingers up his nose, forcing his head back.

I was about to come to his aid when a flash of beard and kilt brushed me aside as Fulton took control. Just as Wayne threw Colin from his back and raised his fist to give him a bloody good hiding, he grabbed the goon by his already torn lapels and rammed his head against the hard wooden bench. As he lay stunned, Fulton booted him in the face and left him to dream.

Ant-knee leapt to his sibling's aid with a smile on his face – a man who enjoys a ruck! He drew back his arm and aimed a forceful right cross towards the Scotsman's head, but with what appeared almost superhuman speed Fulton caught his fist in the palm of his hand, then twisted it in his other hand and squeezed a pressure point. Ant-knee dropped to his knees whimpering, a look of disbelief spreading across his face. This was a situation he wasn't used to. Fulton smiled. Well I guessed he was smiling, as his beard kept the exact location of his mouth a mystery at the best of times.

Fulton growled, then smashed his forehead against the bridge of Ant-knee's nose. The sound of Scottish skull breaking English conk rang around the church with a sickening echo. Uncles pulled faces and turned away, while aunties called for smelling salts. Knowing he was beaten, Ant-knee made a break for it and walked dizzily back down the aisle to safety. Fulton straightened up and rearranged his sporran. 'Cheers for the invite, Charlie. This has been the best wedding I've been to since my cousin Mickey chinned the vicar for looking down his bride's top.'

Colin stood amazed and surveyed the wreckage of his big day. He saw his bride-to-be trying to drag her battered offspring to his feet. He saw the Reverend Tring dabbing the end of his bloodied nose with a large handkerchief. He heard Geoffrey Wilde apologising for causing 'all this bother'. He turned and took at the faces of the stunned congregation. And he laughed, quietly at first, then louder and louder until he was almost out of control. His shoulders heaved and his face turned beetroot red. I was joining in too, as were others, when Jackie rushed towards us in a flap. 'You're not going to believe this Charlie, but during all the excitement Mel's waters have broken!'

'You are kidding,' I said, looking over to where my beloved was sitting. The crowd of excited relatives that had her circled told me this was no joke. 'Has anyone called an ambulance?'

'Yes, but the road is closed Charlie and she says she needs to push, so I don't think it's going to be long.'

I raced over, nearly tripping over the still-groggy Wayne in the process. 'Are you all right Mel?'

'Does it bloody look like I'm bloody all right?'

'Hey careful, we are in church you know.'

'Aaaaarrrrrrghhhh!' she bellowed, as another contraction

built within her. 'Do something Charlie!'

I stood there open mouthed. 'Can't you cross your legs and hold it in until the snow thaws?'

'Out of the way Charlie you goon,' said Auntie Vi as she approached. 'How regular are the contractions luv?'

'About every couple of minutes,' she groaned. 'Ellie only took a couple of hours. This little bugger seems to be in even more of a rush.'

'Right, there isn't time to waste. Charlie, ask the vicar if there's a side room that we can move Mel to.'

'Will do,' I said, relieved that someone else seemed to know what to do. I found the vicar in a small room to the side of the altar. He was checking out his nose in a small ornate mirror. I guessed this must be the office where he attended to vicar-type things. 'Sorry to barge in Reverend, but could we possibly commandeer this room for an emergency? Oh, and if you could lay your hands on some towels and hot water that would be great.'

'What?' he replied, still checking the contents of his handkerchief for blood.

'Don't worry, it doesn't have to be holy water, anything out of the tap will do.'

CHAPTER TWENTY-TWO

It's turned out nice again

Colin smiled contentedly as he bent down over the Moses basket and placed the gentlest of kisses on the baby's tiny soft pink hand. I could swear his eyes were more watery than normal as he stroked the tiny cheek with the back of his index finger. 'He's perfect Charlie, just perfect. Have you decided on a name yet?'

'No, we've been debating that the last couple of days. I fancied something traditional like George or Samuel, but Mel is pushing for Orlando or God forbid, River.'

'River?'

'After the actor.'

'What actor?'

'River Phoenix.'

'Never heard of him,' said Colin. 'It sounds like some kind of waterborne disease.'

'He was an actor. I'm not surprised you don't know him, I think he only made a couple of films before he died of drink or drugs or something.'

'I'm not having my grandson named after some junkie. Feet need to be put down here, Charlie.'

'You're not kidding. Because of the place of his birth she wants his second name to be Jesus.'

He spluttered into his coffee, spilling it onto the floor. 'Tell me you're joking Charlie, please?'

I nodded. 'Yes, don't worry,' I said, fetching a tea towel from the kitchen. 'He's having two middle names, yours and my dad's.'

'Nice touch,' he said, smiling and nodding.

'Has Grace been back to collect her stuff?' I asked.

'Yes, I bagged it all up in bin liners and left it in the porch. When I got back from Sainsbury's it had gone.'

'Now you've had a couple of days to let the dust settle, how are you feeling?' I lifted George/River's legs up to give his bottom a sniff. There was a funny smell coming from somewhere.

'Sorry Charlie, that was me,' said Colin guiltily. 'To cheer myself up last night I got a six-pack of real ale and one of those ready meal curries. It's been a long time since I had a really hot one, and this was a scorcher.'

'Well, I'd watch yourself if I was you. I don't mind putting a nappy on this little chap, but I'll be buggered if you think I'm going to do the same for you.'

Mel had finished loading the washing machine and joined us. She looked tired and fatigued, not surprising really, seeing as the new addition could not seem to go more than a couple of hours without needing his milk fix. She sniffed and wrinkled her nose distastefully.

'Don't worry, it's only Colin,' I said. 'He's got a bit of the old Gandhi's revenge. I offered him a wet wipe but he declined.'

'Guess who I had a couple of pints with yesterday,' piped up Colin.

'Bishop Desmond Tutu and the Cheeky Girls?'

'Close, Charlie, but not quite on the button.'

He left a pause for a second guess, but Mel and I were both struggling.

'Geoffrey, the mystery man who dropped the bombshell at the church.'

'What, Grace's secret husband, number God knows what?' I asked disbelievingly.

He nodded. 'He's a nice guy actually. In fact we found we had a great deal in common. We both share a weakness for Charlie Dimmock and getting our seed potatoes in as early as possible, and that's just for starters. Anyway he put me in the picture, and it turns out we've had a very close escape indeed. He's been doing plenty of investigating since she absconded and he reckons there's definitely one other and possibly two who she's married, split from and not bothered to divorce. The definite one lives in Wakefield, he's a quantity surveyor. Other suspects are a chef in Southampton with a lively gastro pub and a mature student from Dudley who's studying the declining numbers of hedgehogs in urban areas.'

'Blimey!' exclaimed Melissa. 'The scheming cow!'

'He's also on the trail of a bloke called Kevin who sells burgers from a layby on the A303, but that might just be hearsay and gossip.'

'I told you she was trouble from the start Col. It sounds like you're well rid of her. Have you contacted the police?' I asked.

'Not personally, but Geoffrey is keeping me up to speed and he was told they will probably get in touch if and when it goes to trial. Yes, they've got a file on her already, and those two idiot sons of hers. Wayne has already spent a couple of years detained at Her Majesty's pleasure for fraud and actual bodily harm, and the other one has a string of convictions as long as your arm ranging from credit card copying to bribery and corruption and even assault with a deadly weapon. He's a nasty bit of work, I tell you. Geoffrey told me that at a family party he took an exception to someone calling him a third-rate Ronnie Kray. He grabbed him by the lapels, dragged him outside and smashed his head against the pavement until the poor bloke lost consciousness and most of his teeth. I tell you Charlie, we were dead lucky your Scottish pal was there to save the day. We must thank him for his timely assistance. What does he like?'

'Beer, fighting and the poetry of William Blake and Robbie Burns.'

I'll send him a bottle of Glenfiddich, a Muhammad Ali DVD and that thin paperback of Pam Ayres your mother used to like.'

'He'll be thrilled. So getting back to the evil Grace, what is her modus operandi?'

'Well, from what I gathered from Geoffrey, once she gets her claws into you and sets up a joint account she learns all your bank details and the location of any large sums of money you've pugged away for a rainy day. Then, bit by bit and on the sly she sells off your family knick-knacks over a period of months without you knowing they've even gone. Then she does a flit and empties your accounts on line or with the access she has been granted by the banks.'

'Blimey, that's the type of thing you read in the *News of the World*. You don't expect it to happen on your own doorstep,' said Melissa.

'Absolutely, and then to top it all off, years down the line, still being legally married, or illegally as it has turned out, she cops the rest and a widow's pension to boot when the poor victim finally turns up his toes.'

'Flipping heck!' I said.

Colin's face brightened. 'I nearly forgot, our adventures in the church have not only made us famous locally but now the nationals have caught a whiff of it and are sniffing around. I'm due to meet a guy from the *Sunday Mirror* tomorrow to give him my first-hand account of my life with the bosomed bigamist. That's their title, not mine by the way. They want to negotiate exclusive rights to the whole sorry affair. I'm sure they'd love a word with you guys and a picture, and the little man as well. I tell you Charlie, this might indeed turn out to be a godsend. I reckon once the bidding war is over we'll be ten grand better off out of all of this.'

'Well, you can count me out for a start,' said Mel. 'The last thing I want is my face splashed across the tabloids.'

'And what have you got to hide then? I said. Have you

got another couple of husbands you're keeping quiet about as well?'

She poked out her tongue.

'I'll tell them to keep your names out of it,' said Colin.

'Hey, let's not be too hasty,' I answered. 'Play this right and we could become famous. This time next year I could be a judge on the X-Factor, Mel could be eating kangaroo's testicles on *I'm a Celebrity Get Me Out Of Here* and Colin, you could have your own spot on *Test Match Special*.'

We laughed, and baby awoke with a sniffle and a yelp. I picked the little fellow up and gently handed him to Colin. Just then Ellie, who had finally turned off her Tracy Beaker DVD and come down from her room in search of food, caught sight of her grandpop and rushed up for a cuddle.

I put my arms around Mel. 'Do you know, all my life I've been trying to find contentment, inner peace and a reason to be happy. I think I've just realised it's been here all the time,' I said, sighing.

'About bloody time,' said Mel. She started to unbutton her blouse for my newborn son's feed.

'Hello, dinner's ready,' I said. 'Come on Colin, let's go for a pint and we can discuss my cut of your windfall. How does fifty percent sound? These nappies aren't cheap you know.'

www.ingramcontent.com/pod-product-compliance
Lightning Source LLC
Chambersburg PA
CBHW070531260626
47161CB00002B/332